BY PASSION BETRAYED

✦ ✦ ✦

Desire won over fear and Lady Juilene reached to caress his cheek. Arimond raised himself over her, his body covering hers. She placed one hand on his chest, and gasped.

The sapphire ring, her mother's legacy, blazed brighter than thousands of gems combined. She stifled a scream and her eyes met his and in that moment she knew she looked into the eyes of a stranger.

There was nothing of Arimond's love in those eyes, only lust and desire and something that could only be hate.

His face changed before her eyes. His hair lightened from sun-bleached gold to nearly white, his cheekbones heightened and became more prominent. His lips thinned.

"Lindos!" she cried.

✦ ✦ ✦

"Bush displays vivid imagination."

—*Publishers Weekly*

ALSO BY ANNE KELLEHER BUSH

Daughter of Prophecy
Children of Enchantment
The Misbegotten King

PUBLISHED BY
WARNER BOOKS

ANNE KELLEHER BUSH

The Knight, the Harp, and the Maiden

A Time Warner Company

WARNER BOOKS EDITION

Aspect® name and logo are registered trademarks of Warner Books, Inc.

Cover design by Don Puckey
Cover illustration by Valerie Sokolova

Warner Books, Inc.
1271 Avenue of the Americas
New York, NY 10020

Visit our Web site at
www.warnerbooks.com

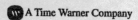 A Time Warner Company

Printed in the United States of America

First Printing: July 1999

10 9 8 7 6 5 4 3 2 1

For my dearest Katie Liz—my rose without thorns—
with love beyond reason or measure.

—Mommy

The Knight,
the Harp,
and the Maiden

Prologue

Silent as the flicker of the candle he clenched in his fist, the young thurge stole through the halls of the sleeping house. His white robe, bordered with the glyphs of the House of the Over-Thurge of Khardroon, shivered around him. His bare brown feet, smooth as the soles of an infant, made no sound on the marble floors, which even in the height of the summer heat were cool.

But the chill that ran up his spine and lingered like a lover's hand on the back of his neck had nothing to do with the temperature of the stone beneath his feet. He had labored long over his books that day, wrestling with the formulas concerning the tides and the moon phases of the approaching autumn. He had gone to bed with a headache from the arcane combinations that danced jigs before his closed eyes, and a prayer that somehow it all make sense in the morning. Now he doubted he would see his bed again before dawn. A summons in the middle of the night from Her Transcendence could mean only one thing. Someone or something had displeased the mighty Over-Thurge of the third most powerful city in the Sylvrian League, and he, sleepy Siss-Obed bel 'Damin, the nineteen-year-old son of a mere demi-thurge, was about to be called upon to arrange whatever might be necessary to restore Rihana's good humor. In no way did Siss believe himself to be anything but expendable, even though his growing reputation for discretion had earned him the favorable notice of Her Transcendence. But now he wondered what quality had made her call for him in the middle of the night: his discretion or his expendability? He gripped his smoking candle until his nails dug into his flesh, and tried to convince himself it was only the heat that made his palm sweat.

The flame threw up huge shadows against the white walls of the corridor, and as he passed by, the light glimmered off the unlit sconces of polished gold set high upon the walls. The palace of the Over-Thurge of Khardroon had never been so magnificent before Her Transcendence had come into her power. He entered the long gallery, where the wide windows were thrown open to catch the breezes off the sea. The summer night was sultry; the gauzy shrouds draped over the windows to discourage insects hung still as corpses on the hangman's tree. He could not even hear the ships in the nearby harbor creaking on their moorings. It was as if the whole city held its breath, in anticipation of something—or someone, he mused as he pushed open the elaborately carved doors at the end of the gallery. But what could have so disturbed Her Transcendence on such a night, when surely all the good citizens of the city slept in heat-drugged stupor, and even the rest were likely to lie in snoring oblivion in their rat-infested warrens?

He paused a moment and took a deep breath. With only the slightest waver of the candle, he opened the door and stepped into the antechamber of Her Transcendence's suite. The light of a hundred candles stung his eyes, and an incessant buzzing rose to a fevered pitch upon his entrance. He allowed the suggestion of a frown to cross his face, even as he dropped his eyes and composed his features into the impassive mask it was wisest to wear. He gathered the folds of his robe more closely about him, and hoped she wouldn't notice that his fingers trembled.

"You're late."

The voice cut through the thick air with the precision of a scalpel, soft and biting all at once. He raised his eyes without the least hesitation, for that was never wise, and met the dark, hooded eyes of Rihana, the Over-Thurge of Khardroon.

She was still a young woman, not yet passed her childbearing years, but her beauty emanated from the power that clung to her like a garment, not from any symmetry of face or form. Her full lips were red in the candlelight, and her skin had that subtle glow that told him she had used her power but only a short time ago. Her black hair was piled in a careless knot upon her head, and her dark nipples made round shadows beneath her thin white shift.

He dropped his eyes again, and stood just inside the door, his posture that of perfect submission. "My Transcendence," he murmured.

Just as he spoke, the mantling on her desk shrieked. The hair on the back of his neck prickled. Immediately, from across the room, a sympathetic moan arose from the gilded cage that contained at least a score of the things.

"Ssh," she said, one long fingertip gently touching the tiny head of the thing writhing upon the smooth surface of the desk, its pink human-shaped head at odds with the black carapace of its insect body.

Siss-Obed swallowed hard. How could she stand the presence of the mantlings, let alone to touch one? They were a legacy of the long-ago Age of Anarchy, before the Goddess Dramue had set the world in balance, when the thurges quarreled among themselves and used their power indiscriminately. The mantlings had the faces and features of humans, with the bodies of insects. They could grow as long as a man's longest finger, and their young were as affectionate, it was said, as puppies. Not that he would know. He had never touched one of the things, and would have sooner shared the room with dwarf dragons. At least they didn't look at you with human eyes.

Bile rose in his throat and he swallowed hard with effort. It would never do to let the Over-Thurge see his disgust. She might order him to touch the thing itself.

Beneath her finger the creature had calmed, and the angry buzz from the gilded cage subsided to a low hum. He raised his eyes to hers once more. "Forgive me," he murmured. "I had gone to bed early, and your servant had a difficult time waking me."

She ran the edge of her tongue over her lips and continued to stroke the head of the mantling. "Please"—she gestured toward the gilded chair on the opposite side of her desk—"sit."

The black carapace of the insect tapped from side to side as the creature squirmed in mindless ecstasy. He sidled closer and sat down. Better to concentrate upon Her Transcendence than the creature on the desk.

"Word has reached me from Gravenhage," she began without looking up.

"Oh?" He kept his face carefully neutral. Gravenhage lay to the north, second in power only to Sylyria of all the seven city-states of the League. The Conclave of Thurges was due to meet there in less than a month. He remembered the cold winds that blew off the mountains and shivered. He most fervently hoped the lady had not taken it into her mind to send him there any sooner than was absolutely necessary.

Her eyes flicked over him, colder than the memory of that mountain air, impersonal as the sting of a whip. "I know you like your comforts, Siss, but I'm afraid I must send you there. Sooner than I ever expected."

He clasped his hands on his lap, willing them to relax. "As you will it, Transcendence, I obey."

She circled the mantling's downy head with one fingertip and smiled as it preened. "The young heir of the King of Gravenhage has gotten himself into a fine coil of trouble. And it seems to me we can turn it to our advantage."

Of course, thought Siss-Obed, settling back. Of course it would be turned to her advantage. For if Her Transcendence didn't take advantage of whatever tangle the young Prince of Gravenhage had happened to find himself in, the other thurges of the other city-states surely would. He leaned against the thick cushion and waited to hear more. It was never wise to try to second-guess Rihana's intentions.

This time she smiled directly at him. The dark depths of her eyes glittered with power and something else, something hard and hungry. He preferred to think that it was curiosity that caused his throat to close as if seized by a predator. He allowed himself one "Oh?"

"He's gotten his half sister with child."

"What?" Involuntarily he started out of his chair. "The heir of Gravenhage has no—"

"Ah." She held up her hand. "That's what they wanted everyone to think. Queen Mirta kept her mouth shut a little too tightly, for no one ever guessed that General Keriaan was the father of her son. However . . ." Her voice trailed off and she dropped her eyes once more to the thing undulating beneath her finger. A small smile played at the corners of her lips, and Siss-Obed once again suppressed a shudder.

"However," he finished for her, "your spies are well paid. But what is the use of such information to Khardroon?"

"I intend to help, of course." Her expression was so perfectly guileless he wanted to laugh in spite of his fear. "Something must be done about this, or the entire House and City of Gravenhage may be disgraced. Mirta has had a hard enough time controlling the various factions with the House, especially the one led by Lord Amon. What if the House of Gravenhage falls?"

He sucked in a long slow breath. The question was merely rhetorical. He knew as well as she what would happen if the House of the Thane of Gravenhage was to fall. The delicate balance of the world order would be upset, and suddenly he felt cold all over. Could Rihana's sudden interest mean that the throne of Gravenhage was in imminent danger of falling? But her next words were even more startling.

"And in order to prevent such a calamity, I intend to offer my power to Galanthir."

"Galanthir? He's no more than a master-thurge in the service of the Over-Thurge—why does he deserve such an honor?"

"Keriaan is his brother—and that makes the young prince his nephew. He will do anything to spare his family and that of the ruling house the disgrace of incest. Think of what the nobles of Gravenhage would do were it known that the young prince and his own half sister . . ." Rihana's words ended in a sly smile.

"Galanthir's appealed to you for help?"

"No." She snorted impatiently and the mantling whimpered its displeasure at the abrupt change in her touch. "Of course not. But I've read the Book this night. There may be a way to overthrow Lindos, and secure the power of the Conclave for ourselves.

Now he was beginning to understand. Rihana had only a passing interest in the affairs of the thanes of Gravenhage. It was Lindos who was her target, Lindos, Over-Thurge of Sylyria and High Thurge of the Conclave. As High Thurge, Lindos was the most powerful thurge in the entire world. Rihana would do anything to bring about his downfall in order to take his place. "What do you intend to do?" She smiled once more, and this time he shivered visibly. He reminded himself to relax. "And what do you want of me, Most Transcendent?"

Her lips quirked a little at a title. It was the one reserved for only the High Thurge, whose will was considered a divine manifestation of the goddess. "You know me well for someone who's been in my service only a few years, Siss-Obed," she murmured as she allowed her eyes to linger on him.

A needle of fear slivered through him. Was this a good thing, or a bad? He lowered his eyes. "I have always been observant, Transcendent One."

She laughed softly. "Yes. So I've noticed." She stroked the head of the mantling, which had fallen into a deep sleep. "And that's why I want you to go to Gravenhage. Ostensibly, as my agent, you will make the arrangements for my arrival—find suitable lodging, arrange for servants, that sort of thing, you know." She paused and he waited.

"But most importantly, you are to seek out this Galan-thir. And when you judge the time to be right, you are to offer him the help of Khardroon. Do you understand?"

He spread his hands, more than a little confused. "But what help am I to offer, Transcendence? How can the Power of Khardroon assist?"

She paused once more. She stroked her chin with long fingers, pinning him to the chair with her pointed gaze. At last she pushed her chair back from the desk and rose. Noiselessly, she padded to the wide window and gazed out at the silent courtyard far below. "What I am to tell you, Siss-Obed, you will reveal to no one. Do you understand?"

"You have my word, Transcendence."

She turned and the smile on her face made him shudder. "I'll have much more than that if you betray me, Siss-Obed. But never mind." She turned back to the window and spoke softly, so softly that he had to lean forward to hear her. "We do not so much wish to bring down the throne of Gravenhage as we wish to bring about Lindos's doom—do you understand?"

"Yes, Transcendence."

"And the Book is clear—Lindos's doom is the non-born knight."

"Non-born knight? What's that? How can there be a knight who isn't born?"

This time her smile was genuine. "I have puzzled over that for longer than you can imagine, Siss. And the answer came clear to me tonight. So this is what we are going to offer to Galanthir. We will offer to send his nephew— Cariad, that's his name—back in time. And we'll tell him that the Book reveals that the House of Gravenhage will be secured if he does."

"And will it?" asked Siss, momentarily confused.

She waved her hand impatiently. "How should I know? The Book only hints of the present future—not one which will be incurred should the past change. But it won't matter. For once Cariad is in the past, he will *be* the non-born knight of Lindos's doom. I will send him to a time before Lindos was ever Over-Thurge of Sylyria—when Lindos was only a master-thurge—not much more powerful than the demi-thurges who served him. Lindos's fate shall be sealed before he ever has the chance to become Over-Thurge of Sylyria." She paused once more, and drew a deep breath, her breasts swelling under the thin white fabric of her gown. "And nothing—and no one—shall prevent me from becoming High Thurge of the Conclave."

So that was it. Siss-Obed stared at her, his thoughts now a jumbled swirl of terror and confusion. Not only was the House of Gravenhage about to pay a high price for the help that would come from Khardroon. But he suspected that the real price was hidden far more deeply than anyone, even Rihana herself, might ever know. "Back in time?" he whispered, more to himself than to the lady. "Is such a thing possible?"

She smiled again, and turned back to face the night. "All things are possible, Siss, if one but dares. You're a thurge—a young one, but a thurge nonetheless. You should know that."

"But—but to alter time? Won't that upset the Balance—the Order?" Genuinely perplexed, all his fears forgotten, as well as his careful control, he gazed at his mistress.

"It may," she said softly, so softly he had to lean forward once more to hear. "But the Covenant was only meant to last ten thousand years, Siss. And the tenth millennium approaches."

"And what if you anger the goddess herself, lady?" whispered Siss. His gaze dropped to the abomination sleeping on her desk.

"I don't believe in the goddess, Siss. And here's a little secret: neither do most of us. The Covenant is nothing but an outworn set of rules that haven't changed with the world. It's time new ones were written." She turned back to him, a smile stretched across her full bloodred lips, and this time he recognized the look in her eyes. It was the one worn by predators when the prey is finally within reach.

"But what of the other Over-Thurges? Never mind Lindos—what of the others?" Shock made him persist even in the face of her most dangerous expression. "Do you think the Conclave will sit idly by and allow—"

"Allow?" She spat the word back at him. "Those fools in the Conclave—what use is the Power if they are afraid to use it? Think of them all: sanctimonious old men who allow themselves to be bound by an outworn writ, a writ that constrains us to study but almost never to use. Bound magic. Faugh," she spat. "What use are such men to me? What use is such magic to me? And what have I to fear?'

"Wild magic," Siss whispered. "You mean to use wild magic."

"I've been looking for the secret to unlock the magic ever since I was a child. I'm not the first." She leaned across the desk and he had to steel himself to stop from shrinking. "How do you think Lindos became High Thurge? He's known how to use the wild magic for longer than you've been alive—and he won't share the secret with anyone. But that's changed now. And I intend to change everything with it."

Siss glanced around the room, casting about for something, anything that would make her change her mind. Every demi-thurge, even the lowest and meanest, even his father, understood the danger of wild magic. His mind flashed a memory of the hovel he'd only too recently left, and he wondered what advice his father would have for him now. Even for the greatest and most powerful of master-thurges, wild magic was something never spoken of, let alone even attempted. Wild magic was the power unbound, untamed by the complicated series of rules and balances imposed by the Covenant upon the thurges. No one even understood how to invoke wild magic. At least, he had thought no one did. He had suspected for some time that his mistress might have attempted it once or twice. But now she intimated that she not only could invoke it; she could use it. As she willed. And if that was true, Rihana was not only the most powerful thurge in all of Khardroon, but in all the Sylyrian League as well. He stared at his mistress. In the candlelight, her skin glowed, as if she were lit from within by some incandescence. He felt the blood rise in his face and in his loins. She was beautiful and terrible all at once and Siss knew beyond all doubt that she was capable of crushing every single one of them all at once. He wet his lips and tried once more. "But what if this Galanthir goes to the Over-Thurge of Gravenhage, and tells him what you offer? How will you answer before the Conclave? Before Lindos? There's nothing to stop them from turning the Power against you." In the long silence that followed Siss-Obed wondered if his expendability had outweighed his talent for diplomacy.

To his surprise, Rihana burst out laughing. "I like that about you, Siss. You aren't afraid of me. I can't quite decide if you are truly courageous, completely foolish, or potentially powerful enough to challenge me someday. But we won't wonder about that now, shall we?" She waved her hand dismissively. "Galanthir go to the Over-Thurge of Gravenhage? Or to the Conclave? I am glad you anticipate such eventualities, Siss. Because that is the very reason I'm sending you, my dear demi-thurge. You are to see that Galanthir accepts my offer—and that no one—and I do mean no one—knows of this. Ever."

He swallowed hard and met her eyes. In Rihana's stare, Siss-Obed thought he could almost read his own doom. "Yes, Most Transcendent. As you will it, I obey."

Chapter One

"You! Old woman!" The harsh voice echoed across the meadow beneath the cloud-studded autumn sky, and reached the old woman as she stamped her foot, impatiently trying to dislodge a troublesome pebble from the sole of her worn leather shoe. She frowned a little and raised her head in the direction of the sound. Little wisps of grey hair escaped her hood and obscured her vision. She swept her hair out of her eyes and gripped the straps that secured her harp to her back. Across the long wind-bent grass, three horsemen bore down on her so swiftly she knew she had no chance to step aside. She picked up the small pack that held the rest of her worldly possessions more out of reflex than need. If it were Dramue's will that her life was to end here on this rock-rimmed highway, so be it. "As you will it, I obey," she murmured.

She narrowed her eyes as the riders cantered up, their huge round-rumped horses obviously bred for war. Their cloaks were a uniform shade of dark red, bordered in intricate designs of black. Some master-thurge's house guard, she surmised. She noticed that one carried what could only be a woman's petticoat, white and flounced with lace so delicate it was no more than a gossamer banner in his black-gloved hand. She straightened her back, sensing trouble. This was a public road that led eventually into the City of Sylyria. There was no reason any should deny her access.

The riders reined their mounts a few paces from the roadside, and the animals tossed their heads, snorting and pawing impatiently. She struggled not to show her fear. One blow from one of those horses' hooves would be enough to knock her unconscious. "Goddess blessing," she said, her voice steady by virtue of years and years of travel upon rougher roads than this.

"State your business here, old woman." The speaker wore a short pointed beard and his hair was the color and texture of tousled straw. It stuck up in all directions, and the old woman was suddenly hard-pressed not to laugh.

"I say the songs the goddess sends," she replied, the old ritual answer falling off her tongue without thought. "I travel to the keep of Thane Jiroud at Castle Sarrasin. I am invited." She raised her chin defiantly. These ruffians would not intimidate her. She noticed that one of them had ragged scratches, still raw and bleeding, across his face, and the other's cloak was torn along one seam. What had these men been doing? she wondered. She peered at them more closely, and saw that beneath their cloaks, their clothing was disordered, and that their breeches were muddy at the knees.

Scratch-face leaned forward and spoke in Straw-hair's ear. All three men guffawed, and Straw-hair looked at her with contempt. "I'm sure you are, old woman." He waved his arm. "Off with you. You've another two hours on foot."

She nodded, not taking her eyes off the men. The one who held the petticoat thrust it down on the far side of the horse, out of her sight. Her uneasiness turned to fear. Something had happened here, something that involved a woman, and one gently born by the looks of that petticoat. There was a furtive air about the men, an air of guilt. She stood her ground as Scratch-face dropped his eyes and pulled at the reins of his horse so quickly that the animal reared and wheeled. "Off with you, old woman," he said with a quick gesture to his companions. As one, the men touched their heels to their horses' sides and galloped off.

She stared after them for a long moment, then scanned the line of willows that surely must bend over a brook. Nothing moved, and she thought of taking off her shoes and bathing her tired feet in the cool water. The pebble that had lodged in her shoe somewhere on the long walk between Eld and Sylyria was growing into a boulder, or at least, so it felt.

Another gust of wind swept over the meadow, and the grass rippled and the swaying branches of the willows dipped and signed. She looked down the road, and fancied she could see the faint smudge of the walls of her destination on the horizon. If she kept on, she would arrive well before dark. For a moment, she wondered if she should investigate. But if she paused to find out what mischief those men had involved themselves in, she might be on the road after nightfall. The looks of those men decided her. The world was a cold place when one traveled alone, without so much as a roof to call one's own. She would not invite trouble. She stamped her foot in one more futile attempt to dislodge the troublesome stone, and gripped the straps of her harp harder against her back. She coughed. The familiar tightness in her chest clenched around her heart. She thought of her old friend and student, Reyerne, now music master at the keep of the thane. One more student to assess, one more prodigy to recognize, one more Festival, and then it would be time to rest. The goddess was calling her home. With a sigh, she shrugged her pack to her shoulder and continued on her way.

"No!" The word hung, almost visible, not six inches from the long nose of the man who stood in trembling obeisance before Jiroud, Thane of Sarrasin. "How many times and in how many ways must I say it? Invite all the songsayers you please beneath my roof; let Juilene play 'til her fingers bleed. But no daughter of mine shall make a public spectacle of herself, at the Festival or anywhere else, and that's my final word." Jiroud folded his arms over the gold medallion of his rank and leaned against the high carved back of his chair. The late-afternoon light slanted across his face, and the red glow of the fading sun only made him seem more formidable than he already was. Sarrasin was one of the largest domains in all of Sylyria, and anyone who met Jiroud never forgot it. The medallion gleamed upon his chest, throwing off golden glints of light in all directions, and his grey hair, once an auburn as ruddy as the light, hung loose and curling about his shoulders.

From the safety of the far side of the hearth, Juilene allowed her fingers to skip lightly over the brass strings of her harp, and watched her music master raise a stubborn chin, even as his shoulders shifted with a barely concealed sigh. The tentative notes faded, even as Reyerne's persistent pleading continued.

"But, Thane Jiroud," said Reyerne, a man more known for his musical talent than his diplomacy, "this will be her only chance, her last chance, to sing and play before the goddess. Can't you see the opportunity, the honor she will bring to your house? Not one of the noble houses—"

"Precisely," Jiroud said. "Not one of the noble houses has ever sent a daughter—or a son, either—to join the ranks of the songsayers at Festival. And that is precisely why I will not allow it, either."

Reyerne sighed and ran his fingers with their callused tips and long nails through his shock of unruly white hair. Fourteen years in Jiroud's service had inured him to the thane's wrath. "My lord, I beg you. Your daughter has a rare and unique gift. I know that most of the songsayers who appear before the Festival are mere charlatans, mere amateurs. But the Lady Juilene is the genuine thing—she more than any other pupil I have ever had deserves the honor and the recognition. One of the greatest of them all will be here before nightfall—just to hear your daughter sing."

"That's as may be," answered Jiroud. He looked up and for a moment, Juilene felt her father's keen eye fall upon her. She bent her head and hid her face behind the curtain of her curly auburn hair. It wouldn't be wise to attract too much of his attention at the moment. "Any songsayer is welcome beneath my roof. But my answer is still no. The songsayers may be sacred to the goddess in theory, Reyerne, but you and I both know that too many are little more than—than—" Jiroud glanced at Juilene, clearly struggling for a delicate way in which to express himself. "The reality is far different. Most of them are nothing but common harlots who offer much more than a song in exchange for a bed. I won't have my daughter mistaken for one of that sort."

"But, lord, can't you agree that when one is given a gift by the goddess as precious and rare as the Lady Juilene's, it should be used, appreciated, not hidden beneath a barrel to shine all alone by itself? What would the goddess have been thinking when she bestowed this gift upon your daughter?"

Jiroud's thick grey eyebrows rushed together and met above his hawk nose. "I don't presume to guess what the goddess was thinking when she bestowed the gift, as you call it, upon Juilene. But I remind you she also saw fit to make her the daughter of one of the most important families in all of Sylyria—in all the League, I might add. And there are certain things a daughter in Juilene's position just doesn't do—and parading around at Festival in the company of harlots and drunkards, thieves and cutpurses, surely is one of them." His face flushed, and he snapped his fingers at the seneschal, who, along with two other men, idled uncomfortably just inside the doorway that led from the kitchens. "Damn it, man, stop fingering that message like a whore. Where's that demi-thurge? I thought I paid well for fair weather, and now you bring me this." Jiroud held out his hand for the rolled parchment that the seneschal reluctantly laid in his palm.

Reyerne stiffened. When Jiroud was in one of his rages, it wasn't wise to confront him. Accordingly, the music master dropped his eyes and allowed his shoulders to sag an infinitesimal, albeit visible, amount. He sighed audibly as he withdrew. Juilene clutched the harp closer, and shifted on her stool. She held her finger up to her mouth as her music master approached with heavy steps. It definitely wouldn't do to call any further attention to themselves right now. She watched as the demi-thurge, a slight, stoop-shouldered man of middle years, shuffled to the front of the dais. Dust clung to the front of his robe, his hair looked as if it had never seen a comb, and Juilene could never remember his name.

"With all due respect, Thane Jiroud," he began, "there is no way to guarantee safe passage of a cargo. Not from pirates *and* weather. What you demanded was simply too complicated for this time of year, when the winds off the Outer Ocean are too unpredictable—"

Jiroud glared at the demi-thurge. "Excuses. You like the security of my roof—of my kitchens well enough. You'll take my money and my food. And in exchange, what do you give me? Excuses. All you thurges—some days I think we'd be better off without the lot of you hanging 'round."

"I beg your pardon, Thane Jiroud," said the demi-thurge, "but not every thane agrees with your assessment of our worth. Why, only last Festival, the thurges of Sylyria were commended for their—"

"Quiet," snarled Jiroud. "I was there." He shook his head. "What do you suggest now, Master Demi-Thurge? My cargo's in the hands of Parmathian pirates—what's left of it."

"I will, if my thane wishes," replied the demi-thurge with an air of injured dignity, "consult with Master-Thurge Lindos. It is entirely possible that I made mistakes in my calculations—I am ready to take responsibility for whatever difficulties that has caused."

Juilene bit her lip. Her father was behaving like a boor and a bully. The poor thurge looked so uncomfortable. Beside her, Reyerne looked no less discomfitted. One of these days, her father was likely to burst a blood vessel in his head with all his bellowing, and it looked as if today might be the day. Certainly it was not a good day to ask her father anything. But every year since she had turned fourteen—the minimum age for a songsayer to appear at Festival and perform before the goddess—Reyerne had approached her father and asked, no, begged permission for her to play and sing before the city. And every year her father said no.

This year was different though. Her exasperation flared into full-fledged resentment as her fingers fell across the strings more heavily than they should, and Reyerne raised an eyebrow. Her mouth twitched an apology. But why apologize? This was the last year she would ever be able to appear before the Festival. Songsayers were supposed to be single—they couldn't be married, for the Goddess Dramue in her incarnation had remained unmarried. And this year, on the eve of her twentieth birthday, she was to be married to her childhood sweetheart and the heir to the neighboring domain, Arimond of Ravenwood. Thus, with one stroke, her father accomplished two things at once: his daughter's happiness and the uniting of two distant septs of one of the oldest families in all the Sylyrian League. Though, really, thought Juilene as she caressed the smooth strings of polished brass, really he had accomplished three. He had insured that she, his only daughter, would never seek employment as a songsayer.

She plucked a few strings experimentally and watched her father beneath carefully lowered lids. For all the lip service her father paid the goddess, he had no idea what music meant to her or to anyone else for that matter. He was a tall man, still in his prime, still vital, still a force to be reckoned with, and his whole life was consumed with the cares of his domain. Jiroud's scowl deepened as he chewed a stick of uster-wood, reading and rereading the parchment scroll from his agent in the port city of Khardroon. The pirates who roamed the waters of the Parmathian Straits were a notorious menace to shipping and trade, and Jiroud had sought to ensure a safe passage by means of the magic. Juilene pressed her lips together in a suppressed sigh, and glanced at Reyerne.

The music master's hair stuck up in all directions, a sure sign of distress, and his whole body quivered. "I am sorry, my lady," he began. "I tried. I thought this year—surely, this year, your father would relent. Perhaps after Galicia hears you sing—"

She shook her head and shrugged. "I doubt it, Reyerne. Look at Father's mood. Could the goddess herself change his mind? I know you meant well, asking her to come and hear me, but I'm not surprised. I never thought for a moment Father would allow it. You know what he thinks of songsayers."

Reyerne sighed again. "Yes. I do. And for the most part I agree with him. It is a most debased occupation. But you—you, my lady—your gift is real. Who better to honor the goddess in her own profession?"

Juilene looked down at the harp she held, at her long nails necessary to play the brass strings. "It won't be the same after I marry Arimond, Reyerne, you know that. I won't have time for singing or for playing. Maybe it's just as well that I stop now." She finished with an angry glance in her father's direction.

"No, my lady, please don't say that." Reyerne bent down and covered her hand with his. On the broad palm, she felt the same smooth calluses as on hers.

She looked into his faded brown eyes, and all the anger she felt for her father melted into sympathy for her tutor. She had studied with Reyerne for more than twelve years. In all that time, Reyerne had refused offers of other employment, the opportunity to move on to other households, even to teach at the Academy in Sylyria, where the best of the songsayers trained. There were some unkind enough to say that Reyerne did not so much refuse to leave Juilene as he refused to leave his sinecure. But Juilene knew the depth of the old man's devotion.

He drew another deep breath and slowly straightened. "Forgive me, my lady. Galicia is a very old friend of mine, a songsayer of highest repute. Perhaps she will be able to change your father's mind."

"If she does," Juilene said with a sad smile, "she will be the first."

"I have known her since I was very young, for I was fortunate enough to study under her when I was not much older than you are now. Surely the goddess herself has willed that Galicia intends to be in Sylyria for the Festival this year. For even if your father won't change his mind, I want her to hear you play. She cannot help but be impressed."

Juilene smiled. Everyone who heard her play said the same things. It would be good to play just once at the Festival—just once to sit before the anonymous, faceless crowds and offer her songs to the goddess. It would be a fitting end to her years of study. For a moment, she allowed herself to imagine the scene—the crowds clustered close about her feet, the flickering torchlight, the eager faces fastened on her hands and on her harp. With her hands and her voice, she would weave a spell as real as any thurge, and she would feel the acclaim, know that with her music, she had pleased them all and taken them to a place only she could show them. But Reyerne was speaking, and the vision faded abruptly. "I—I have begun to make arrangements, in fact."

"Arrangements, Reyerne?" Juilene set the harp aside, and gestured for her teacher to join her on the bench. Her father was bellowing for his scribe; it was extremely unlikely he would even remember Reyerne's request if no one mentioned it again.

Reyerne sat, pulling his robes around his thin shoulders. "I have a little money saved, my lady. Your father was a most generous employer—his wages to teach you were far more than I ever needed. And so I am thinking of finding a little house in the city, after you marry, and perhaps taking on another pupil or two. Something to occupy my time, but nothing taxing." He paused and smiled ruefully at her. "I doubt I shall ever have a student as able as you."

"Oh, Reyerne." Impulsively, Juilene kissed the old man's cheek. "I am sorry Father is so—so stubborn about letting me perform at the Festival. He just has such strong ideas about what is right and proper."

"And I don't blame him, my lady." Reyerne rested his age-spotted hands on his knees. "He should be concerned with the proper order of things. It only makes me sad to see such talent as yours wasted. Everyone here loves your playing and your singing, and all the children love the stories you tell—" Abruptly he broke off, staring into the distance. "Ah, well. Soon enough you will have children of your own to tell them to, my lady," he finished. "Perhaps it is nothing but an old man's pride in the best student he has ever had the privilege to teach."

Pride made her straighten and hold her harp tightly. She basked in the music master's praise, even as something in her rebelled at the restrictive circumscriptions of her life. But better not to think of it now. She might as well make the most of the time she had left. "Listen to the variation I made up, and tell me what you think."

Reyerne smiled once more, and settled back, nodding his head, as she ran her fingers over the strings. The notes rippled and she frowned a little, trying to remember the particular combination she had thought so pleasing.

From the corner of her eye, she saw her father's eyes shift toward the door, and he broke off speaking in the middle of a word. His scribe paused in writing, and Juilene saw the man's mouth open, even as the great doors of the outer entrance to the hall slammed open with a loud bang. A voice as familiar as it was unexpected rang out, "My lord Jiroud, my mother begs your help in the hour of our need."

Amazed, Juilene turned to stare, the harp strings vibrating beneath her suddenly still fingers. Arimond stood in the doorway, poised at the top of the shallow steps that led down into the great hall. His cloak was carelessly tossed over his arm, and his hair was windswept. Without even pausing to scan the hall for her presence, he strode down the steps, toward her father's central chair, one hand outstretched.

"What's wrong, boy?" Jiroud half rose from his seat, waving away his scribe with one hand as he beckoned to Arimond with the other.

Arimond swallowed hard and wiped a dirty glove over his face. "It's my sister. She was found an hour or so ago in the lower meadow by the river. She'd been set upon by—" Abruptly he broke off, and Juilene handed her harp to Reyerne.

She sprang from her seat and ran to his side, gripping one arm. She could feel the tense muscles beneath his muddied tunic. Hair was plastered to his neck and cheeks, and he looked as though he had come straight from the practice fields without bothering to change.

"By whom?" bellowed Jiroud. "Outlaws? I thought we'd cleared the last of the scum—"

"No, my lord." Arimond's hand tightened on Juilene's but it was the only sign he gave that he was aware of her presence. "She says it was Lindos's men. And she managed to tear off a scrap—" Here he fumbled in the pouch he wore at his waist, and pulled out a dark piece of fabric. "These are their colors."

Jiroud rose to his feet at the name. His face darkened considerably. "Are you sure of this, boy?" His voice was soft, but in it Juilene heard the edge that made even the most hardened of all her father's soldiers quiver in their boots.

Arimond nodded and handed the tattered scrap to Jiroud, who met Arimond's eyes briefly, then turned the piece of material slowly in his hands, examining each side of it. "This blood—"

"My sister managed to inflict some damage of her own," Arimond answered.

Jiroud nodded. His grim gaze fell on Juilene, and he shook his head. "And you, my lady, think I'm harsh because I won't have you wandering the countryside dressed up in songsayer's rags." He shook his head and gave a short snort as he turned to the seneschal. "Have my horse saddled. I'll go to your mother directly, boy." His eyes flicked over the couple, from Juilene to Arimond and back. "Stay with my daughter if you wish. You've done all you can for your sister."

Arimond glanced down at Juilene and squeezed her hand. "Thank you, my lord."

Without another word, Jiroud turned on his heel and left the hall as anxious servants scurried in his wake. Juilene gazed up at her betrothed. He was tall and blond and just a few years older than she, and she was closer to Arimond and his sister, Arimelle, than she was to her own brother, Lazare, who was more than a dozen years her senior.

"Come and sit," she murmured as the flurry of activity subsided and the hall was once more peaceful.

He drew a deep breath and turned to her, bringing her hand to his lips. "Forgive me, sweetheart, for not greeting you properly."

Juilene shook her head impatiently. "Tell me what happened to Melly." She led him to one of the benches before one of the high hearths, and drew him down beside her. She glanced around. Reyerne had withdrawn with her harp. Except for two servants the hall was deserted. She beckoned to the nearest. "Would you like something to drink?"

He nodded. "Anything."

"Bring us some cider," Juilene said as the servant approached, wiping his hands on his apron.

Arimond waited until the servant had gone and the other was out of earshot. His clothes reeked of sweat, and the odor of the stables. "I'm sorry, Juilene. I know I don't look—or smell—very good."

"Never mind that, just tell me what happened."

Arimond drew a deep breath as though to compose himself by force. "I can't. It's too terrible."

Images raced through Juilene's mind, every terrible thing she could possibly imagine. "Arimond"—she gripped his arm—"please, you have to tell me—how bad can she be?"

"She'll be lucky to live. How's that? And if she does live, she'll be lucky to walk. They broke both her legs, one of her hands, they tore out locks of her hair—" He stopped at the look on Juilene's face. "I told you it was terrible. But I'll make him pay—by the goddess, I will make him pay. I swear it." He gazed into the hearth, where a small fire smoldered.

Juilene could feel the tension in the muscles of his upper arm as she pressed next to him. A long shudder went through his body, and when he turned his face to look at her, she saw tears forming in his eyes.

"I'll kill the bastard, I swear it. I'll take him apart with my own hands—thurge or not, he'll pay."

"Arimond," Juilene whispered, smoothing the tangled strands away from his face. "Father will know what to do. But please—will she live?"

He ran a grimy hand over his forehead. "I don't know. Branward doesn't know. They stopped just short of killing her. I suppose even they didn't dare that."

"Oh, goddess," whispered Juilene. The thought of her friend, beaten and abused, was more than she could stand. She clutched Arimond's arm. "And you're certain it was Lindos's men?"

"That scrap proves it, doesn't it? Those are his colors. And you know as well as I do he doesn't even attempt to control them. He lets them rape and plunder and pillage where they will—you know it, Juilene—don't try to convince me otherwise. They roam this countryside in gangs. Soon not a woman will be safe if this keeps up."

"You must appeal to the Over-Thurge."

"Old Blaise?" Arimond shook his head. "He's weak, sick—why else would Lindos so blatantly defy all the rules of decency?"

"But he is the High Thurge of the Conclave, not just the Over-Thurge of Sylyria. All of them answer to him. Surely they will have some say over this master-thurge—Lindos is only a master-thurge after all—"

"Ah, my jewel." He interrupted her with a rueful smile and a shake of his head. "You are so young—you believe the best of everyone. The Conclave cares nothing for the common folk—haven't you guessed that? What goes on among the master-thurges in obscure corners of Sylyria doesn't concern them—"

"Then Father will appeal to the King."

He shook his head again. "And what will the King do? Send an emissary?" He gave a soft snort. "I don't think so. And you know as well as I do that even if your father himself confronts Lindos, he will only deny it was his men. He'll say the scrap came from a stolen tunic or something. And by the time he gets around to denying it, the scratches Melly did manage to inflict will have healed, and there will be no proof at all. Just the word of an hysterical girl, they'll say."

Juilene looked up as the servant approached bearing a silver tray with two goblets. She nodded to him to put it down, and handed Arimond one of the goblets. "Here. Drink this." She raised the other to her lips and sipped, amazed at how her fingers shook.

"There's only one thing to do, Juilene. If Lindos is going to be stopped, I shall have to stop him myself." He sipped the cider and stared into the hearth.

"Stop him? But how? You can't go riding up to his gate and challenge him. He'll laugh."

"Let him laugh. And what's to say I can't? There're no rules against challenging a thurge."

"Arimond, think of what you're saying." A tremor went through Juilene. She knew this mood. Ordinarily Arimond was the kindest and gentlest of men. But once he had his mind made up to do something, nothing stopped him—not the threat of death or serious bodily injury. Nothing. If he had it in his mind to confront the wizard, there was little she was likely to do about it. Even her father was not likely to change his mind. "Please wait and see what Father thinks, Mondo," she said softly, using the old childish name for him. "You know at the very least he'll call a Gathering."

A bitter smile twisted his mouth. "That's what you both called me, wasn't it? We were Mondo and Melly and Jewels—and nothing was ever going to separate us, was it? She might die, Juilene. When I left, Mother didn't think there was much hope. And even if she does get better, she won't be the same. Never."

Old memories of childhood flooded back, and Juilene's eyes filled with tears. She bit her lip as her mouth quivered. "I know Melly is very bad," she managed. "But I don't want you to risk your life. I couldn't bear to lose you."

For a long moment he stared at her, and then he gathered her in his arms, drawing her close. He pressed his lips into the thick mass of curls, and wrapped his arms around her. She nestled close to him, savoring the comfort of his strength. "Don't you see, Jewels?" he whispered against her hair. "If someone doesn't stop him, no one will be safe. It's bad enough that peasant women have been assaulted in broad daylight. And Melly only wandered down to the meadows where we used to play—if she was vulnerable, so are you. So are all the women of the entire district, noble or not. And I couldn't bear it if anything happened to you and I knew that there was something I could have done to prevent it."

She twined her fingers in his tunic. "Please, please, talk to Father. How could you alone possibly prevent it?"

"What if I told you I thought there was a way?"

She pulled back a little and frowned into his eyes. "What do you mean?"

"A way to rid the land of Lindos forever."

"Invoke his doom, you mean?"

"A thurge's doom is always true, and he makes no secret of it. It's why he's so brazen, why he lets his men do as they will. He thinks no one can stop him."

"I suppose I understand that," she said, turning the goblet in her fingers. "For what in the world is a non-born knight?"

"I think it's me," he answered slowly.

She stared at him in disbelief. "Arimond—" She bit her lip. Could he be mad with grief? "What makes you think such a thing?"

"My real mother died giving birth to me," he said. "You know that. I had to be cut from her womb after she was already dead. I wasn't born the usual way—and my mother never gave me birth. Surely you see—if I am not the non-born knight, who could be? Such a thing is surely impossible."

She sank beside him on the bench, her hands fallen still in her lap. "When did you realize this?"

"I've been thinking it for some time. I guess what really made me start to believe it was when the attacks by his men began to escalate. And Lindos never made any secret of his doom. His men laugh and brag of it on every street and in every tavern of every village in the district. He's so sure such a thing is impossible, but listen, Juilene, isn't that the way it works? The very thing you think you'll never

meet is often right under your nose? Isn't that how the goddess herself incarnated?"

Juilene knotted her fingers together, thoughts darting
through her head like scattering fish. "Arimond," she said
at last. "If this is true—"

"It *is* true," he said. "You know it is."

"I know the story of your birth is true. I don't know
whether that makes you the non-born knight or not."

"A thurge's doom is always true, isn't it?"

Juilene opened her mouth, then shut it. Was there any
point in arguing with him? A thurge's doom was always
true, that much she knew and understood. A thurge's doom
was revealed when he or she accepted his or her power. It
was no simple thing—to know the manner of one's death.
Although the foolish sometimes proclaimed it a blessing,
wiser ones knew it for a curse. It was a terrible price to pay
for the power, thought Juilene, and a terrible thing to live
under the burden of the knowledge of one's own death.

"Yes," she said at last. "A thurge's doom is always true.
And I know that Lindos is unusual, in that he makes no secret of his. But I cannot believe . . ." Her voice trailed off.

"That I could be his doom? Just because you know me?"
Anger and sorrow vied in his shifting expression.

"No," she said. "I don't want anything to happen to you.
If I lose you, I won't have anything left either."

His expression softened and he drew her close. "Ah,
Jewels. No harm will come to me, I swear it."

She relaxed against his chest. His fingertips stroked her
scalp through the thick curly mass of her hair, and she
could feel the roughened skin, the scars and calluses he
bore even at his age. He meant to comfort her, but the scars
only made her think of wounds, and that only made her
think of Melly, lying close to death. She sighed. "What will
you do? Lindos hardly ever lets anyone into his castle—
and it isn't likely that his guards will let you in, especially

if you ride up to the gate and announce yourself as his doom."

"No," he said, his cheek against the top of her head. "I know that. I have to find a way into the castle—a way to sneak in preferably at night, when the thurge will be in his bed, asleep. It will be an easy thing to kill him as he sleeps."

Juilene shivered. Easy, easy. Arimond kept using the word as though anything to do with Lindos was bound to be easy. She shook her head. "And just how do you think to accomplish that? The walls are always heavily guarded, even in the dead of night."

"Except on the nights of the Festival."

She pulled away from him. The Sacred Festival of Dramue, the nine days that celebrated the goddess's life and death as a mortal woman, was less than a few turns of the calendar tree away. "But you still can't simply walk into the castle—you know as well as I the stories that are told about that place. Some say that there are all sorts of traps, of things—horrible things—to protect the thurges. Lindos isn't the first thurge to live there, and who knows what all the others have left behind?" Juilene shuddered, remembering all the times the tales of the nursery maids had made it impossible for her to sleep. "And there're bound to be some human guards as well. Lindos isn't going to let all his guards and servants go to the Festival every night. No one does."

"I know," he said. "And that's where I need to ask you to help me."

She pulled away from him. "Me? How can I help you?"

"You can get us into his keep. Once we're in, you can distract him and I'll find a way to kill him."

"But how can I get us in?" She stared at him in shock.

"Because you can pretend to be a songsayer. Soon the

countryside will be overrun with them. You know that as well as I."

Juilene drew a deep breath. It was true that even the smallest houses were expected to house at least one of the songsayers, the traveling musicians who went from town to town, telling stories, providing music and entertainment for the populace. At the Sacred Festival, they flocked to the cities in droves, since that had been the calling of the goddess in her earthly incarnation. Reyerne's old teacher, Galicia, was not likely to be the only songsayer who would seek shelter beneath her father's roof. And although many of them were legitimate, not all of them were gifted equally. But even the ones who were, as her father said, little more than traveling prostitutes, were supposed to be considered sacred to the goddess, and at Festival time, all were made welcome.

"So you want me to pretend to be a songsayer—"

"No, Jewels, not pretend. You could be a songsayer, you know it. You have more talent in your little finger than most of them. It's only your position here that means you can't do it."

Juilene stared at him. Was this truly the work of the goddess? It seemed impossible to think that just a few minutes ago, Reyerne had been pleading with her father to allow her to go to the Festival as a songsayer. What had the old man said? "What had the goddess been thinking?" Was this the goddess's plan for her? She wet her lips.

Arimond knew he had struck a nerve. "Surely you remember, all those years ago? The games we used to play? You were always the songsayer. And remember when we told our parents that that's what you intended to become? Remember how shocked they all were?"

Juilene dropped her eyes. She well remembered that day, and the looks of amusement, then horrified derision. For although there were plenty of talented songsayers, the women who chose to enter such a life were often little more than prostitutes and sold their bodies with their songs.

Such a life was unthinkable for a girl like Juilene, whose father was lord of a great domain just outside Sylyria. No nobleman's daughter would even contemplate such a life. Their parents had laughed, and then the laughter had turned to anger when she had persisted. It simply wasn't done, and that was the end of it. Until now.

She raised her eyes slowly and met Arimond's. He knew her childish hopes and dreams. He knew how much she still longed to take place in the sacred ceremonies of the Festival. It was one of the reasons she loved him, for he had never laughed or met her dreams with derision. He had dreamed along with her, had allowed her to believe, even if only for a few brief years, that such fame could be hers. Even Reyerne didn't know how much it meant to her, how much she longed to play and sing before an anonymous, faceless crowd, and to be loved and applauded only for her music and her stories. Was this a chance that would surely never come again?

She drew a deep breath. "How—how will we do this?"

"I don't know," he admitted. "It's more than I can answer right now. We have to think and plan it out very carefully. You and I both know there are too many dangers involved and we haven't much time. And we can't tell your father."

Juilene shook her head slowly. That was an understatement. He was likely to lock her in her room for the duration of the Festival if he thought she was likely to try such a thing. And old Reyerne—that was his dream to see her play for the goddess, on the Festival stage. But even he mustn't be told. He would be so proud he was sure to let something slip.

"Jewels," Arimond whispered. He took both her hands

in his and raised them to his lips. "I'll speak to your father as soon as he comes home. At the least, we can raise enough of an outrage that Lindos might rein his men in for a few weeks. It will buy us time. And then after the Festival, no matter what happens, we'll be married and we'll live happily together for the rest of our lives."

Unless something goes wrong, she thought involuntarily as a cold chill went down her back. She gazed into his grey eyes. Arimond loved her, she knew that as surely as she knew her own name. He would never let her be put into jeopardy. And yet, what if he was wrong? It was entirely conceivable that she would be able to get in and out of Lindos's keep with none being the wiser, for the songsayers were under the protection of the goddess at Festival time and anyone who dared to harm them would be seen to commit sacrilege and would be shunned by the whole of society whether thane or thurge. But Arimond put himself entirely at risk. And what if he was wrong?

He twisted his fingers around hers, and brought both her hands to his lips. "Juilene," he whispered. "Don't you know I would never do anything to jeopardize our life together?"

She could only shake her head in mute response. He drew her close, and involuntarily she leaned into him, forgetting the earthy odors that clung to him. He bent his head and pressed his mouth on hers. Her lips opened in answer, and gently, his tongue teased the very edges of her mouth. A long shudder went down her spine, and she felt her breasts flatten against his chest as his arms tightened around her.

"Oh, Juilene," he whispered into the thick fall of her hair, "I can't wait 'til we're married. This waiting's been the hardest part."

She smiled despite her qualms. Arimond was as forceful in this as he was in everything else. Only the rigid code of proper behavior constrained him. She leaned back a little in his embrace. "I love you, Mondo. I just don't want to see any harm come to you."

He pressed her head against his shoulder. "I swear it won't, I swear it."

"Ahem!" Loud throat clearing from the opposite side of the room made them spring apart. With an overly exaggerated clump of heavy riding boots, Juilene's brother, Lazare, came striding into the hall, stripping off his riding gloves. His boots were flecked with mud, and here and there, leaves clung to his cloak. "If you two love doves can bear to drag yourself apart, maybe you can tell me where Father went."

"Lazare!" Juilene jumped up, brushing at her skirts. She knew her cheeks were rosy. "We weren't expecting you."

"I know." He pressed a quick kiss on the top of her head, and nodded to Arimond. "But there's news in the city and I thought Father ought to know. Greetings, Arimond."

"What news?" Juilene beckoned the servants who peered into the hall.

"Old Blaise is dead. Sylyria has a new thurge, and the Conclave must name a new head."

Juilene gasped and Arimond reached out to shake her brother's hand.

"I must say, Mondo, you don't look much better than I do. What on earth have you been doing? Having a roll in the hay?"

Juilene blushed even more violently and shook her head. "Arimond brought news of his own—bad news. That's where Father went—"

"What's wrong?" Lazare cast a quick glance over both of them.

"My sister was attacked. My mother sent me here to ask for your father."

"Arimelle? By whom?"

"Lindos's men."

There was a long silence and the eyes of the two men met. Lazare gave a long, low whistle. "Well now. Well, well." There was another pause, and Lazare asked, "Is she badly hurt?"

Arimond nodded shortly.

Lazare looked from one to the other. "I see. I'm sorry, Arimond. Is there anything I can do?"

"Not at the moment."

"Let me know if there is anything. Anything at all. I mean it."

The men exchanged another long look and Juilene wondered what they were thinking. Too many times she had heard Arimond declare that Lindos was a plague upon the countryside and should be removed. But her father always insisted that the situation was far more complicated than that.

The arcane hierarchy of thurges was even more complex than that which governed the thanes and demi-thanes. Anyone who aspired to the rank of master-thurge began an apprenticeship as a demi-thurge. And only after long years of study, by virtue of demonstrated skill and proven ability before the Conclave comprised of all the Over-Thurges of the League, could any demi-thurge hope to rise to the ranks of the master-thurges. Many never rose so far at all. In contrast, the rank of thane and demi-thane was hereditary. Lazare would inherit Jiroud's title upon his death.

But Lindos, Juilene knew, was unusual. He had risen far more quickly than any other demi-thurge—his ability was legendary. Even old Blaise, the High Thurge of the Conclave, had been said to have consulted with him while he was still nominally a demi-thurge. So although Lindos might be the plague Arimond and his friends claimed he was, the proposition of unseating him was no small matter. But as she watched her brother's face, Juilene realized that older and presumably wiser as Lazare was, there was always the chance that he could decide to aid Arimond.

Arimond cleared his throat softly. "I'd better be getting back home. Shall I tell your father you're here?"

"Yes, please do. It's nearly dinnertime and I planned to stay the night. There's no chance I can get back to the city before dark. Eliane doesn't expect me back until tomorrow."

Arimond bent to press a quick kiss on Juilene's mouth as a wild gust of wind blew through the hall. Juilene looked up.

A small woman wrapped in a ragged cloak of homespun wool, a lumpish pack strapped across her back and another clutched in one gnarled hand, stood just inside the doors, leaves swirling at her feet. Juilene blinked. The old woman's gaze fell upon her, the pale blue eyes watery but clear. "I say the songs the goddess sends."

There was nothing of an old woman's quaver in the silvery cadence, nor of an old woman's weakness in the set of her broad shoulders. This must be the songsayer Reyerne had invited, the woman who had been his own teacher so many years ago. She stared, wondering what it was about the woman that seemed at once so commanding and so frail. Lazare spoke the words of ritual welcome: "Come speak to us, who listen for her voice. Come, be welcome at our hearth."

As the old woman handed her pack to a servant and limped down the steps, Arimond bent once more to whisper into Juilene's ear: "I'll send word to you tomorrow. You'll be one songsayer Lindos will be sorry he ever welcomed beneath his roof."

Chapter Two

❧❀❧

The pale pink moon had risen above the castle walls and the sky was a cluster of stars when Juilene returned to her chambers at last. She sank to her knees beside the windows and rested her burning face against the smooth fabric of her sleeve. She stared out into the night. Galicia's words still echoed in her ears, the old woman's voice damning her performance with faint praise. "A fine technician," she'd said. "Her delivery is well timed." As if the sum of Juilene's playing were no more than that of a time-keeper!

Even Reyerne had been disappointed. Juilene had seen how he had been unable to prevent his face from falling. He had even protested, "But does she not sing as if the goddess herself were alive?"

Galicia had smiled, gently, pityingly, thought Juilene, as

she answered: "The goddess is alive in all of us, Reyerne. Have you forgotten so much?"

At that, Reyerne had opened his mouth, and then shut it abruptly.

Galicia had taken his arm and led him a little way off as she continued, "Certainly the young lady has great potential, and her playing in many ways shows great promise. But the songs the goddess sends are not just meant to be well played and well sung. There is a certain passion, a certain understanding that only comes with months and years upon the roads. It is only to be expected that your student should lack this experience, Reyerne, and it would indeed be most unusual if she'd acquired it, at such a young age, and in such a sheltered place. You've done well with her, my student, and I commend you. Certainly her performance is better than most whom I've been asked to hear. But she is not the next incarnation come to earth, I assure you that."

And listening, Juilene had felt the blood in her face burn hotter than the fire in the hearth, and it took all the discipline she could muster not to throw her harp into the flames and rush from the hall, mortified.

Now Lazare and her father still sat before the hearth, nursing flagons of last season's summer ale between them, her performance and Galicia's long forgotten, a thing of no more consequence than the dregs of the ale. Reyerne had long ago retired, and Galicia was likely to have been given a snug room near her old pupil, her age and reputation ensuring that she received more than the customary blanket and space by one of the hearths.

Juilene was glad that her father had returned even though it had been clear he had listened to her playing with only half an ear, for the news from Ravenwood was not good: Arimelle clung to life by a fragile thread. Her injuries were far more serious than Arimond had known when he had arrived at her father's house. Already the news had gone out to the neighboring thanes, and there was talk of a Gathering as soon as the day after next.

Surely, she thought, as the soft gleam of the brass strings of her harp caught her eye, that accounted for the fact that her playing was not at its best. Reyerne should have explained to the old woman that they'd had very bad news just that day, that her childhood playmate lay close to death. Surely that explained why Galicia found any deficiencies at all in her music.

Juilene plucked at the embroidery on the sleeve of her gown, remembering how her father had watched her with a puckered frown, while Lazare whispered in his ear. She hoped her father and the other nobles would have a calming influence upon Arimond but privately she doubted it. Arimond never changed his mind once it was made up. She remembered all the times when they were little, when she and Arimond had played together in the very meadows where Arimelle had been attacked. Although most of the time Arimond was the sweetest of boys, he had been in the habit of stamping his foot and bellowing when he had truly made up his mind. Even Arimelle used to laugh at him.

She leaned her head against the sill and felt a lump of unshed tears rise in her throat. What was wrong with her? Here she was lamenting because a ragged old woman found fault with a few songs, and Arimond's sister lay close to death. Pray the goddess Melly lived.

Melly had been the perfect counterpart to her brother, all golden curls and light blue eyes, her cheeks round and rosy. No dare was ever too daring, no prank too provoking, no punishment too daunting to temper her spirit. Juilene could imagine her reaction when the thurge's men had come upon her. Melly would have fought; she would never have given in easily. If she had surrendered herself, thought Juilene sadly, she might not have been so badly injured.

But Arimond would be no less intent upon revenge, she knew as she watched a star shoot across the black sky. Far in the western sky, the twin blue stars called the Eyes of Dramue burned low and steadily.

Oh, Dramue, she prayed, look down on us. Ease Melly's suffering and keep Mondo safe. Guide us all in the direction of your will.

Juilene rose to her feet and picked up her harp from its stand beside the window. She sank down on her little stool, gently turning her harp in her hands. The polished wood was warm beneath her fingertips, and the harp strings quivered gently, almost as though in anticipation. Some believed that harps took on lives of their own if their owner's music pleased the goddess herself. The harp was sacred to the goddess, that much Juilene knew, and those who played and sang were under her special protection. Dramue protect us all, she mused as she fingered the strings, her smoothly callused fingertips sliding easily over the brass. Her nails were long and strong, a blessing in itself, for without the long fingernails, the brass strung harp could not be played. A few notes rippled randomly.

Juilene paused. Just over the walls, the tops of the orchard trees were visible, the branches nearly bare of leaves. A low wind whined against the window, and the pane of glass rattled gently. This had been her home for as long as she had been alive, and even though in some ways Arimond's house was as familiar to her as this, it would be very strange to leave her father's keep.

Her father would be all alone in the great house, and there had been talk of Lazare and his wife, Eliane, coming to live here. And that would be strange, too, to see another woman assume the duties that her mother had done for so long until her death nearly five years ago. She liked Eliane well enough, but she had the feeling that her brother's wife looked upon her with faint disapproval.

Such a feeling had only grown stronger as she had grown older, and Juilene was always puzzled as to why that was. The goddess knew she labored as long at her housewifery lessons as she did at her music, as long at the chores as she did at her books. Was it her fault that she had always found the songs and stories of the songsayers more fascinating than the nine hundred and twenty-one ways to roast a fowl? It had always seemed to her that there were far more important things in the world than whether or not the linen was properly bleached. But then, she reminded herself with a sigh, she had always lived in a world where such things were taken for granted. It would never occur to anyone in her father's rank that there might be anything of more importance than one's duty. And if you were a woman in the ranks of the thanes and the demi-thanes who comprised the nobility of the Sylyrian League, your duty included not only the management of your husband's estates, but all the day-to-day cares of the immediate household as well. She had been lucky that her father had indulged her as much as he had.

Now she rested her cheek on her knee, and leaned the harp against the window. The strings shivered of their own accord, and she cocked her head and frowned a little at it. It had been made of the wood of the darvion tree, the tree that had borne the weight of the goddess all those years ago, and now flowered in midwinter when all the world was wrapped in snow and ice.

There was magic in the darvion tree, just as there was incipient magic in everything in the world. The power of the magic flowed, through every rock and tree and living creature, and even the smallest child knew the stories of the Anarchy, when the Ancient Thurges ran rampant with their power, using it as they would.

That power could still be raised in everything, even in inanimate things, by the thurges and the demi-thurges, whose lives were lived outside the stultifying code that governed the lives of the nobility. They lived according to their own code, according to the Way set down for them in the Book of the Covenant. Every so often, the ability to work the magic would show itself in one of the members of the noble houses, and the child would be allowed to escape the dull routines of the life she was bound to lead.

But wasn't that what she wanted? she wondered. Didn't she want home and hearth and husband? Children to sing to, to hold, to love? It was, she knew in her heart. All she wanted now was a taste, a glimpse of a shining moment to enjoy the talent with which she had been blessed, to let the goddess know how much she appreciated all she had been given. Was that so wrong? And Arimond . . . her thoughts trailed off into a troubled mire.

If Arimond was not the non-born knight of Lindos's doom, he was as good as dead. The awfulness of that possibility made her stomach clench and her heart pound. No, she decided, she wouldn't even consider that a possibility. There was no way he could not be the non-born knight; the circumstances of his birth were too idiosyncratic, too amazing. That he was even alive at all was a gift of the goddess. She had never heard of such a thing happening before. She ignored the warning voice in her head that cautioned her that she knew hardly anything about midwifery.

She had already thought of how she would slip away from the castle, under the guise of Arimond's company. They would tell her father and her brother that they were going to the Festival; once in the crowd, it would be an easy thing to separate from them, even if her father or brother were to insist upon accompanying her. And then together, she and Arimond would approach the gates of the master-thurge's keep.

She believed she had the skill to lull the wizard and his underlings into believing she was just an ordinary songsayer. She only hoped she would be able to divert his attention completely enough so that Arimond would be able to do what he had planned. The few snippets of information she'd managed to overhear about Melly's condition had convinced her that Arimond was right. No woman—noble or not—should ever be subjected to such treatment. And it wasn't only Lindos's lack of control over his men—she'd heard the servants whispering of what went on in Lindos's own bedchamber. They'd broken off when they'd noticed her, of course, but she'd heard enough to convince her that master-thurge or not, Lindos should be stopped. And if the Over-Thurge was unwilling to remove him, well . . . let the task fall to those who were willing to do it.

She rose to her feet and the harp strings quivered in response. The notes rippled like a sigh under her fingers.

She rummaged through her closet for her plainest and most serviceable gown. Wandering songsayers weren't rich; they had only a few possessions that they carried on their backs. No, she thought as she smoothed the folds of the blue woolen gown, which even though plain was strong and beautifully woven, they had no need for many things.

A light step behind her startled her out of her reverie. She jumped just a little but didn't turn. Only old Neri, her nurse, had a step like that, and a scent, warm and sweet as caramel, that seemed to follow her wherever she went.

"It's time you were to bed, child."

Juilene nodded, pressing her eyes closed against the sudden flood of tears, even as she felt the old woman stand beside her. When did Neri get so short? Juilene wondered. The top of the old woman's white head barely came to her shoulder. She sighed, though it was more a hiccup than a sigh, and she tightened her fingers around the fabric.

The old woman laid her gnarled fingers on top of her smooth hand, gently laying aside the gown Juilene clutched. "I know," she said. "I know."

Juilene pressed her lips together, and drew a deep breath. "Father and Lazare are discussing what's to be done, but, Neri, really, what *can* be done? There's nothing any of the thanes can do—Lindos is too powerful. Every thane in Sylyria can gather all they please, but will that help Melly? Will that stop Lindos?"

"Ah, child." Neri drew her close. "Your father and the other thanes have more recourse than you might think. After all, the Over-Thurge of Sylyria—"

"Is dead, Neri. The new Over-Thurge will have all he can do to maintain the balance of power, with the old one's passing. And the Conclave won't meet now 'til spring, and until then—who's to say how much trouble Lindos and his men can cause? Oh, Father thinks they'll lie low for a while, because there will be such an outcry, but even so—"

"Now, now, child. You're overwrought. Come to bed. It's late, and you can do nothing tonight, but make yourself sick with upset. Come."

With gentle tugging and prodding, the old nurse drew Juilene away from the window and sat her down before her dressing table. The gnarled old fingers removed the pins that held Juilene's thick auburn hair in some semblance of order and picked up the brush. "But, Neri, what if Melly dies? Arimond will be mad with grief—"

"Child." Neri did not pause in the brushing. "There is nothing—nothing at all that you can do now. Worrying about something that may not come to pass won't help. Lady Melly's fate is in the hands of the goddess. You must trust in her wisdom to set the balance right."

"I don't think I could bear it if Melly died, Neri."

The old woman said nothing, her touch steady and soothing.

"And I don't know what Arimond will do."

"It would be best if he left it in the hands of the goddess, child. But if he chooses not to, that won't be for you to prevent."

Juilene drew a deep breath and stared at her reflection in the mirror. The polished steel reflected the light of the candles, and the light gleamed on the wood of her harp where it rested on its stand by her bed. "Nenny—" the old childhood title slipped easily from her lips unnoticed. "If I tell you a secret—do you promise to keep it?"

"Well, I don't know, child." Out of the corner of her eye, Juilene saw the old woman cock her head and raise her eyebrow in the familiar gesture of disbelief, even as she continued to brush steadily. It was one she had seen often enough, when Arimond and Melly had gotten her into trouble. "It depends what the secret is."

"I've been thinking all evening, Nenny. Ever since Mondo came and told us about Melly. Melly has always been the bravest of us. She never hesitated to try anything."

The old woman was silent, waiting.

"If I told you I wanted to go to the Festival as one of the songsayers, what would you say? Would you go and tell Father?"

The old woman hesitated, and loyalty to her master and love for her charge warred clearly on her face.

"You know by Year's End, Mondo and I will be married. And then I will never have the chance to join the Festival, never. You always told me I sang well enough, and now tonight you told me—"

"Oh, child," the old woman sighed and her voice was

heavy with age. "You always were one to turn my own words against me."

"Nenny, listen." Impulsively, Juilene turned and kissed the old woman. "You know the songsayers are sacred to the goddess; what harm can come to me? And Arimond will be with me—he won't let anyone come within yards of me. Just this once—just this last time before I marry and take up all the cares for which you and the others have prepared me, for so long? It isn't fair you know—"

"Not fair?" The old woman blinked.

"Not fair that Father gave me music lessons and hired tutors to come and teach me, and doesn't mind trotting me out whenever there're guests. You know he was to have me sing tomorrow night, though he will probably excuse me now . . ." Her voice trailed off, and her hands tightened involuntarily again. Every time she thought of Melly her throat tightened and she thought she might never be able to sing until she knew her friend was out of danger.

"You think that's something Lady Melly might have tried, if she'd been given your gifts?" Neri's voice ended on a quaver and Juilene knew that the old woman shared her worry.

Juilene nodded, unable to speak over the lump in her throat.

"Well, child." The old woman paused and drew a deep breath. "I can't see there's much harm to it—but how—"

"Leave the how to Arimond and me. We'll think of something, and it's better if you don't know anything at all, don't you think?" Juilene stole a glance at her old nurse under her lashes. "That way you can't lie to Father, and if anyone gets into trouble, it will only be the two of us."

Neri shook her head. "Indeed, child. Only the two of you. I can't imagine what sort of trouble there could be over Festival, but you never know. It would do you both well to be careful—extremely careful. Your father will not look kindly upon being fooled, no matter how harmless the prank."

"I won't be long." Fallona, Arimond's stepmother, laid a gentle hand on his cheek as she rose to her feet from the chair beside the bed. "Branward said if she lived the night, she had a better chance of surviving. And now that she has—" It was the sixth or seventh time Arimond had heard her repeat that phrase since dawn, as if it were a charm or an incantation, warding away death.

"Yes, Mother." Arimond bowed as Fallona left the room with a heavy step. He had never seen his stepmother look so old. She had been a beautiful woman when his father had brought her to the keep, and in the sixteen years since her marriage to his father, she had never seemed to age. The only other time he had seen her look so old was the night his father's body had been borne home from the Gathering at last Year's End.

Was it truly less than a year since his father had died, he wondered, leaving him the heir of his small domain? Arimond had thought Fallona would never smile all those dark winter days. It was only recently that some of the heavy shroud of her grief had begun to lift. And now, if his sister died . . . He let his thoughts trail off into the unthinkable. His stepmother was likely to retreat into a deep depression if his sister died. They were all she had left, Fallona would say, gathering both of them to her and pressing them close. She had never treated Arimond as anything less than her own son, and she was all the mother he had ever known.

Now he stood just inside the doorway of his sister's bedchamber, where a low fire burned in the polished grate, and a shaft of pale morning sun cut through the drawn drapes like a blade. Melly lay on her back, her arms by her sides, her hair spilling over the clean white linen of the pillow.

The covers were drawn up to her chin. Her cheeks were swollen bruises and one eye was as huge and purple as a plum.

He sank down into the chair beside her, wishing he could hold her hand. But both her hands were wrapped in bandages, her right had was swollen to three times its normal size. If she did recover, there was some question whether she would ever have the use of her right hand again. Food for Parmathian sucker vines, he thought. I'd like to wrap each and every one of Lindos's men in one of them, and watch while the suckers did their work, leaving only empty shells. The vines spread like brushfire across any area where they gained a foothold, and were more feared than animal predators. Lindos's men richly deserved such a fate.

"Arimelle," he murmured. "Melly." He leaned forward, as close as he dared, watching the labored rise and fall of her chest beneath the white sheets. "I swear to you, Melly, and before the goddess, I'll see you avenged. I'll see Lindos dead, and his men brought to answer before the Gathering. They aren't thurges—those misbred whelps of his. They're only men like the rest of us, and I will see them answer before the thanes, I swear it. And Lindos will go to his grave, knowing you were the one who ultimately brought down his doom."

In the dim room, the only answer was the soft snap and hiss of the fire. He stared at his sister, trying desperately to see if there was some hope, some flicker of response. But there was nothing, and he sighed, closing his eyes. He'd not slept at all.

"Arimond?"

Juilene's soft voice startled him out of his reverie and he jumped in his chair. "Juilene?" he said in a loud whisper as she stepped into the room, her harp in her arms. "What are you doing here?"

Juilene pushed her hood off her face, staring down at the bed. "Father came to speak to your mother again. I wanted to come, too—I brought my harp . . ." Her voice trailed off as she gazed at Arimelle, lying still in her bandages on the bed. "Oh, goddess, Arimond, I didn't realize how bad—" She pressed the back of her hand to her mouth as Arimond leaped to his feet.

"You shouldn't be here, Juilene. You shouldn't see this." He strode around the bed.

Tears spilled down her cheeks, and she cradled the harp close. "Arimond, Arimond, how could anyone do this—"

"Come with me." He wrapped one arm firmly around her shoulders and propelled her out of the room. He held her close to his chest and stroked her hair. "You shouldn't have seen that, Juilene. She's beyond your music, right now. There isn't anything any of us can do for her, but wait and hope."

Juilene took a deep breath and swallowed hard. "They must be monsters. How could anyone do such a thing?"

Arimond looked grim. "Now do you understand why I must see Lindos punished? Now do you understand why someone must stop him?" When Juilene nodded, he pressed a quick kiss on top of her forehead. "Go on, now. Go back to your father. I must wait here until my mother comes back. I'll take you home when I can."

Wordlessly, Juilene turned away. Arimond watched her go, anger churning in his gut. He went back into his sister's sickroom and sank down once more into the chair. He wished he could touch her, but he didn't dare. With another muttered curse, he spoke aloud. "I'll see that dog dead."

"Strong words, young thane."

At the sound of a man's voice, he looked up, his hand instinctively reaching for the dagger at his side.

"Forgive me, Thane Arimond." The house physician,

Branward, stepped farther into the room, his bag of instruments held in his hands. "I didn't mean to startle you so."

"Physician." Arimond sagged. "I could have killed you."

Branward nodded. "You're in a killing mood, young thane."

Arimond raised his eyebrow. The physician was not so very old, perhaps only five years or so older than his mother, and he had served in his father's household since the time he and Fallona had been married. He had more times than Arimond could count bound up fingers and toes in the endless scrapes Arimond had gotten into as a child, had patiently attended Arimond through all the customary illnesses of childhood. "And would you blame me, physician?"

Branward raised his brow. "We are sworn not to kill, my lord." On silent feet, he moved to Arimelle's bedside. "If you will excuse me?"

With a short nod, Arimond rose. At the door he paused. "Physician?"

Branward glanced up. "My thane?"

"You—you have some touch of the power, do you not?"

The physician made a little gesture with his hands, and straightened. "I am merely a demi-thurge, my thane, and my training in the use of the power is limited to the healing arts. I have never had a reason to study further."

Arimond nodded. "But you do know certain—certain charms—certain spells to dispel certain effects of the magic?"

"Only the most rudimentary, my thane, although I, like any other thurge, am capable of discerning the effects of the power when it is used upon another. And I can assure you, it may have been the thurge's men who did this to your sister, but there is no trace of the power upon her. Her ills are only those of the flesh, nothing more."

Arimond nodded. "Yes, I know, physician. Thank you." His whole body thrummed with suppressed tension. If Branward could provide him with even the simplest protection from Lindos's power, his plan had a much better chance of succeeding. Now was simply not the time to broach the subject. In the shadowy corridor, he met Fallona.

"Branward was—" she began.

"He's with her now."

Fallona sighed and squeezed his hand. "Thank you for sitting with her. I want someone with her if—when she wakes." She gazed up at Arimond with misty eyes.

"I understand, Mother." He patted her hand. "I'm going to take Juilene back to Sarrasin—I'll be back in—"

"Arimond, you won't do anything foolish?" Fallona drew back and stared up at him, her brows knit together.

"I'm only going to take Juilene home. I might stop at the tavern on the way back here. But I'll be within calling distance if anything—" He broke off when he saw the stricken look in Fallona's eyes. "If Arimelle wakes," he finished.

"Please"—she clutched at his sleeve—"you mean it? You won't do anything foolish? If one of *his* men come in, you'll ignore him, won't you?"

"Mother." Gently, Arimond disengaged her hand. "I said I wouldn't do anything foolish. I'll be back very soon. I just need to—to think by myself for a while." He patted her hand once more. "Gilles will know where to find me."

The door to Arimelle's chamber opened, and the physician peered out into the hall. "My lady." He motioned to Fallona. "Will you send for more linen?"

Fallona nodded sharply. "At once, physician."

Arimond leaned down and kissed Fallona's cheek. "I won't be later than sunset."

* * *

Despite the relatively early hour, the tavern was crowded with smoke and men, and the conversation rose higher and higher as voices argued and fell in jerky rhythm. Arimond heard the excited babble as he rode up, tossing the reins of his horse to one of the stable boys who swarmed in the yard of the tavern, eager for a tip. The sun was not yet past its zenith, and already it sounded as though it were standing room only at the bar.

He pushed open the massive door and stepped into the crowd. The air was smoky and hot, and the tavern was packed full, so full that there was scarcely room for Arimond to negotiate his way to the bar. Word had traveled quickly. He could see it in the expressions of those who recognized him, in the murmured greetings, and in the suddenly subdued atmosphere that descended like a shroud the closer he got to the bar.

On the other side of the polished oak bar, he recognized the coppery hair of his closest friend, Benoit, who broke off speaking when he caught sight of Arimond.

Arimond leaned over the bar to order a mug of ale when he heard Benoit say, "On my tab, good Janney—here, Arimond, come join us."

With quiet greetings to men he knew at least by sight and reputation, Arimond managed to make his way around the bar. Benoit waved him closer, ale foaming over the lip of the mug he held out. "My friend," said Benoit as Arimond took the mug and nodded gravely to the others in Benoit's group, "we've all heard the terrible news. I am so sorry."

The other men muttered greetings and condolences, and Arimond shook hands with at least half a dozen who pressed in close. "Thank you, Ben, thank you all. Melly's not quite on the mend yet, but Branward says each day she lives, her chances are better."

"Is it so bad?" Benoit's grey eyes searched Arimond's, and Arimond hesitated. Benoit had hoped to marry Arimelle, had even spoken to Fallona, and had never made any secret of his intentions to Arimond. Arimond, who loved Benoit like a brother, had welcomed the thought of Benoit married to Melly. The two families, which had lived peacefully for generations side by side with Juilene's, would continue to do so.

Finally Arimond nodded, a brief, short nod, and Benoit lowered his eyes and turned away for a moment.

"We've all been talking, Arimond." An older man of more than thirty leaned closer. Edourd was a demi-thane from a nearby village; his keep was a two hours' ride or more, and Arimond was surprised to see him. "I just happened to be riding home when I heard the news. Something must be done."

"This isn't the first time Lindos's men have overstepped themselves," put in another.

"Nor Lindos, himself," added a third. "He's taken over a fifth of my domain, little by little, and my case is clogged in the King's courts, while every day, Lindos takes more and more. I'll have no domain left at all by the time the King makes a ruling."

"I say the thurges are festering pimples on the land," put in yet another. "Don't hush me—I'll have my say. They're like bloodsucking vines, sucking the meat out of all of us. What do we need them for anyway?"

Arimond nodded slowly, listening to the bitter litany of continuing complaints. Lindos grew stronger each year, and each year he constantly sought ways to increase his power.

"The tenth millennium approaches," said Eduord, beneath the other voices. "Some say there will be great change—"

"And others that it's all superstition and nothing will

change at all," interrupted Benoit. "Well, I say it's time to take matters into our own hands. The King can't—or won't—act, the Over-Thurges are senile old men. Lindos isn't the only thurge who seeks power. It's in their nature to take as much as they can. And who is there to stop them, if not us? We can't let this continue—we have to act, and act now."

Arimond nodded. There was nothing in what Benoit said he didn't agree with. Arimond glanced around. It seemed that everyone glanced their way, even the men on the other side of the room who gathered by the roaring hearth. Everyone here knew who he was, and everyone here knew what had happened to Arimelle. But could he trust everyone here not to go to Lindos? His eyes met Benoit's and the two exchanged a long look. It might be better to continue this conversation in a place without so many ears.

The door opened with a cold gust of wind, and shut with a loud bang behind a slender woman dressed in a dark cloak. She shrugged her hood off her head and tugged at the straps that held a small pack strapped across her chest. She carried a small lute in one hand. Those nearest the door looked up at her expectantly, and the barkeep paused in wiping the clay tankards with a grimy rag. "Well?" the huge man barked.

"I say the songs the goddess sends," responded the woman. Her voice was deeper and richer than Arimond would have expected from so slight a woman, and Arimond was reminded of Juilene, whose voice had a similar musical quality. Arimond noticed the dark shadows beneath the woman's eyes, and the paleness of her thin cheeks, as well as the inadequacy of her cloak against the cold autumn wind. It was as well, he thought, that Juilene would never know the reality of the hardships and the deprivation of such a life.

"There are ears to hear in plenty," said the barkeep. "Give her a place by the fire, lads."

With only a little good-natured grumbling, a space was cleared beside the hearth, and the songsayer sank down on the warm stones, holding her hands over the flames. Her dress was not so ragged as some, observed Arimond, but there was about her the stark cast of starvation. Juilene would play at being a songsayer, and then, he would see that nothing ever happened to her, nothing at all.

A plaintive melody rose from the songsayer's lute, above the hum of conversation, and Arimond saw many of the men turn in the woman's direction, speculative, measuring looks on their faces. No, he thought, it was truly as well Juilene would never be forced to sell either her music or herself for a few bites to eat.

He touched Benoit's arm. "Let's speak more of this tomorrow, friend. I told my mother I wouldn't be late."

"Tomorrow, then," said Benoit. "Here?"

"No. Come to Ravenwood. I have a few things in mind, but I think it best if we discuss our plans in privacy. Jiroud of Sarrasin will stand by us, but he's loath to move. You know how the older thanes are. But I've no wish to have even the slightest breath of suspicion reach Lindos. There're too many ears here—too many who might think it more profitable to go elsewhere—if you know what I mean."

"I know exactly what you mean," Benoit said, casting a look over the entire room. "I'll come. You know you can count on us."

Chapter Three

❧

The Eyes of Dramue burned a steady blue in the black night sky when Juilene slipped out of the gate by the kitchen gardens. In the shadow of the orchard outside the walls, Arimond stood waiting, a faceless shadow wrapped in a hooded cloak. The night was cold and the stars burned in the sky and the night birds sang only sporadically. A cold breeze rustled through the last few leaves clinging to the branches of the fruit trees. Winter would not be long in coming this year.

"Any trouble?" he murmured as he bent to press a swift kiss upon her cheek.

She shook her head as she turned to meet his mouth with hers. She heard the swift intake of his breath as their mouths met. He wrapped his arms around her and pulled her close.

"By the goddess, Juilene," he whispered. "This night, my blood runs hot . . . it's good we have an errand, or I vow you'd be mine before the morning—" he broke off. Beneath the thick wool of his cloak, she could feel the stiff leather breastplate he wore, and she was reminded that this was no lovers' tryst.

"It was easy," she said, more to cover her discomposure than anything else. "Especially with Neri helping—no one even noticed. And look—look at what she gave me—" Juilene tried to pull off her glove hastily.

"Not now." He cut her off with a gesture. "Come. The horses are over here." He led her through the stand of fruit trees. Damp wind whined between the trees, and the twigs tangled in her hair. She clutched her harp, which she had wrapped in an oiled skin to protect it from the weather, to her chest, as he lifted her onto the horse's back.

The trees dipped low in the whining wind, and the black branches reminded her of the grasping fingers of the skeletons carved over the family tomb. With an effort, she pushed that thought from her mind. Now was not the time she wanted to think about death.

She gripped the reins, feeling the unfamiliar weight of Neri's gift on her finger. She was vaguely disappointed that Arimond had dismissed her so abruptly, for the ring Neri had given her that evening was not so much a gift but a birthright from her mother. She let her thumb caress the thin band on her ring finger while Arimond tied the harp securely in place and whispered another prayer. "Be with us now, Dramue," she pleaded.

Arimond swung up onto his own mount and flapped the reins gently. They rode out of the orchard and onto the dark road that led to the thurge's keep.

Lights shone from every house they passed, and the road was crowded with Festival-goers. The first ceremonies of the Festival were at dawn tomorrow, and many of the common folk came the night before, to set up a campsite from which they could see as much as possible of the yearly ceremonies. They passed dark shapes clustered around flickering fires by the roadside. Without fail, music filtered through the night, some songs low and mournful, others, fast and cheery. In the light of the flames, Juilene caught glimpses of dancers with skirts hiked around their knees, swirling to the tunes the songsayers played upon their instruments. For the first time she could remember, Festival time didn't seem like a time to be festive.

As they reached the approach to the thurge's keep, Arimond slowed his horse and dropped back to her side. "I've talked this over with Benoit and a few of the other younger thanes. They will meet us just over the last rise in the road. Here's our plan: you and I will go into the keep, while they wait outside. After you play awhile, you'll leave, and I'll stay behind. When they see you come out, that will be the signal for them to attack the keep. Don't wait for me, or anyone else. Get home as fast as you can—I want you out of danger as soon as possible."

In the dim light, she stared up at him. "What if you are recognized?" The other possibilities, that Arimond might not be the non-born knight, were too terrible to even shape into words.

"I'll keep my head down. And when you see me in the light, you'll see I'm not dressed as a young thane. But I am not about to let you go in there alone."

"But what if the captain of his guards or some of his soldiers recognize you? What if he knows you himself? There's no way any of them will know *me*, but you're a different matter."

He stared at her for a long moment. The horses' hooves beat a steady tattoo on the road, and a gust of wind whistled and tugged at her cloak. She shivered. "I can't let you go in there alone, Juilene. I've seen how men look at songsayers, especially young ones, pretty ones. I'd rather risk discovery than risk you being in danger—any kind of danger. I wish there were some other way we could get into the keep without involving you. But right now this is the best way, and I'm not sending you in alone."

She knew further arguing was useless. Arimond had made up his mind; there was nothing she could say to sway him. She urged her horse on, and they rode in silence the rest of the distance. When they reached a small copse of trees just beyond the thurge's gatehouse, Arimond pulled his horse to a halt once more, and swung out of the saddle. He held up his arms and she slid off the saddle. For a long moment, he held her close again, his cheek pressed against the top of her hood. "You'll see, Jewels," he whispered. "Everything will be fine, I promise."

She lifted her head. In the starlight, only the ghostly outline of his face was visible. She tried to suppress a shudder. *Goddess, why must everything make me think of death?* She shook her head to clear such thoughts away. "Look," she said, pulling off her glove, her voice a little shrill, "see what Neri gave me tonight? It belonged to my mother." She held up her hand. A dark, dull band of stone encircled her ring finger. "It's the sapphire ring—do you remember it? The one that warns whenever danger is about—"

"That's nice, dear." He pressed another kiss on the top of her head. "And I have something for you, too." He fumbled inside the neckline of his tunic and withdrew an oddly shaped pendant on a long leather string. "Here"—he placed it over her head—"put this under your clothes."

She fingered the thing. Whatever it was gave off a vaguely peppery scent. She felt something cold and hard, like a stone, and something that could only be a feather. "What is this thing?"

"Branward gave it to me. It's a charm, a protection

against magic. It should help protect us from any spell Lindos might try to use. Make sure it's under your clothes."

While Juilene tugged and arranged her clothing so the charm was covered, Arimond gave a long, low whistle followed by three short ones. Juilene frowned as she patted her neckline into place. She was as important a part to this scheme as any of the others and Arimond was treating her like a child. She pulled her glove back on, hoping that the ring didn't manifest its legendary power at all. She held her cloak tighter around her shoulders as dark forms carrying shuttered lanterns emerged from around the trunks of the trees. As they drew closer, she saw the colors of many of the neighboring houses of thanes, and that nearly all the houses in the entire district were represented by at least one or two members. One or two of the younger members, she realized as the lantern light illuminated their identities. They bowed and murmured greetings in her direction, and then looked to Arimond in silence.

A bright shock of red hair flashed in the dim light, and Benoit bowed low before her. "Lady Juilene of Sarrasin," he said, "I'm sorry to see you in such dangerous circumstances."

"Dangerous but necessary," said Arimond. "Is everything in order?"

"Everything. We but await your signal."

"Good. Wait here. When Juilene returns, you'll know what to do."

"As you will it, my thane, I obey." Benoit grinned, and Arimond clasped his arm.

"Then come, let's go." Arimond motioned to Juilene. She clutched her harp in its oiled wrappings. Her heart pounded slowly in her chest. Surely Lindos would hear it over her music.

She heard soft words of encouragement, murmured wishes of good fortune as they started up the road. Her hands shook so much she hoped she would be able to play the harp. She swallowed hard and forced a smile at Benoit. "Yes," she said, surprised at how strong her voice sounded. "I'll meet you here—afterward."

Arimond wrapped an arm around her shoulders, caressing her, as he drew her close to him. She felt the swell of the muscles beneath his clothes, and momentarily, she felt a strong urge to refuse to continue. What madness was this, she wondered, what if they failed?

The danger to her was negligible—even if she were recognized, what was the worst that was likely to occur? She could be dragged back to her father's keep, protesting it was all a girlish prank. Oh, she would be punished, but no real damage was likely to occur. But what if Arimond was wrong?

Goddess guide us, she prayed silently. She held her cloak close against her throat as a sudden gust of wind blew harder, whipping her skirts around her legs.

"Here." He took the harp from her, and beneath its protective wrap the harp gave a sudden thrum. Startled, he looked at her with the first vestige of fear.

"It's all right," she said. "You just made the strings vibrate."

She gripped his arm more firmly and gathered her skirts to keep them from flying so wildly in the wind. "Come," she said. "Let's go." She knew the others watched as they started off down the road. "Arimond," she began, when they were well out of earshot, and not yet in sight of the walls of the keep, "how much do you know about the Power? About magic?"

He shot a quick glance at her. "Why do you ask?"

"Because we, you and I and all your friends, are about to go marching into the keep of one of the most powerful master-thurges in Sylyria, according to all the talk."

"We have several advantages," said Arimond slowly,

"for a thurge needs time to prepare his spell. He can't act in the moment—you know that. They're vulnerable to surprise—and we intend to exploit that. And the kinds of spells he can perform—that's limited, too, by the time of day, the position of the sun and the moon, the conjunctions of the stars, the tides, even the direction of the winds. Believe me, it's not his magic we have to fear—it's his men at arms who pose the gravest threat. And getting in with you will give me a chance to assess just how well prepared they are."

Juilene sighed. Arimond's words made sense, but why then was she plagued by such a deep sense of foreboding? Perhaps it was only her lack of experience, combined with Lindos's reputation. She shifted her harp in her arms as the road turned sharply to the left.

The walls of Lindos's keep rose before them in the night, the walls limned with thurge-light, which glowed a weird yellowish green against the black sky. Juilene gripped Arimond's arm harder. Her mouth was dry and her hands shook. Arimond murmured something encouraging and drew her on. At the gates, they paused. Guards loitered in the gateway, although the gates themselves were flung open wide. Just inside, she could see into the open courtyard of the keep, and men and women gathered around bonfires, laughing and joking. At Festival, surely even Lindos relaxed, she thought.

She drew a deep breath and squared her shoulders. She clutched her harp closer and this time it gave an angry twang as though it resented the rough handling. Goddess, help me, she whispered, and started forward.

"Come to sing for us, sweetheart?" The guard closest to the gate leered at her as she approached.

"I say the songs the goddess sends," she whispered, clinging to the ritual phrase as though it were a protective charm.

"Eh, what?" There was a loud chorus of laughter behind her as a voice rose, shaky and unsure, more a wail than a song in the night.

I sound better than that, Juilene thought, and this time she spoke up. "I say the songs the goddess sends."

"Only if you can say them better than that one in there." Another jerked his thumb over his shoulder. "His Transcendence sent that one out to us—not good enough for the hall, he says."

"Maybe we should let her sing for us, Teck," the first said.

Juilene summoned every ounce of courage she possessed. "I must sing for the master of this keep, and then, should the goddess grant, I will sing for you as well." She tried to speak with the same simple dignity she had heard the songsayers use who came to sing before her father.

"And what about this one?" The second soldier frowned at Arimond. "You sing, too?"

"He's—he's my brother," Juilene stammered. "He must stay with me."

"Why?" asked the first, trying to peer under the heavy hood Arimond wore low over his face.

"The—the goddess has his wits." Juilene's jaw was stiff with tension. "We go to the temple tomorrow to beg them back."

"Let them in, you fool." A third leaned over the first's shoulder. "It's Festival. You know how *he* feels about this sort."

"Don't we all," the second leered.

Juilene swallowed once more, and hoped they wouldn't notice how the hand that held her cloak shook, nor how white-knuckled was the hand that held the harp. The torches turned her cheeks to orange, and the guards nudged each other and snickered and nodded as she passed. Her face burned. These were the men who had used Melly so shamefully. Thank the goddess they honored the Festival, if nothing else.

Once inside the courtyard, she saw at once that despite the chilly night, the wide doors of the hall were thrown open. In the light of the leaping fires, she saw that the people danced in wild abandon, and sang loudly and drunkenly. Such disorder had never occurred at her father's keep, and suddenly, Juilene was afraid once more. What if the Festival laws were honored in name only?

In the doorway, she paused. The vaulted ceiling soared at least a hundred feet in the air, and looking up, she saw the ceiling was painted with scenes of every description, in colors that swirled into the shadows. She glanced to the right and left. Men and women lounged by the hearths that lined the walls, goblets in their hands, beside platters piled high with fruits and cheeses. A few of the women had their bodices unlaced and most of the men were shirtless.

"What kind of house does this man keep?" muttered Arimond, his voice a low growl in her ear.

She only cleared her throat and tightened her grip on her cloak, thankful that it shrouded her from neck to knee. She took a deep breath and spoke as loudly as she dared. "I say the songs the goddess sends."

All eyes turned to stare at the two of them, and she thought she heard a low chuckle emanate around the room.

"Come in, come in, goddess-sent. Come into my hall and be welcome." The soft voice seemed to filter through and under the crowd in a way that made her hands tremble and her knees knock together under her thick woolen gown, and reminded her of the sound of a snake slithering through tall grass.

She squared her shoulders and glanced down at the ring. It glowed a soft blue, the stars that the light reflected in its depths barely visible. She started forward. It seemed that the fires that burned on either side of the hall didn't give

off the same quality of light as those in her father's hall. It
was as if the light was contained, controlled, so that instead
of being cast out into wide pools of warmth, the light
seemed to hover on the edges of darkness. She felt rather
than saw the people turn toward her as she walked between
what seemed like endless rows of benches. All her attention was focused on the tall form that seemed to uncoil itself as she drew closer.

At the base of the dais she stopped and pushed her hood
off her face. With every ounce of courage she possessed,
she gazed into the face of the thurge. Could it be true that
Lindos was only a master-thurge but newly come to his
power? she wondered. The power that surrounded him
seemed as tangible as any she had ever felt, even in the
presence of the Over-Thurge of Sylyria. No wonder he's
feared, she thought. And Arimond's brave words came
back to her. Oh, Arimond, she thought, I think you're
gravely wrong, if you think this man is not one to be reckoned with.

He was fair, fairer even than Arimond, for he lacked the
ruddy glow of sun-bronzed skin that Arimond wore, even
in the winter. And his eyes were blue like Arimond's, but
pale and cold as ice. An aura of power hung around him,
but it was of a different sort of power than any she had ever
felt before, emanating from anyone else. He reminded her
of the icicles that formed on the edges of the highest towers at Sarrasin, hanging sharp and poised and dangerous to
anyone who ventured too close at the wrong time. A scaled
form uncoiled itself from the base of Lindos's chair and
growled, showing pointed rows of yellowish teeth. Juilene
jumped. She had never seen a dwarf dragon, but she knew
thurges, especially master-thurges, were fond of keeping
such things as pets. Her father sneered at such things, believing that all such abominations should be destroyed.
The dragon tossed its tail higher and settled itself once

more. Juilene shivered in spite of the heat of the hall. "I say the songs the goddess sends."

"Say on, then, little songsayer. Play for us, if you will it," Lindos replied. He bowed his head gravely, and sat down on the high-backed chair, as elaborately carved as her father's.

Her hands trembled so much she could scarcely hold the harp Arimond held out to her, and she thought she might stumble as she saw the stool Lindos indicated. "Come, come, little songsayer—how young you are! Don't be afraid. We've more than plenty ears to hear your songs."

The ancient words seemed almost sinister as he leaned upon one hand and smiled, a smile that stretched his mouth across his face but did nothing to warm his eyes.

Juilene swallowed hard again. Her mouth was dry, and she knew her hands shook. Of its own accord the harp rippled beneath its wrappings, and she froze. She had heard the songsayers who came to her father's hall say that such a thing meant the presence of the goddess. Dramue, be with me now, she prayed.

She sank to a low stool placed just before the dais and felt her cloak slip from her shoulders. Someone moved behind her, easing the heavy fabric away from her plain gown, and she heard the low murmur of the crowd rise and then fall away into silence. With shaking fingers she unwrapped the harp, and saw the gleam of the polished wood as the light fell on it. Even the thurge's magic couldn't keep the light from the harp, and under her hands, she felt it stir like a living thing, the brass strings shimmering in the gloom of the hall. It seemed that the harp gathered the light to itself, and beneath her fingertips she felt the strings quiver. She let her fingernails run over the strings, feeling the gentle vibration beneath her fingertips, and the sound swelled in the silence. She drew a deep breath and sang.

> "The world was dark, the sky was white
> The earth was fair but knew no light
> And all around each flaming hearth
> The people labored in the dark."

It was the simplest song of all, nothing more than a child's nursery rhyme, really, which told of the coming of the goddess to right the balance and restore the world to order. She sang it softly, gently, almost as though it were a lullaby. The music shuddered in the air, as though something prevented it from soaring to the vaulted ceilings of the high hall. With more courage than she ever thought she possessed, she gazed at the wizard, and saw that he leaned upon his hand, his fist curled beneath his chin.

> "The goddess heard her people's cries,
> She knew their greatest fears
> And with a vow as deep as night,
> She came to aid her people's plight."

What did he think, Juilene thought, as her voice gained strength, sitting there so secure in the power that seemed to throb throughout the room like a heartbeat. Did he find her voice pleasing? She saw his eyes drop to her breasts, and even as she sang the last verse, she knew she blushed, and knew he noticed.

> "And so we sing the older songs
> As Festival draws near—
> The goddess bring us peace and hope
> And order all the year!"

Only Lindos applauded as the sound died away, the harp's voice curiously dulled. Juilene pushed a strand of hair away from her face, and wondered why no one else seemed to have reacted. She looked up and was thankful to see Arimond leaning against the wall, watching her. His arms were folded over his chest, and his cloak was slung back over his arms, as if to show he wore no visible weapons. The others stared at her with fixed eyes. Were they all so inured to the songsayers that even the simplest of the songs had no meaning to them? She dared a look at the faces around the thurge, and gasped. All of the people standing near him seemed to be shrouded in a mist, so that their features were indistinct, and only the vaguest shapes of their forms remained visible.

"Play on, little songsayer," he whispered, motioning with his hand, and obediently, as though there were no other choice, she bent over the harp once more. Her fingers plucked out song after song. She had no idea how long she sang for the wizard, but she knew the fires on either side of her snapped and hissed and flamed. She was vaguely aware that men moved behind her feeding the fires huge logs thicker than a man's body, and that every now and then conversation seemed to rise above the music. Out of the corners of her eyes, she caught glimpses of movement, yet when she turned her head, nothing was there. Her fingers shook and once or twice the music faltered, but no one seemed to mind or notice.

And then Lindos stood before her, a smile still on his lips, the same one he had worn all night, she thought, and he was leaning down over her, touching her cheek with the very briefest of kisses, the customary acknowledgment of the master of the house to the songsayer. The hall grew darker. A woman touched her shoulder, offered her a thick blanket, and pointed to a place by the hearth.

In a deep daze, Juilene stumbled over to the spot. It was warm near the flames, but the fire seemed to be contained in that same peculiar way, as though its energy was controlled. But this time, it seemed to be no matter to puzzle over; she simply accepted that this was the way things were. She wrapped the harp once more in its protective covering, and curled up with her blanket and her cloak. All around her men and women were lying down, and in the shadowed light, she saw couples writhe together under the cover of the blankets. Once again, she had a sense that something, someone, danced just on the periphery of her vision, and she sat up, squinting in the gloom. Someone touched her back and she started, stifling a little cry.

"SShh," Arimond whispered. "It's only me. Come, we have to get you out of here."

"Arimond," she breathed. She clutched at his cloak, and a sensation seemed to grow between her legs, heavy and warm, and she shifted uneasily and shut her eyes.

"Juilene." He shook her urgently. "You can't stay here— there's a powerful charm at work here—a spell. Lindos uses his power to keep his people—" He broke off as a couple writhing near them groaned aloud.

She gasped and blushed, and Arimond pulled her to her feet. "My harp—"

"Here." He handed it to her, and she stood for a moment, wondering why they ought to leave. The hour was so late, and surely it wouldn't hurt to rest—rest for just a little while— "Come on," he hissed, tugging at her hand.

She stumbled after him. The harp gave a throb, a low rumbling of the strings, as they reached the open door, and the cold air hit her in the face. Suddenly the fog seemed to clear from her brain, and she looked at Arimond, and wondered why he wasn't affected by whatever spell was at work upon the hall. She glanced down at the ring Neri had given her and gasped. The sapphire blazed a clear and vivid blue, the white stars within its depths clearly reflected. She gasped. So Neri was right—the ring did have the power to warn of danger close by. She reached for Arimond's arm and held him close.

"But, Arimond," she whispered as they hurried out of the hall and into the courtyard, "the charms—why am I affected and you aren't?"

"Branward's only a demi-thurge," he said. "He warned me this was merely a low-level spell, but I figured it was better than nothing. As to why you are more affected than I, I don't know. Maybe it's that Lindos had more of his attention on you—I was just a bystander in the back of the hall. He uses his power, or some of it, anyway, to keep his people in check. That can only work in our favor. They should be easy to overcome. Now let's go."

He caught her firmly under the arm, and led her through the deserted courtyard. As they walked, he spoke in a terse whisper. "Now listen to me. You go—go to the clearing where we left the others. I'm going back in there. You aren't to worry about me. You get on your horse and you ride back to your father's house. I'll come to you as soon as I can, do you understand?"

She nodded, wordlessly, looked up at him desperately, wishing she could think of something, anything that would convince him not to take this chance, not to risk their entire future for the sake of revenge. He bent down and gathered her to him, kissing her hungrily, and she thought she might faint. Then he drew back, and nodded toward the gate. "Go."

She dashed out to the gatehouse, where the soldiers who had let her in still leaned upon their spears.

"Our master not to your liking, little songsayer?" The one who had told the others to let her in laughed softly as she pushed past them and out the partially opened gate. She made a noise, low and indistinguishable, and ran, the sound of their laughter burning in her ears. On and on she ran, half expecting to be stopped, to be dragged back into the presence of that horrible wizard. She didn't slow until she was almost at the copse. A dark shape emerged from the shadows of the trees, and she gasped.

"Juilene?" Benoit's familiar voice brought tears to her eyes. "Is it you? By the goddess, we've been so worried. Are you all right?"

She sank to the ground, breathing hard, cradling her harp in her lap.

"Lady, what's wrong? Did he hurt you? Are you all right? Is Arimond still there?"

All around them dark forms were emerging from the shadows, clustering around, muttering as weapons gleamed here and there in the starlight. "Yes—yes, he's there. Go quickly—he's on his way to Lindos now—he has some sort of charm against the power, but it's not very strong—please, go." Her voice shook.

"Lady—Juilene—will you be all right?"

She nodded. Benoit looked up. "Richaume—you stay with the lady. Take her home— You others, come with me."

She leaned against a tree as the dark mass of men rushed down the road toward the keep. The harp hummed against her chest, and a deep sense of foreboding overwhelmed her. She bent her head and wept.

"My lady?" The soft voice of Benoit's squire made her look up. "Let me see you to your father's house."

"No." She shook her head, settling back against the tree. "No, I've come this far—I'm going to wait right here for Arimond to come back."

"But, my lady—"

"It's no use. I'm not leaving unless you drag me. And that would be a gross breach of propriety. So here we stay."

The squire made a little sound. She wiped her eyes with a corner of her cloak, and turned her head to watch the road. She leaned her head against the tree, fingering the ring, and felt her heavy lids fall over her eyes. The last thing she heard was Richaume saying, in voice low with resignation: "I shall keep the watch, my lady."

The next thing Juilene knew, a dark shape was bending over her. She startled wide awake and sat up, nearly knocking her head against the rough bark of the tree. For a moment, she was groggy and disoriented, and then Arimond's face sharpened into focus. "Arimond, my love, are you all right?"

Arimond nodded, sinking back on his haunches. In the light of a flickering campfire, she could see that his hands were bloody, his clothing torn. He sagged against another tree, and she leaned forward and wrapped her arms around him.

"Arimond, what's happened? Are you all right?"

"Yes," he whispered. "Everything went just as we planned."

"But are you hurt?" She ran her hands hesitantly over his arms.

"No."

"But you're exhausted—" She looked around in the dim light for Richaume. "Where's that squire? Where's Richaume?"

Arimond waved one hand. "I sent him on to keep—to his master. Benoit was hurt."

"How badly?"

Arimond shrugged.

"And what of Lindos? What of the others? Where are all the rest of your friends?"

"Back at the keep. Will you come?" He rose to his feet and held out his hand.

"Lindos is dead?" She got to her feet a little unsteadily, her cramped joints protesting.

He reached for her hand, and his grip closed around it so

firmly her knuckles cracked and she stifled a little cry. "Come."

"Arimond, you're hurting me." She twisted her hand in his.

He relaxed only a little. "Your pardon, my lady. We're going back to the keep, of course. Don't you want to see the wizard dead?"

She stared up at him in disbelief. Show her the body of a man slain in battle? Had Arimond suddenly taken leave of his senses? She stumbled a little in a rut in the road, and her long skirts tangled about her knees. Arimond did not lessen his stride. She glanced at his profile and the expression on his face was cold and unforgiving. "Arimond, are you all right?"

He turned his head so swiftly she gasped, and his teeth flashed white in the starlight. "Oh, yes, my dear. I'm fine."

The gates of the keep were flung wide, and the torches burning in the massive iron brackets sputtered. It must be close to dawn, thought Juilene as she clung to Arimond's hand. The courtyard was deserted. "Where—where is everyone?" she whispered.

"I told all my men to take the dead and put them in the kitchen gardens," Arimond answered without a break in step.

The hall doors were opened wide, as well, and inside, Juilene could see long rows of sleepers, wrapped in dark blankets, beside hearths that smoldered and leaked grey ribbons of smoke. They were utterly still, utterly silent, and Juilene stared at them on either side as she and Arimond marched down the middle. She wriggled her hand in Arimond's grip. Something was wrong here, something was very wrong here. "Arimond," she whispered loudly. "What's wrong with these people?"

This time he didn't look at her, only smiled and continued. "Nothing's wrong, my dear. Nothing at all."

They went down a dark corridor to a wide flight of steps. Arimond took the shallow stairs with ease, while Juilene scrambled to keep up. "Arimond—" she said when they reached the top, "I don't want to see Lindos. Just take me home." Here and there on the periphery of her vision, she thought she caught glimpses of things that moved faster than her eye could quite see. She whipped her head around once or twice, and each time saw nothing but the stone blocks of the walls. "Arimond, just take me home."

He swept her up in his arms. "Oh, my sweet little love, I don't mean to frighten you. You don't have to see the wizard dead if it upsets you. But come, there's something here so beautiful I don't want you to miss it."

His arms around her were as unyielding as iron, and Juilene held her breath, twining her fingers in the rough fabric of his tunic. Three paces from the steps a door yawned open. Arimond ducked his tall head a little and carried her inside. "Look."

She gazed around in disbelief. This must be Lindos's bedroom and she had never seen anything so magnificent in her life. The great bed that dominated the center of the room was draped in white linen, linen so finely spun it resembled gossamer. Sewn into the linen, worked in intricate patterns, tiny gems of every color twinkled in the firelight, like a shower of thousands of stars. "How beautiful," she murmured, forgetting her fear.

"I thought you would like it," he said. He leaned against the door frame and crossed his arms over his chest.

She walked over to the bed and touched the hangings with one tentative finger. "It's amazing." The light sparkled in the jewels, throwing off rainbow glints, shifting as the fabric moved beneath her touch. "It's the most beautiful thing I have ever seen." This was what it meant to be a thurge, she thought, protected and sought out, valued by everyone for the knowledge to manipulate the power of the magic. No wonder the young thanes envied the thurges.

Arimond came to stand behind her. "Do you really like it?" He ran his hands down her shoulders to her upper arms, and a ripple of pleasure went through her. She nodded, unable to answer. He reached around her throat and unclasped her cloak. The garment slid to the floor unheeded as he pulled her back against his chest. He slid one arm beneath her breasts and the other around her belly. He bent his head and teased her earlobe with his tongue. She shivered, and moaned a little.

"You like that," he whispered, his breath making her feel hot and cold all at once. She could only nod.

She felt his fingers in the tangle of the lacings of her bodice, and she arched back against him. What did it matter, really? No one was here to see them, and she and Arimond would be married soon. She closed her eyes, offering no resistance as he slipped his hand inside her chemise and cupped her breast.

She turned her head toward him, making a little sound in her throat. For answer his mouth sought hers, hard and hot and more insistent than anything she had ever felt before. His arms seemed to crush her, and for one brief instant, Juilene shrank back, inexplicably afraid. This was a side of Arimond she had never seen. She pushed back and turned her head. "Please," she murmured. "Gently."

She thought she heard him chuckle, a low sound deep in his throat that made her shiver. He swept her up in his arms and placed her on the bed, his hand fumbling for the lacings on his breeches. He pushed her skirts up to her thighs and rolled on top of her, the hard length of his desire pressing against her flesh. "Forgive me—I guess I'm just a little overwrought tonight."

Desire won over fear and she reached to caress his cheek with the back of her hand. He raised himself over her, his body covering hers, his legs forcing her knees apart. She placed one hand on his chest, and gasped. The sapphire ring, her mother's legacy and Neri's gift, blazed brighter than all the thousands of gems combined. She stifled a scream and her eyes met his, and in that moment, she knew she looked into the eyes of a stranger. There was nothing of Arimond's love in those eyes, only lust and desire, and something that could only be hate.

She struggled harder, pushing against his chest with all her strength, twisting and turning beneath him. His face changed before her eyes. His hair lightened from sun-bleached gold to nearly white, his cheekbones heightened and become more prominent. His lips thinned. The man poised above her was not Arimond. "Lindos!" she cried.

The glamour of the spell fell away from him in that instant, and surprised, he loosened his grip on her. She struggled out of his grasp, and rolled to the opposite side of the bed, holding the edges of her bodice together as her feet touched the floor. "Where is Arimond?"

The thurge chuckled. "Ah, little songsayer. You have the truth of it. I am indeed Lindos, and your beloved is right there." He pointed over her shoulder, and she turned. The illusion of a solid wall melted away before her eyes, and she saw Arimond hanging chained, his clothes hanging in shreds off his body, his head sunk to his chest.

"Goddess," she whispered, bringing her fist to her mouth. "What have you done to him?"

"Only what he would have done to me." The thurge shrugged.

"Arimond?" She drew a little closer. His torso was streaked with blood, and she could see the gaping edges of his wounds, from which blood still seeped, through the tattered fabric. His flesh was pale, and there was a bluish cast round his mouth. "Arimond?"

"He's quite dead, my dear."

Juilene turned to face Lindos. The walls of the room seemed to close in on her, the ceiling seemed to drop toward her. Her vision clouded and then focused. "You've killed him."

"It's only what he would've done to me." Lindos smiled almost apologetically.

"What of the others?"

"I'm afraid they're dead, too. Most of them. The ones who aren't soon will be, thought I might let one or two live long enough to go back to the thanes and show them what happens when anyone tries to interfere in my affairs. I don't like interference, you see."

She felt faint and dizzy. Surely this was all a dream, a nightmare, from which she would awaken screaming at any moment. How could they all be dead? Arimond, his friends, the heirs of noble houses all. How could they all be dead? And Arimond—her mind refused to consider the awfulness of his death. She closed her eyes and when she opened them, she saw a small head peering from beneath the bed, a head with huge black eyes that bulged from a face that was narrow and grey with high slanting cheeks. She stifled a scream and the black eyes glowed with a weird yellowish green light.

Other faces crowded from beneath the bed, from around the corners of the bed, faces attached to huge bald heads and skinny bodies with spindly limbs. She gasped and drew back involuntarily.

Lindos's mouth stretched into a snarl. "Away with you, all of you." He cuffed the nearest on the side of the head and the creatures recoiled, disappearing in a blink.

Juilene tugged the laces of her bodice closer. She tried not to think about what those things were. What had Melly done when her attackers had come upon her? She had faced them bravely and fought. Juilene was determined that she would do no less. She raised her chin and tried to keep her voice steady. "Are you going to kill me, too?"

He laughed. "Kill you? Oh, no, my dear, you're sadly mistaken. I don't intend to kill you. Why that might bring down every outraged thane in the entire League to my door, and as I said, I can't abide interference. I brought you here for another purpose."

"You'll have to kill me before I let you touch me again." Some rational recess in her mind told her her voice was shrill in the unnatural quiet.

"Rape? Oh, no, my dear, how crude. You really don't know me at all, I see. No, I brought you here to offer you a choice, an honorable choice."

"What do you understand about honor? You allow your men to rape helpless women—abuse them nearly to death. What could the word honor mean to you?" She balled her fists and squared her shoulders.

His eyes glittered like the jewels. "My men are men, my dear. It isn't my fault their appetites are sometimes a little—well—fierce. And as for my honor, at least I don't masquerade as something other than what I am in order to invade someone's house. With the intention of aiding in their murder, no less. That's hardly an honorable action, do you think?"

Juilene bit her lip, feeling that her charade of courage was close to cracking. "My honor is not the issue here."

"Well," he said, plucking at the coverlet of the bed, "that's a matter for debate, I think. But never mind now. You've had a long night, and I am sure you want to return home. So here is the choice. It has occurred to me that an alliance with one of the thanish houses might be a good thing—enable me to control certain elements, shall we call them? And so this is my proposal: marry me, and there will be no more reprisals from this night. Everything will be the same as it was."

"The same?" she whispered in disbelief and horror, acutely conscious of Arimond's corpse behind her. "How could anything be the same? Nothing will ever be the same again."

"Not exactly the same," he replied. "But very nearly the same, especially for you."

"Nothing will be the same. Never."

"I had hoped you would be able to see things differently," he said, gazing at the underside of the canopy.

"Why?" Her whole body shook with the strain of trying to maintain her calm demeanor.

"Because, my dear." He rolled to face her. "If you should refuse me, I will have to punish you. What you did was inexcusably wrong, and I think even your father would agree."

Juilene glanced at the tiny jewels. Their sparkle seemed dull and lusterless. The door seemed impossibly far away. She closed her eyes and Arimond's expressionless face rose before her. "That's between me and my father."

"Under other circumstances, I would agree. But you see, these are not ordinary circumstances are they?"

"Do whatever you want to me. Kill me, if you please. I don't care."

Lindos waggled a finger at her. "Now, now. You're very young. Think about what you're saying carefully. You might just live to regret it."

She glanced over her shoulder once more, and gathered the edges of her bodice more firmly in one hand. With squared shoulders and the last bit of strength she could muster, she walked to the door. "You've taken from me the only man I will ever love. What does it matter what happens to me?"

He watched her go, but made no move to stop her. As she reached the door, he said, "Go, little songsayer. You've made your choice." She reached the door and he began to laugh, louder and louder, and the sound echoed through the corridor and down the stairs, until she was forced to cover her ears. She shut her eyes as something, some force as strong as thunder without sound, dragged her to her knees.

Lindos's voice filled her mind, and her whole body thrummed with his voice, as though she were a harp string, too tightly strung. "Now listen, girl, and listen well. You will never have anything, except that which you earn by your own hands. Charity is denied you, for any who try to help you will bear the curse I set upon you. You are condemned to earn your own way in this way—neither eating nor wearing nor having anything which you do not purchase by your own effort. Only the love of a man who loves you for yourself alone will lift my spell—and you'll see how few those are."

Juilene swallowed hard, gulping back tears. With every ounce of will that she possessed, she got to her feet and turned to look at the thurge once again. Arimond was dead. What did anything else matter? She gathered all the spittle she could and spat at him. "Goddess damn you, thurge. Damn you to the coldest pit."

She gathered up her skirts and ran, his laughter ringing in her ears all the way out of the keep.

Chapter Four

❧

His laughter echoed in her mind as she hurried down the road. In the clearing, she paused just long enough to retrieve her harp. She found Richaume's body lying a few feet from the tree where she had fallen asleep. The horses were gone.

She clutched the harp tight against her chest and started off down the road. Dawn was only a grey sliver across the horizon but the air smelled like morning. She trudged down the dusty road. Her feet began to ache, and her head throbbed. Her back hurt and her arms were sore from carrying the awkward shape of the harp.

But although her mind registered the aches of her tired body, a pall seemed to hang over her awareness, and she felt curiously numb, curiously detached from her surroundings. How was it possible Arimond was dead?

The worst that could have happened had come to pass. Arimond and all his friends had failed—failed in the foolish, brave attempt to rid the land of thurges like Lindos. What would happen when it was known that half the heirs of the noble houses were dead? Juilene kept walking.

The dark walls of her father's keep rose before her just as the sky began to lighten. She skirted the perimeter of the walls and slipped into the kitchen garden through the orchard. She heard noises in the kitchen as she stepped over the threshold into the house, the first stirrings of the cooks and scullions as they began to prepare the household's food for the day. She scurried up the back steps, down the corridor, and into her rooms. She found Neri slumped in the window seat, her grey hair disheveled, a blanket pulled up to her chin. As Juilene slipped the latch back into place, the old woman opened her eyes. "Oh, my dear," cried Neri, "I've been half sick with worry."

Juilene knelt beside her. Neri wrapped her arms around her, and Juilene pressed her face into the woman's thin shoulder.

"Child, child, what's happened?"

Juilene shook her head, unable to speak. A lump had formed in her throat and in her chest, and her eyes stung with tears. All she could do was cling. Neri stroked her tangled curls. Finally with a sigh that was more like a shudder, Juilene raised her head. "He's dead."

Neri looked back at her, fear in her pale eyes. "Who's dead, child?"

"Arimond. He went to kill the thurge, but Lindos killed him instead."

"Child?" Neri shook her head as if she didn't quite understand what Juilene had said.

Juilene gripped the old woman's hands in both of hers. "Not just Arimond, Neri, but half the sons of all the noble houses in the district—they went with him, to wipe him out, but Lindos was too strong—too powerful." Juilene heard the hysterical edge in her voice, heard the shrill tone as the words tumbled out of their own volition. "And now they're dead—he's killed them all. They're all dead."

Neri cupped one hand under Juilene's chin. "Child, what are you saying?"

Juilene pulled away, tears spilling down her cheeks. "They're all dead, Neri, all of them. And it's all my fault, because if I hadn't agreed to go with them, if I hadn't said I would help, they would never have tried such a thing, I know they wouldn't have. So it's all my fault."

Neri narrowed her eyes. "Child, you talk foolishness. What woman has ever stopped a man when he has his mind made up to do something? But what have you done this night? Where did you go?"

Light flooded the room as the bright rim of the sun rose over the high walls, and Juilene shut her eyes. "Because I was there, Nenny. I was there."

"Tell me all of it, child." Neri twisted one curl gently around her finger. "Tell me everything."

Slowly, haltingly, Juilene told the story, which even to her ears sounded more like a songsayer's tale than anything that might have actually occurred. Neri listened, saying nothing, only shaking her head every now and then. Finally, when Juilene had finished and had placed her head in the old woman's lap, Neri clucked her tongue. "Child, child. I don't know what your father will say. Or do."

"Neri, I can't stay to talk to Father. I must leave. Don't you understand? The spell Lindos put on me won't allow me to stay in this house. There is nothing here that I have earned—nothing at all, except perhaps my harp. And if I don't go, something awful will happen to the people who live here—I can't let anything happen to anyone here."

"You can't leave, Juilene. You're a child—"

"I'm nearly twenty. I can sing, I can play my harp. I can

tell stories. It's Festival. I'll go down to the city and take refuge there. It will be easy to earn my way, and perhaps by the end of Festival . . ." She let her voice trail off. By the end of Festival, would anything have changed? The outcry would only have just begun and each moment that she spent beneath her father's roof was only one more opportunity for harm to fall upon everyone who loved her or whom she loved. "I have to go before Father knows, before anyone is hurt."

"Child, I don't like this. You must stay until something can be done."

"And what happens if something happens to Father because of me? What if a servant is injured because of me? What if something happens to Lazare? I'll be safe enough in the city with the songsayers, Neri. I've seen Lindos's power, Neri. And you have to understand that I cannot stay."

Neri frowned. "I don't like this. I don't like this at all. I wish you would speak to your father—let him send someone with you to protect you—"

"Nenny, listen. I can't pay anyone to protect me. If Father sends someone with me, either Father or that person would be hurt. I can't let anyone else be harmed—Lindos has caused enough grief tonight. I can't look to anyone for help. You have to believe that."

Neri shook her head and opened her mouth as if she would speak. Then she sighed and rose to her feet. "Let me fetch you a few things, child. You must be hungry—I'll be right back."

Juilene rocked back on her heels as the old woman left the room. She gazed around the room as if seeing it for the first time. The wide bed with its worn blue cover, the lamp with the crack from the time she had thrown something at it during a childish tantrum. The little stool where she had sat and practiced her harp— She rose to her feet and took her harp out of its wrappings. The wood shone in the morning light, and the brass strings gleamed. Gently, she replaced it, covering it carefully.

Did she dare to take it? The harp was her only means of support—without it, she would be lost. Technically, it could be called stealing, but she didn't care. There was no one here who would want it. She went to her dressing room. The days were getting cold, the nights colder. She chose two of her heaviest, plainest dresses, and two sets of her warmest underwear, her thickest socks and her sturdiest shoes. She bundled everything but the shoes into a pack with a blanket, and lifted it. It was heavy, but not so heavy she wouldn't be able to manage it, she thought. It looked bigger than the one Galicia had arrived with, but then the old woman had practically no possessions at all. On impulse, she tucked a pair of her prettiest slippers into the pack. They were practically weightless and she could wear them if she was invited to play before any of the noble houses.

She lifted the pack once more and went out to the bedroom, just as the door was closing behind Neri.

"There you are, child." The old woman kept her head down, and Juilene could see that the old woman had been weeping. "I brought you some food—there's enough for at least a few days. And some coins—not much, but as much as I could get my hands on at such short notice."

"Oh, Neri." Juilene wrapped the old woman in a hug and kissed her wet cheek. "I'll come back—I promise I will."

"You take care of yourself, child. Be careful—the world is not what you think it is. I-I-I—" The old woman shook her head, unable to continue.

Juilene strapped her harp across her back as she had seen Galicia do, and picked up the wrapped blanket with her clothing. Neri held out the parcel of food, and as Juilene took it, the old woman's hands burst into flames.

Neri screamed. Juilene screamed, too, and grabbed her pillow to smother the flames. In a few seconds, the fire was gone, but Neri's hands were blistered and raw. "Goddess, oh, goddess, forgive me, Nenny," whispered Juilene in horror.

Neri sagged to the floor, her hands held before her, her face blanched, her lips drawn with pain. "Go, child. Don't worry about me. Go before you're discovered."

Horrified, Juilene stumbled out of the room. The curse was terribly real. She looked left and right down the corridor, her eyes darting in her skull like a hunted thing. She clutched her pack tightly to her chest, gathered her skirts in the other hand, and ran, heedless of all who tried to stop her. It was not safe for anyone to help her.

It was nearly dark when she arrived at the gates of the City of Sylyria. Torches burned on the walls, and she could see the banners announcing it was Festival time. Streams of people were flocking to the gates. The guards were laughing and joking with the people who passed through. It was the best holiday of the year.

Juilene paused beside the road, her arms aching, her back bent beneath the weight of the harp. Her feet had swollen into two lumps of blistered-covered flesh, and she felt sticky and dirty, her whole body gritty. The horror of the last day and night weighed heavier than the pack that seemed to have grown to twice its original size. She watched the people streaming by, their voices loud with laughter, their faces flushed with smiles. It didn't matter what happened to her here. Arimond was dead, and nothing would ever be the same again.

She took a deep breath and hoisted her pack once more. Several times this day she had thought she would burst into tears, but the tears didn't come. There was only a lump that

seemed to rise from deep within her chest, and then slowly
sink back down.

She started down the road, caught in the flow of the
crowds. Someone bumped against her, an elbow dug into
her back. She gasped and stumbled.

"Your pardon, sister," a man's voice spoke in her ear,
and a firm hand gripped her elbow and set her upright.

She glanced up. He was of medium height, his hair and
eyes dark in his swarthy face. He looked like one of the
Parmathian pirates her father was always cursing, or a native of Khardroon. "Thank you," she murmured.

"You've come a long way this day, sister?"

For a moment, she was confused, and then she realized
he addressed her the way all songsayers were addressed. At
least she looked the part. "Yes," she managed. "It seems
that way."

He laughed at that. "I know your meaning. Some roads
are much longer than others. It's all in how you travel, not
where, I say." His accent was definitely of Khardroon, she
decided, the soft lisp over the sibilant sounds, the gentle
roll of the r's.

"Eral!" A shout made him look back. "You getting back
in the wagon or not?"

"Goddess blessing, little sister." He smiled at her, and
faded back into the crowd.

She bit her lip, feeling the lump rise again. She had to
stay in control, she thought, she mustn't give in to the feelings of panic that were threatening to overwhelm her. She
knew exactly where she was going. She squared her shoulders and raised her head, looking around at the people who
pressed in on her from both sides as they reached the gate.
The guards waved everyone through. When it was her turn,
the guard smiled down at her. "Goddess blessing, little
songsayer," he said, showing crooked and broken teeth in
a sunburnt face.

"Goddess blessing," she replied, keeping her voice firm.

She let the crowd carry her through the broad avenues, her heart pounding in her chest. Wasn't this what she had wanted? The goddess did indeed have a plan for her, she thought bitterly.

"You there—" A voice made her look to one side.

A man stood on the corner, outside a house.

She glanced around, and the man nodded and spoke once more. "Yes, you—are you a songsayer or not?"

She nodded, feeling sweat break out on her palms. "Yes, yes, I am—I-I say the songs the goddess sends."

"Good—come with me, if you will? My wife is sick— she wants a song to cheer her—you'll have a bed to sleep in this night, if you please her."

Juilene followed the man into the house, her heart pounding in her chest. The bottom floor was a shop, for she could see bolts of fabric piled against the walls, the tables covered with thin parchment patterns. Pins gleamed in the soft candlelight and two young boys sat cross-legged on the floor, sewing.

"This way," he said shortly, motioning her to follow him up a narrow flight of steps.

Her heart beat so loudly she was amazed he did not hear it. Goddess bless me, she prayed as her hands grew slick with sweat.

The stench hit her as she reached the top. The man walked down the hall, oblivious. "This way," he said again, his hand upon a door.

Juilene tried not to breathe through her nose. No wonder the man had to stand on the street and find a songsayer. Anyone who smelled this stench was unlikely to want to spend a night beneath this roof. She walked down the hall and peered into the sickroom. A woman lay on a wide bed, covered with a sheet. She might have been beautiful once, but her skin was yellow and her features were sunken into her flesh. There was about her mouth the same bluish cast Juilene had seen on Arimond's lips. Why, she's dying, thought Juilene. And she can't be too much older than I am.

"Kara," whispered the man. "Look, my dear, I've found a 'sayer—she'll ease you, I'm sure."

Somewhere in the house an infant squalled, and the woman on the bed fluttered her eyes. The heavy lids opened with obvious effort, and the dark eyes slowly focused in the direction of the man. "Jonnah?"

"I'm here, love—look, the goddess has sent you a 'sayer—" He gestured to Juilene and nodded.

Fighting back nausea, Juilene unstrapped her harp and sank down on the low stool by the fire. It felt so good to have the heavy weight off her shoulders at last, so good to rest her weary feet. For a moment, she closed her eyes, trying to ignore the stench that filled her nostrils.

"'Sayer?" The master of the house looked at her expectantly.

"Forgive me, sir." Juilene touched the strings once, experimentally. Her damp fingers slipped on the strings. She wiped them on her dress, made a few adjustments here and there, and prayed once again to the goddess. She played a few soft notes here and there, testing the harp, trying to give herself to the music. But the music didn't come, didn't flow, and so she tried instead a song, something she could play with her eyes closed in her father's keep. Her fingers skipped over one or two of the notes, and the music was discordant, the harmony ruined. One rough-edged nail caught in a string, and she looked up to see the husband frowning at her.

At once she muttered an apology and switched to something different, something even simpler, forgetting that the key was entirely different. This time the strings seemed to shriek, and the man pursed his lips.

She shut her eyes. Why was she so nervous? She had thought she had known these songs better than her own name. She struck a chord and took a deep breath. The voice that came out of her throat shocked even her ears. Her voice was high and thin and reedy, and hovered alarmingly off-key. The woman on the bed did not move. She took another breath, feeling the color rise in her cheeks. She kept on singing, hearing the awful noise, wishing she knew a way to end it gracefully. Jonnah was looking at her with a mixture of impatience and disgust.

When the song mercifully came to an end, he rose to his feet before the last of the notes faded from hearing. "Thank you, songsayer." He made a gesture with his hand, indicating that she should go.

Juilene flushed. She gathered her pack and her harp, not even bothering to cover it, and ran from the room, her footsteps echoing. She thought she heard him call, but she ran out into the street, her palms sweating, her cheeks red with embarrassment. What would Reyerne have said about that performance? He would have been shocked, disbelieving. No one would ever want to listen to her if she sounded like that. She would have to remember all her lessons, all her control. She couldn't even soothe a dying woman.

She looked around. The hour was late and the night was dark, but the torches flared and burned on high poles all along the streets and the crowds still ebbed and flowed through the cobbled streets like water. She set her pack down and strapped her harp on her back. When she reached for her pack, it was gone.

She looked around for it frantically, not comprehending what could have happened to it, and then she remembered her father's words: "Thieves and cutpurses, pickpockets and whores." She sagged. Now what? She had nothing except her harp and the clothes on her back, and the few coins Neri had pressed upon her. Even her food was gone.

She scanned the crowd, searching for a familiar face, a friendly face, anything. She thought of her brother's house in the city, where her brother lived with his wife and his children. Briefly she thought of going to him, but she realized she could never go to her family. Not after what she had seen happen to Neri. Lindos had ensured that she could never accept charity, and never even ask for it, especially from the people who she cared about the most. What was she to do?

She bit her lip and shivered as a cold wind whined through the streets. Couples and groups of people passing laughed and drew closer to each other. No one else seemed to be without a companion. She had never felt so alone in all her life. She looked down the street, trying to remember what she knew of the city. This was the way to the temple district, where the largest temple of the goddess in all the city-states of the Sylyrian League stood. The doors of the Temple of Dramue stood open all throughout Festival. There would be a corner there for her to get out of the cold at least, and perhaps she could spend a penny or two for bread. Her stomach rumbled alarmingly, and her head swam. She was so tired. No wonder she had been unable to sing or play.

She took a deep breath and started off down the street. A rough hand gripped her shoulder and she turned, startled.

"Little sister," leered a grey-bearded man old enough to be her father. "Looking for a warm place to spend the night?"

She gasped, too frightened to reply.

"I have a place for you," he said, a crooked smile stretching across his face. His hand tightened on her shoulder and his other reached to twine in her hair.

With a frightened shriek, Juilene pulled away. She darted into the crowd and stumbled into a few of the Festival-goers. There were a few good-natured "Watch yourself"s and one or two grumbled curses, and she staggered down the street, the lump in her throat feeling as though it would suffocate her, her heart pounding so loudly in her chest she thought surely it was audible to all. She kept her head down as she hurried along, ignoring every greeting, every advance. Her cheeks flamed and her ears burned.

Finally the street opened into a great square, where the temple of the goddess rose five stories or more into the air, taller even than the towers of her father's keep. She stared up at it in awe. Light flooded from the open doors, from the colored windows in the high spires of the towers that rose from each corner and at the very center. Behind the great central tower, a white dome gleamed like a moon in the glow of the light. The crowds clustered on the shallow steps, and the smell of food of all kinds reached her nostrils.

Vendors and merchants from every city in the League crowded into the square, hawking merchandise of every description. The air was thick with their cries, with smoke from the grills and charcoal fires of the food vendors, and above and over all the shrill noise, the plaintive melodies of songsayers rose high in the night. Juilene wandered wide-eyed through the crowds.

She saw the burly natives of Albanall, bare-armed and bare-chested despite the cold, who lived far to the north and the east, selling the fine skins of the mountain sheep and goats, garments made of leather and trimmed with the softest, costliest furs. Merchants from Gravenhage, Sylyria's nearest neighbor and closest ally, offered fabrics spun of the leaves of the silkenwood tree, bags of nuts, pottery of every description and color. She saw the desert dwellers of Khardroon, the most thickly wrapped in their white robes against the chill, lounging by the sides of their wagons, their hands held out over fires that leaped and sparked in the breeze, selling sweetmeats and spices, rare wines and perfumes. The little men of Parmathia, the island off the coast of Khardroon, were there, little brown men who wore blankets brightly dyed with colors so fantastic they hardly seemed real, who crouched and spoke a language so heavily accented it was barely understandable, and watched her avidly as she passed. Her cheeks flamed and she lowered her eyes, hurrying by with a false sense of purpose. Only Eld of all the city-states of the League was not represented, but Juilene knew that the inhabitants of the Sacred City, as it was called, rarely ventured forth into the others. It was as if having been the home of the goddess, Eld had no need to seek for earthly things.

Juilene's mouth watered once more as the smell of roasting meat and fresh bread wafted by on the wind. She fumbled in her pocket for the coins. There they were, still solid and blessedly substantial. They made a pleasing jingle. She roamed through the crowd, looking for the stall that would offer the greatest value for the best price. As the rich smell of meat reached her once more, she knew that was what she needed. She sidled through the crowds and stood on the edges of the line that had formed around the cart.

Thick pieces of meat hung from long wooden skewers. She saw the gleam of copper as money changed hands, and she heard the clink of the coins in the vendor's apron. He was a short man, balding, his hair in a fringe over his ears. He wore an apron stained with grease and blood, and Juilene's mouth watered uncontrollably. Finally she reached the cart. "Please," she managed, "I want one of those."

"Ah, little sister, songsaying is hungry work, eh?" He reached for one of the thickest skewers. Juilene held out her coin and the vendor shook his head. "Little sister, that's only half—well"—his face softened—"but you do the work of the goddess. Take it."

Horrified, Juilene drew back. "No, no, I mustn't. Give

me a smaller one—or here—" She fumbled in her pocket. "Take this."

"Little sister, you do me dishonor," he said good-naturedly. "Take the meat. You look as though you could use a good meal."

She shook her head, pressing two coins into his palm.

He shook his head and gave both back to her, handing her the skewer. She held up both hands and backed away. "No, I mean no dishonor, but you don't understand—"

He reached for her hand and closed the skewer in her fingers. "Please—" His face was creased with gentle insistence.

As her fingers closed around the skewer, there was a loud snap from the grill, and hot fat flew in all directions. A gob landed in his eye, and the vendor screamed. Juilene pushed backward through the crowd, horrified that once more, someone who had tried to do her a simple kindness had suffered.

She ran to the very steps of the temple, breathing in sobbing gasps, and paused in the shadows beside them. How was she ever to manage? Two men idling near her smiled at her and beckoned. She turned her back, horrified. What man would love her for herself alone? She could hear their laughter ringing through the night. A drop of grease fell on her hands and she realized she still held the skewer of meat. The scent was more than she could bear. She sank her teeth into the chunks in despair and gnawed like a hunted animal. What in the name of the goddess would she do?

Chapter Five

❧

Cold wind gusted through the shadows, and Juilene sank to the ground, shivering, as the juice from the meat ran down her chin. She closed her eyes and gave a little sob, and a few notes rippled randomly from her harp. She was tired and dirty and still hungry, and all she had were a few coins and her harp. She couldn't stay in the city very long; her father was sure to send men to come looking for her, and among the songsayers was the first place they would look. And what sort of havoc would the curse wreak upon her family, if she went back to them? Poor old Neri had done nothing more than hand her a pack of food, and the meat-monger had done her only the smallest kindness, and look at the price they had paid. Juilene shuddered to think what might befall her family if her father insisted she stay beneath his roof.

And that was exactly what would happen—he would insist that she stay—no matter what price he had to pay, for the obligations of family meant everything to him. She didn't dare risk the potential danger. She had to get away, get as far away as possible. But where should she go?

The harp rippled once more, mournful little notes in a minor chord, and Juilene reached for the straps, fumbling with the knots with her greasy hands. She wiped her fingers on the underside of her skirt. In the dim light of the shadows beneath the great temple, the wood of the harp gleamed with a gentle shine. Juilene touched the strings, feeling the cool metal, the vibration in the brass as the notes fell, soft but clear, beneath the rumble of the crowded streets all around her.

She bent her head and her hair tumbled down, falling around her shoulders like a cloak. In the dark, it didn't matter if her fingernails were dirty, if her skin was grimy. In the dark all that mattered was the music. She closed her eyes, listening for the chords, cradling the harp as though it were a child. She pressed it close, holding its warm, familiar weight, her head bent down, for it was the only thing of home she had left. Unthinking, she played a lullaby, a song that Neri had sung to her from before she could remember, and the music floated in the dark, surrounding her in a little bubble of tranquillity in the cold night. She shut her eyes tighter, humming a little. The words of the song meant nothing. It was the music, the swelling notes, the silvery cadence of the harp that had meaning. She rocked a little in time, crooning low in her throat, and when the song ended, her fingers changed their pattern and without thinking, she began another song, this one a lament, for a lost love. She pressed her lips together. She had no voice for this song.

"When the goddess speaks, the goddess sings." The man's voice startled her out of her reverie, so that she broke off in midphrase, the harp still quivering beneath her hands.

She gave a little cry and stared at the man who peered into the shadows. "Wha—who—what do you want?"

"Forgive me if I've frightened you, little sister." The man spread his hands wide apart, as though to show he meant no harm, and gave a little bow. His face was dark and his hair and beard were nearly black in the dim light. "My name is Eral bel Afflyn, and my troupe and I had just spotted this corner here by the steps as an excellent location for our stage. I didn't mean to startle you out of your music."

She peered at him more closely. There was something familiar about the man, about the way he smiled in the dark, and suddenly she remembered him. He was the man from the road to Sylyria, that very day. "I saw you on the road today."

"Ah," he said, "you, too, are but newly come to the city?"

She nodded as she rose awkwardly to her feet. "Goddess blessing."

"But where are you going?" he said, holding out his hand. "Are you spoken for? Have you another engagement this evening?"

She laughed. "No. But you wanted this spot for your stage. I'll go."

"But we also wanted a songsayer to play the background for us, and see—in the very spot I thought would be the best place to honor the goddess, I find she sends me a songsayer, too. What more could we ask?"

"You—you want me to play?" Juilene took a step backward.

"It is just the background music," he said, almost apologetically. "But to my way of thinking, it's the most important part—it sets the mood. And we would pay you, of course, we would divide our offerings with you." This last he said with haste, almost as if he was afraid she would turn him down.

"I—I suppose—of course," Juilene stumbled over the words, scarcely believing her good fortune. Even a few coins would enable her to buy something to eat, maybe even a place to sleep.

"Good." Eral smiled, and turned, waving his arm. "Here—over here, Maggot," he called. "Bring the wagon over here."

Juilene sank back to the ground, the harp cradled in her arms. She watched as a horse-drawn cart materialized in front of her. This Eral bel whatever must be a member of a traveling troupe of actors, who went from town to town, district to district, plying their trade, sometimes selling potions or simples, sometimes a demi-thurge accompanied them, plying potions or simple charms, and most often, at least two or three songsayers made up members of the company. She watched, fascinated, at the behind-the-scenes activity of the troupe. Each knew his or her assigned role. There were about seven actors and actresses, she thought, five men and two women, as far as she could see. One of the men, a thin-faced, sharp-nosed boy, offered her a three-legged stool on which to sit. She accepted with a murmured thanks.

Eral was clearly in charge, she thought, watching him direct the activity. Torches were set up and flared into life, and in the light she saw that there were six men and two women, and that one of the women was old, older than any of the men, and that Eral had a lot of grey in his dark hair and beard. The other woman was not much older than Juilene herself, she thought, as she watched the other woman move here and there, unpacking boxes, sorting costumes. Once or twice, she thought she saw the woman look at her with derision, and she felt the color flare in her face. Who was this woman to judge her? thought Juilene, and she raised her chin defiantly.

In less time than Juilene thought possible, the stage had been set and the actors wore their costumes. They gathered in front of the stage, and Eral raised his arms. The thin-faced boy banged on a drum, and Juilene, peering from the back, saw a few faces in the crowds turn expectantly toward the actors.

"Harken, all with ears to listen . . . led by the goddess to obey . . . we who tell the timeless story . . . come and watch and hear us play." His voice was rich and deep and rolled like thunder over the rumble of the crowds, and Juilene saw more and more faces turn. Several stopped and began to cluster at the base of the makeshift stage.

It was, thought Juilene, who had seen so many of these same kinds of troupes appear at her father's gates, and who had seen more than one performance of this kind by actors in residence within the city itself, not a terribly bad performance of its kind. Eral looked over his shoulder straight at her, and Juilene struck a chord. He nodded approvingly. This was not going to be so terribly difficult, she thought. Hidden behind the stage, out of the sight of the crowds, it was easier to find the chords, to remember the proper harmonies. And the story was familiar: it was nothing more than a version of the goddess's own incarnation story, one which everyone throughout the length of Sylyria knew practically from infancy. Her fingers quivered only a little as the actors pranced and postured upon the stage, and once or twice, she thought Eral threw her an approving little smile. Slowly she warmed to the task, as the life of the goddess played out before the assembled crowds. The old songs came easily to her fingers, and she played them softly, one after the other, as the story of the goddess wound down to its inevitable conclusion.

The prone body of the younger woman was borne away

by the other actors when the crowd started to applaud. Eral leaped to center stage again, bowing and smiling, and the sharp-faced boy circulated through the crowd, holding a hat in which many placed at least a penny or two. Several threw coins at Eral's feet, and more than once, Juilene thought she saw the glint of silver. A note or two was pressed into his hands by plainly dressed men, and with a little shock, Juilene realized that these must be from the carriages that had stopped at the very perimeter of the crowds.

Eral kissed the notes, tucked them away, bowed. "Thank you, thank you all—come again . . . our next performance will be at noon tomorrow." As the crowd slowly dispersed to find another diversion, Eral leaped off the stage, running his fingers through his hair. He swept all the coins that had fallen on the stage into his pocket, and motioned for the sharp-faced boy to bring the hat over. "A goodly take tonight, Maggot," he said cheerfully.

Maggot—if that was truly the name he bore, Juilene doubted her hearing—nodded and grunted something unintelligible. Eral came around behind the stage, his arm over Maggot's shoulder. "Gather round, my children, gather round," he said, making the same expansive gesture he used before the crowds.

"Oh, drop it," said the younger woman. She still wore her bloodstained goddess costume, and the greasepaint on her face gleamed in the torchlight. "We've all seen that act time out of mind—there's no need to practice on us."

Eral grinned as though she had complimented him to the skies. "And each time it's as fresh as a day-old rose, eh, sweetheart?" He pinched her cheek despite the greasepaint, and she slapped him away, ducking out of his reach.

"You keep your hands to yourself, Eral, or you'll be shy a few fingers less of a hand," she snarled.

"Oh, my little kitten has such claws." He laughed, waving the hat, which made a loud clinking noise.

Juilene watched the faces of the others, sullen and surly all of them, except for the old woman who hung back, arms crossed over her bony bosom.

"Let's see the color of the coin," she said.

"What will it matter," muttered one of the men, "we know our share is all copper and brass."

"Copper and brass buys warm food and a soft bed," Eral said. He walked over to Juilene and smiled down at her. "And there's more of it tonight than ever, mostly due to the efforts of our songsayer, here, don't you all agree?"

The others nodded and shrugged, muttering noncommittal responses. Juilene smiled at them tentatively. To the crowd they had appeared happy, like one large family working in concert, but behind the scenes, she could see that was not at all the truth. If anything, they behaved more like strangers than people who spent most of their lives with each other every day, and every night.

Eral's hand fell on her shoulder, and she could feel the strong fingers massaging and caressing the muscle beneath her skin. Involuntarily she stretched a little, her back and her neck ached from the long day, from carrying her possessions, and she saw the younger woman snort and turn away.

"What's wrong, Mathy?" he asked. "Don't want your share of the take tonight?"

"Aye," the girl turned back. "I'll take my share of the whole take, if you don't mind. Let's see you empty those pockets of yours into the pot."

He stopped caressing Juilene and drew himself up with an expression half shock, half hurt. "You shame me, Mathy, and before our new songsayer, too. You make me sound like a cheat."

Juilene stared at him, shocked. New songsayer? When had she become that?

But Mathy kept speaking, her tone bitter and angry. "Aye, that's my intent. You are a cheat, Eral. And why don't you tell our new songsayer what happened to our old one, before she decides to berth with us? Just to let her know what she's getting into?"

Juilene glanced around the circle. The men were watching with guarded expressions, the boy crouched with his eyes fastened on the small hoard. The old woman turned away, her mouth set. She seemed determined to ignore the discussion.

"My arrangement with each of you is private," he said, with a trace of anger in his tone. "And each of us takes a fair share of the take, an equal share. That never varies and it never changes."

"Faugh." Mathy spit to the side. "Give me what's mine. You leave a bad taste in my mouth every time I have to speak to you."

Eral crouched down, sorting the coins, his lips moving as he counted out the money. In the end there were nine piles of a dozen coins each. "And here," he said, "since I am so generous, and the hour is so late, and you all worked so hard and so well, I'll take one coin out of my share for each of you—call it a Festival bonus, if you like."

Juilene wondered what hold he had on the rest of the troupe that made them turn away so obediently, the money jingling in pockets or purses. But not Mathy.

"Yah," Mathy said with a sneer as she counted her coins, feeling the weight of them in her hand. "We'll try not to spend it all in one place tonight." She turned away, the coins tied up in a kerchief she tied into the lacings of her bodice.

The others slowly dispersed, muttering and grumbling among themselves, and Juilene was left alone with Eral, her harp still cradled in her arms, a small pile of coins at her feet.

He smiled at her, as if the incident with Mathy had never happened, and picked up the coins. He took her hand and poured them into her palm, closing her fingers around the small copper and brass pennies. "Never mind Mathy," he said, holding her hand closed around the greasy feel of the money. "Some of us never know our place. She thinks she should have made it on the legitimate stage, with a King's company, or maybe an Over-Thurge's. Not all of us recognize our own limitations, my dear. It leads to rash and foolish acts."

Juilene stared at the man who knelt before her. Weariness washed over her, making his face suddenly swim before her eyes. He wagged a finger before her nose. "You don't look like the type to hit the rude-wine."

"The child is exhausted, Eral." The sharp voice of the older woman pierced the fog that was clouding Juilene's vision. "You come with me, child. You've earned a safe place to sleep tonight." The old woman stood over Juilene like a mother hen, holding out her hand.

Eral laughed as the old woman led Juilene away. She looked over her shoulder as the old woman said something that sounded like a curse, but might have been an admonition, and then all she knew was a nest of moldy blankets, which seemed softer than a feather mattress as she sank down into sleep.

The sun had not yet risen above the rooftops when Juilene opened her eyes. For a moment, she lay looking up at the cloudless sky above her head and wondered what on earth she was doing out-of-doors. Then the smell of the old wool and her own body came to her, and she remembered everything that happened in the last two days. She felt the weight of the coins in her pocket, and saw the harp in its wrappings lying next to her. She sat up. Three of the other actors, including Mathy and the older woman, and the sharp-faced boy, snored gently beside her. There was no sign of the rest. Her joints were sore and cramped, and every muscle in her body ached. She rose unsteadily to her feet, wincing as her blistered feet touched the ground. She felt the jingle of the coins in her pocket, and she remembered everything. She had to get out of the city. It was only a matter of time before someone from her father's house or Lazare's recognized her. This was probably the first place they would come looking. In the grey light of morning, she counted out the meager store of her coins. She bit her lip when she saw how few there were. Barely enough to buy a day's meals, she thought, not to mention the fact that she would dearly love to buy a bath at one of the inns in the square. She sighed, tucking her hair back around her ears. She bent to fold the blankets that had made her bed, and a voice startled her so that she nearly stepped on her harp.

"Early riser?"

She turned to see Eral standing with folded arms, leaning against a corner of the wagon. "I suppose I am." She remembered Mathy's words of the night before. What had happened to the other songsayer, she wondered.

"That's good," he said. "Going for breakfast?"

She shrugged. "I—well—I—yes, I suppose I am."

"Good. The tavern across the way is the only one open right now, but the landlord is generous with his bread and beer." He pointed across the square.

Juilene picked up her harp and sidled past him. "Thank you."

"Your harp will be safe here." He caught her under the elbow.

"I might earn my breakfast," she said, amazed at how easily the lie slipped off her tongue. Something about this man and the way the others had reacted to Mathy's accusations made her uneasy.

"Good for you," he said, and she knew he watched her as she limped across the square.

The tavern door was open and the smell of frying meat pervaded even the square as she made her way toward the door. A woman was on her hands and knees, scrubbing the cobblestones in front of the tavern.

"Goddess blessing," she said as she saw Juilene.

"Goddess blessing," Juilene answered. She bit her lip. "I say the songs the goddess sends," she said after an awkward pause.

The woman laughed a little, running her red, work-worn hand over her forehead, pushing back an errant strand of grey hair. "I'm sure you do, child. But you'll find no ears to listen inside. Still, if you have coin, you'll find a hot breakfast."

The woman nodded toward the door, and went back to scrubbing. Juilene backed away, the smell of the meat making her mouth water, the blood stinging her cheeks. Surely she would have to get over some of this embarrassment, or she was going to spend the rest of her life with a permanent flush on her face. She skirted the wet area on the cobblestones, and went into the inn. The only patron at that hour of the day was slumped in a chair before the cold hearth, his boots on one chair, his mouth hanging open, his eyes shut. He snored in happy oblivion.

The landlord behind the bar looked up at her. "Greetings to you," he said shortly, forestalling any on her part.

She nodded, pressing her lips together.

"Breakfast?"

"Well . . ." she hesitated, feeling in her pocket, wondering how to ask the price. It occurred to her that she had never in her life had to ask the price of anything. "How much?"

"Fried bread and meat together cost you six, bread only cost you three. A tankard of beer is another two," he said, frowning a little.

Juilene fingered her coins. "And—and a bath? Do you—?"

He nodded. "During Festival, always. The tub's in a room off the kitchen—it's nothing fancy, mind." He gave her a long measuring look as if considering what she might consider fancy.

"How much?"

"Three pence. And this time of day, the water will be fresh and hot, just off the stove. You won't have to share it with anyone."

She gaped at him. The thought of sharing another's bathwater, water that a stranger had bathed in, had never occurred to her. "That—that's fine," she managed finally.

"Be another penny for soap and another for use of a towel."

"All right," she said. "A bath, and I'll have the fried bread and beer."

"Sit yourself down—I'll call for the mother." The landlord slung his rag over his shoulder and went to the door as Juilene took a chair by a window. The woman paused in her scrubbing as the landlord spoke, and said something Juilene couldn't hear through the thick leaded glass.

The burly man came back inside, reached for a tankard from beneath the bar, and filled it with foamy beer. He set it down in front of Juilene. "Eat first. She'll have the bath ready for you in a few minutes."

She nodded, reaching for the tankard, hearing her stomach growl alarmingly. Except for the meat last night, she had eaten almost nothing the entire day yesterday. He curved his huge hand over the top of the tankard. "You'll pay for everything first."

She fumbled in her skirt, and counted out the coins. Two

for the beer, three for the bread, three for the bath, two more for soap and a towel. She had eight coins left. But at least, she thought, as she watched him slide the money off the table, she still had the original coins Neri had given her. She clung to the thought of those coins as if they were a good luck charm, a talisman against everything that could happen to her in the harsh world in which even the use of a towel cost a penny, where water could be shared with a stranger, and where even a pack of clothing could be stolen without a moment's thought.

She sighed and sipped the beer, the harsh, acrid taste bitter on her tongue. The landlord set a plate of golden fried bread before her, the fat pooling and gleaming on its surface. The scent of the meat rose from the bread, and she realized it had been fried in the same fat as the meat. Her mouth watered, despite her stomach's rumbles of protest. She tore off a small piece. The fat-soaked bread at once repulsed and seemed as if it must be the most delicious morsel she had ever tasted. Tentatively she placed it in her mouth.

The landlord leaned against the bar, wiping glasses with his rag, laughing. "By the goddess, I never saw a songsayer eat so sweetly—you have a dainty bent, I see."

She smiled at him then, apologetically, and wondered what he would say if she told him the truth, that she was no songsayer, that she was the daughter of one of the noblest houses in Sylyria, and that just down the street and over a few blocks was a house three times the size of this mean little inn that belonged to her brother, and if only she dared, she would have gone there by now, and thrown herself on their mercy. But she did not dare, did not dare to put all the people she loved so much at risk, and the thought of Neri's blistered, bleeding hands rose before her like a vision. The bread lodged in her throat like a heavy lump and she choked a little, almost a sob.

He looked at her critically as if just noticing her. She thought he might speak, and then he went back to wiping the glasses. When the woman came in, lugging the bucket and her mop and her brush, he said, "Just a few minutes, and your bath will be ready."

She nodded, chewing the food slowly, sipping the bitter beer every third or fourth bite. She stared out the window. Four or five other patrons had come in, and the landlord was busy, drawing beer, fetching food from the kitchens. The people paid her no mind. She was no more and no less than any other tired, hungry songsayer in the city for the Festival.

A young man with sun-bleached blond hair went by, and her heart seemed to stop. Arimond, she thought. No, she reminded herself, it couldn't be Arimond. It would never be Arimond again. Grief flooded through her like a wave and a hard lump rose in her throat. She choked on the bread and forced herself to swallow, but the taste of it was bitter on her tongue. Her eyes burned with unshed tears. Best to put it all behind her and go on. Nothing was ever going to be the same again. Her life had changed irrevocably, there could be no going back.

The landlord's wife emerged from the kitchens and paused in the doorway. "You, girl. This way, if you will." She beckoned with rough curtsey.

Juilene took one more sip of the beer. There was no way she could ever finish it; it was too bitter and too foreign to her taste. But it had quenched her thirst, and washed some of the morning's scum off her tongue, and so she rose and followed the woman down a low corridor to a rough door.

"In there," the woman said. "You'll find the towel on the chair, fold it and leave it there when you're finished. And here"—she fished in the pockets of her capacious apron—"you paid for soap." She handed Juilene the smallest sliver.

Juilene nodded her thanks. This was as good as she

could expect, she supposed. She went into the room, where
a huge wooden tub steamed, and pulled down the latch.
She stared at the ceiling, black with age and dank with
mold in spots. At least the place seemed clean enough.
Suddenly, she felt as though her skin crawled.

She fumbled with the lacings of her bodice. As she
slipped her dress off her shoulders, she heard the jingle of
coins in her pocket. She would have to find a better
arrangement for her money, she thought. She thought of
how Mathy had kept her coins from sight, tied securely to
her bodice, and wondered if she might manage something
like that. Perhaps if she could find the means to purchase a
needle and a thread—the dressmaker's shops she had fre-
quented before always had plenty. But how to acquire such
a necessity was beyond her; she had no idea whether or not
she could simply walk into one and ask for a needle and
thread. She sighed as she slipped into the water.

The hot water enveloped her like a blanket, and she took
a deep breath and leaned back against the wooden edge.
She closed her eyes. She could feel all the muscles in her
back and shoulders and neck, the soreness in her feet and
calves from the long walk of the day before. Who would
have thought that a songsayer's life was so hard? No wonder her parents had been horrified at the thought.

And what would her father say now? she wondered.
What would he do, besides go rage at the new Over-
Thurge? Nothing could lift a thurge's curse, not even the
thurge himself. No, Lindos had known what he was doing.
And what man would love her now? she wondered. She
thought of Mathy, of her hard, calculating face and the way
she had argued with Eral over a few pennies. It wouldn't
be much longer before she too was reduced to quarreling
over pennies, and she knew that whatever was soft and innocent about her would be more of a liability than an asset.

Mathy was a far cry from the girl her father had raised her to be.

Slowly, she worked the scrap of soap into a lather, working it over her shoulders and breasts and arms. She let down her hair and wet it, working the harsh lather through it. Who knew when she would next have the luxury of a bath? She looked at her clothes and where she had left them on the chair. No Neri now to whisk them away, to replace the soiled underlinen with snowy fresh, no maid to brush and shake and air her dresses. She reached for her underlinen. It was badly creased. If she washed it, here in the water, and put it on, it would dry on her body. She wet it, scrubbed it with the soap, and wrung it out as best she could. Then she shook it out and laid it over the rim of the tub. She reached for her dress. She dabbed at the stains as best she could, and tried to scrub the underarms with the sliver of soap. Then she splashed the water on the fabric, rinsing as much of the soap away as she could. She rose unsteadily on her feet and shook the dress out, placing it flat over the back of the chair.

A knock on the door startled her. "You drown yourself in there, Sissy?" It was the landlord's rough voice.

"No, no, I'm fine," she managed. "I'm nearly finished. I'll be right out."

"Someone's asking for you."

She heard the heavy clump of his boots as he went down the hall and froze as she reached for the threadbare piece of linen that passed as a towel. Who could be asking for her? No one knew her name—she had been so careful not to go anywhere she might have been recognized. She dried herself thoroughly, then stepped out onto the cold stone floor. She put on her damp underlinen. The fabric clung wetly to her skin, and she grimaced. This was going to be uncomfortable.

She shook out her petticoats and put on her chemise, her

fingers fumbling with the buttons and the fastenings. She reached for her dress. The wet spots under the arms chafed terribly as she laced it. She dried her hair with the damp towel, and braided it loosely. She thrust her feet into her shoes and picked up her cloak. She folded the towel neatly over the back of the rickety chair.

Well. The goddess had seen her clean and fed, her first day as a songsayer. She had a few coins in her pocket, and her harp. Time to face the day.

She strapped her harp on her back and went out into the passage. The landlord's wife gestured her to go on ahead. "There's a man been asking for you, sister."

Juilene bit her lip and peered into the tavern. Eral stood beside the bar, laughing and joking with a few of the men who had gathered there. The morning was well along, the sun was high, and she could see people hurrying past in the streets. The square was crowded again.

He smiled broadly when he caught sight of her. "There you are, little sister." He waved her over to him. "It's nearly time for the noon performance. You must have known we couldn't start without you."

Juilene blinked. He seemed to take for granted that she was a member of the company. She gave him a puzzled frown. "I—I didn't realize my presence was wanted."

"Not wanted?" He clapped an arm around her shoulders and she winced. "Surely you realize how much of an asset you are. What's a troupe without a songsayer? We couldn't have performed last night if it weren't for you—you know that. And you profited, too, didn't you?"

He winked at her broadly and for a moment Juilene wanted to pull away. Then she thought again. It was true, she had profited and a dozen coins or so every performance would be enough to earn her bread and a few other necessaries. It wasn't much but it would be a start. "Yes," she said at last. "I did."

"Good," he said with a laugh and a smile so broad, she thought his face must ache with the stretch. "And we can count on you to come with us, when we leave here?"

Juilene blinked. She hadn't considered that possibility—that the actors troupe would be leaving the city. "When—when will you leave?"

"Why, right after Festival, of course." He laid a silver coin down on the bar and gently propelled her toward the door. "We'll head south, south to Khardroon. We don't want to be stuck up here in the winter—already the nights are getting too cold for my blood." He steered her through the crowded square. "Ever been to Khardroon? No place is prettier, to my way of thinking. Of course, that's where I was born, so you might say I am biased. If you want to come with us, you're welcome and I offer the same terms I offer the others—an equal share of each performance's profits."

"But if I come," she said with a puckered frown, "there will be less for the others—won't they mind?"

"Goddess bless you, you've a head on your shoulders," he said, hugging her so close, her bones ached, and she had to stop herself from instinctively drawing away. "Why, think, foolish child. Without a songsayer, we'd be lost. It was the grace of the goddess which led me to that dark corner by the temple, where you had hidden—you were hiding, weren't you?" He cocked his eyebrow at her.

So that's it, she thought, he thinks I am a thief or worse. Well, it's true I have something to hide, and the less he knows the better. Let him think I only want to get out of the city. "I—I just have one question," she said.

"Anything, goddess-sent, anything."

"Last night, I played behind the scenes and no one saw my face. Is—is that how you want it done, all the time?"

He raised one eyebrow. "Well. Let's do it that way for now, shall we? Once we're out of Sylyria, we'll see.

Mathy's been overstepping herself lately—you might try the role of the goddess herself once or twice."

"No." Juilene blushed furiously. "That isn't what I meant at all—"

"No?" He smiled and his teeth were white, so white against his sun-browned face, and inexplicably she was reminded of Lindos. She shuddered before she could stop herself. "Well. We'll just leave well enough alone for now. You stay in the shadows, little sister. It's the music you make the people will pay to hear. No one need know who makes it. For now. Do we have a bargain?"

Juilene took a deep breath. This was surely the most immediate answer to all her troubles. She looked into Eral's dark eyes. They danced and gleamed with a merry light. She remembered the misgivings Mathy had raised, and dismissed them from her mind. Just as she nodded, a group of excited men burst past them into the tavern. They were gesturing and talking loudly among themselves, and Juilene thought she heard the names "Lindos" and "Ravenwood."

She peered around Eral, and he, at once catching her interest, turned around. He glanced back down at her, his eyes narrowed. "Good sir," he said as the group jostled past, "what news is there, so early in the day?"

The man stopped and stared. "Can you not have heard? The whole city is alive with it."

Eral shrugged and spread his hands. "Alas, I'm just a poor actor newly come to the city but late last night. I have scarce found a place to water my horses, let alone hear the latest news. Pray, tell us." With one sweep of his hand, he included Juilene.

The man eyed her briefly. "Arimond of Ravenwood and half the young thanes and demi-thanes of the outlying districts were slain night before last."

"By whom?"

"It's said by Lindos, one of the master-thurges. He denies it, yet the thanes have sworn revenge, and the whole district is in turmoil. There's talk of wild magic—that Lindos has found a way to unbind the magic. He's locked himself within the walls of his keep and they say he's plotting to take over the entire city. There is to be a Gathering in the city day after tomorrow, and Thane Jiroud swears he will have this Lindos strung upon the walls—wild magic or not."

Juilene raised her eyes. Eral was watching her closely. She hoped the expression on her face did not betray her.

The man shook his head. "If you're an actor, my advice to you is to leave the city as soon as possible. There's likely to be rioting and who knows how the new Over-Thurge will put it down?" He nodded toward the open door, and in the square, Juilene could see throngs of people.

" 'Tis Festival," said Eral.

"Festival be damned, friend." The man shook his head. "You earn your bread on the road—there'll be nothing here for you if the thurges retaliate to the demands of the thanes. Do you know what I'm saying, friend?"

Eral nodded slowly. "I do, indeed. Thanks for the wisdom."

The man shrugged and hurried off to join his companions at a table on the other side of the room.

"Well, little sister," Eral said, turning a speculative look upon Juilene once more, "it seems our stay in the city is to be briefer than I ever thought. What do you say? Will you come?"

Juilene nodded. What choice did she have? She clutched her harp close and whispered a prayer. "As the goddess wills it, I obey."

Chapter Six

❦

The fire snapped and hissed as Juilene crouched in the flickering light, her hands wrapped around a tin cup full of thin broth. Behind her, she could hear Maggot's snorts as he tossed in his sleep. She wondered what dreams tormented him every night, for only toward dawn did he fall into an exhausted slumber. Then he lay as still as the dead, his mouth hanging open, his hair falling over his sharp-boned face. But as deep as it might appear he slept, he was easily roused by even the slightest noise, leaping to his feet, with one hand at his waist, the other clenched in a fist.

She heard the old woman, Nuala, stir. Nuala shook the boy and murmured something, and Maggot quieted down. Every night that ritual was repeated more times than Juilene could count. She was learning to sleep through it, though; the last few nights she had been so tired, she had fallen asleep as soon as her head had touched the blanket, and had not awakened until the smell of the breakfast gruel had reached her nostrils.

She sipped her broth, watching the flames dance and sway in the cold breeze. On the other side of the fire, in the shadows beyond the periphery, she heard Mathy's sharp whisper and a muffled slap. There was a grunt, and a man's low murmur, and Juilene waited to see whether it would be Yoshi or Thaddam who would emerge from the shadows. But there was silence, and Juilene realized that Mathy must have reached an understanding with either or both of her two admirers.

None of the men had approached her, although they eyed her speculatively. Nuala kept a sharp eye on her, and more than once, each of the men, including Maggot, had heard the sharp side of her tongue where Juilene was concerned. The old woman seemed to notice everything.

Juilene shivered and pulled her cloak closer around her body. The heat of the fire was seductive—it made her reluctant to leave its warmth and seek the thin nest of blankets that served her as a bed. By unspoken agreement, the women had the use of the wagon at night, while all the men but Maggot slept on the ground. Except for Mathy—she was as likely to disappear of an evening as was Eral and the other men.

He was gone now, Juilene knew, off entertaining one of the women who had crowded around the base of the stage that evening, and had perhaps wrapped her coins in a note of invitation. And the other men who formed the company—Yoshi, Thaddam, and Ruell—one was with Mathy, and the others must be off gambling or drinking or doing whatever it was that kept them occupied until the small hours of the morning.

More than once Juilene had been awakened by their

voices, in the greying light of a wintery dawn, and had
known that they were just coming back from a night spent
doing what she could probably not even begin to imagine.

But she kept to herself. Nuala made her nervous in a
way even Eral did not. The old woman might be tough and
proud and sharp as ten-year-old cheese, but she was kind.
And there was nothing Juilene feared more than kindness.
The others left her alone, too, after a few attempts at conversation. She was too different and they all seemed to
know it.

A twig snapped, and Juilene jumped. Mathy stood on the
other side of the fire, a ragged shawl clutched over a shape-
less gown that served as her nightdress. She shrugged a
greeting. "Can't sleep," she said as she settled down beside
the fire, one hand held out to its warmth.

"It's cold tonight," Juilene said.

"Mm," the other girl agreed. The firelight was kind; she
looked not much older than Juilene in its rosy glow. "Another week or so, we'll be through the last of these mountains, and the weather will be warmer. Thank the goddess
Eral at least has the sense to take us south for the winter."

"You go there every year?"

"Of course. A troupe that doesn't have a regular berth in
one of the cities or with a thane or thurge would be foolish
to wander through the northern cities during the cold
weather. Gravenhage must be a very dull place." She
laughed a little.

Juilene frowned a little and cocked her head. "Why's
that?"

"It's so cold there." Mathy looked at her as if Juilene had
spoken in another tongue. "Have you never been there?"

Juilene shook her head. She had never traveled beyond the confines of the district where she had been born
and raised. Her only experience with cities was Sylyria,
and even that had been confined to the immediate vicin-

ity of her father's house. She had heard the stories, of course, of the traders and the songsayers who had come to her father's house, but her life had been circumscribed by her station.

Mathy cocked her head. "You come from Sylyria, don't you?"

"Close by," Juilene said.

Mathy shrugged. "You needn't tell me anything. We all have things we'd rather not speak of—you're no different from the rest of us in that way."

Juilene raised her head. "In that way?"

Mathy leaned forward, her arms folded around her knees, her toes in their torn slippers peeping out from beneath the hem of her gown. "You're very different from the rest of us. And you know it, so don't deny it." She looked around, over her shoulder, and squinted into the dark behind Juilene. "Look. I don't want to know you, don't want to hear your story any more than I want to tell you mine, but you've been good for the troupe, and it's because of you we've all earned bigger takes. So let me tell you this much, in exchange for the better money you've brought us. Don't trust anyone. Don't think of anyone as your friend, because they aren't. This life isn't like the one you've known—oh—" She held up her hand. "Do you think none of us recognize your accent? The quality of your clothes? They might soon be as shabby as ours, but they aren't yet. And don't you think I can see how they were made for you?" She shook her head. "You are an innocent.

"Eral's got two things in mind for you. First of all, he intends to use your talent, your skill, to make as much for himself as possible. If we happen to benefit in some way— if you happen to benefit—so be it. But don't think for a moment he has your best interest at heart."

Intuition told Juilene what the second thing Eral might have in mind, but her curiosity was piqued by Mathy's uncharacteristic communicativeness. "What—what happened to the other songsayer? The one who left the company, before Sylyria?"

"Left us?" Mathy gave a harsh laugh and shook her head. "Yes, I suppose you could put it like that. No one's told you? Not even Nuala?"

Juilene shook her head.

"She died." Mathy looked away. "That rat-bastard wouldn't take the money out of his own hoard to pay for a demi-thurge, let alone one who was also a physician. So she died."

"She got sick?"

Mathy snorted softly. "You could say that. She got with child. And she didn't want to carry it, you see, so she tried to rid herself of it. And she died."

Juilene looked into the fire and down at her lap. Anywhere but to see the naked grief etched on Mathy's face. Mathy made a little noise that might have been a sob, and rose to her feet. She disappeared into the shadows without another word.

Footsteps and a low whistle made Juilene turn. Eral emerged from beneath the low-hanging branches of the trees into the clearing. "Greetings, little sister," he said with an air of surprise. "I didn't expect to see you at this hour."

Juilene shrugged a brief greeting. Mathy's revelation had only come as a partial surprise. It was obvious that Eral intended to get as much from her as possible. It made her feel comfortable. There was little danger of causing any trouble as a result of the curse. And if he got more from her than he gave, so what? At least she wouldn't be responsible for someone's injury or worse.

"It's cold," she said. "I couldn't sleep."

"Ah." His white teeth gleamed. "And you aren't the sort to seek out a body to warm you, are you?"

She blushed. "No," she managed.

He chuckled. "I didn't think so."

He sat down within the narrow circle of the fire's heat and tossed a leather bag in his hand. "The goddess was smiling on me, tonight, little sister. I won ten aurelles at dice tonight—and a berth for us for the morrow. You won't have to worry about cold toes for at least a night!" He smiled at her and ran his eyes over her body, and Juilene blushed again. The look he gave her reminded her of Arimond in a way, and yet—he was so different. She didn't doubt his interest, and yet, in some strange way he didn't frighten her either. She had too much value to him, she realized with a start.

She swallowed all the broth, lukewarm now, and got to her feet. "Good night, Eral." She met his eyes fearlessly. She was beginning to understand, she thought. Was it possible only a few weeks had passed since that terrible night in Lindos's castle and her frantic flight from her father's house? Perhaps she would survive this strange new life.

"Good night, little sister," he answered with grave courtesy. "The goddess guard your sleep."

With another smile and a nod, Juilene turned on her heel and went to snuggle among the blankets, the dank smell of the wool scarcely bothersome.

Brave slivers of sunlight pierced the lowering sky as the little troupe jolted across the lowered drawbridge of the keep that was only a few hours south of their campsite of the previous night. Juilene held her harp against her, to protect it from the bouncing of the cart, and stared at the grey towers that rose before her. A chill went down her spine. Thank the goddess that no such invitation had come from any of the thanes or thurges closer to Sylyria. There was not a thurge or thane within a week's radius of the city who would not have known her. And the word had gone out, she knew. News reached them at every stop. The thanes and the thurges of Sylyria were nearly at war. Everywhere they met people fleeing into the safety of the outer districts, and more than once, she had heard her own description given. Thank the goddess her role in the company did not put her face before the public. There was far less danger in her being recognized by anyone as long as she stayed in the background and played according to her cues.

And the goddess knew she made enough mistakes. Once, someone had the presence of mind to ask Eral if the songsayer was by any chance the runaway lady. And he had laughed, saying, "You heard her play. Was it the playing of the paragon described?"

And the other man had turned away, nodding in agreement. Juilene had listened from the shelter of the cart, her face burning. But it was her very mistakes that had kept her safe, she thought. At the time she hadn't thought whether or not Eral might have wondered who she was, but after last night, she was almost certain that he, at least, had guessed her identity long ago. As long as it profited him to keep her secret, she would be safe.

She leaned outside the covered interior of the wagon and gazed at the faces of the household that were gathering as the cart entered into the inner court of the keep. The people stared eagerly, expectantly. It was far enough past Festival time that a performance would be a treat.

Eral drove the cart up to the very foot of the stairs leading into the main hall. "Goddess blessings, good people," he cried, standing up. He tossed the reins to a groom, and grinned that infectious smile that Juilene had seen few resist. "Goddess blessings upon you all."

"And you," said a woman's voice, clear and soft and deep all at once.

Juilene looked up. A woman of about forty-five stood

upon the steps, her long white dress bordered in a series of complicated designs. A master-thurge, she thought. She had seldom seen a woman thurge, although she knew that in one or two of the other cities of the League, there were more female thurges than male. The woman was smiling at Eral in welcome, her blue eyes vivid and startling in a face pale as milk.

"Welcome to my house," she said, lifting her eyes to include the entire company.

Together, they murmured thanks and greetings. Eral leaped from the cart and bowed low before the woman. "Lady Deatrice," he said as he offered her his arm, "will you allow us the honor of offering our humble performance for your pleasure?"

The woman smiled up at him. "I expect your performance will bring me pleasure, my dear Eral. From you, I expect nothing less." She took his arm with something like a girlish simper and Juilene felt herself blush. No wonder they had been invited to spend the night beneath the thurge's roof. Behind her Mathy snorted. "His performance, indeed. The rest of us might as well baa like sheep and cluck like hens. 'Tis only the crow of that cock she wishes to hear."

Nuala elbowed her with a quick glance at Juilene, and Mathy snorted once more. "She'd do well to understand what he is."

"She shows no signs of going the way your sister did," said Nuala as she shoved aside the flaps of the opening. "You, Maggot, help an old woman down, will you, and stop gaping at the girls. Haven't you ever seen one before?"

Juilene stared after Mathy as she scrambled from the cart. So that's what it was. The songsayer who'd died had been Mathy's sister. No wonder she was so bitter. She gathered her skirts in one hand and her harp in the other and allowed a groom to help her out of the cart. The people gathered around her, murmuring greetings and blessings, and she smiled in return. There was much about this life she could find pleasant. As long as she remembered that Eral was going to exploit her in any way he could, and that her bread depended entirely upon her own ability to feed herself. As long as she remembered all that she would be fine. The farther they journeyed from Sylyria the freer she felt to show herself before the crowd. And everyone always applauded wildly at the end if she shyly emerged from behind the curtain. More than once, the crowd had called for a song or even two, and Juilene had obliged, while Eral circulated through the crowd, hat in hand, beaming.

In some ways she was the most valuable member of the cast and they knew it. It meant that her place among them was assured. Mathy caught her eye. "Come on." She motioned toward the door. "There's a room for us to rest, and bathe and even change."

Juilene extricated herself from the crowd as quickly as she could. She managed to bathe at least twice a week, and even Mathy and Nuala thought her predilection for bathing peculiar. They didn't understand her reluctance to use water that had been used by others, nor her need to bathe more than once every two weeks. And the fact that she rinsed her underlinen every day, and changed it every night, was a matter for merriment among the entire company.

And here was a chance to rest, to lie back against a great tub, surely as she had done in her father's house—she froze, as she remembered the curse. Would her performance be worthy of what she was about to receive? And if not, who would suffer? She shivered. A maid touched her arm. "This way, sister."

Juilene followed, biting her lip. In the hall they passed

the master-thurge and Eral, where they sat on high-backed chairs and drank wine from gem-studded goblets. Juilene lowered her eyes as the master-thurge glanced at her, but not before she saw the woman's eyes narrow.

"You—girl." The master-thurge beckoned.

Juilene paused. "Yes, lady"

The woman motioned her closer. "Come here—closer." Her head was cocked and she watched Juilene's every movement. "There's a taint of magic on you—" She blinked her eyes, as if trying to see more clearly. "Come here."

She held out her hand and Juilene reluctantly took it. The woman closed her eyes and squeezed Juilene's hand gently. From out of the corner of her eye, she saw Eral lean forward, speculative interest in every line of his face.

The woman gasped and drew back her hand as if Juilene's touch had hurt her. She rubbed the palm as she stared up at Juilene, an uneasy frown on her face. "You've run afoul of powerful magic, haven't you, girl?"

Miserably Juilene nodded.

"What's wrong with her?" demanded Eral.

Juilene knew at once what he was thinking. The handsome sum he had no doubt been promised was in danger of slipping away. And every shred of security she had managed to achieve for herself in the last few weeks was about to go with it.

The thurge leaned back in her chair, still cradling her hand. "That's for her to say, if she wills. But there's a powerful spell upon her, placed there by one more powerful than I. More powerful than most, I'd wager—you weren't wanted by the Over-Thurge, were you?"

Juilene shook her head, too frightened to speak.

The woman shook her head. "I can protect my people from you, at the least I can do that. But you'd be wise to be wary, my friend," she said, looking at Eral. "The spell she carries is of no demi-thurge's making. The power that binds itself to her is stronger—and of a stranger sort—than any I have felt in quite a while." She cocked her head, her eyes roaming Juilene.

Eral looked suspiciously from Deatrice to Juilene and back again. "A stranger sort? In what way?"

Deatrice frowned. "A spell leaves a certain pattern, rather like a blanket knitted in a particular weave. It should be possible for another thurge to read the weave, so to speak, to understand how the thurge who cast the spell worked the power, so that under some circumstances, especially in the case of a spell as dangerous as this, the magic can be undone by a thurge as powerful as the one who cast the spell. But this—" She shook her head and stared, frowning at Juilene. "Either the master who cast this spell was more powerful than any I have ever met, or—" She paused, biting her lip.

"Go on," Eral demanded.

Deatrice raised her head. Her expression was cold, and Juilene realized that infatuated by Eral as the thurge might be, there was still a great line dividing them. "There are things of which I need not speak to you, my traveling friend." She beckoned to a maidservant. "Take the girl to her room." Deatrice rose, her white robes swirling gracefully around her slim body.

"Where are you going, my lady?" asked Eral.

"I must consult the grimoire," murmured Deatrice, her eyes fastened on Juilene. Juilene flushed and glanced at her ring. The sapphire band was a dull blue-black. Whatever the woman intended to do posed no immediate danger.

Eral grabbed at Juilene's wrist as she went by, his grip hard and demanding. "We'll speak of this later, my dear. After the performance."

Juilene nodded and followed Deatrice's servant, wondering what Eral would say if she told him it was his own greed that kept him safe.

It was nearly midnight when Juilene slipped out onto the balcony. The night was clear and very cold, but the stars shone steadily above, and the Eyes of Dramue gazed in blue beneficence upon creation. Juilene stretched her hands upon the stone balustrade. Her fingers ached, her wrists throbbed. She had played for more than six hours straight as well as at a rehearsal Eral had insisted upon that afternoon. The joints in her hands felt as though they were on fire.

She rubbed her hands together, trying to ease the ache. The sounds of revelry filtered through the door, and suddenly she felt achingly alone. More than one of the young men in the service of the master-thurge had smiled at her, more than one had approached her, some shyly, some bold, and had spoken to her, offered her morsels, a goblet of wine.

She had refused everything. It wasn't safe. How could she know where the limits were? She had watched Mathy flirt with the men who flocked to her side, and even old Nuala had smiled, her ancient face flushed from the attentions of a seasoned sergeant at arms. But Juilene did not dare accept even the smallest offering. She had no way to know what Deatrice had meant when she said she could protect her people. And Juilene did not want to risk alienating her acting companions. The troupe was more than a means of livelihood; they were her way to put real distance between herself and whoever might be seeking for her. Behind her, she heard the door open, then close, and she stiffened.

"Here you are," Eral said.

She glanced at him over her shoulder. He had disappeared with Deatrice shortly after their performance. Now he padded across the stones in soft leather boots to stand beside her at the railing. His collar was open, and his linen shirt was rolled up. He stood close enough for her to see the coarse dark hair that curled on his arms and at his throat.

"You played well tonight," he said after a brief silence. "Better than I have ever heard you play before."

She bowed her head. "Thank you."

"There was something about your playing tonight that struck me—something one doesn't often hear in a wandering songsayer, as young as you are." He waited and Juilene said nothing. "You were classically trained, weren't you?"

She sucked in a deep breath and clenched her hands together. "I—I was taught a few things."

"More than a few things, I'd say." He crossed the space between them in two long strides and gently turned her to face him. "Who are you, little sister? What did you do to merit a curse from a thurge—a powerful thurge—so young? And from what do you run?"

Juilene glanced away, over the balcony to the wide courtyard beneath. A stone fountain stood dry in the center of the garden, the intricate rows of shrubs clipped close in preparation for the winter. Even so far south snow would fall shortly after Year's End. "I mean you no harm," she said at last.

He laughed, his teeth flashing white in the torchlight. "I never thought you did. But come—tell me—what happened? What could a child like you have done to so displease so mighty a master-thurge?"

She drew a deep shuddering breath and shivered.

"Come," he said, drawing her toward the door. "Come inside. You're cold and tired. You need something hot." She made a little sound of protest, but he ignored it, coaxing her to follow him back inside. He led her past the great open doors of the hall, and down the wide corridor, to a little private sitting room where a warm fire burned in a polished grate, and soft pillows were spread before the fire. On a low table set before the fire, two silver goblets glowed with a polished sheen. "Will you sit?"

She glanced around. Weariness was overtaking her. It would be so good to lie down before the fire, on the thick rugs, and lay her head on the cushions, let the warmth and the softness carry her away to the time before Lindos, before everything had changed so irrevocably. She swallowed hard and looked at him. "I should go to my room."

He smiled. "You should. And you will. But you must know I have questions for you—you must know ever since I met you, I've wondered about you. And now, since this afternoon, when Deatrice spoke to you, I've wondered even more. Won't you sit?"

She wet her lips and sank down before the fire, tucking her skirts carefully around her legs. The fire blazed hot and high, and the light shimmered on the polished grate, gleamed softly on the tiles of the hearth. The tiles were creamy shades of peach and rose and green, arranged in an intricate design, and fleetingly she wondered how much such things cost. She was reminded of her father's house, where she had not even thought to notice such things as how the fireplaces were made, and a lump rose in her chest.

Eral sat across from her. He poured a little liquid into one of the silver goblets and sipped. "Has she spoken to you?"

"Deatrice? No—not since this afternoon." Juilene felt herself flush.

Eral watched her with narrowed eyes. He licked the wine off his lips. "You know you should have told me in the beginning. It wasn't fair of you to put the rest of us in jeopardy."

"But you weren't," she said, her voice quivering just a little. Was he about to turn her away? "You weren't, ever."

"How can I know that?" Suspicion was set in every line of his face. "Can you tell me?"

She hesitated. Would it matter? Would it change or alter anything? And didn't she owe this man and the troupe something, after all? He had taken her out of Sylyria, provided a refuge and a means to earn her bread. Surely the truth and the assurance it would bring was the least she could give him. She took a deep breath. She searched her mind for the proper way to begin, and the words came, slowly, faltering from her tongue. "I—I was born in a house near Sylyria."

"So you are noble."

She nodded, staring into the flames. How to tell him, she wondered. The easiest way was the simplest, she supposed. She took a deep breath and began. "There is in that district a master-thurge, who is cruel and cares nothing for the people within his domain, and nothing for the authority of the Over-Thurge, or the Conclave. He lets his men do as they please, and the whole district speaks of nothing but how to be rid of him." She paused, realizing how true that was. She could scarcely remember a time when the people had not grumbled about Lindos.

"Go on," he said, turning the goblet slowly in his hands.

"I was to marry a young thane of a neighboring house. But his sister was attacked and beaten by the thurge's men, and so Arimond swore revenge. He went to the thurge's house—" She broke off as her throat closed.

Eral leaned forward. "I can guess what happened next. This master-thurge didn't look kindly upon the challenge, I take it? This is what has sparked the situation in Sylyria, isn't it?"

Miserably, she nodded.

"But what made him think he could handle the thurge? Especially one with such a reputation?"

Juilene raised her head, her eyes brimming with tears. "He thought he was the thurge's doom."

"Ah." Eral sat back with a low whistle. "I see. But how were you involved?"

"I helped get him into the castle. I pretended to be a songsayer—it was the night before Festival, you see."

"Ah." Eral nodded. "And so you brought down the thurge's anger against you?"

She looked away. "He gave me a choice. Either marry him or be cursed. But he had killed my love. I could have nothing to do with him."

"What's the nature of this curse?"

"I can accept nothing save that which I earn by my own hand, neither kindness nor charity, not even the smallest crust of bread without having first earned it. And it can only be lifted by someone who loves me for myself alone."

Eral raised an eyebrow and sat back. He put the goblet down. "I see. Quite a predicament you found yourself in."

Juilene nodded. "Yes."

"No wonder you had such a scared lost look about you. And no wonder you are so very different from the others."

"I've learned a lot in the last weeks."

He laughed. "Yes, you have. Who else knows about this?"

She shook her head. "No one, except my old nurse. She tried to help me, you see, and she was horribly, terribly hurt. The curse is real. I dare not—"

"Hush." He held up one hand. "Your secret is safe with me. It certainly explains everything. No wonder you keep to yourself. I'd be frightened, too."

She turned away to stare into the fire. Frightened. She had been so frightened these last few weeks. Could he even begin to understand? She heard the rustle of fabric behind her, and felt his arm go around her, drawing her close. She stiffened, started to pull away, and then relaxed in spite of herself.

"Poor little songsayer," he murmured. "Poor little sister."

His shoulder was strong, his arm comforting. It felt so good to be held, to be touched and soothed. It had been weeks since she had been hugged. She gave a little sigh.

"Ah, there, that's better." He smoothed her hair back, his fingers sure and steady. She felt her eyes grow heavy. His arms tightened around her, and she felt herself shifted and lifted, so that he cradled her against his chest. She sighed once more, and opened her eyes. He smiled into them, and lowered his mouth to hers.

She gasped.

"No, no, sweet, hush," he murmured against her throat. She felt her hair tumble down her back and over her shoulders, and he twined his fingers in the curls, his fingertips brushing against her body. She gasped once more, shocked a little by the sensations he was rousing in her, and tried to turn away. But he only smiled and forced her face up to his. She opened her mouth to protest, and his lips came down on hers. It was nothing like Arimond's kiss, she thought, and she tried to struggle, tried to close her mouth shut against his probing tongue. But his arms were too strong, his mouth too insistent. Involuntarily, she clung to him, as his fingers skillfully slipped through the lacings of her bodice, and found the warm, heavy weight of her breast.

Fire shot through her, a burst of heat that made her turn in his arms, and he drew back, stroking and caressing the round flesh and pebbled tip that suddenly seemed as though it were made of something far more hot than flesh could ever be.

"I can't break your curse," he whispered in her ear, and

his breath sent little sparks down her spine. "But I can make you forget, for a little while, at least. Shall I?"

"N-no, please," she said, her hands plucking fretfully at his wrists, trying to displace his fingers from the opening of her bodice. He was kneading her breasts now, moving back and forth from one to the other, claiming both of them.

She tried to force his hands away, but he only chuckled and held both of hers in one of his, while he rolled one nipple gently in his fingertips. "So sweet. So very, very sweet." He raised her in his arms and kissed her then, hungrily, while his hand worked at her dress. Somehow, despite her struggling hands, he got it off her shoulders, exposing her to the waist. She gasped, shrugging and twisting as she tried to cover herself.

"No, little love, you're much too beautiful." He moved her hands out of the way, holding them above her head in one hand while with the other he fumbled with the lacings of his breeches. She felt him push her skirts out of the way, felt his fingers probe the swollen flesh between her legs. She screamed against his mouth as his tongue probed her mouth once more, stabbing deep as he moved her legs apart and lowered himself between them. Suddenly the implication of his intentions penetrated her tired, wine-fogged mind. If he took her virginity, here and now, she lost all hope of ever marrying. A thane's bride must be virgin—she would be disgraced, even more outcast than she was now. She pushed up with her body, clenching her fingers around his arms, digging her nails into his flesh. "Eral, please leave me alone—I can't do this—not like this—I'll scream—"

"Ah, but you can." He tightened his grip on her wrists. Something thicker than his fingers pushed against her, something harder and more insistent. "Scream all you please—I'll like it just as much." He lowered his face to hers and she twisted her neck away.

"I don't want you to do this, Eral," she pleaded more insistently. "Leave me alone—please—"

"Let me do this for you," he whispered against her ear, pressing harder. "Let me show you this—" He raised his hips and thrust. She cried out, as loudly as she could and tried to move her legs together, but his weight pinned her firmly, and he covered her mouth with his, so her loud protests were swallowed by his tongue. Pain radiated, a blinding stab that made her shudder and lie still. She screamed and he covered her mouth with one hand."

"That's better," he whispered. He raised his hips and thrust again as she turned her face and closed her eyes and concentrated on trying to fight him off. But he pressed forward, driving into her struggling body with short stabs. Finally, she felt another sharp stab of pain and something gave way. "There," he murmured. She bit her tongue to quell the nausea that rose in her throat. He raised his chest and smiled down at her, pressing her hands above her head. "Now—" He thrust back and forth three times, his eyes glazed, his breathing ragged. He tensed above her, grimacing, as she willed herself to lie still. He rolled off her, panting.

She drew a deep shuddering breath, and slowly backed away, drawing her clothes into some semblance of order. He sat up, pulling his breeches together. "Wasn't so bad, was it?"

She clenched her teeth to keep from screaming. Her whole body felt dirty, the tender flesh between her legs was wet and sticky and so horribly sore she wondered how she would walk.

"Look." He leaned over and kissed her forehead. "In your situation, it was going to come to that, you know. Sooner or later, you're going to have to sell yourself. And don't you think it's better to have someone like me the first time? Someone you know? Would you rather have had a stranger?"

She could only stare at him. She had trusted him, told him her story, and he had taken the cruelest advantage of her. What a fool she was. No wonder Mathy was bitter. But never again. She would bear this violation the way she was learning the bear all the other burdens—with silence and with strength. She pulled her bodice closed, holding it tight with one shaking hand, and extended the other.

He raised his brow. "Are you expecting me to pay you?"

She narrowed her eyes and hated him. She nodded.

He threw back his head and laughed. "Nervy little thing, I'll give you that." He reached into the purse he wore at his belt, and flipped a brass coin at her. "There you go. You really weren't too bad for a first-timer."

She stumbled to her feet, feeling fluid trickle down the inside of her thigh. She twisted her hair in a loose knot.

"But, sweetheart—"

His words made her pause with her hand on the door-knob.

"You've got to learn to intensify your protests a little more if that's how you like it. Really kick and squirm. There's plenty who'll pay you highly for that kind of performance."

She shuddered, scarcely believing what she heard, and fled, his laughter ringing in her ears.

Chapter Seven

❦

They left the castle as a grey dawn broke over the towers three days later, a cold wind whining in the trees. Winter was hard upon them, and even Eral looked worried as he bowed a jaunty farewell to Lady Deatrice.

"Might snow," he said, to no one in particular, as he flapped the reins and the cart jerked over the drawbridge.

Juilene huddled in the back, her cloak pulled tightly around her. She wasn't sore anymore, but both her body and her mind were numb. Mathy avoided her eyes. They all knew, she was sure. They all had to know. She had sold herself for money, had allowed Eral to take the very thing that made her so precious to the men of her own class. He was nothing but a cruel opportunist who had taken her innocence with no more thought than he might help himself to a morsel of food. What would her father say, now? Even if she could go back to him, even if by some miracle she found a way to return so that she was no longer a danger to him or to anyone else who lived on his estate, there was no way any thane would have her. The life of an unmarried, unwanted disgrace loomed before her. There was nothing left for her but this life upon the roads.

She raised her head, and stared at towers of the castle as they disappeared behind the tops of the leafless trees. The grasping branches were like skeleton claws, reaching blindly in all directions. She shuddered. Eral behaved as though nothing had happened. So would she, she decided. Let Dramue give me strength.

She tossed her hair behind her shoulder and peered past Nuala and Mathy through the opening in the front of the wagon. Beyond Eral's broad back she could see the high mountain peaks looming on either side of the road. On the other side of the pass through which they traveled now lay Khardroon.

The name shivered down her spine. The ancient city of Khardroon was shrouded in legend. It was said to be the oldest of all the city-states, with the exception, of course, of Eld. But Eld lay high in the mountains, inaccessible much of the year, a center of religion and learning. Hardly anyone went to Eld. But everyone, everyone Juilene had ever known, spoke of Khardroon. It rivaled Sylyria for riches, and only its position between the Great Desert and the Parmathian Sea meant that it was squeezed smaller than Gravenhage. It was said that one could find anything in the world in Khardroon. Maybe, thought Juilene, as a little bitter smile raised the corners of her mouth, maybe she would find what she was looking for in Khardroon. And she had heard snatches of conversation in the hall and among the servants. War between thane and thurge was imminent in Sylyria: even Deatrice had looked uneasy when Eral broached the subject with her one evening after dinner. Better that they all put as much distance between themselves and Sylyria as soon as possible.

She glanced at Eral, at the dark hair that curled at the nape of his neck and spilled over his collar. He whistled something tuneless under his breath, just loud enough for her to hear, and the sound grated on her nerves. She unwrapped the harp and cradled it between her knees. Gently, she ran her fingers over the strings. Nuala lifted her head and smiled.

Juilene only met the old woman's approval with a quick upturn of her lips she hoped could pass as an answering smile. At least no one could take her music away from her. Eral turned around and winked at her over his shoulder. She ignored him. Let him think what he would. Somehow, in Khardroon, she would find a way to get away. Mathy had said lots of traveling troupes went to Khardroon for the winter. Surely she would be able to find another position for herself. The weight of her money sack had grown over the last weeks. She had many more than the six coins with which she had fled her father's house.

She concentrated on the music. It was easier than ever now, to give herself over to the music in a way she had never been able to do before. Where once she had played to amuse herself, to impress her teacher or her family, now she played to soothe herself, to escape. The fragile threads of sound were like a blanket, protecting her from the world in which she found herself. As long as she could weave the music around herself like a protective web, she would be safe.

It was just before dusk when the little company lurched to a halt outside a roadside tavern on the other side of the mountain pass. The air was warmer, the light softer, the shadows deeper. Juilene raised her face and sniffed. The smell of something cooking was on the air, and the scent was flavored with unfamiliar spices. Eral leaped out of the cart, and spoke to the young stablehand who came forward to take the reins. Mathy and Nuala stirred, and Juilene climbed out of the wagon, without waiting. A soft puff of air caressed her face, gentle as old Neri's touch.

The tavern was built of some white stone, the windows wide and open to catch the breezes. Long benches on either side of the door invited patrons to lounge. To the right of the main building, an earthy odor announced the stables, while to the left, clangs and bangs and a woman's shrill voice indicated the kitchens.

"Good to see this place again." Nuala climbed down from the wagon, her face drawn and tired. She had slept most of the way from Deatrice's castle. "These bones are too old for that cold. I say next year we hightail it here before Festival, Eral."

"Ah, but what excuse would we have to snuggle?" Eral chucked her under the chin.

Nuala playfully slapped his hand away. "My days for that are long over, you rogue, and you should have respect for such an old lady."

Eral pressed a kiss on Nuala's cheek. "Never too old, my love, 'til the goddess calls you home, right, my Jewel?"

Juilene stiffened. No one had used that name for her since Arimond. She pressed her lips together and turned away from the byplay. "Right, Eral. Of course."

She reached into the wagon and grabbed her money bag, which had grown to a comfortable weight. She was too hungry to stand and watch his performance.

Later, Juilene sat before the hearth, her hands loosely in her lap. For once, she was content to sit and watch the patrons. They were for the most part darker-skinned than the natives of Sylyria, their faces lined and browned by the sun. More than a few wore the flowing robes and cloth headdresses and spoke in the liquid accents of the desert dwellers. More than once she had been the object of scrutiny, for her auburn hair was rare in Khardroon, and more than once, she had seen men nudge each other and stare. The few women who had come into the tavern were accompanied by men, kept their heads down, and their eyes lowered.

On the other side of the hearth, Mathy yawned. The hour was not so very late, but Nuala had already disappeared up the stairs to a room above, and Eral and the men were gaming in the yard outside the tavern. Once in a while, she could hear the voices raised in cheers or jeers, and once, Juilene was sure she had heard Maggot's excited cry.

Mathy stood up. "I'm for bed," she said. "You?"

Juilene nodded. "I'll be up. I just need to get my things from the wagon—I should have brought them in with me before, but I've been so comfortable by this fire—"

Mathy nodded. "I know the feeling. Nothing like a place beside a warm hearth when you've been on the road." She smoothed her skirts and glanced around the room. The eyes of a dozen men were watching. "I'm off. Good night."

Juilene watched her walk across the room, an exaggerated sway in her hips, her stride as languorous as a cat's. One of the men leaning against the bar raised his glass to her as she passed and Mathy paused and smiled. Juilene pulled herself to her feet. How could Mathy be so brazen and so bold? Had she no fear?

Juilene slipped outside, her cheeks burning, aware of the same scrutiny as Mathy. She wished she had been clothed as soberly as the other women, the respectable women, the ones who were protected by husbands and brothers and fathers. But that was denied her forever. And the sooner she accepted that fact, the better off she would be.

She was painfully aware of the shabby condition of her dress, of the patches and the stains that even Deatrice's laundry had been unable to remove. Maybe here in

Khardroon she would buy something new. Maybe she would even buy one of the loose pairs of trousers and the knee-length gowns the women of Khardroon wore. With her hair covered by one of their flowing veils, who would know her? Lady Juilene of Sarrasin in Sylyria would truly be no more than a memory.

In the yard, the men were gathered in small clusters, some kneeling in the dust, throwing dice, others sitting on the long benches. A few smoked long clay pipes, and the scent of burning uster-wood filled the air. A pang went through her. It reminded her of her father, on the long winter nights when, it seemed, the scent of Jiroud's pipe invaded every corner of the castle and clung to her clothes and her hair. She remembered all the nights she had flounced off, her nose held tightly shut, complaining loudly of the stink. What she wouldn't give for one more chance to sit under her father's roof and smell that pipe again. She would gladly smoke it herself, she thought.

She sighed and continued across the yard to the cart. Something scuttled in the dust before her, and she gasped. It was long and black, and moved like an insect, but she was sure it had a round, pinkish head. She shivered. Could it have been a mantling? They couldn't survive the cold winters on the other side of the mountains, but Juilene had heard tales of the things. Khardroon was crawling with them. She suppressed another shudder and continued on. In the shadows of the stables, she saw two men talking. There was a furtive air about the way they stood, and with a start, she recognized Eral.

"—knew as soon as I met her something was up," he was saying.

Juilene flattened against the side of the wagon, instinctively wary. She sidled around the back to get a closer look, and with a shock recognized her father's colors, though not the man who wore them. She froze.

The stranger made a low reply, something indistinguishable, and Eral nodded and laughed. "Yes, we've taken good care of her. She's the same as ever—no harm done at all. Now—what about the reward?"

"You'll get the reward when I get the girl, my friend."

Of course, thought Juilene. Eral had betrayed her for the money her father would have offered for her return. Was it by chance she had been found, or had Eral planned this all along? It didn't matter now, she decided. She had to get away, and quickly. Who knew how many of her father's men were here? And if she went back to her father's house, it was only a matter of time before something terrible happened. She could see the lumpy shape of her harp in its wraps beside her pack. Could she possibly grab both? She reached inside the wagon and seized the pack. It made a dull thud against her side as she swung its strap over her head.

"What's that?"

Juilene heard both men moving at the front of the wagon, and willed herself to be absolutely still.

"Who's there?" called Eral.

Juilene held her breath. What would she do if the men caught her?

"There's no one there," he said at last. "Now, just how much were you saying—"

Her father's man gave a soft snort, as though he recognized Eral for what he was. "Five hundred gold—"

Juilene waited no longer to hear her own worth. She seized the harp and dashed out of the stables.

"You there—"

She heard her father's man shout as she ran as fast as she could toward the gate. And then she slowed. The road was the first place they would look for her. What were the odds of her getting away from men on horseback? She scampered into the inn, through the common room, past the barkeep and the patrons, and through the kitchen door.

A couple of the maidservants looked at her with some surprise. "Please," Juilene cried, holding her stomach. "I need the privy."

"That way—" one of the pointed.

She darted through the door. The smell of garbage hit her nostrils like a wall. Refuse rose in high piles on either side of a narrow brick walk. She pressed her lips together against the stench and picked her way down the path, holding her skirts high above the muck as best she could. The only light was a single wavering torch in a sconce set high near the door. She opened the low gate with trembling fingers, the metal crusted with rust. She pushed it, out of frustration, and the gate swung open with a bang. She looked back over her shoulder as she scampered through.

She darted a quick look around. The low stables rose in front of her. She could hear shouts and cries coming from the stables, and the pounding of hooves in the inn yard. To the right lay the inn, and if she was correct, if she went to her left, she could skirt the inn, avoid the stables, and end on the road. She drew a deep breath, grimacing as the odor of the garbage, now strongly mixed with the stables, reached her once again. She picked her way through the shadows, which grew deeper as she moved away from the meager light. In the dark, she heard the muck squelch under her feet. She tried not to think about what she might be walking through.

She followed the edge of the building, one hand held before her to feel her way. At the corner, she paused and looked around. A stand of trees rose immediately to her right, on her left was the inn, and before her was the inn yard, where most of the men still bent over their gaming, the smoke from their pipes, thicker now, lazily hanging over their heads.

She swallowed hard. This was the hard part, she thought, looking up, where the road lay perhaps a dozen yards ahead. If she could just get through the inn yard, if she could just gain the open road, she would be free. Sweat trickled down her sides, and stung her armpits. Once or twice, a man glanced in her direction and she froze, sure she had been seen. But each time, the man glanced away, and Juilene breathed a sigh of relief. She tightened her grip on her bundle, checked the straps of her harp, and let her skirts fall. She would walk across the inn yard as though she were any songsayer, moving on to a more congenial location. She started across, keeping to the side, her head down and her eyes lowered as she had seen the other women do. None of the men paid her any attention at all. She reached the entrance and slipped through the open gates. Just outside she paused and drew a deep breath. She was free.

"Thought you'd be abed, little sister." Eral's voice from the shadows startled her so much that she almost dropped her bundle. She turned, gasping. "Forgive me. I didn't mean to startle you. It's just I had no idea where you might be going—it's so unlike you to be abroad at this hour."

Color rushed to her face, and her mouth was dry as the dust on the road. Her heart was pounding so loudly she was certain he could hear it. "I—I wanted some air."

"Air?" His white teeth flashed in the shadows, and his body loomed over her. "It's a bit late for that." He reached for the harp she carried. "And a bit late for this, isn't it? Where do you think you're going, little sister? With your pack and your harp? Surely you can't be thinking of leaving us?" More quickly than she could react, he pulled the harp out of her hands. Juilene made a futile grab for it.

"What's it to you, Eral, if she decides she wants air? At any hour of the day?" Eral swung around as Mathy walked up behind him.

"What are you doing out here?"

Mathy snorted. "Earning an extra bit of brass, if you want the truth. And what's that to you? We're not bound to you, Eral, not me, not her. We come and go as we please."

Eral threw her harp aside and Juilene cried out as she heard it smash against the stone wall. She shrank back when she saw Eral reach for the long dagger he wore behind his back.

"Is that so, Mathy?" His voice was hard and Juilene shivered.

"Mathy, watch out," Juilene cried.

Eral snarled and whipped his head around, and in that moment, Mathy sprang at him with a dagger of her own. He sagged suddenly, and his face reminded Juilene of a bladder suddenly bereft of air. She had to bite her lip to keep from laughing as he crumpled.

Mathy pulled the dagger out from between his ribs, and looked at Juilene. "Go on. Go now. I know you mean to leave—go, while you can. Even in Khardroon there'll likely be some questions asked, and you want nothing to do with this."

Juilene hesitated, the urge to laugh gone. Eral lay bleeding at her feet, and in the dim light, she could see blood bubbling at the corners of his mouth. His face was slack. "Mathy, what have you done?" she whispered.

"What I've wanted to do for a long time. Now go on and get out of here. There's another inn not too far down the road. You can find shelter there for the night. Go. Now!"

This last Mathy said with a raised dagger, the blood dripping off the gleaming edge. Juilene saw the flash of madness in the girl's eyes, and with a little gasp, heedless of her broken harp, she fled down the road into the dark night.

Chapter Eight

❧

Juilene trudged down the rock-rimmed road. The sun was high and little dust clouds puffed beneath her feet with each step. The straps of her pack dug into her shoulders. Three days on the roads of Khardroon had given her an appreciation for the troupe's wagon she hadn't had before. She sighed and shifted her bundle to her other hand and shrugged, trying to redistribute the weight. The pack had never seemed so heavy before. She had learned to appreciate so many things in the last months, things she had never even thought to notice in the time she thought of simply as "before." She was tired, so very tired. Her money hadn't lasted very long, nowhere near as long as she'd hoped it would. And without her harp, she had little means of earning more. The two inns she'd passed had been squalid places, dung and refuse heaped in the inn yard, the women who lounged in the doorways looking disheveled and dirty. The few patrons she glimpsed had a dark and furtive air; she had shuddered and passed both those places by. Why invite trouble, when it so easily found her on its own? Neither of them looked as though they'd welcome a songsayer who merely wanted to sing.

She paused, listening. From a small thicket of trees, she thought she heard the rush of water. She stepped off the road, ducking under the high brambled weeds that grew chest-high along the roadside. A broad stream tumbled through the trees, the banks as rocky as the road. The sun sparkled on the water.

She shrugged off her bundle and let it fall against a tree. She kicked off her shoes and sank down on the rocky bank. The water foamed over sharp rocks, tumbling past her with a speed that was deceptive. Arimond used to warn her to be wary of such places. "You could be swept away in a minute, Jewels," he'd say, his blue eyes wide and steady, his arm placed securely around her waist, as though the water might surge over its banks and carry her away. The thought of Arimond, of the carefree days of her childhood, flooded her eyes with tears. She gazed into the dark green water, at the sharp, pointed peaks of the rocks that broke the surface of the water, hinting at what lay below. Was it possible she had lost so much?

She bit her lip and stripped off the shredded remains of her stockings. In the first days of her flight, she had thought to save them, and had quickly learned that her feet blistered without them. She dipped her feet in the water and the cold water stung her skin. Dirt was embedded beneath her ragged toenails. Her hair was matted and she itched. She had never been so tired or so dirty in her life. The tears welled up and spilled down her cheeks. She twined her fingers in the pathetic remnants of the stockings Neri had knitted for her, so long ago, and wept.

Everything and everyone was gone, everyone she had ever loved, everything she had ever treasured: all were lost to her. She was truly an outcast, no home, no roof, no place to call her own, and without her harp, no real means of finding a place, either. The man who had loved her was dead, the family she had loved was cut off from her forever. She had lost her innocence to a schemer who had tried to betray her trust for money. She was alone, in a strange place, where she had no friends, no family, no one to care about or to care for her at all. What difference would it make if she slipped into the water, and let the river carry her away?

She glanced down at the dull blue sapphire ring on her finger. It had been many days since she had thought to look at it, for it seemed to her that the stone never glowed its warning since that night in Lindos's keep. She twisted the ring while she watched twigs, leaves, and other bits of debris swirl past in the foaming current. Although it might have value as a jewel, it could never be sold for money. The family legend said it would only fit the hand of one to whom it had been given. She sighed. Even something that might buy her bread was worthless. It would be so easy, she thought, as the tears slipped down her cheeks, so very easy to let herself ease down into the water, and lose herself to the current. Easier than the life she had lived in the last months, she thought, easier than trying to survive. Her family surely had resigned themselves to her death. No one would miss her or know that she was gone. She would let the water wash her away.

"Room for a fellow traveler?" The hoarse voice startled her out of her reverie. She jumped, turned, and reached for the little dagger she had taken to wearing concealed in her bodice. It was one of Mathy's tricks.

Just on the edge of the thicket, a woman, stooped with age, leaned upon a staff. Her hair was white and fell in a tangled snarl to her shoulders, but her eyes, despite their web of wrinkles, were as clear and blue as a noon sky. "I mean you no harm, sister. I'm just looking for a place to rest."

Juilene hastily wiped at her cheeks, her fingers still curled about the dagger. The old woman looked harmless enough, but Juilene had learned not to trust appearances. She narrowed her eyes. Another songsayer—this one looking so old and tired, she wondered how the woman managed to bear the weight of the pack she carried on her back. Juilene hesitated. She wanted to be alone. The old woman had not moved. She was clearly waiting for an invitation. Juilene dabbed at her eyes once more and gestured vaguely in the old woman's direction. "Sit, if you please."

The old woman nodded her thanks and slumped to the ground. She leaned back against a tree and shut her eyes. Insects hummed and the water splashed and gurgled, but over the sounds of the clearing, Juilene could hear the harsh rattle of the old woman's breathing. She glanced around, wondering as if she ought to do or say something. She glanced at the ring on her finger. The stone was dull as one of the pebbles at the bottom of the river. There was no danger from the old woman.

"Come a long way, girl?"

The old woman's voice startled her once more. She raised her eyes from the water and met those of the old woman, and this time she was struck by the penetrating quality of the woman's gaze. "From Sylyria."

"Long road."

Juilene nodded. The old woman was staring at her with a fixed and almost glassy stare, and her chest rose and fell with each labored breath.

"Songsayer, are you?"

Juilene made a little gesture. "I was."

"Was? Don't you know that once the goddess sets her

finger on you, girl, there's no turning back? You can leave the life, if you will it, but you bring something of the road and something of the songs in everything you do." At the end of this speech, she drew a huge breath, and the air rasped in her throat. She narrowed her eyes. "What are you thinking of, girl? Here, by the water? Where's your harp?"

Juilene stared at the woman. "How do you know I play the harp?"

"You have the look of it in your face. And the marks of it upon your hands. Oh, Merie might be old, but I can still see."

Juilene bit her lip. "I lost my harp."

"Lost it? Or was it taken from you?"

Juilene looked into the water. It foamed and swirled, pattern upon pattern, ever-changing, always moving. "I suppose you could say it was something of both."

"I'll give you mine on one condition."

"What did you say?" Juilene stared at the woman. Was she mad?

"I said you can have mine on one condition." The old woman shifted uncomfortably and coughed. "You must take the road to Eld."

Juilene scarcely believed what she heard. A harp was far beyond the reach of her purse; there was no way she could take the old woman's means of livelihood. "Sister—" she murmured, shaking her head, "I thank you—you are truly kind—but I cannot take your harp—"

"How long do you think I will need the harp, girl?" The old woman closed her eyes and winced as though a spasm of pain passed through her. "I can barely stand to carry it any farther—I will not lift it again to make a song upon it. Take it—but you must promise me to take the road to Eld."

Juilene moved a little closer. The sun had changed position and the shade was deepening beneath the trees. "Sister, I wish I could take your harp, but, you see, of all the songsayers in Sylyria, I—I cannot. If I take your harp, harm will befall you—I cannot repay kindness with evil."

The old woman fixed her with a stare. "We both have a need, have we not? And look at me, girl. Do you think it looks likely that I will ever rise from this spot again?" She made a feeble gesture with her hand. "The goddess is calling me, child," she said in a gentler tone. "Take the harp and leave me to her. Only promise me to take the road to Eld." She raised her hand and beckoned. "Unstrap it for me—I have not the strength to do that, even." She smiled and she shook her head. "Who would have thought the goddess would come so quickly when she calls?"

Juilene rose slowly and walked to the old woman. She saw the deep lines that marked her face, the thinness of the woman's frame, the bluish pallor around her mouth. The old woman's breathing was loud and labored. Juilene bent down. The old woman's head fell back and their eyes met. With surprising strength and swiftness, the old woman grasped her wrist. "You've come far, and learned much, daughter. The ending shall be worth the journey." Her voice was a harsh singsong. "The only way out of the fire is through it. Some burn to ash, some melt away, but the toughest are strengthened. Which you will be is your choice."

As Juilene stared at the old woman in amazement, the light died from her eyes, and her lids fluttered closed. Her hand dropped to her side and with a little sigh, she went limp. Juilene gasped. As gently as she could, she reached around the woman, unstrapping the harp from her back. What in the name of the goddess had the old woman been talking about? It had sounded like madness. Poor old woman, she thought. She lifted the wrapped harp and slung it over her shoulder. So this was how a songsayer died, she thought, alone, unmourned.

She straightened and stared down at the limp corpse.

She bowed her head. She could do nothing for the old woman, but take the road to Eld. She leaned down and touched the old woman's wrinkled cheek. "Rest well, sister. Sleep long."

Juilene climbed back to the road, the weeds lashing at her face, the sun falling heavily as a weight across her shoulders. She drew a deep breath. Pray the goddess there was at least an inn on the road to Eld.

The shadows were long and the sun was red when Juilene reached the first inn on the road to Eld. Not that one road or another made any real difference. Eld lay high in the mountains. Only a fool would go there in the middle of winter. Better to stay in the lowlands of Khardroon at least until spring made the heat intolerable. She could search for Eld then. But one road was as good as another, and at least the inn looked prosperous. The inn yard was crowded. A merchant train newly arrived, she thought, for many of the men wore the white robes and elaborate headdresses of those who plied trade between the city-states, the heavy wagons filled with barrels and boxes and long fabric-wrapped bundles. Grooms scurried to unhitch the huge horses from the wagons, and wiry stablehands swarmed through the wagons, maneuvering them into some semblance of order. She brushed a hand across her face, suddenly conscious of her shabby appearance, and hoped the landlord would let her stay.

She sidled across the courtyard, narrowly escaping being bumped and jostled. She stepped into the common room, where a young man was setting out glasses on the bar, and three women dressed in drab scurried in and out of the kitchens. She paused uncertainly in the doorway. He looked up. "I say the songs the goddess sends," she said before he could speak.

He looked her up and down, and his mouth twisted. For

a long moment, she thought he would send her away. And then he called, without turning, "Elizondo! Elizondo, come here."

There was a heavy pounding on the steps behind the bar, and the glasses shook. An enormous man, blackly bearded, emerged from the low doorway, his bulk covered by an elaborately embroidered robe. "Now what?" His speech was so thickly accented Juilene understood his tone better than his words.

The younger man behind the bar gestured in Juilene's direction. "A 'sayer."

Elizondo threw up his hands. "Thanks to the goddess." He rushed around the bar, his robes billowing, and grasped Juilene by the shoulders. He ran his eyes up and down her body. "A songsayer? Truly? You speak the truth?"

Astonished by both his girth and the warmth of his reception, Juilene could only nod.

He narrowed his eyes, his brow furrowed. "You're a bit thin—I can see you've been on the road a long time, but I suppose you'll do. You, Allia—a bath for our songsayer—" He snapped his fingers impatiently as the girl appeared dazed. "Now!" He turned back to Juilene. "This day of all days, our 'sayer lies abed—" He leaned down closer and Juilene was blasted by his spiced breath. "A fever! And the physician says there is naught to do but let her lie. Bah— these 'sayers can be so temperamental—but you, now you are here, and you will play and sing and entertain us all tonight, no?"

Once again, Juilene could only nod. He beamed and clapped his hands. At once, hands took the harp from her back, reached for her bundle.

"Go with Allia—she'll show you where you can refresh yourself—get her something to drink, someone—some of that hot stuff Drussa drinks—that's right—"

Allia touched Juilene's arm shyly. "Sister, will you come?"

Juilene, feeling a little dazed, allowed herself to be led away from the flurry, Elizondo still bellowing in a swirl of brilliant colors. "What's all the fuss for?" she managed to ask in the corridor.

Allia looked over her shoulder and shook her head. "Master's all a dither. Lord Diago is coming tonight. He's on his way back to his castle, and he'd got his lady with him. And so Master's ordered the best, the finest for dinner, and wouldn't you know it, our songsayer falls ill and says she can't sing." The girl looked stricken for a moment, and then leaned closer to whisper in Juilene's ear. "He's called in a demi-thurge, who assures us all it's not the Fever, but I say you can't be sure, and Master ought to call the physician. But Master doesn't listen to me, or to any of us, and so . . ." She let her voice trail off and shook her head, looking aggrieved.

Juilene bit her lip. "So no one knows what's wrong with her?"

Allia shrugged. "Who's to say we won't all be dead by dawn?"

No wonder she hadn't been turned away, Juilene thought. "And no one else knows of this, I suppose?"

"No! And he doesn't want anyone to know, either. Master has the finest inn in all of Khardroon—he would never want word that there might be Fever in his house to get out."

"It isn't Fever, you silly knock-worm." An older woman, grey hair sticking out from under a white linen coif, stood in an open doorway, her face pink, hands on her ample hips. "Stop scaring this poor girl—she looks half worn out already. Master has guests to entertain, and it will be your fault if this 'sayer can't entertain them any more than Lucca can." She stood aside, motioning to Juilene.

"Come in, sister. Here's a hot bath for you, and a cup of honeyed wine. Is there anything else you require?"

Juilene shook her head. "N-no. Thank you." She set her harp and her pack down beside the door. The room was small, but spotlessly clean, its only furnishings a huge wooden tub, steaming with herbs, and two low benches against the walls. Towels were piled on one of the benches, and on the other, a tray containing a clay goblet steamed with sweet-scented herbs.

The older woman was looking at her critically. "You've been on the road a long time, sister?"

Juilene nodded, and glanced down at her gown. It was muddy at the hem and stained in many places. The fabric itself showed evidence of hard wear. It was the only dress she owned, since she had never earned enough to buy another. During performances, she had worn a gown that belonged to the troupe, but that had stayed in a chest with the other costumes.

"Well, it's the way of the goddess, I suppose." The woman shrugged. "Though why anyone would choose such a life is beyond me. Allia, take her dress to the kitchens—there's time to make it presentable at least. Lucca is taller than you and broader; I'm afraid nothing of hers would fit you, anyway. Now out of that gown and into the bath with you—there's time, but not much."

Juilene unlaced her gown and stepped out of it, feeling awkward and inexplicably ashamed. What would the woman say if she knew this life hadn't exactly been Juilene's choice, either? She handed the garment to Allia, who disappeared without another word. The older woman nodded in satisfaction. "Wrap yourself in towels; I'll have one of the maidservants bring you your dress. Take as much time as you wish in the tub."

Juilene flushed. It would be the first bath she'd had since coming to Khardroon. The woman turned to go, but Juilene managed to blurt out: "Excuse me—but what is wrong with the songsayer?"

The older woman turned and gave Juilene a measuring look. "She's afraid of Lord Diago."

"But—but he's a great lord, is he not?"

"And a man with most peculiar tastes." With another pointed look, the older woman closed the door behind herself.

The common room was crowded, and the air was smoky when Juilene made her way across the room to a place beside the hearth. A low fire burned in the polished grate, but the windows were open to catch the cool breeze. She took a seat and paused for a moment, looking over the men who clustered at the bar and in smaller groups at the tables arranged throughout the large room. The smell of roasting meat and baking bread permeated the room, and though Juilene's mouth watered, she didn't dare accept any offer of food. She might be dangerously close to the edge of charity, for the bath and the wine, and the light biscuits that Allia had brought her with her dress. The evening was still young; there was time to earn her dinner and perhaps even a place to sleep tonight. She had learned that although the days were warm in Khardroon, the nighttime temperatures could still dip low enough to make the outdoors uncomfortable.

With a little sigh, she ran her fingers over the strings of the old woman's harp, and the instrument rippled pleasantly, like the greeting of an old friend. She leaned down and examined it more closely. It was smaller than her own harp had been, and clearly of great age. The wooden frame was dull, and scratches and gouges bore testimony to a long life upon the road. There had once been a pattern carved into the wood, but over the years, it had been largely erased. Now the scratches and the gouges overlaid their own pattern upon the wood. But it was her only real possession now, her only means to earn her bread. Perhaps not quite the only means, she thought, remembering the coin Eral had pressed into her hand the night he had taken her virginity, but the only respectable means, the only way that did not lead to servitude and ultimate degradation. Lindos had tried to ensure that, she thought.

A few of the men were glancing at her now, at her hands as they moved over the strings, at her hair. One or two of the bolder ones ran up and down her body with their eyes, and she felt herself flushing. She lowered her head to the harp and closed her eyes. Her fingers plucked at the strings, easily as water rushing over rocks. She felt as if the harp played of itself; that her fingers were the instrument's, not the other way around. She hugged the harp closer, and the sounds vibrated through her body. It was like a living thing, responding to her touch, and she felt as if she wove the music from the air, from some hidden place, to grace the crowded inn. The last notes rippled and faded away, and she opened her eyes.

The inn was packed. A man and a woman, more richly clothed than all the rest, stood in the very center of the semicircle surrounding her. The woman's smile was tinged with sadness, and the man's made Juilene cringe for some reason she could not name.

"You play like the goddess," he said. His eyes were black and steady in his sunburnt face, and he gazed at her as if she were a morsel on a tray. She looked up into his eyes, and suppressed a little cry. His eyes reminded her of Lindos, for the pupils were as flat and as expressionless as a reptile's.

Juilene shivered but kept her back straight, refusing to be cowed. She knew that she had just played better than she ever had before. Something had happened here, although she could not put it into words. "When the goddess speaks, the goddess sings," she replied, trying to meet his eyes without fear.

He broke into loud laughter, and the cold gleam disappeared, but Juilene thought he only masked it. "That she does, little sister." He turned away, clapping one of the other men on the back. "Elizondo—Elizondo—where are you, old pirate? Give us the best of your cellars."

Juilene watched the men cluster, their faces eager as a dog's at the hunt. This must be Lord Diago, and the lady must be his wife. She looked at the woman, who still stood a few paces from Juilene's chair and smiled at her. "Goddess blessing, lady."

"And to you, little sister." Her accent was different from her husband's. The woman smiled back. There were dark shadows under her eyes and her face was thin, her complexion, unlike most of the people of Khardroon, pale. Juilene realized that the lady had not been born in Khardroon—had likely come here upon her marriage. She looked at the woman more closely. Her hair was hidden by a linen coif, but that only added to her pallor. She looked as though she had been ill for a long time. She took a chair on the opposite side of the fire, and Juilene marked how slow her movements were. The woman could only be at most ten or twelve years her senior, but she moved like a woman more than twice that age. "Play on, if you will."

Juilene glanced over at the bar, where Elizondo and his servants bustled back and forth, pouring wine, serving platters piled high with meats and cheeses and delicacies of every description. "Will you eat, my lady?"

The woman's thin fingers plucked restlessly at her skirt. "I—I have little appetite, my dear—" She was interrupted by a slim, dark-haired man who leaned over her chair and whispered in her ear. "Ah, very well, Cariad, if you insist. Fetch me something, anything." She smiled up at him, and he glanced in Juilene's direction.

Their eyes met, and something about him made Juilene hold his gaze for a moment. There was kindness in his look, and an impersonal fleeting interest, and for the first time in a long time, Juilene wanted more. But why, she wondered, as she dropped her eyes, a blush creeping up her cheeks. He turned away to do his lady's bidding. She noticed that while he was slim, his shoulders were broad. He wore a short tunic and a white shirt. The sleeves were rolled to the elbows, revealing well-muscled forearms. His breeches and his tunic were the same dark blue the other men wore, and she realized he must be one of the lord's knights. A slim dagger at his belt was the only weapon he wore, but the sheath was richly decorated. It was no house soldier's weapon, but his boots, though polished to a high sheen, were well worn. He negotiated the crowd with a sure grace. His hair and eyes were dark, and his skin was nearly as dark as the other men's but there was something different about the look of him that told her he was no more a native of Khardroon than either she or the lady."

"I am Lona," the lady said simply. "And Cariad—" The Lady nodded in his direction. "I do not know what I would do without him."

Juilene nodded and bent her head over her harp once again.

"And you, little sister? Your name?"

"I—I—my name is Juilene." Her hands shook a little on the strings and she willed herself to regain control. What on earth had this man done to so unsettle her? There was nothing of the look of Arimond about him—he was as dark as Arimond was fair, slim in build where Arimond had been broad. But all Arimond's strength had not saved him, Juilene thought, and unbidden tears formed at the corners of her eyes.

"My lady."

His voice made her open her eyes. He stood before Lady

Lona, holding out a plate piled high with fruit and a few dainty tarts.

"Ah, you appeal to my sweet tooth." Lona smiled up at him, and he smiled back, a sweeter smile than Juilene might have expected from one who had such an air of gravity about him.

She let her fingers find a tune on the harp, something low and coaxing, the sort of music she had heard her father's musicians play at mealtimes. Cariad settled down in a chair just behind Lona, in the shadows, and Juilene sought to lose herself in the music once more. The rest of the men in the tavern were milling around, talking excitedly, and few paid her any attention at all. Elizondo still hustled from kitchen to bar and back, sweat rolling down his cheeks, his gaudy silken robes billowing in all directions.

"Can you give us a tale?" Lona leaned forward, her fingers hovering over her plate. Cariad rose and walked across the room to the bar. Juilene felt a vague disappointment.

She looked at Lona. "If you wish, my lady." She glanced into the fire, where the flames licked gently at the slow-burning wood. There was kindness in this woman's eyes, more kindness than she had seen in many weeks, and an idea came to her. Why not, she thought, and she struck a minor chord on the harp.

"In a distant land, not so long ago, there lived a lady who loved a thane. They had known each other from childhood, and they had loved each other for nearly as long. It had been decided that they should be wed, and so the plans were made. They were both very happy. But there was in that same district, a thurge who was cruel and abused his power. The young thane decided that this thurge should not be allowed to continue in his evil ways, so he set out with his companions to stop the thurge, and put an end to the trouble which he was causing in the district. The lady had great foreboding in her heart, but because she loved her betrothed, she tried to help him. And one night, the thane came to the place where the lady slept. 'It's done,' he said to her. 'Come with me, and I will show you.'

"So the lady rose up and went with him, because she loved him with all her heart. And he led her to the place where the thurge lived. He took her to the thurge's very bedchamber, and there, as he tried to force himself upon her, his disguise fell away, and the lady saw that it was truly the wicked thurge himself."

Lona gasped a little, and Juilene glanced over her shoulder. Cariad sat in the shadows, his face hidden, but his whole aspect told her he was listening intently. " 'What have you done with my beloved?' asked the lady," Juilene continued. " 'Where is he?'

"The evil one laughed, and waved his hand, and the illusion on the room fell away. The lady saw her beloved hanging in chains upon the wall—dead. 'There is your beloved,' answered the thurge.

" 'Why have you brought me here?' asked the lady.

" 'To show you what happens to those who would stand in my way,' he answered. 'And to offer you a choice.'

" 'What choice have you to offer me,' asked the lady. 'My life is over now—my lover is dead.'

" 'Become my bride,' replied the thurge, 'or live with the curse I shall set upon you.'

" 'Better to die than be your bride,' answered the lady. 'Never will I wed you.'

" 'Then your choice is made,' said the thurge, and fast as light, the spell was made. And the lady shuddered as the power wove itself around her, encircling her with chains forged of light and air and power, and she cried out. 'Now,' said the thurge, 'this is the curse I set upon you. Nothing shall be yours but that which you earn by your own hands.

You will know the harshest deprivations, the coldest nights, the hungriest days. For if you accept the least kindness, the smallest charity, the curse will befall on all who would befriend you, and you will watch their suffering and know you were the cause of it.' "

"How cruel," murmured Lona. "Is there nothing to save her?"

" 'Only one who loves you for yourself alone shall break the curse,' said the thurge, and the lady fled into the night. In despair she went to her father's house, and sought comfort in the arms of her old nurse, but when the poor old woman tried to help her, the nurse's hands burst into flames. The lady disappeared into the night, carrying only a few possessions, and her harp, by which would come her means to earn her bread. And so she wanders from town to city to village, across the roads, accepting no charity, no kindness."

"But what happens to her," asked Lona. Cariad had set a goblet of apple-scented wine beside her, and she reached for it unconsciously. She took a long drink. "What happens to the lady?"

Juilene looked down. What a foolish thing to do. How was she to end the story? "I—I cannot be sure, lady. Though I am certain she met a kind man who loved her for herself alone, and broke the spell and together they lived happily." She glanced up and saw Cariad watching her. There was that same compassion in his eyes, and she had the feeling he had heard far more in the story than she had told.

"What a sad, sad story," Lona mused, munching on a grape. She popped another into her mouth. "And you tell it well, with such feeling, I would think you had it from the lady herself." She looked up and narrowed her eyes. "Have you a place to sleep this night, little sister?"

Juilene hesitated. There was too much kindness in this

woman's face. The landlord had said nothing, but surely there was some nook she could curl up in. "I—I will stay here, my lady."

Lona gave her another sharp look. "Fetch a plate for the 'sayer, Cariad, if you will—she's earned a fine supper, don't you think?"

"Assuredly, my lady." At once he was on his feet, bowing, and before Juilene could protest, he was halfway across the room.

"No, no, my lady." Juilene gripped the frame of the harp. "I—I have already eaten—"

"Hush, child." Lona waved her hand. "You look thinner than I do. And I would wager you cannot remember the last time such a handsome young knight served you with his own hands?"

Juilene flushed. She could remember all too clearly the last time she had been so served, and she lowered her eyes lest Lona see the tears that sprang once more to her eyes. "You are too kind, my lady," she murmured. She looked up to see Cariad leaning over her, a large dish piled high with every kind of food from the platters. "I—I cannot."

"Take it," he said, his voice as gentle as a nursemaid's.

She shook her head, pleading with her eyes. "I cannot."

"Take it," he said once more. "Nothing will happen. I promise."

She drew a deep breath. There was such assurance in his voice, in his eyes, in his face, that inexplicably she believed him. "I—I have no money to pay—"

"Take it." He held the platter out.

Slowly she set her harp upon the floor, and gingerly reached out. Her hands closed around the edges of the plate, and as she took it, he released it. She realized she was holding her breath, staring at his hands, waiting for something awful, something terrible to happen to him, and for the outcry that must surely follow.

But nothing happened, nothing at all, and he withdrew
with a little bow. He turned to Lona. "The hour grows late,
my lady. Shall I see you to your room?"

Lona looked around. "Eat, child." She sighed. "I think
so, Cariad. The day's traveling has quite exhausted me."
She rose heavily to her feet and smiled once more at Juilene. "Goddess blessing, little sister. Your playing has
eased me greatly, this night, whether you know it or not.
Sleep well."

The knight offered her his arm. Lona took it, and without a backward glance, the two left the common room. Juilene picked up a morsel of meat wrapped in dough and
slowly chewed it. Her mouth watered, and she closed her
eyes, savoring the delicate spices, the juicy flavor of the
well-roasted meat, the flaky texture of the buttery crust.

"I see you pleased the lady."

Her eyes flew open. Elizondo stood before her, his
hands laced over his ample belly. He smelled of sweat and
musk and the kitchens all at once, and for a moment Juilene lost her appetite. "Yes, sir. It seemed I did."

"And you pleased everyone else, too, it would seem, for
more than one has commented to me on your skill. Lucca's
got lazy, I suppose. Maybe it's time I booted her out on the
road. Well, no matter." He paused and an expression she
could not read flickered over his broad features. "I wish I
could offer you a proper room this night, for you have
played well. But I am full to the attics, and well—if you
want you can sleep in the stables. There's a room off the
side that the stablehands use if one falls sick. You can sleep
there if you like, if you'll play 'til closing."

Juilene nodded. It was better than sleeping by the road,
and there was a chance that Cariad might return after seeing Lona to her room. He might wear the lord's colors but
he was clearly the lady's man. Perhaps they were lovers,

she wondered, as Elizondo turned back to his guests, and she bent her head to the harp once more.

Diago and his men were laughing at the bar, making so much noise that the harp's gentle music was nearly drowned out. It didn't matter, thought Juilene. She caught Diago's eye inadvertently. He smiled and raised his glass to her. There was something about the way he looked at her that made her shiver despite the heat of the fire. But she had better get used to the way men looked at her, she scolded herself, and become more adept at handling their advances than by blushing and turning away. She was no longer the shy daughter of a noble house. At least for this night, she was safe and clean and well fed, and there was the promise of a warm place to lay her head. It should be of no consequence that the lord of the district should choose to look at her as if she, too, were one of his possessions. Tomorrow she would move on. The old songsayer was right. So far the road to Eld was a good one.

The fire had burned down to no more than grey ash, the platters were empty save for crusts and crumbs. Dirty goblets and cups were everywhere. Juilene paused in her playing. The last of the patrons was snoring in the corner by the window, and Elizondo leaned upon the bar, his robes hanging off his shoulders like broken wings, counting pieces of silver. "What a night, what a night," he said, over and over again, as he shook his head and sifted through the coins, not so much counting them as caressing them.

The young barkeep looked up from polishing the glasses and smiled, but said nothing. The serving maids crept from the kitchens and began to gather the debris into shallow baskets. Elizondo looked at the young man behind the bar and grinned. "A better night I've not seen in many days." He heaved his bulk away from the pile of gleaming coins and shuffled over to the door. He pulled the outer door tightly shut, and ceremoniously slid a thick piece of wood through the lock. "There," he said, to no one and everyone, "the night's done." He gave a self-satisfied sigh and turned to face the servants. "Clear up this mess as quick as you can, and then to bed. Those merchants from Parmathia want to be on the road to Gravenhage early." He swept the coins into a huge leather bag, savoring the weight. "A very good night, indeed."

Juilene watched him disappear up the steps behind the bar, the wood groaning beneath his weight. How lucky he was—rich and overfed and self-satisfied, the master of his own little world. She rose to her feet, holding her harp close. Now to find the stables, and the room Elizondo said might be hers for the night.

A serving maid with a tired face and a stained apron pointed through the kitchen doors with a suds-covered hand. She made her way out into the yard. Stars flickered in the black night sky. There was no moon, but dim lamps burned in some of the windows, casting enough light for her to pick her way across. The stables were large and immaculately kept, as one would only expect in an inn of Elizondo's standing. The odor of horses was strong but not offensive, and in the dim light, she could see the bulky shapes and hear the soft whickers of the animals as they slept. A thin line of light beckoned beneath a door set in the far wall, and Juilene followed it. She placed her hand on the rough-hewn wood and gasped, for the sapphire ring glowed a low but steady blue. She glanced over her shoulder, but saw nothing. She hoped the door had a lock. Swallowing hard, she pushed open the door and peered inside. The room was small, but clean, and a narrow bed, covered in a coarse blanket, stood against the farthest wall. There was a rickety table, on which burned the stub of a candle, beside a basin and a pitcher. Her pack lay on the floor at the foot of the bed. She sighed and hugged the harp. "It's nothing but all being in a strange place, surely, old friend," she whispered as she stepped inside and closed the door. She placed the harp carefully beside the table. "Let's rest while we can."

"Rest, indeed, little sister." A man's voice drawled from the shadows, and Juilene gasped. Thane Diago lounged on a small stool in the corner behind the door.

"M-my thane," she stammered. "What are you doing here?"

"Come, little sister, don't play so naive. Of course you know why I'm here—Elizondo told you to expect me, didn't he?" He rose to his feet and stood between Juilene and the door.

She glanced desperately at the door behind his back. "N-no, my thane," she replied, struggling to regain her composure. "He did not."

He cocked his head and put his hands on his hips. "Oh, I think so, my little songsayer. All those looks and soft glances you gave me—and that playing of yours, so full of gentle passion—and you, yourself. You intrigue me, you know that?" He grinned. In the meager light of the candle, his face was very dark and his mouth looked very wide, his shoulders very broad. He towered at least a foot over her.

Juilene instinctively drew back. "Please—I'm very tired. I have no wish—"

"Ah," he said softly, dangerously, and Juilene felt the edge of the bed against the back of her legs. "It doesn't matter what you wish. You've glamour on you—what sort of magic is this that you carry?"

Faster than she could imagine, he reached out, grabbing for her. She shrieked and tried to dodge, but as his bare hand made contact with her upper arm, he pulled it back just as quickly, as if stung. "What the goddess?" He stared down at her, his whole body menacing. His eyes were narrowed slits. "There *is* a spell on you. I thought I saw it in the tavern, but you were in front of the fire and I couldn't be sure. And there's something—something odd about it, isn't there?" He paused.

Juilene stared at Diago in disbelief. Could the man be a thurge as well as a thane? He fumbled in his belt for his gloves and pulled them on, the tight leather snapping against the flesh of his wrists. He leaned down and Juilene shrank back. "I want you to tell me who put it on you." He jerked her face up to his.

"I'll scream," she managed.

"Scream all you please. Elizondo knows what I require—he takes great pains to meet the needs of all his guests."

A chill went through Juilene. So that was why she had been welcomed, bathed, and fed. No wonder the curse hadn't affected Elizondo or his servants. There was a price she was expected to pay, and it wasn't with her music. Damn them all, she thought suddenly. I'll not be used. "Let me go and I will."

For answer he pushed her down on the bed and fell across her, his weight pinning her. She struggled with all her might, but he only held her down easily and laughed.

"Quite a little dragon, aren't we?" He felt for her nipple through her gown and pinched it. She gasped and tried to slap his hand away. "Now. The name." He pinched her nipple again, harder, and grinned as her face twisted in pain. He reached for her arms and held them above her head with one hand. With the other he fumbled at the skirt of her gown. He pulled it up roughly and she closed her eyes as she heard the worn fabric tear.

Tears filled her eyes as she felt the coarse wool of his breeches and the cold leather of his boots on the smooth skin of her legs. He ran his hand up and down her thigh, probing between her legs, stabbing his fingers deep into her secret places. She struggled against a nausea that flooded her throat. She clamped her knees together, but he was too strong.

"Now," he whispered, and his hot breath burned her ear. She heard the sound of a dagger sliding out of its sheath, and he held it up before her eyes. The blade was long and jagged on one side, and it gleamed silver in the dim light. The hilt was black leather, banded and bordered in silver. "The name," he said, "or I put this in you—and I might not care which end goes first."

Juilene gasped and closed her eyes. "Lindos," she whispered. "Lindos of Sylyria."

He threw the dagger aside and rolled on top of her with a chuckle of triumph. Her face burned with shame and humiliation. This was exactly what Lindos had in mind for her, she knew. But instead, she heard the door open and another man's voice, Cariad's voice, she recognized, and her heart leaped.

"Leave that girl alone."

Diago looked up. "Get out of here, young whelp. Go crawl back to your mistress's skirts 'til you're ready to play like a man."

"Men don't play this way," Cariad answered. "Even animals don't play like this."

Diago rose and Juilene scrambled up, pulling at her skirts. She drew her knees up to her chin and wrapped her arms around her legs.

Diago's face had darkened to an ugly mottled red. "You insolent puppy—shall I teach you what it means to play with me?"

"Go ahead and try," Cariad said calmly. He stood motionless. "Especially if you wish to answer to both King and Over-Thurge. Darmon is itching to bring a complaint against you. Give him the excuse he's been waiting for. I don't think you want to endure too much scrutiny, do you, my thane?"

The veins in Diago's temples bulged and he pressed his lips so tightly together they nearly disappeared. Dust swirled on the floor, and the whole room shook. A crack appeared in one wall, and from the stables a horse screamed, but nothing else happened.

Cariad stood impervious.

Finally Diago pushed past him, his face twisted with rage. "I'll deal with you another day," he bellowed, his voice echoing across the silent stableyard as he disappeared into the night.

Juilene swallowed hard, scarcely believing he was gone. "How—how did you dare to withstand him?"

"He knew I was right," he said with a shrug. "Diago has no wish to call the attentions of either Conclave or Council upon himself. He's not trusted by either as it is. And in my country, my uncle is a thurge. He gave me a charm to protect me against the use of magic."

Juilene eyed him closely, not sure whether to believe him or not. But Cariad was speaking and she could scarcely gather her thoughts sufficiently to ask the questions swirling through her head. He gestured to her harp. "Come with me."

"Where?" she asked, not sure whether to trust him or not. There was something in his face that said he could be trusted, but how many others had she thought she could trust, and how many times had she been mistaken?

"I have a room in the inn," he repeated patiently.

"Oh." Juilene raised her eyebrow. So he had saved her for himself. She drew a deep breath and let it out in a long sigh. If she was going to be used this night, it might as well be by one whom she found attractive. "All right." She picked up her pack. Her wrists ached and she shuddered to think at the way Diago would have used her.

"Ready?"

She nodded.

"Come."

He offered her his arm and she took it after a moment's hesitation. What was it about this man that was at once so noble and so—she groped for the word—sad? He was young—maybe only a few years older than she—certainly no older than Arimond—but there was about him an air of gravity, utterly different from Arimond, as though he had known great suffering in his life, and carried the memory of it with him always. She realized that not once that whole evening had she seen him smile.

He led her back across the yard, and through the kitchens, and finally up a flight of steps to the rooms above the inn.

She bit her lip, and hoped that what she could offer would be worth her night's lodgings. Something about this man made her not want to see anything bad come to him because of her.

She allowed him to lead her down the corridor, and finally he paused before a door. He opened the door, and stood aside to let her pass. She walked into the room. It was not large, but it was comfortably furnished with a wide wooden bed. The sheets on the bed were white, the blankets fine wool dyed a soft rich shade of blue. A fire burned in the small hearth. She looked around, and was surprised he did not follow her inside. She turned back with a question on her face.

"Good night, sister." He bowed with grave courtesy and began to close the door.

"Wait," she cried. Immediately he paused. "Aren't you—don't you—where are you going?"

"I'll be just outside the door. Diago is a stubborn man when he gets in a mood like that. If he's frustrated, there's no saying what he's capable of doing. Goddess help whatever poor wretch he's found to use instead of you."

"But, but, can't something be done to stop him?"

Cariad's face was grave. "I'm only one man, my lady. If I believed that I, alone, could stop Diago, believe me, I would've tried to do so, a long time ago. But there're too many deaf ears and blind eyes . . ." His voice trailed off and he shook his head as his shoulders heaved in a sigh. "I do what I can. You, at least, will be safe here, my lady. Lady Lona is in the next room. I can watch over both of you this way."

"But—" She dropped her pack and her harp on the bed and ran to grab the doorknob. "You—you don't understand—I can't stay here unless—"

"Unless what?" he asked gently.

"Unless I pay," she said miserably.

He was silent for what seemed like a long time. "You paid with your songs, my lady. I require no other coin."

Juilene shook her head violently. "No, you don't understand. Unless I pay, something will happen—something terrible."

He hesitated once more, looked right and left down the corridor and slipped inside the room. "That story you told tonight—that's your story, isn't it?"

She bent her head and nodded, plucking fretfully at the skirt of her gown. "You have to let me—let me earn my place here—or—"

"Or the thurge's curse will affect me the way it affected your nurse."

She nodded again, biting her lip as her eyes flooded with tears.

"My lady—"

"Why do you call me that," she whispered. "I am no one's lady."

"I was taught to respect women, no matter their rank or social standing. In my country, my mother is—greatly respected by all, and I would accord that respect to every woman."

She could not look at him, for the tears were threatening to spill down her cheeks. Not only was he offering her shelter for the night, but protection as well. There were not enough songs in Sylyria to pay for that. She shook her head. "I can't let you do this—you must—"

"Make you pay?" he said. "With your body?" He shifted on his feet uncomfortably. "No. I would rather risk the curse than make you do something which you would rather not do."

"I don't want anything to happen to you," she managed.

"I told you my uncle gave me a charm," he said. "It's very effective. And I think you've earned a good night's sleep—a safe night's sleep. No more now—the hour grows late."

She looked up into his eyes and saw they were blue— blue with flecks of gold. He bent down and kissed her forehead, so gently she scarcely felt the pressure of his lips,

"Sleep well, little sister." He was gone before she could answer, the door firmly shut behind him.

She stared at the door a long time, debating whether or not to open it and protest. But there had been such a finality about the way he had spoken that she doubted she could change his mind, without embarrassing both of them.

Finally she undressed. Goddess protect him, she prayed as she slipped between the clean linen sheets. Whatever pain his past concealed, he did not deserve to suffer more for her sake.

Chapter Nine

❦

The sun slanted across Juilene's face, bothersome as an insect. She stirred and opened her eyes, and for a moment could not remember where she was. The ceiling above her was white, the window with its diamond panes of glass sparkled in the sun. She stretched her arms above her head. The last night she had slept in a bed like this had been at the castle of the thurge Deatrice, and then she had to share it with Nuala and Mathy. It had been so long since she had had anything like this to herself.

What a spoiled darling she had been, she thought. Had she ever truly appreciated the life she had led? She thought of her childhood fantasies of the life of a songsayer. No wonder her parents had been so horrified. She thought of Arimond. She had allowed him to lead her into utter danger—what a naive fool she had been. She should have heeded all those inner warnings.

She rolled over on her stomach. Arimond had paid with his life. She snuggled deeper into the pillows. And she—she had paid with her innocence.

There was a knock on the door.

"Come in," she said, drawing the covers up to her chin as she rose up on one elbow.

Allia, the maid who had shown her to the bath yesterday, peered into the room. "My, uh, sister, the day is half over. There is breakfast waiting for you. And the master wishes a word."

"With me?" Juilene blinked and sat up, her mind racing. Were there to be repercussions from the incident with Diago last night? At least she'd had the best night's sleep she could remember. "Very well, Allia. Thank you. Tell your master I will be there directly."

The maid curtsied, and Juilene raised her eyebrow. What had happened in the hours since she had slept? "There's a can of hot water out here for you, sister. And a clean towel."

"Thank you," Juilene managed. When the girl had gone, she clambered out of bed. This was entirely unexpected. Songsayers could expect certain courtesies of course, certain decencies, in any noble house, but this hardly qualified as the house of a noble. She expected Elizondo to boot her out for refusing Diago. But she was being treated more like an honored guest than an unwelcome itinerant.

She washed and dressed as quickly as she could. The doors all along the corridor were open, and Juilene could see that the rooms were empty of any signs of occupation. Everyone had moved on. She thought of Cariad with a pang, of his silent, uncomfortable vigil through the night, and wondered if she would ever see him again. Had anything happened to him? she wondered. And if not, was there a possibility that the curse could be lifted, dispelled, in some way? His uncle must be a powerful thurge indeed. Was it even possible to think of finding him?

She stepped over the threshold of the silent common room, and found Elizondo seated at one of the tables, a long ledger book before him.

"Ah, you're awake at last, I see."

"Allia said you wished a word with me."

He gestured to a chair. "Sit." For a long moment he gnawed at the end of his pen. Finally he made a notation in the ledger and looked up. "I don't know what magic you wove last night, but you certainly cast a spell over that young knight in Diago's service. He's paid for a month's lodging for you. I agreed to let you sing here of the evenings, and earn your bread. He said if that didn't meet with your approval, I was to give you the money. Well? What shall it be?"

Juilene stared at the innkeeper in disbelief. She shook her head slightly as if to clear it and lean forward. "Lodging? For a month?"

He nodded. "That's right. There was some—" He glanced over his shoulder and then turned back to Juilene. "Some unpleasantness last night, with Lucca. She took a turn for the worse."

"A permanent turn for the worse," said the young barkeep, lounging in the doorway. "Tell her the truth, Elizondo. Diago got a little carried away last night."

Juilene gazed in horror from one man to the other. How could they take the death of another human being so lightly? She knotted her fingers together, thoughts racing through her head. Did she dare to stay here, where her life was obviously counted so cheaply. And yet, she wanted to see Cariad again, more than she cared to admit even to herself. "Where has he gone?"

"Diago? Back to his estate today—message came early

this morning that the keep was ready. He hightailed it out of here faster than you can blink and left me to deal with his mess." Elizondo grunted. "So I've a need for a 'sayer, and you, if you don't mind my saying, look as if you've a need for a roof over your head. You look too soft for the road."

Juilene hardly heard his offer. "Where is his keep?"

"Right over the rise, practically. You can see the towers from the top of the inn. Less than a turn of the glass away." Elizondo leaned forward, his jowls quivering. "But don't worry. That young knight of his is likely to be back sooner than the master, and there's something about that one that even Diago is wary of. So what do you say, sister? You want the job, or you want the money?"

Juilene blinked. "I'll take the job on one condition. I want nothing to do with Diago. If he's killed someone, something must be done."

Both men laughed and Elizondo shook his head. "Who would miss a 'sayer or two? Now, you, missy, you're different. That knight told me the very same thing—"

"Indeed," interrupted the barkeep, laughing, "but he had a keener edge to his request."

Elizondo glared at the barkeep. "Enough, Lem."

With a snicker, Lem turned away. "Don't worry, little sister," he said over his shoulder. "Even Elizondo has the sense to fear a knight in love."

Juilene glanced at the men. In love. If only such a thing could be true. But a man like Cariad would have no interest in someone like her. His nobility was as tangible as a cloak. She knew what he was—the son of some noble house, sent away to learn the arts of war, or to cement an alliance with a distant faction. If he were not betrothed since childhood, likely his parents were hard at work finding him a suitable bride. He was not for her. She drew a deep breath as Elizondo drummed his fingers impatiently on the tabletop. "Very well," she said. "I'll take the job."

Elizondo snorted. "Good. Though in the name of the goddess, I am not sure what use you'll be. I've never had a songsayer with a champion before." He waved his hand dismissively. "I'll expect you down here by sunset. Understand? And you'll play 'til closing, do you hear?"

Juilene nodded.

"Then go practice or whatever else it is you do. The room you slept in is yours."

Juilene rose. "Thank you."

"And I won't be sending anyone to remind you. Sunset. Oh—there's breakfast in the kitchen." He picked up his pen again and scratched his temple with the end. Juilene thought she saw Lem wink as she left the room.

The fire snapped and crackled as Cariad leaned against the hearth, staring into the flames. The day wasn't really chilly at all, but the keep had been vacant for so many months, the rooms were damp and musty. He toyed with the hilt of the dagger in his belt. His muscles ached from the afternoon's drills. He had fought like a madman, until even the sergeant at arms paused to watch, and a circle gathered around his sparring partner, the son of Lady Lona from her first marriage. Finally young Darmon threw down his sword and raised his hands in mock surrender. "Kill me quick, if you will, Cariad," he said, breathing hard, his face flushed.

"Kill you?" Puzzled, Cariad lowered his own weapon.

"Better a quick, clean death than the slow one you're leading me to," Darmon replied with a grin. "Why not get my stepfather out here, if you're in a murdering mood?"

The grins and good-natured catcalls ended immediately. Cariad handed his sword to someone in the crowd and stalked away. It was all well and fine for Darmon to voice his hatred of his stepfather privately, but speaking so openly, especially beneath his stepfather's roof, before men sworn to serve him, was more than foolish. It was dangerous.

He sighed heavily as a woman's voice broke through his reverie: "What troubles you, Cariad?"

He turned to see Lady Lona standing on the threshold and automatically straightened. "My lady. Is there anything you require?"

She shook her head and sighed. "Nothing but an explanation for your long face, Cariad. I heard about the display in the practice yard this afternoon. You seem troubled. What's wrong?"

"Nothing."

"You must be tired."

He shook his head and turned back to the flames. "No."

"Cariad, please talk to me. I don't like it when you brood—you know I would do all in my power for you. I could not ask for a better friend than you." Her skirts made a heavy whisper on the floor as she shut the door and walked across the room.

"Your husband troubles me, lady. And short of murder, I know not how to deal with him."

"You must do as we all do, Cariad. Tread softly. Say little. Hope always."

He stifled the urge to snort. Nothing would be served by challenging Diago. He was too powerful, a thurge and a thane all at once, theoretically bound by two sets of restrictions and in reality bound by none. "I am not sure I did the right thing, Lona."

"Are you talking about the little songsayer?"

He smelled the essence of lilies as she came closer. At times her perceptions amazed him. When she had opened her door that morning, to find him stretched out in the hall, his head pillowed on his cloak like a soldier in the field, she had known at once what had happened. Neither of them had been surprised to learn of Diago's rage that had resulted in the death of the songsayer. He was not used to being thwarted. Cariad nodded. "Was it wrong of me to try and find her a place at the inn?"

"The innkeeper needed a 'sayer." Lona sighed. "She will be warm there—off the roads—she looked so delicately made, it was hard to believe she's known that sort of life."

Cariad looked at Lona pityingly. For all her perceptiveness when it came to some things, she could be amazingly blind about others. It had been clear as glass to him that the girl was speaking of herself as soon as she had begun her tale. What a life she had found herself in—and for a girl, gently born and raised from the looks of her, a shock. He was amazed she had survived at all. And he had been touched by her unspoken expectation that he would take her—and touched, too, by her desire that he not come to any harm. But better for all if she had taken the money instead of the job. "I should have given her the money, and left it at that," he muttered.

"But then, she would have been out on the road, and it could have been stolen from her. And then where would the poor child be? I would have her here, but . . ." Lona's voice trailed off into silence.

Cariad stared at the fire. He knew as well as Lona why the songsayer was better off at the inn, better off anywhere than under Diago's roof. But what was he doing, worrying about the fate of some nameless songsayer? Keeping Lona and Darmon safe and out of harm's way was charge enough. Did he have to add a half-grown girl to whom he owed nothing to the list?

"Cariad." Lona's voice was soft. "Why don't you go to the inn?"

He jerked his head up. "What?"

"Go see her. If she's there. Maybe she's taken the money. I can see she—she affected you." Lona smiled.

Cariad shook his head as though to clear it. "You must think me a fool, Lona."

"No," she answered. "Not at all. A man whose eye's been caught, perhaps. But not a fool."

He felt his face grow warm. Surely he was too old to blush? She laughed. "Go on. We can manage without you. I promise." She hesitated just a moment, and then went on. "And while you are there, see if Elizondo knows anything about that poor woman. The other one. We should—we must offer her headprice to her family."

Cariad hesitated a moment, then bowed. "I will go now, then, if you allow it, lady."

"Allow it? I insist."

Cariad bowed once more. "As you will it, I obey." He found himself hoping against hope that the songsayer—whatever her name was—would be at the inn when he got there.

All evening, Juilene found herself looking up whenever the door opened. She plucked the harp strings by rote, scarcely sure of what she was playing. But something must be pleasing, she thought, for the patrons turned and smiled and nodded whenever she paused, and more than once, she caught snatches of murmured appreciation. A few even approached her and pressed small coins in her hand, whispering "Goddess blessing, little sister." It made her realize just what a boon Cariad had given her. She would be able to pay for her own lodgings soon, if this kept up. Tonight there were even more people in the inn than usual, and the talk was all of Thane Diago's return. She was growing used to the more liquid vowels of Khardroon, the sibilant sounds of their speech, and she could almost understand them as well as she could her own people. She had known at once that Cariad and Lona were not of Khardroon, but she was uncertain where they were from.

She paused for a moment, and caught Lem's eye behind the bar. He nodded, filling a goblet for her, of cool watered wine. The mixture soothed her throat. She set her harp carefully on a stand that just that evening had suddenly appeared before the hearth, and walked to the bar. Lem set the goblet before her and winked again. He leaned across the bar. "Doing well, sister. Keep it up, and Elizondo will hold Diago back himself."

Juilene blushed. She remembered her first awful performance, if it could be called that, in that wretched sickroom in Sylyria. She had changed so much from the shy girl who was too terrified even to manage a few chords. She took the goblet and smiled at Lem. He was such a marked contrast to Elizondo, for he was thin to the point of skeletal, and his clothes hung so loosely off his shoulders it gave the impression there was no body beneath them.

She raised the goblet to her lips, and as she drank, the door opened and shut. By habit, she glanced at the door. Cariad stood just inside the threshold, shaking off his cloak. A few of the patrons seemed to recognize him, for they greeted him and called to him to join them. He glanced at her, nodded a greeting, and went to sit with three or four men grouped around a table in a corner by the window.

Juilene tightened her fingers on the stem of the goblet. "My thanks, Lem—I'd best go back to playing."

He nodded and smiled, and she made her way back to her seat by the hearth. A sudden downdraft made the fire leap up and she kept her face down. Her cheeks felt hot. What had she expected? That he would come in and fall down at her feet? She berated herself for being a silly girl even after all that had happened to her. She picked up the harp and played a jig, skipping over the strings and the intricate notes with all the skill she had. The music rose above the general buzz of conversation and more than a few of the people turned to look at her as she played. She kept her head down and concentrated upon her music. She didn't want to know if Cariad watched her or not.

The song ended and the inn rang loud with applause. Men pounded the tables and stamped their feet. Elizondo burst into the room from the kitchens, wearing a grease-spattered smock. He was greeted with louder clapping, and more than a few comments to improve all the staff, not just the songsayer. His moon face beamed, and he kissed several of the men on both cheeks, before waving and disappearing back into the kitchens.

Juilene played a softer air. The hum of conversation resumed as the patrons went back to their drinking. She stole a peek in Cariad's direction. He was talking with his companions and hadn't seemed to notice either her playing or the applause. She allowed herself one soft sigh, and pressed her cheek against the scarred wood. She was behaving like a moonstruck girl, and surely, she was anything but that.

"I see you decided to stay." Cariad startled her so that she plucked the wrong string and the mistake resonated to the rafters. More than one person turned to look at her.

Juilene flushed. "Yes. Yes, I did. Thank you, for what you did for me."

"It was nothing, my lady. I was glad to do it. But I disturb your playing." He bowed and turned to go.

"Wait," she cried. She stopped in the middle of the song. He looked back, one eyebrow raised. "I—I just wanted to ask you—are you well?"

He gave her a quizzical look. "Well, my lady? Do I look ill?"

"No—not at all." What was it about this man that addled her thoughts and tied her tongue? "What I meant was—I can't believe that nothing happened to you—you are quite well?"

He turned back to face her as a slow smile spread across his face. It lifted the somber corners of his eyes, and lit the golden flecks within the blue, and Juilene thought she had never seen a man smile so beautifully. "Yes, my lady. I am quite well, quite unaffected." He spread his hands. "Do you see? No bumps or bruises, save those I earned myself."

"Oh," she said, flustered. "Good. I—I didn't want anything to happen to you, because of me."

"Rest easily, my lady." The smile was gone as quickly as the sun on a cloudy day. "If any harm comes to me, it will be by far more dangerous hands than yours." He bowed once more and walked away, his shoulders stiffened, as though braced against an unseen enemy.

Chapter Ten

❧

The leaves of the calendar tree turned, a rapid succession of such peaceful days that Juilene scarcely believed her good fortune. The little money pouch she wore in her bosom grew heavy with coins, and when the pouch bulged to capacity, she went to Elizondo, who changed the brass and copper for silver. These she sewed into a secret lining she had made in her cloak. She scarcely needed a cloak, for she was never out at night, and the days were seldom cool enough to warrant more than a light shawl.

Cariad appeared every evening. He was always dressed in the now familiar colors of Thane Diago's house, and he always sat with a small group of soldiers from the keep. She was able to recognize many of the patrons by sight now, if not by name, though Lem was happy to tell her as many tales as she would believe after the inn closed its doors for the night.

Cariad spoke to her every evening, an almost courtly exchange of pleasantries that only served to puzzle her further. There was so much about him she didn't understand. His air of command, his gallantry, was more like the men of her father's rank and even higher, than that of an ordinary knight in the service of a thane. Sometimes she had the unnerving feeling she was speaking to someone even more highly born than she. And she had the sense that in speaking to her, he found an equal, someone who knew and understood the things he knew and understood. But his speech was oddly accented, a few of his expressions and turns of phrase wholly foreign. He referred to his home as "my country"—something no one ever did. The city-states of the League were as firmly bonded together as any family. Did that mean that Cariad came from a country even farther away? From across the Outer Oceans? She had heard of travelers with strange customs arriving in the port cities, and she supposed that such a thing was not so uncommon, really. But if he was from across the sea, why did he seem so familiar with all things of the League?

She tried to remember if any of the merchants and travelers who had visited her father's keep had sounded like Cariad, and she tried to draw him out as much as she dared. But each time the conversation turned to his background, he found an excuse to end it. She was learning not to ask questions.

But he watched her, she knew that, and he smiled at her with growing frequency. She knew she blushed under his scrutiny, and she knew she had never played so well. He had given her a great gift, and somehow had managed to escape harm. But he refused to speak of his home or his family, and answered her only with the briefest and most cursory of replies if she broached those subjects. He would talk to her of Lona and her children, and she learned from him that Diago had gone away again, on some unknown business that only brought a frown to Cariad's brow whenever the subject happened to come up.

Year's End passed, and Juilene found her days slipping into a pleasant routine. She rose late, for seldom did she see her bed before the small hours of the morning, and practiced in the afternoons. Her evenings were spent before the fire, lost in the music of the harp. Her singing had improved, as well, she thought; she was no longer so shy and the acoustics of the inn made her voice seem to fill every corner.

The old harp gleamed beneath her care, the brass strings resonated with a quality of sound she attributed to the instrument's age. And if of a winter's night, it seemed that the gouges and the dents in the wood frame seemed less and less, Juilene pretended not to notice. She knew that each time she played especially well, the harp rang with a richness she had never heard in any other instrument, and in the firelight, it seemed to pulsate like a living thing. There was something odd about the harp, something that made her nearly afraid to touch it, at times. But there was also a deep sense of peace that accompanied her playing, and so she scolded herself for any qualms. Besides, in the cold light of day, the harp appeared as shabby and as dull as ever.

One evening, she slipped into her usual place and saw Cariad already there. He was sitting alone at a table near her chair, and she smiled when she saw him. She had noticed some days ago that he was gradually moving closer.

She murmured a greeting, and picked up her harp. He leaned back in his chair, head cocked, listening. She played a song that she remembered learning only just before her life had changed. She had struggled with it, for the words and music had not come as easily as other songs, and she wondered as she shifted the chords why it suddenly seemed so easy.

"Still in the winter, deep in the darkness,
All the world wrapped in white and in cold.
When I cried out, your voice came in answer,
So softly, so calmly, speaking so near.
At the window, the snow fell, the first of the year,
You said to me, hear how the bells ring so clear.
Then I knew nothing of safe harbors in storms,
But hot tears brought healing, and patient you waited,
My candle in the night, silent as light.
I watched you through long days of yearning,
Days that were empty as blank, starless skies
And you offered to me a hand like the dawning,
You made me smile when my heart should have broken,
You ended the darkness, you shone like the morning,
You fell like rain upon parched summer earth,
And I bloom like a rose in the depths of the winter."

The music swelled, the melody as fluid as water. Juilene's fingers plucked surely at the strings, her body swaying a little in time. The last notes faded, and she looked up. The inn was silent. The maids peered around the door from the kitchens, Lem leaned upon the bar, a faraway look in his eyes, Elizondo's bulk filled the outer doorway. All the patrons were still. A few stared at her, a few into their mugs and goblets, a few into places she knew she would never see. She dared to peek at Cariad.

He was staring past her, into the flames, wearing an expression she couldn't read. She lowered her harp. Lem began to clap, and the others followed suit. "Well sung, little sister, well sung!"

Juilene blushed. Mugs were raised in her direction, and Elizondo gave her an approving look as he disappeared back upstairs.

"When the goddess speaks, the goddess sings," Lem

called from behind the bar as he poured a goblet of her favorite apple wine. "For you, little sister."

Cariad rose and fetched the goblet. Juilene raised her eyes to his. He offered her the wine. "Well sung," he said.

She laid her harp down and sipped the wine. The liquid stung the roof of her mouth. "Is there anything wrong?"

Cariad sank down into the chair. "No. Nothing to concern you."

"You look troubled. Is Lady Lona all right?" She had gleaned from their conversations that the lady was in frail health, and that Cariad feared for both the lady and her oldest son.

He gave her a quick smile that didn't quite reach his eyes. "That was a beautiful song." He glanced over his shoulder as a cool gust of wind accompanied the entrance of a bent figure in a dark cloak who leaned upon a cane.

Juilene followed his gaze. The old man pushed a hood away from his face and made his way to the bar, where he rested his walking stick and slid awkwardly onto a stool.

"Welcome, traveler. What can I bring you?" asked Lem from the far side of the bar.

Cariad narrowed his eyes.

"What's wrong?" Juilene leaned forward and touched his sleeve.

"Ale," answered the old man, and Juilene looked up, wary. The old man spoke with a Sylyrian accent.

"Travel far?" Lem placed a brimming mug in front of the old man.

The old man nodded, and lifted the mug. He swallowed hard and set it down, wiping foam off his beard. "All the way from Sylyria. Have you heard the news?"

Lem shrugged, glancing around at the other patrons. "All the news from Sylyria has not been good lately. Have you anything more to tell us?"

The old man nodded again in the middle of a swallow. "Indeed," he said. "There's a new Over-Thurge in the city."

"Ah, you're a month or more late with that news, stranger." Another man, dressed in a rich tunic of unrelieved black, spoke from the shadowy corner on the far side of the hearth. His face was indistinct, and Juilene realized with a shock he had been sitting there a long time. She had not seen him come in. "We heard weeks ago that Nod won the title."

"So he did," said the old man. "But Nod is dead. And a new Over-Thurge sits in his place. A master-thurge but lately come into his power. Such a thing has not happened in the span of the Covenant."

The shadowed man made a little noise of disbelief. "What master-thurge rises so quickly? What's his name, and who are you, that you know so much?"

"I have just come from Sylyria," answered the old man. "And the master-thurge who reigns there is named Lindos."

Juilene gasped. Out of the corner of her eye, she saw the color drain from Cariad's face. He gripped his dagger with a white-knuckled hand, and that surprised her even more. What did Lindos mean to Cariad that he should react so to the name?

The stranger rose in one fluid motion, and as he left his place in the shadows, Juilene saw the intricate gold belt that he wore around his waist. His cloak was black and bordered with intricate glyphs of gold and Cariad sucked his breath in, his eyes narrowing. "What's wrong?" she whispered.

He shook his head, motioning her to silence, as he watched the interaction between the richly dressed stranger and the poor one.

"Why do you travel so shabbily, brother?"

The old man smiled, and his teeth were long and looked very sharp. Suddenly Juilene shivered. Brother? Surely it wasn't possible that the old man was a thurge, and yet the black-clad stranger addressed him as the thurges addressed their own. The old man looked like a wolf. "I travel quickly. Khardroon is but a stop on my journey. I have business in Parmathia. And you, brother? This is not your home, either."

The black-garbed stranger smiled and spread his hands. "I await the return of the Thane Diago, the master-thurge of this district and the thane of this domain."

"So it begins." Cariad spoke so softly Juilene wasn't certain he had spoken at all. She looked from the old man to the thurge and back at Cariad. He had sat back in his chair, and he was staring into the flames, but she knew he was listening intently.

She cleared her throat. She had to know. If the old man were indeed a thurge from Sylyria, perhaps there was word of her father. "I beg your pardon, Transcendence, but may I ask a question of you?"

The moment was broken as the old thurge's eyes shifted to her. "Of course, little sister. Say on."

"What word of the thanes? The thanes of Sylyria, who challenged Lindos, at Festival time?"

The old thurge's face grew grim. He rose from his stool and made his slow way to sit at a table beside her bench. His eyes were cloudy, the color obscured by whitish disks, and Juilene realized with a shock that the old man was blind. "It is not a good time to be a thane in Sylyria, my child." His voice was low, but there was a rough kindness in the timbre. "Be glad you are not a member of such a house."

"Why not?" whispered Juilene. "What has happened there?"

"Be glad it does not concern you, little sister. You've run into enough trouble with thurges in your time, haven't you? The spell you carry blazes like a black light under the moon. Say your songs, and be grateful the goddess has placed you outside the sphere of such events."

Juilene opened her mouth and shut it quickly. There was

no way to ask any more without blurting out too much about herself. Everyone was likely to wonder why she cared so intensely about the fate of the thanes of Sylyria. She twisted her fingers in her gown.

Cariad rose to his feet and held out his hand. "Will you walk with me, my lady?"

She stared up at him, wondering how he could even think of walking when the news was so terrible. He gazed into her eyes intently, and she understood. There was something he wanted to say to her alone. She rose and placed her hand in his. "If it pleases you, my knight," she said with forced gaiety. The old man's eyes were closed; the black-garbed thurge had seated himself once more in the shadows. The other patrons were deep in conversation or their mugs. No one paid the least attention to them.

"Come."

She got to her feet, brushing off her skirts with her free hand. It shook a little and she wondered if he noticed. His hand was warm, the palm smoothly callused. His grip was firm but not uncomfortable. He held the door open for her as she paused long enough to say to Lem: "I'll only be a few minutes."

Lem waved to her with a wink.

The door closed behind them with a whispered sigh. Cariad offered her his arm.

"Where are we gong?" Juilene asked. The night was very clear but a cool breeze whispered through the long leaves of the willows that shaded the courtyard of the inn.

"I needed some air," he said. "And if you'll forgive me for saying so, you looked as if you could use it, too." He shrugged his cloak off his shoulders and wrapped it around her. "There. That better?"

She smiled up at him. The cloak was warm from his body. She snuggled it up to her chin, and his scent, woodsmoke and horses and leather and something else, something indefinable but most definitely him, enveloped her like a blanket. He led her across the road and seated himself on a low stone fence across from the inn.

Yellow light blazed from nearly every window, and smoke, pale pink in the light of the red-orange moon, twisted in lazy curls into the black sky. She sat down next to him, acutely conscious of his thigh next to hers. She clasped her hands together on her lap. The full moon cast everything in a rosy hue.

"You're worried about your family." It was a statement, not a question.

She nodded. "I hear so little of so much—snatches of sentences, a word here, a phrase there. I know there's trouble in Sylyria, but I don't dare ask too many questions. I just wish I knew what was happening with my family."

He glanced around, as though to ascertain they were alone. "There's trouble all over."

"Why do you say that?"

Cariad shook his head. "I'm not one of those who believes there isn't room for thane and thurge within the League. But Sylyria isn't the only place there's conflict." He sighed. "I wish there were more I could do to ease your fears, but what little I can do, I will. I can ask Lady Lona to send a messenger to Sylyria, to inquire about your family. You do understand, though, that the news is not likely to be good?"

Juilene drew a deep breath. "Cariad, that's very kind of you, but I can't let you do that. If a messenger were to suddenly appear, asking about my family, my father is not a foolish man. He would guess that I was involved somehow, sooner or later. He would probably have the poor messenger apprehended and would refuse to let him return until he told my father everything he wanted to know."

Cariad smiled, a sad, gentle smile that made Juilene swallow hard and twine her hands tight into her lap. "I think the messenger would be discreet, my dear. But we hear things, too, you know—messages come for Diago, even in his absence. There's talk that the King of Sylyria has gone into exile."

"Exile? The King leave Sylyria?"

Cariad shrugged. "It may be a rumor, nothing more."

Juilene opened her mouth, but no words seemed to want to shape themselves upon her lips. What was it about this quiet, slender man, who seemed to make every thought she had turn to confusion in her mind?

He patted her hand. "Think about it. The offer stands." He lapsed once more into silence.

Juilene reached out timidly and covered his hand with hers. "Cariad, what troubles you? What did you mean inside, when you said, 'so it begins'?"

He pressed her hand between both of his so swiftly it took her breath away. "I wish I could tell you." Their fingers twined together of their own accord. He turned to her, and the look he wore took her breath away. "Juilene, what would you say—" He broke off, and turned his head away, swearing softly beneath his breath.

"To what, Cariad?" she prompted gently. "What would I say to what?"

"Lady Lona has asked me to ask you if you would be so kind as to come to the castle and teach the three little girls—"

"Teach?" Juilene sat back, feeling profoundly disappointed, for a reason she could not name. Damn this man, and the effect he had upon her. What was it about this quiet, courtly stranger that so unsettled her, as no man ever had, even Arimond?

"In the afternoons, of course, so it wouldn't interfere with your work here. I—I would escort you—you need not travel alone."

"I have been on rougher roads than this."

"I know," he answered. "Since you were cursed." She felt

the heat rise in her cheeks, but in the dark he didn't see it, or chose to ignore it. He gave her a sad smile. "Lady Lona has also spoken of your coming to live at the castle, but—"

"But Thane Diago must come home eventually."

"Yes. Exactly. But she is a kind and gracious lady, and her husband is a disgrace to both his titles."

"Her very kindness makes her vulnerable to the curse. Surely you can see that."

He dragged the tip of one boot through the dirt. "Lona wants to talk to you. She didn't realize at first that the story you told that night was your own, but later—well, believe it or not, when Diago's not around and she's not afraid for her life, she is very perceptive. And she wanted me to bring you to the castle tomorrow, if you wouldn't mind."

Juilene shrugged, a little mystified. "No, of course not. But, why does she want to talk to me?"

"I think she wants to talk to you about the thurge who put the spell upon you."

"Lindos? Why does she want to know about Lindos?"

Cariad stared at her in dismay. "Ah, by the goddess, I see the pattern unfold. It was Lindos who cursed you? Killed your betrothed?"

Juilene nodded. "Who just became Over-Thurge of Sylyria."

"And who will be High Thurge, next, unless he is stopped—" Cariad broke off abruptly. He swore softly under his breath.

"High Thurge? What makes you think that?"

Cariad hesitated. "Well, it makes sense, doesn't it?"

"I—I suppose. But don't all the Over-Thurges have to agree, before the High Thurge is elected?"

Cariad shook his head. "I don't know, Juilene." He rarely used her name, and she liked the way his accent elongated the vowels. It sounded like a caress. "Some say that just as the Incarnation of the goddess was preceded by an age of anarchy and chaos, so, too, will the end of the tenth millennium. Now that this Lindos had made himself Over-Thurge—" He shook his head again and sighed. "Will you come and talk to Lona?"

"Certainly," Juilene answered, feeling bewildered. "But how can anything I tell her change anything?"

"It may not," he said, brushing a stray curl out of her eyes. "But it may warn of what's to come. And one never knows where one will find a friend." He smiled, a little sadly, and Juilene suddenly had the urge to take him in her arms and comfort him.

The road to Diago's keep was long and straight as an arrow, the land cleared for at least a mile in each direction. Juilene clung to the back of the little mare Cariad had brought for her. She didn't like the idea of entering Diago's castle, despite the fact that she knew the thurge was not in residence and that Cariad would be with her. She glanced at Cariad. He rode his gelding with practiced ease, his lean body molding itself to the motion of the horse as though he were merely an extension of the animal. In his presence, she felt safer than she had in a long time, but the thought of confronting the wizard on his home ground made her shudder.

The white walls of the keep rose sharply from a steep moat, dazzling in the light of the winter sun. Juilene felt a shiver of fear as she passed beneath the open gates. This place reminded her of Lindos. The towers spiraled to the sky, contorted and tortured, and faces leered from the stone rims of the walls, repressive and cruel. The guards and the men at arms in the inner ward greeted Cariad with respectful nods, but there was some wariness in their expressions that told her that Cariad was not quite fully accepted as one of their own.

So she was not the only one who sensed his difference. She wondered exactly what Cariad's fellow knights thought of him. She pulled her shoulders straighter as

Cariad slid off his saddle and held up his arms to help her down.

He smiled down at her as he drew her arm beneath his, tucking it close. "Shall we go in, my lady?"

She nodded, a little flustered. His use of that form of address made her feel more girlish than she had felt in a long time. Only a few months had passed since that terrible night, but it might have been an age. She felt a thousand times older than the girl who had fled her father's house on that cold morning.

But there was an ease with which the title fell from Cariad's lips, and a grace with which he guided her up the steps, and suddenly she was struck with the knowledge that he, too, was somehow more than he pretended to be. He might appear to be a mere knight in the household of this arrogant thurge-thane, but she knew with a sudden certainty there was more to Cariad, much more than he had told her.

A woman's light step on the stones of the entryway made her look up. Cariad bowed as the slight form of Lady Lona rounded the corner. "Lady Lona."

Juilene glanced from Cariad to the woman before her. Lona seemed much healthier than she had at their first meeting, and it struck Juilene that Diago's absence had done her good. She was not as pale, the dark circles under her eyes not nearly as pronounced. She was still thin, though, and her hands fluttered like birds as she extended them to Juilene.

"My dear," said Lona, "how happy I am to see you again. Will you come and sit?"

Without waiting for an answer, she turned and led the way to a small room off the main corridor. Juilene peeked through the open doors on the opposite side of the entrance as Cariad drew her forward. She glimpsed the sight of a huge hall, easily twice the size of her father's in Sylyria. The walls were whitewashed stone and rose more than two vaulted stories. Vivid colors swirled on huge tapestries, and Juilene craned her head to see more.

"Yes," said Cariad, leaning down to speak into her ear. "Diago's house is magnificent. If only his outer display matched his inner self, he would be a great man, indeed."

Lona sat down in a chair beside a small fire that burned in a hearth of polished brass and shining tile. She indicated two chairs opposite. "Please, sit. Would you care for some refreshment, little sister?"

Juilene glanced around, taking in the sumptuousness of the furnishings, the obvious expense of the silver goblets, the tiny pastries piled high upon a silver platter. And yet something about this pale, slender, almost sickly looking woman seemed terribly out of place, here as well. What were they all, she wondered, a gathering of misfits?

Lona glanced up at her and flushed. She plucked at the lace that edged the sleeves of her gown and glanced at Cariad. "You are more perceptive than you realize, my dear," she murmured.

Juilene started. Had the woman heard her thoughts?

Cariad leaned forward. "Has there been any word of Diago, Lona?"

Juilene glanced at Cariad. In the privacy of this room, he spoke to her as though he were her equal. Although he spoke gently, there was no trace of the obsequious squire. Who were these people, she wondered, and why did Lona not react to the subtle change in his tone?

"We will try to explain as much as we can to you, my dear," said Lona. She shook her head at Cariad. "No. As far as I know, he's still with Rihana."

Cariad sucked in his breath. "And no word as to how much longer he intends to pleasure his sister with his company?"

Lona shook her head, her lips a thin line in her white face. "No. But for all I care he can stay with her as long as he pleases."

Cariad sighed and got to his feet. "I know. But the trouble with that is we've no idea what mischief he may be up to while he keeps her company."

Lona shrugged and waved her hand. "Enough about Diago. I am delighted to see you again, my dear—may I call you Juilene?"

Juilene nodded. "Of course, my lady, if it pleases you."

"I know you have questions, child. If I had not been so wrapped up in my own grief, I would have realized that the story you told on the first night we met was indeed your own. I wonder if you would answer one or two questions for me, and then I will answer as many of yours as I can."

Juilene glanced from Lona to Cariad. He was watching her carefully, a concerned look on his face, as though he feared she might refuse. He looked suddenly older than she had ever seen him look before, so that he seemed much older than she. Her new sense of caution tugged at her, but another sense, an instinctive trust of both of these people, told her she was among friends. "As you will it, I obey, my lady."

Lona nodded. "Thank you. I know you've learned in the last months not to trust anyone. And I will tell you as much as I can, I promise. But first, what was the name of the thurge who put this spell upon you?"

"His name is Lindos. Cariad was there last night when we heard that he has been made the new Over-Thurge of Sylyria." Juilene took a deep breath. Such a development could not bode well for her family.

"I'll send a messenger—a discreet messenger—to Sylyria this day to find out what we can about your family," Lona said. "But tell me, if you can, what happened when Lindos laid this spell upon you? What happened—what words did he speak? Can you remember?"

Juilene closed her eyes and drew another deep breath, clenching her hands into a tight ball. There was nothing she would care to remember less.

"Try to tell us what you can," Cariad murmured, and in the sound of his voice, Juilene found the courage to confront her memories.

"I was in his bedchamber—trying to get away from him. And I felt something—a force—like a wind, but without air—do you know what I mean?" She looked from Lona to Cariad and back. They nodded. "And I remember feeling—trapped . . ." Her voice trailed off.

"Was it night?" Lona leaned forward.

Juilene thought, then shook her head. "No—it was close to dawn, I think—yes, it must have been, because when I left the keep and made my way home, it was not so dark as it had been."

Lona glanced at Cariad and the two of them nodded. "I know this is painful, my dear, but you must try to remember as much as you possibly can. Was there fire, water, crystals—anything?"

"His bed—the hangings—they were all woven with gems—beautiful stones, in truth, I have never seen the like. It was like a web of such beautiful light—there was a fire in the hearth, and the power—the magic—as it went through me—it felt piercing me—" She broke off and bit her lip.

"Was there anything or anyone else in the room?" Lona asked gently.

Juilene swallowed hard. "There were these horrible creatures—with big eyes and skinny legs and arms—"

"Thurge sprites," Lona said, her lip curling in disgust.

"And Arimond was there. Or his body."

"Your betrothed?"

Juilene lowered her head and stared at her hands. "I remember how the blood trickled down his face. Slow, slow drops, like tears. It was as if he wept."

Lona made a little noise, and Juilene looked up. She glanced at Cariad. "What is it?"

His face was grim. "Corpses don't bleed."

Juilene stared back at him. "You mean—Arimond wasn't dead?"

Lona rose and paced the room. She glanced up at the walls, at the ceiling, as though she feared that someone might be hiding in the recesses of the room. "Not dead then. Yet." She paced back and forth, her hands clenching and unclenching. "But there was nothing you could have done for him. Nothing at all. You must not think you were responsible for his death."

Juilene looked at Cariad, her eyes filling with tears. She closed her eyes. "Don't cry," he whispered. "Truly, there was nothing you could do."

She drew a deep breath and forced herself to stay composed. She looked at Lona. "But, why?"

Lona grimaced. "Have you ever heard of wild magic, child?"

"Wild magic?" Juilene shook her head. "No. I don't know very much about magic at all."

"In the beginning, when the world was new, you know that the thurges who lived upon the land used the magic as they willed, that there were no restrictions upon them, and they lived as they pleased."

"Yes, of course," answered Juilene. Did the woman think she had never heard the legends? "And I know that that is the reason for the incarnation of the goddess—that she came to earth and lived among us, and her legacy is the Covenant."

"The Covenant is more than simply an agreement between the goddess and the people. The Covenant binds the magic, caused it to be bound to the world, to certain restrictions. It is no simple thing to use the magic, you know that. And it is those restrictions which make the magic so difficult to use."

"But what has this to do with me, and Lindos, and the way Arimond died?"

"Ever since the beginning of the Covenant, there have been those thurges who have sought to unbind the magic, to undo the restrictions of the goddess, to find a way to access the wild magic, the magic which some say exists just outside the material world, which others say is the same magic, only unbound by the terms of the Covenant. Whichever it is, it doesn't matter. For if a thurge were to access such power, it would mean that he or she could use the magic as he or she wished, with no restrictions, no concern or thought for the proper order of things, no fear that anything could go wrong. In short, he or she would have all the power of those ancient thurges, before the Covenant."

Juilene stared up at Lona. "You mean you think Lindos is one of those?"

She laughed shortly. "I know Lindos is one. As is my husband. And his sister, Rihana—young as she is, the magic is even stronger in her than it is in him. Believe me, it isn't brotherly love that keeps him dancing attendance upon her. And the fact that Lindos was able to curse you as effectively as he did—it makes me fear—" She stopped speaking abruptly, as though she could not stand to give voice to the words.

"Lindos may have discovered a way to use this power," finished Cariad softly. "His position, his rapid rise to power in Sylyria—such signs bode ill."

"But—but what makes you think such a thing? Lindos is known as a thurge of great promise—what makes you think that he could have this—wild magic, as you call it?"

Lona sighed and sat heavily in her chair. "There are—certain natural boundaries between things, you understand—day and night, cold and hot, wet and dry—do you understand?"

Juilene nodded.

"And the Covenant binds the magic to the natural order—makes it impossible to work the certain forms of magic except at certain times, you understand? But the Covenant is weakest when it has to deal with those places which are not quite one thing, not quite another—the time of day between day and night, for example, when the one is fading into the other, or at the changes of the moon, at the changes of the season—this happened at Festival time, did it not?"

Juilene nodded again. "At the very beginning."

"That is what I feared. At the time of year, at the time of day, with a man who was not quite dead, though passed the point of saving—within a web of precious stones, woven into a deliberate pattern, I have no doubt—do you see, my dear? Lindos used this power most effectively—have you ever heard of such a thing being done before? Diago saw there was something about you. And I saw it, too, but I was tired, so weary, I took little notice of it. The magic binding you is tangible, visible, to the right eyes, and yet it has a different quality—" Lona paused and looked away. "And I believe Diago knew it, and that's why he went to Rihana." She broke off once more. "If only we were in Eld."

"Eld?" Juilene echoed. "I was on my way to Eld when I stopped at the inn."

Lona and Cariad both stared at her. "Why?"

Juilene clasped her hands loosely before her. "Why do you wish us in Eld, lady?"

Lona exchanged a glance with Cariad. "She's earned a few answers of her own, I think." She smiled and drew a deep breath. "I am a native of that city. I came here only a few years ago, upon my marriage to Thane Diago. My father was one of the Guardians of the Ancients who sleep in that city—do you know the legend?"

Juilene shook her head. Cariad had moved so close to her she could see the pulse beat in the hollow of his throat. Her own heart beat faster. Lona seemed to take no notice.

"Eld is not like any other city in the League—it was the

goddess's own city, and there is still a certain holy sense to the city—have you ever been there?"

Juilene shook her head again.

"But it is not merely the presence of the goddess so long ago which makes Eld a holy city, a blessed place. Surely you have heard of the Twelve Sleepers?"

Juilene stole another peek at Cariad. She realized with a sinking sensation that it was the spell and her story that held his fascination. She should have know better than to think he could have been interested in her. He was absorbed in Lona's story. And yet, the things Lona spoke of—wild magic, Twelve Sleepers, they were the stuff of legend and dreams—no one took such tales seriously. Did they? "Of-of course I have," she stammered. "But no one thinks such things are true. Do they?"

Lona smiled, gently, pityingly. "In some places they still do. Of course. But it isn't your fault you don't know that, child. Our age has degenerated sadly." She sighed, and for a long moment gazed into the fire in the hearth, as though she would find comfort in the flames. "Of course the Twelve are real. My father was one of the Guardians."

Juilene stared at the woman. So much, so quickly. Her head was spinning with everything she had been told. The legends said that Twelve of the original Council—six thurges and six thanes—slept beneath the mountains of Eld, deep in rock caverns carved when the Covenant was new. They slept until the dawn of the New Covenant, when they would once again be needed. But they were only twelve, and fourteen were needed to make the Council complete, and so it was said that a new thane and a new thurge would complete the number, and the harp that had belonged to the goddess had to be played, in order to make the Sleepers awake. "You have seen the place where the Sleepers lie?"

Lona nodded. "I have never seen the Sleepers. But I have seen their crypts."

Juilene looked at Cariad. "But what has this to do with me, or you, or any of us? What has this to do with Lindos, or your husband, or his sister? What has this to do with the troubles in Sylyria?"

"War in Sylyria," Cariad corrected her softly. "It will soon be war between thane and thurge in Sylyria, if it isn't already. I think the rumors that the King has gone into exile are likely to be more than rumors. And then it will only be a matter of time before it spreads over the mountains into Khardroon. Already Gravenhage is affected, as is Albanall. Unless the Council and Conclave intervene, there will be war throughout the League by spring. And if Lindos does indeed have the use of the wild magic—" He gazed into the fire. "Perhaps it can be changed."

Lona frowned. "Hush, Cariad. Enough."

Juilene looked from one to the other. "But isn't there anything that can be done?"

Cariad rose to his feet. "There is a chance, perhaps, not much of one, but a chance. Now that we know, or suspect that Lindos may have the wild magic, we can alert the High Thane of the Council, who is the King of Gravenhage. He must be told. Before, we had no evidence, only suspicion that such was the case. But now—"

"Before what?" asked Juilene, confused.

"Hush," said Lona, even more emphatically. "Before doesn't matter, Cariad. We can send him a message."

"King Mark is—is sickly." Cariad stared into the fire, an unreadable expression on his face. "He leaves much of the business of the Council to his Queen."

"Mirta is a fine woman," said Lona softly. Their eyes met in a long look Juilene did not understand.

"Then—then surely you must send a message to the Queen and tell her," said Juilene. "Surely everyone must know all this as soon as possible."

Lona and Cariad nodded and sighed in unison. "It's easier said than done," said Cariad. "Far easier."

"Juilene," said Lona, after a silence, "why were you going to Eld?"

"I—I had met an old songsayer upon the road that day. I had lost my harp, and truly, I was in even more distress than when you met me. I was hungry and tired, and I hadn't slept. I had stopped beside a river, and there the old woman found me. She gave me her harp, and told me to take the road to Eld."

Lona gasped. "Who was this old woman? What did she look like? What else did she tell you?"

Juilene shrugged. "She was very old and close to death. In fact, she died beneath the trees, before I took the harp. She said the goddess was calling to her and she had no more need of the harp. And when I would have refused to take it, she said that the harp had need of me. But, I just thought that was the raving of an old woman."

Lona stared. "What—what does this harp look like, child?"

"It's old," Juilene went on. "You saw it that night when you were at the inn. And Cariad has seen it every night he's been there. It's ancient—the carvings are nearly erased, but it plays beautifully." She glanced from one to the other. "What is it?"

Lona gripped the arms of her chair with a white-knuckled hand. "And where is the harp now?"

"At—at the inn," Juilene answered. "Why?"

"And the old woman told you to take the harp to Eld?"

"No, not exactly. She told me to take the road to Eld. And to keep the harp safe. That it was her oldest friend in all the world—why? What has an old harp to do with this?"

"Dramue's harp is lost," whispered Lona. "And the legend says it will return to Eld when it is needed. A search went on for hundreds of years, but finally it was abandoned. It was thought that the harp was destroyed."

Juilene looked at Cariad and then back at Lona. "You think the harp the old woman gave me is the lost harp? The goddess's harp?" She gave a short laugh of disbelief. "That hardly seems possible."

Before Lona or Cariad could reply, there was a knock on the door. "Enter," called Lona.

The door swung open on well-oiled hinges, and a manservant bowed, holding out a parchment packet. "A message just arrived for you, my lady."

Cariad retrieved the letter and handed it to Lona. The servant bowed once again and disappeared down the corridor. "Shall we leave you to your reading, lady?"

"No, no," said Lona, looking up from the letter with a white face and thin lips. "It's from Diago. He and Rihana will be here by nightfall tomorrow."

Cariad glanced at Juilene. "Then we better see about getting a messenger out today. Two messengers. One to Sylyria, and the other—"

"To Queen Mirta in Gravenhage," said Lona. "We have to do something, before Lindos and his wild magic destroys everything." Without another word, she rose and swept from the room.

Cariad held out his hand to Juilene. "Come, let me see you back to the inn. It will be safer for you there, now that Diago is on his way home. It's entirely possible he could be here by nightfall tonight. I don't trust a word that—" He checked himself just in time. "I don't trust him at all."

Juilene laid her hand in his, and he closed his over it, his smooth callused palm wrapping around her smaller fingers gently. "Thank you for your concern for my family and for everything you've done for me." The words sounded pitifully inadequate.

He smiled down at her, and he did not release her hand.

"You've done more for me, my lady, than ever I can tell you. I have more to thank you for, believe me."

"I don't understand what you mean."

For a moment, he looked as though he would say something, and then he flushed. "I know," he said, looking away. "I know."

"Cariad," she began, wishing she knew the right words to break through his reserve, "you listened to my story. I will listen to yours, when you are ready to tell me."

He drew a deep breath. "You deserve the truth, lady."

She gazed up at him, puzzled. "Have you lied to me, Cariad?"

"No." He shook his head. "But the truth—the truth is more complicated than you could even begin to imagine." He looked away, and once again he looked as though he wanted to speak.

"Cariad," she said softly, nearly a whisper. "Let it wait. You'll know when the time is right. It isn't anything—bad, is it?"

He smiled then, a sad smile that made the corners of his mouth lift, even while his eyes seemed to darken. "I'll let you be the judge, Juilene. Now, come. I don't think you should be here when Diago returns."

She waited until they were on horseback, trotting down the rutted road on the way back to the inn. The road to Eld, she reflected. She lifted her head and stared off at the blue mountain peaks, barely visible on the horizon. "Cariad," she began, a little uncertainly.

He visibly roused himself from his own thoughts. "My lady?" The title fell naturally from his lips, and once again Juilene wondered who and what he was.

"What does my harp have to do with any of this? Why was Lona so interested in it?"

Cariad looked grave. "Three things are necessary to awaken the Twelve, it is said, and those are a thane, a thurge, and the harp of Dramue. Only the true harp will awaken the Sleepers."

"What will happen if the Sleepers don't wake?"

Cariad sighed. "You test me, lady. I wish I understood such things better than I do. I'm not sure anyone knows the answer. But there are those who say that if the Twelve do not awaken, then the Covenant shall end, and the magic shall be unbound, and wild magic will be loosed once more upon the world. And when I think of the horrors which are with us still, after the last Age of Anarchy, I shudder to think what could happen next."

Chaper Eleven

❧

Cariad bid her a quiet farewell, promising to return that evening. With a curiously heavy heart, and a deep sense of foreboding, Juilene went to her room and unwrapped the harp. Could it even be possible that such a thing could once have belonged to the goddess herself?

The old wood shone with a low luster in the glow of the late winter sun. Deep nicks, gouges, and scars marred the surface of the wood, and it was impossible to guess what had been carved deliberately as part of a pattern, and what the years had carved at random. A shaft of light fell across the brass strings, dull with age and use, and she gently touched them with the very tips of her fingers. The harp quivered of its own volition, and Juilene drew back as if she had been stung. How could such a thing have survived so relatively intact through thousands of years?

But trees did, and rivers, said a voice in her mind. The land itself was ageless. There were things that lasted almost as long. And if Dramue herself had played upon this harp, who could say that it had not acquired some vestige of her divinity?

Juilene sighed and placed the harp upon its makeshift stand. She glanced at the window. The sun was low in the sky; soon it would be time for her to go down to the common room and play. More than a few had said there was magic in her harp. Maybe they were more correct than they had ever guessed.

She had just seated herself beside the hearth when a girl's voice, high-pitched and imperious, made her look up from tuning the harp. A man's lower voice answered her, although the words of both were indistinguishable. She glanced out the window and saw the large train of horses and men milling in the inn yard. With a pang, she recognized the colors that Cariad wore. The door slammed open with a loud bang, and a slight woman strode into the room, the upper half of her face obscured by the black hood trimmed in amond fur. Her entire cloak was made of the priceless material, and it gleamed in the inn's dim light. Even from across the room, Juilene recognized the quality of the garment.

The woman swept the hood off her face, and her dark hair tumbled about her shoulders, black and lustrous as the fur. Juilene was startled. The girl was young, younger than Juilene, for she could not be more than fourteen or fifteen years old at the most. But her obvious youth was at odds with the imperious glance with which she swept the inn. She looked over her shoulder and called outside, "Well, Diago, where's that innkeeper friend of yours?"

His answer was lost beneath the thrum of the harp, but the girl laughed at his reply. Her dark eyes took in every detail of the inn. She strolled to a table in the center of the room. She placed what looked like a very small gilded cage upon it. Something moved inside the cage, and startled, Juilene's attention was diverted.

Her fingers stumbled and the discordant note echoed to the rafters. The thing in the cage shrieked, and Juilene jumped. The girl's gaze fell upon Juilene. A chill of revulsion ran down her spine as the girl's black eyes lingered on her face. This must be Diago's sister, Rihana. And looking at her, Juilene understood why Lona was so unhappy.

"Well, well," said the girl, her eyes boring into Juilene's, "you must be the 'sayer my brother speaks of so often. You have no idea how eager I have been to meet you."

"I—I say the songs the goddess sends," Juilene managed, and she gripped the harp in both hands.

"Yes." Rihana smiled. "I'm sure you do." She squinted a little and cocked her head, as though trying to see something better. "Let's hope she sends you better ones than she did the last one," said Rihana. "There's nothing worse than a 'sayer who can't sing. Personally, I think there's only one thing that ought to be done with them. Would you like to meet my pet?" She picked up the cage, and for a moment, Juilene thought she might thrust it into her face. She fought not to recoil visibly.

But at that moment, Thane Diago strode into the room, his dark cloak billowing around his wide shoulders, his face heavily bearded. He wore a curved dagger in his belt, and Juilene bit down hard on her lip. It took all her self-control not to run from the room.

Diago glanced in his sister's direction, and recognized Juilene. "Ah, how happy I am to see you're still in residence, little songsayer." He grinned, and his teeth looked even whiter than Juilene remembered against the black beard. "I've told my sister so much about you, she's been most eager to make your acquaintance. You will give us a song or two?"

"It will be my pleasure, my thane," Juilene said. She lowered her eyes. She shuddered to think what this man could have told his sister. Nausea roiled in the pit of her stomach as the two of them peered down at her. If the two of them did not stand back, she was afraid she would vomit into the hearth. Thankfully, the door to the upper floors behind the bar swept open and Elizondo stumbled out, his cheeks red in his pasty face, his eyes huge.

"My-my thane!" he stammered. "We were not expecting you—this is truly an undeserved honor—"

"Be quiet," Diago said, snapping his fingers. "My sister—you remember my sister, Rihana, don't you, Elizondo? Of course you do. Rihana had a strong desire for a decent meal before we descended upon the castle where my beloved wife keeps such pecuniary splendor. Can you accommodate us, or no?"

"But of course, my thane, of course." Elizondo paused long enough to wipe his sleeve across his broad brow and turned to call up the steps. "Lem! Lemuel! Come down—we've guests!" Elizondo sidled around the bar. He bounded over to Rihana, who had shrugged off her cloak and now stood beside the table in the center of the room, looking amused at Elizondo's obvious discomfort. "My lady, my dearest lady, of course I remember you. Who could forget you? You honor my poor inn like the goddess herself. Sit, please, sit. I'll have something brought out immediately—the best I have, what would you prefer?"

Rihana laughed in his face, and Juilene cringed. She saw Diago's lip curl with scorn, and he cuffed the innkeeper lightly on the side of the head. "Off with you, man. Bring us wine—we'll know if it's the best you've got or not."

Elizondo scuttled off, his robes flying. Lem ducked into the bar, his shirt barely laced. As Diago's men streamed through the front door, maidservants entered from the kitchen, bearing trays of cheese and bread and late winter

fruits. Juilene struck a few tentative notes upon the harp.
Rihana leaned back in her chair and slowly stripped her
black leather gloves off her long white hands. As the babble of voices rose higher, Juilene lowered her head and
softly played, losing herself in her music.

An hour might have passed, or two. More food than she
had thought the kitchens could contain was brought in and
out in a steady stream of platters, which Diago and Rihana
picked over daintily, searching out the choicest morsels.
Wine and ale and mead flowed like rivers from the casks
beneath the bar, and bottles of stronger liquor were passed
among the company. Her music was lost in the general
noise, but Juilene only played more softly, her hair falling
across her face in a heavy curtain. Every time she glanced
at Diago, her blood froze with the memory of the night of
shame and humiliation. The maidservants moved among
the men, teasing and laughing, and the company grew
more raucous. And in the center of it all, Diago and Rihana
sat, calm as if they sat in private on a calm summer day, instead of in the midst of a crowded smoky inn.

The strings of the harp resonated and quivered beneath
her fingers, and she could feel the vibration of the strings
in the whole frame of the harp. The music seemed to
course through her thighs, down her legs, and permeated
her whole body. She lifted her face. There was something
about the music, something about playing that brought her
out and away and into another place entirely. Nothing mattered when she played this harp, nothing at all, and her fingers moved almost of their own accord over the gleaming
brass, finding chords and melodies and harmonies she
would have said she never knew. The music swelled, over
the roar of the men, the shrieks and giggles of the maids.
She threw her head back and closed her eyes, oblivious to
everything but the spell the music wove around her.

Fingers in her hair and a rough voice in her ear shocked

her out of her spell. "Well played, little songsayer." Her eyes flew open and she stared into Diago's face. "You have a magic all your own, don't you?" He chuckled at her distress.

"Please," she whispered. "Let me go."

With a smile, he released her, but not before he gave the strand of hair he held a vicious twist. "Let you go?" he whispered, so only she could hear, his mouth so close she could smell the heavy odor of spices on his breath. "You intrigue me far too much, little sister. I can see you still wear Lindos's mark upon you—and no ordinary mark it is, is it? One of these nights, very soon, I'll come for you. And then you will tell me all about this Lindos and his magic, and then, as your reward, of course, I'll take you and make you mine."

Juilene drew back, holding her harp between them, like a shield. "No, my thane," she said. "You may think what you will, and you may do what you will, as well, but I do not belong to you, nor will I ever."

He laughed then, even as his face darkened. Juilene glanced over his shoulder. Rihana was watching with an expression that bordered somewhere between amusement and intense curiosity, her chin propped against her hand. He leaned closer once more. "And if I took you here, who would help you, do you think? If I bent you over a stool and had my way, do you think any would rush to your aid? That fat windbag of an innkeeper? The empty bladder of a barkeep? Any of the men you see? Why, it would be my wager they'd only cheer me on and line up to take their turn with you when I'd had my fill."

Juilene pulled back, the rounded back of the chair holding her captive. "Leave me alone," she hissed.

Diago chuckled. "Or what? Leave you alone or what?"

"Or feel my steel on your neck, Diago," said Cariad. He

stood directly behind the thane, his hand on the dagger in his belt.

Rihana yawned as Diago slowly straightened and turned. "Well, well, little cock. Didn't take you long to ride from the keep, did it? Your mistress let you out long enough to find a bitch to keep you tame?"

Cariad said nothing, but his back went rigid and his face paled.

"You've been itching to give me a taste of your steel ever since I took your miserable hide into my service, haven't you?" Diago went on. "Kin to my wife, she says. You're no more her kin than you are mine, you miserable half-bred bastard."

Cariad's face flamed, but his hand remained steady and otherwise he did not move. "Call me what you like. Even your writ only runs so far, my thane."

A silence was falling over the common room, the men drawing back and turning to watch, the maids shrinking back near the bar and the kitchen doors. Lem paused in his polishing, watching the two men with narrowed eyes, and Elizondo burst through the kitchen door, hands raised, robes flying. "Gentlemen, gentlemen, please, please—there are no enemies here. You wear the same colors—please, I beg—"

"Quiet, fool." Diago spat the words at Elizondo, but his eyes did not leave Cariad's face. "Shall we see what you are made of, princeling?"

Juilene gasped. Although Diago was older, he was taller and broader than Cariad, and while Cariad was obviously in fighting condition, there was no guarantee that he would be the winner in a fight with Diago. "Cariad," she cried, "don't—"

"Hush, Juilene," he said, his face set and grim. "Let me do this."

Diago snapped his fingers. "Torches, my good

innkeeper. Torches in the yard. I want to see how much blood this young one leaks when I run him through." He left the room with a swagger and an another bow. Rihana raised her eyebrow, shaking her head with suppressed laughter, and followed him outside.

Juilene set the harp aside and rose to her feet. "Are you mad, Cariad? You mustn't raise your hand to him—"

He caught her to him and held her close. "Get your cloak, your harp, and anything else you might want to take. The little mare is saddled and waiting for you in the stables. Lona wants us to leave. It's not safe for either one of us here. I'll explain more on the road."

"But what about Diago? What do you mean to do here? He'll kill you if he can—"

He touched her nose, and smiled almost gaily. "If," he said, raising his eyebrows. "I'll fight him just long enough to distract him and then I'll catch up to you. Let him think I'm a coward and turned tail. It's more important we get away."

"What of Lona?" she whispered, still not believing what he told her. "Will you leave her?"

Cariad looked grim once more. "You know it isn't my choice to leave her, lady, at the mercy of that—that bastard scum. But she has her ways of handling Diago—and it's more important that we—that you—get away." He glanced over his shoulder. Loud shouts and catcalls came from the inn yard. "There's no more time, now. I'll explain everything I can once we're on the road. Wait for me beneath the trees at the second crossroads. I won't be far behind." He brushed a stray curl off her face with the back of a gloved hand.

"Cariad—" she said when he was halfway across the room. "Please be careful. Don't make Arimond's mistake."

He turned back and his smile was gallant but his eyes were rueful. "Have no fear, my lady. I fight to save a life, not to take one." He swept her a low bow, turned on his heel, and disappeared out the door.

A low wind sighed through the branches of the uster trees as Juilene reined the little mare to a halt at the center of the crossroads. The leaves whispered and rustled in the breeze and the animal whickered and stamped its foot. "I know," murmured Juilene, patting its neck. "I'm not used to being out at this hour, either." She slid to the ground and looked back over her shoulder. Pray the goddess Cariad was safe. She tried not to think about being here, in the dark, out in the open, all alone. What would she do if he didn't come? If, despite his brave words, Diago killed him, or at the least, seriously injured him?

Cariad had implied that it wasn't safe for her to stay at the inn, now that Diago and his sister had come. And he seemed to imply that she would be better off somewhere else—somewhere he would take her—but where? Where should she go? The road to Eld, a voice seemed to echo in her mind as the wind sighed once more through the trees. She raised her face to the star-studded sky. A thousand points of light flickered, inscrutable as the will of the goddess. Dramue, protect Cariad, she prayed. Protect us both.

The little mare stamped once more and tossed her head. "Yes, yes," Juilene said, "I know, I know." She led the horse to the little stand of trees, and tied it to one of the low-hanging branches. With some difficulty, she managed to pull one of the packs off the animal's back. She fumbled with the straps until it opened. She probed the inside. Lumps of various sizes, indistinguishable in the dark, met her fingers, and finally she found what she was searching for: flint and tinder. She pulled it out of the pack, set it on the ground, and searched the immediate area for wood to make a fire. As she was gathering a few dry twigs and one heavier log, she heard the mare scream. She rushed back to the trees. The horse was shaking its head from side to side, and neighing. Small, dark objects clustered around its eyes, and with a cry, Juilene rushed forward. She swung a long twig, and the things buzzed and lifted away.

She patted the horse's nose to calm it and looked around fearfully. Something whined around her own head and with a cry she swung her arm blindly. Her hand connected with something, and the creature fell, shrieking, to the ground. In the starlight, she could barely make out a dark, cylindrical body and a pinkish round head. She shuddered. Mantlings. They were nocturnal creatures; a fire would keep them away.

Her hands shook as she piled the wood as quickly as she could and struck a spark with the flint. She raised her head in the direction of the inn as the flames leaped into life. Goddess, protect him, she thought. Please let Cariad be all right.

As if in answer to her prayers, the low drum of a horse's hooves broke the silence. The little mare knickered softly and tossed her head in the direction of the sound. Let that be Cariad, she prayed. The sound grew louder, and a dark shape emerged over the rise of the hill. The horse and rider cantered to a stop and the rider swung out of the saddle.

"Juilene!"

She rose with a little cry and held out her hands unthinkingly. He wrapped his arms around her and pulled her close to him, and for a long moment, they stood together. She heard the beating of his heart, her nostrils full of his distinctive scent. Finally she pulled away, a little awkwardly. The embrace had seemed so natural, and yet, she reminded herself, this man was little more than a stranger.

He smiled down at her, almost shyly, as the light of the fitful fire played across his face, a face she saw was bloody.

"You're hurt!" she cried.

"It's nothing." He waved one hand impatiently and turned away. "I'll be fine. Let's get this fire going, and then we can talk."

She busied herself with wood and brush, and finally, when the flames leaped high in the dark, and both horses were tethered securely just inside the perimeter of light, she sank to the ground. He seated himself beside her, not quite close enough to touch her, but close enough for her to see the thin line of blood that snaked across his forehead and down the side of his face.

"You should let me take a look at that," she said once more.

"Later," he said. "After we've talked." He tore open a package from one of the packs and held out a hunk of cheese. "Hungry?"

Juilene hesitated. She fumbled in the bodice of her dress and held out a brass coin. "Here."

"What's that?"

"The curse hasn't been lifted," she said. "Please, take this. I don't want to take any chances."

He opened his mouth as though he would protest, seemed to think better of it, and pocketed the coin. "Now, will you eat?"

She took the cheese and broke off a piece. "Now, will you talk?"

He smiled. "As you will it, I obey. Lona had the feeling that there was more to Diago's sudden homecoming than he wanted anyone to think. And the fact that he was bringing Rihana made her realize that the two of them might have some plans involving you. And if the harp you carry is Dramue's—" He broke off and started again. "I wish we could have gotten you away from the inn before Diago saw you once again. But—" He paused and stared into the fire. "The fact that he stopped at the inn, so that Rihana could get a look at you—"

"At me," she echoed. "Why would they do that?"

Cariad leaned forward. "I've told you—Lona's told you. The magic which binds you has a different look to it, apparently. Each thurge leaves a certain—signature—I suppose, and there is something uniquely different about yours. Do you remember the thurge in the inn the other night? Not the old man from Sylyria—the one who sat in the shadows and said he awaited Diago's homecoming? He arrived at the keep this afternoon. Lona believes Diago had him at the inn spying on you. Anyway, Lona thinks we should take the harp to Eld and let the Guardians have a look at it. That gets you out of Diago's way, and prevents both of them from trying to destroy the harp."

"They would destroy the harp so that it can't be played at the end of the millennium?"

"Exactly," said Cariad. "The last thing Diago and Rihana or anyone who is trying to unbind the magic would want is for the Sleepers to awake, and for a new Covenant to be made. If that happens, all their questing for the wild magic will be for nothing. But I don't think Diago quite realizes what he nearly had—or what you might have—and so, hopefully, we won't be followed into Eld."

"You think he'll follow us?"

"I think Diago is capable of doing anything in pursuit of his goal. Lona believes that he and Rihana were going to try and untangle the magic which binds you, in hopes of deciphering exactly what the spell was Lindos put on you."

"Why not ask Lindos?"

"The last thing a thurge in possession of the wild magic would do is tell another thurge. Especially one who seems as bent on power as Lindos. If that were the case, all the thurges might rise up against him or, as Diago plans, challenge him as individuals. No, Juilene, it's better that you get as far away from Diago as possible. He would think nothing of using you—not for pleasure—but to study the magic."

"I suppose that wouldn't be so bad," she murmured.

Cariad stared at her in horror. "You don't know, do you?"

"Don't know what?"

"I could tell you stories—" He gazed into the flames. "In—in my country," he began awkwardly, pausing between the words, "the thurge—the High Thurge—" He broke off. "Magic is used to torture people. Even to kill. And it is not easy or clean, to watch a man die by magic."

Juilene stared at him in horror. There was so much she wanted to ask him, so many things she wanted to know about this mysterious country he alluded to from time to time. "What kind of thurges are these?"

He shook his head. "Evil men and women. But that is of no matter now. What does matter is we must find a way across the wilderness and over the mountains into Eld. And at this time of year, that isn't going to be easy."

"Do you think Diago will come after us?"

"I want to hope not. But that's not what I believe." He poked at the fire with a long stick and a log split into a shower of sparks. "Yes, we'll have to be careful. The wilderness is not an easy place to cross—there are all sorts of things which live there—mantlings, dwarf dragons—all kinds of dangers. But if we take the roads, that's the first place Diago is going to send men looking, and we can't afford to let him capture us."

"Us?" Juilene cocked her head. "Why do you say, us, as if we are somehow in the same situation?"

Cariad looked grim. "Because we are, lady. There is a spell binding me, as well, although I carry a glamour to shield me from the eyes of prying thurges. But the glamour is wearing thin, and under the scrutiny of two thurges, such as Rihana and Diago, who are deliberately looking for the magic, I am afraid I would stand out like a beacon in the night, even as you do."

"What sort of spell?" Juilene frowned.

"A dangerous spell, and a powerful one. Don't worry, it carries no threat to you, or to anyone around me, but the marks of the magic are upon me, as surely as they are upon you. And I dare not reveal them to anyone, especially to a thurge like Diago."

Juilene rocked back on her haunches, gathering her knees under her skirts and wrapping her arms around her legs. Who was this man? She looked at Cariad closely, as though some clue to his identity might be evident in his aspect. But in the light of the flickering fire, all she could see was a lean face and high cheekbones, dark brows and a high forehead, with dark, sweat-soaked curls clinging to the bloodstained skin. His eyes were hidden in the shadows, his nose was straight, and his mouth was as carefully chiseled as though some sculptor had traced it out of fine marble. There was an air of sadness about his mouth, she thought, although his shoulders and his back were straight, and he gazed into the fire steadily, as though staring the future in the face. He was very brave, she knew, and yet, it was a very different kind of bravery from Arimond's. Cariad would always think before he acted, and would never act without considering all the consequences. She relaxed as she realized that for the first time in a long time, she felt very safe.

He raised his head, as if he, too, could hear her thoughts, and smiled at her. Their eyes met and held, and Juilene drew a deep breath. She remembered how the gold highlights in his eyes lit up when he smiled and she wished she could make him smile that way at her. Can you so easily forget Arimond, a voice in her mind scolded. Yes, something else echoed, and she dropped her eyes and knew she blushed. Arimond was a boy—but Cariad—her thoughts trailed off into a jumble of confusion.

"You must sleep here tonight," Cariad said, looking around. "No one is going to notice we are gone until tomorrow—you aren't expected to play again until tomorrow night, and Diago won't come looking for me. So we have a little time, and the wilderness is a dangerous place at night—I am not eager to take you there any sooner than I must." He rose to his feet. "Let me get you a blanket."

"What about you? Won't you sleep?"

"Oh, I can manage on an hour or two if I must. Tonight, I'll keep the watch. Believe me when I tell you you will need all the rest you can get in the wilderness."

Silently Juilene watched him retrieve blankets from the back of his horse. She spread them out on the ground beside the fire and lay down, her head pillowed on her arm. Cariad's face was clear in the glow of the flames. She wished he would smile at her, but he only scanned the darkness beyond the fire, staring into some dark and hidden place only he could see.

Chapter Twelve

Cariad woke her before the dawn. The grove was still; the breeze had faded sometime during the night, but the fire still burned steadily, testimony to his careful tending. She sat up and pushed her hair away from her face. He was busy with the packs that he had retrieved from the horses.

"Here." His voice was gruff and Juilene turned to stare at him, wondering why he suddenly sounded so abrupt. He was holding out a bundle of cloth to her. "Put these things on. You'll never make it through the wilderness in that dress, and these soldier's clothes will make it easier for you to ride."

Juilene rose stiffly. Her back was sore, her legs were cramped. She stretched, shivered, and wrapped her arms around herself. "But—but—"

"These things aren't mine, nor Lona's. In Khardroon,

everything a wife has is legally her husband's. So take them. The only one who's likely to suffer is Diago."

Still groggy and disoriented, she took the bundle from Cariad. It was easier to accept what he told her than to argue. Their hands brushed briefly, and she thought she heard the swift intake of his breath. He backed away, pointing.

"You can change behind those trees. Go on—when you come back, we'll eat and be on our way. I want to get as much of a head start as we possibly can."

Obediently, she changed her clothes in the shelter of the thicket. She ripped the silver coins out of the lining of her cloak and stuffed them in the pockets of her breeches. She tied the old cloak into a bundle with the rest of her old clothes. She was tempted to leave it behind, but realized at once it might make a trail for Diago's men to trace. The soldier's clothes were big and baggy, and she had to knot the thin leather belt rather than buckle it, in order to make it fit her waist. But they were warm and well made, and she knew at once that Cariad was right. Riding would be much easier in breeches and tunic, and the thick cloak would serve as shelter from the elements in the day, and an extra blanket at night. She laced the leather riding boots as tightly as she could. They reached over her knees to her thighs, and she blushed to herself in the dark. Not since she was a very little girl had so much been exposed. The leather clung to the curves of her calves. She was glad the light was still too dim for Cariad to see her clearly.

But did it matter, a little voice in her mind whispered. They were about to become far more intimate than she had ever been with any other man in her life. She had never been alone over so long a period of time with any man, nor in such conditions. Even when she had traveled with Eral's company, the presence of Mathy and old Nuala had satisfied her sense of what was proper. But if what Cariad said was true, they went in fear of their lives. What did it matter, if Cariad glimpsed the shape of her legs? The conventions of her birth suddenly seemed silly.

She brushed through the waist-high grass, and found Cariad stirring something in a pot. Two tin cups and spoons were laid out on a flat stone. Whatever was cooking smelled good.

He smiled at her when he saw her, and all traces of his gruffness were gone when he spoke. "Here's breakfast. Come, eat quickly."

"What do you want me to do with these things?" She held up her bundle of clothing.

"Give them to me. We'll get rid of them when we can— I don't want to bring any more with us than we absolutely must, but we can't leave them here."

She handed them over to him without a word, realizing that just a few months ago, she would have been horrified by the idea of handing a man a bundle of clothing containing her undergarments, and worn undergarments at that. What would old Neri have said? She started to push the thought of Neri away, then realized as she sank down near the fire and picked up the mug and spoon that the journey she was embarking upon might very well bring her home. Perhaps the Guardians of Eld could find a way to lift the spell and dispel the curse. They seemed powerful in their own way, not that either Cariad or Lona had spoken of it, but it seemed to her that from everything she had heard, there was great magic in Eld.

Cariad took the bundle. He busied himself with the horses for a few minutes, then disappeared into the same thicket. He reemerged just as she was finishing the porridge. "Ready?" he asked when he saw her scraping her spoon along the sides of the mug.

"Yes." She stood up. He took the cooking things. She felt helpless and unsure. She looked around as he stamped out the fire, covering its traces with brush, and retrieved her blanket. She shook it out well, folded it as tightly as she could, and held it out to him.

"Don't worry," he said, smiling over at her. "I'll teach you how to survive out here soon enough. But right now it's easier and faster for me to do it myself—here, give me the blanket."

In less time than she would have thought possible, he had the camp completely obliterated. He handed her a flask. "Here. This is your ration of water for the day. There's water in the wilderness—we won't die of thirst—but some of the streams are foul, and I don't want to take chances." He nodded. "Let's go."

She slung the strap of the flask over her head as she saw he wore his, and swung into the saddle without assistance. She settled the harp behind her, careful to position it so that it rested against the curve of her back. He said nothing, but nodded approvingly. With a soft cluck to the horses, he flapped his reins. The sky was pale and the first real daylight was soft in the morning sky. "You stay close," he said.

Juilene expected that they would go into the brush. Instead, Cariad started off down the road. After an hour or so, the road branched into a fork. He paused and glanced over his shoulder. She reined her horse beside his. "What's wrong?"

"Nothing," he said. "That's the way into the wilderness." He drew a deep breath. "You have to stay close. The trails are narrow, and the land is treacherous. There's swamp and quicksand, and where the road isn't narrow, there're dangers all around. Believe me, if I thought there was a better way, we'd take it. I don't suppose you have any experience at all with a weapon?"

She pulled her dagger from the sheath she had placed on the belt. "I have this."

"And where did you get that?"

"I—I thought it wise to have one, after Diago. So I

bought it for myself." She raised her chin. Was he laughing at her? "I can use it. I've practiced."

He sighed. "That's better than nothing, though by the time you got a chance to use that, things would be over. Never mind. Come. If my memory serves me, there's high ground about six hours from here. If we can get there, we'll stop and I'll sleep for a couple hours." He flapped the reins and started off.

If, Juilene wondered. If? She glanced down at the ring on her finger. It was glowing a bright blue. What kind of place was he taking her to? She followed as closely as she dared. Soon the road petered out into a track, worn by years of use, and the track diminished into a trail, narrow, but clearly delineated. The trees hung low, drooping with vines and overgrowth, and she shivered. The grey hanging forms looked like ghosts. Although the sun rose, the light remained the same beneath the thick overhanging branches of the trees. The silence was thick. Several times, she thought she heard something, something slithering through the branches, and once or twice, the trees ahead of them shook as though with the force of something traveling through the branches. Cariad didn't hesitate. He pressed on, his mouth set and grim when she glimpsed it, his face resolute. She could see the dark shadows under his eyes and the dark shadows of his beard on his chin. The ground changed beneath the horses' hooves, and soon each step the animals took was accompanied by a sticky squelch of the mud. Cariad held up his hand. They rode more cautiously, ducking the branches, and Juilene swayed from side to side, forced to avoid the tendrils of the vines that hung low and grasping, and seemed to reach out to tangle in her hair.

"Watch out," he said. "See those reddish vines over there—twining around those trees? Those are Parmathian sucker vines—we've got to pick up the pace."

She flapped at the reins. The ground was squelchy and uneven, and she wondered what they would do if one of the horses went lame. Out of the corner of her eye, she saw something dip down, searching the air beside her cheek. With a cry she ducked out of the way and urged her horse on.

The animal responded with a neigh and a grunt. Another vine uncoiled itself from the ground beside the oak, splaying out blindly, just as the horse's leg went by. Juilene shuddered. The vines behaved almost like sensate beings. More and more uncoiled themselves from the trunks of trees. Cariad spoke quietly but urgently from ahead on his horse. "Juilene."

She glanced up. She had been so busy watching the vines from all sides. "Yes?"

"Don't answer me yet . . . but I think we'll have to make a break to the side. I don't like the way these vines are behaving." He glanced back and his face changed. "Behind you!" he shouted.

She ducked, just as a vine snaked out of a tree and narrowly missed tangling in her hair. She screamed and pressed down against the neck of her mare. The animal screamed and reared, and for a horrible moment, Juilene was afraid she would lose her seat. Cariad drew his sword and gathered up the reins of his horse.

"Now!" he cried. He bolted through the trees, and Juilene struggled to regain control of the horse. She clutched the reins in both her fists and pulled as hard as she could. Vines were snaking out from every direction, questing like fingers, seeking to entwine themselves around either her or her horse. She glanced down at the muddy path, where traces of the vines were worming their way through the thick mud, erupting from the ground.

She sucked in a great breath, bent low, and dug her knees into the horse's sides. The little mare leaped forward just as a writhing mass of vines erupted out of the ground where only a moment ago she had been standing. Juilene plunged through the trees, the vines shaking and shuddering in her wake. She felt the very ends of tendrils brush her cheeks and her head, and one twined swiftly around her neck. With a cry, she drew the dagger from the bosom of her tunic and slashed at the thick, hairy tendrils. The mare shuddered and screamed a warning, as a huge, thick vine dropped out of nowhere from a low-hanging tree. The mare reared and by the grace of the goddess alone, Juilene managed to pull the horse around it, and continue through the wood. She could hear Cariad slashing and cursing his way through the trees. More of them seemed to be attracted to him than to her. "Cariad?" she cried when the sounds seemed to fade.

"Ride on," he answered immediately. "I'm all right."

At last, the trees opened out into a swampy fen, and the vines no longer pursued them. Juilene paused on the shores of what looked like a small lake, and looked back over her shoulder. Cariad cantered up when he saw her. "By the goddess," he breathed, "that was close. Are you all right?"

She nodded and hoped he wouldn't notice how she was shaking. She had heard all the stories told about the sucker vines—how victims died slowly and painfully over a period of days and weeks, the life blood and soft tissues sucked out of them. The horses whickered and stamped their feet.

"Forgive me, Juilene. I wouldn't have taken you through there if I had any idea that those things were waiting. Can you go on?" He was looking at her closely, and she smiled bravely back at him. Now was not the time to indulge in any lady-born hysterics.

She brushed back her hair, shuddering at the memory of the hairy touch of the vines. "I'm fine."

He gave her a long assessing look, as though measuring the truth of what she said, and nodded, finally, as though satisfied. "Then come. Let's go on."

She flapped the reins and slowly followed. The terrain was all low, marshy fens from which grew long-leaved swamp weeds, all of fantastic hues of pinks and reds and purples. Here and there, flowers the color of gold and silver seemed to reflect the sun with a light all their own, and more than once, a scent, sweeter than any perfume she had ever smelled, wafted to her nostrils.

"Beautiful, aren't they?" Cariad remarked when the path widened enough for them to ride side by side.

She nodded, speechless, entranced by the colors and the scents. The leaves waved languidly in the gentle breeze, tantalizing as feathers. Touch us, they seemed to say, touch us and feel how soft, how sweet.

"Juilene!"

Cariad's voice made her realize that she was leaning half out of the saddle, dangerously close to the ground.

"Whatever you do, don't touch those things. They're beautiful, but just as deadly as the sucker vines. They just kill more easily." He reached across and shook her hand, as he nodded to the side of one small pool of water.

Juilene blinked. A bloated carcass of some animal lay on its side, insects buzzing and crawling all over it, so it looked as though it still moved. Another lay a few feet away, and she realized the ground all around the weeds was covered with corpses. The odor of the leaves disguised the stink. Nausea rose in her throat.

What kind of a place was this wilderness? she wondered. She remembered the tales of the nursery maids, who used to scare her half out of her mind with their talk of ghosts and hags, and sucker vines and the flowers of sleeping death. Neri had hushed them, and banished them from the nursery, and comforted her by saying good little girls had nothing to worry about. But these things must be the basis of the tales, she thought, and wondered what else the nursery maids might have been right about.

They skirted the pools of silvery water, and Juilene fought over and over again to ride carefully, and not succumb to the seduction of the weeds' scent. At last, the path began to move into higher ground, the higher ground Cariad had spoken of. The track was less muddy, and the trees, while few and far between, offered no cover for Parmathian sucker vines.

Slowly, they wended their way up the track. Juilene could see that they were making for the hills. More than once, Cariad held up his hand and paused, as though listening for something she didn't hear.

Finally, after the fourth or fifth time he had done this, Juilene looked around, and seeing nothing, asked, "What are you listening for?"

"The grimmen," he answered shortly, as though that explained everything.

"The what?"

He looked at her and sighed. "You were very sheltered, weren't you?"

She drew herself up. She had experienced far more in the last few months of her life than she had in all the time before but that didn't mean that she had been sheltered. But, said a little voice in her mind, you know that he is right. Now wasn't the time for ladylike protestations of experience, either. "Yes," she said, finally. "I was. But are you going to tell me what a grimmen is? Or must I discover it the way I have nearly everything else—by blundering into it, unprepared?"

At that he chuckled. "Point scored, my lady. Forgive me. I am no more familiar with this wilderness than you are— I only have a few tales to guide me on, as well as a map given to me by Lona. The grimmen are a race of men—I suppose they were once men, just as you and I. But in the days of chaos, they were altered by the thurges, changed somehow. Like most things which remain from the anarchy, they feed on human flesh and human blood, and they are cunning and more like men in that they use rudimentary weapons and make armor out of whatever they have at hand. They are said to inhabit the deepest fastnesses of the wilderness—I believe that we are still too close to the haunts of men for them to be a danger to us. But our trek will take us close to the lands they are said to haunt, and I think it best that we remain alert."

"But—but how will you know if they approach?" Juilene glanced around nervously. It was becoming clearer and clearer to her that if she had believed that the road to Eld was fraught with peril, it was nothing compared to the dangers they faced within the wilderness. As the goddess wills it, I obey, she murmured, and then wondered what on earth the goddess could have willed for them to find themselves in the midst of such utter danger.

"It's said they make a peculiar whistling sound—they scent out their prey through their snouts, that are so constructed that they make a peculiar and distinctive noise," Cariad explained.

"Have you ever heard it?" She eyed him doubtfully.

"No," he admitted. "But I know what normal noises sound like—if we hear anything suspicious, anything at all, we ride like demons as fast as we can. They have no horses—it will be our one advantage."

Juilene said nothing more. The sun was beginning to fall and the shadows beneath the stubby pines were deepening into dark pools that made her wonder what might lurk beneath them. At last Cariad paused and pointed to a little clearing off the track. "There," he said. "We'll make camp there."

"Will we be safe?" Juilene asked.

He paused a long moment before answering. "As safe as we can be anywhere, lady. It's not to my liking, either, but I must sleep a few hours at least, and so far, it seems that nothing lurks within this wood. When we get deeper into the hills, I won't be quite so sure."

* * *

They made the camp and built a fire, and Cariad cooked a thin gruel over the fire. He yawned and ran one hand over his rough chin as she sipped at it. "Forgive me, lady, but I must sleep." He handed her his dagger, which was longer and thicker than her own. "Call me if anything—and I mean anything disturbs you. I will wake at midnight."

She looked at him doubtfully. "How will you know it's midnight?"

He shrugged and grinned. "It's a trick I have." He stretched out beside the fire, rolled himself in his cloak, and was asleep all in one motion.

Juilene stared at his prone body. She tightened her hands on the tin cup. The horses drowsed and grazed beneath the trees, and the fire leaped up, flickering and burning. She drew her cloak around her shoulders, and unbidden thoughts of Diago intruded.

She shivered and pushed them aside. She wouldn't think about him, she wouldn't. She hugged herself hard, as though thoughts of him would somehow call him to them. The wind blew harder and sighed through the pines. Her head snapped up. Was that a sound, like snuffling she heard? She strained to hear it once more, and heard nothing but the horses nibbling at the graze, and Cariad's soft snores.

She looked at him. His beard was dark on his chin and he looked scruffy and unkempt. Well, did she look—or smell—any better? She smiled grimly to herself. Her fingers itched to touch the curls that clustered at the nape of his neck. His body seemed slight, almost boyish, but the breadth of his shoulders implied great strength. He was so unlike Arimond, she knew, in every way she could think of. With a start, she realized she had not missed Arimond in a long time.

She had thought of her father, and her home and old Neri constantly in the last months, and realized she still thought of them every day. A hundred, thousand things reminded her of what she had lost, and yet, it had been days, or even weeks since she had thought of Arimond. What did that mean? she wondered. Had she not really loved him?

She eyed Cariad, who had risked everything, even his life, to save her, to bring her away from Diago and his sister, who had given her the chance of a better life. He wasn't rich—the knights of great lords were paid an allowance, and she couldn't imagine that Diago was generous to his. The money he had given Elizondo had to have been a large proportion of his funds. And yet, he had never mentioned it, never suggested that she should pay it back. He was brave and generous, and so very very vulnerable, lying there, his mouth relaxed in sleep. He looked so very young.

She shut her eyes and rubbed her hands down her face, trying to fight off the waves of sleepiness that threatened to overwhelm her. Cariad had stayed awake for nearly two full days—couldn't she at least give him a few hours of rest? She yawned and scraped the last of the gruel from the pot. She wasn't hungry but eating gave her something to do.

An errant flame licked out from the side of the pot and burned her finger. She sat back with a little cry and sucked on it, nursing the hurt, and as she watched, the fire seemed to bulge, to grow, and then to shrink. She glanced at Cariad. He lay prone, his eyes shut tight. She opened her mouth to cry out, and instead, felt the air stop in her throat. She narrowed her eyes as a chill went down her spine.

Something was taking form within the depths of the fire, something black and swirling, as though the fire itself was turning dark. A face took shape, and a pair of eyes, lit with the fire's reddish light. Juilene made a little sound, more a whimper than a gasp.

Diago smiled at her, his eyes narrow and glowing. *Little sister . . . there you are . . . running off to Eld? Your knight keeping you safe?* The vision seemed to chuckle, and Juilene bit her fist to keep from crying out. The voice seemed to come from all around her, echoing and reverberating as loudly as a drum, but Cariad slept on and even the horses appeared unaffected. *Run all you please, little sister, run as far and as fast as you can. But we can find you, little sister—your knight thought himself so clever by taking my things, but you see . . . it only gave me a link to find you both . . . it led me right to you . . . oh, it took a bit of work, and will take more . . . but never fear, little sister . . . find you again we will . . . if the grimmen and all the other things which live within the wilderness don't first . . .*

The vision faded out of the flames. Juilene found herself gasping and shaking. Cariad still slept and the horses grazed and the fire only burned tamely within the stone circle Cariad had built. Juilene pinched herself. It was a dream, nothing real. She had nodded off to sleep for the moment, and it was nothing, just some play of her imagination. But even as she tried to deny it, her brain recognized the truth of what she had seen. They were searching for them both, Rihana and Diago, and somehow, Cariad had made a terrible mistake by taking the things to give her from Diago.

She shook her head at Cariad's sleeping body. He was as fallible as Arimond, as likely to make mistakes as Arimond. But would he listen to her, as Arimond would not? She closed her eyes and prayed that Cariad would not be as intractable. She fed the fire and stared at the sky. The stars shone peaceful and serene. She whispered another prayer to the goddess to keep them both safe, and looked down into Cariad's eyes.

"What's wrong," he whispered.

"I saw Diago," she said, even as she wondered how he knew anything had happened.

A question flickered over his face, but he didn't move. "Where?"

"In the fire. I wasn't dreaming."

He sat up with a stretch and a sigh. "I didn't say you were."

"He—he said he would find us again—that there was no escape. He said that the things you took and gave to me made a trail of some sort that allowed him to find us. That he can use it again . . ." Her voice trailed off.

"Damn me for an idiot." Cariad slammed a fist against the ground. "I should have thought of that. Forgive me, Juilene. I've led us into danger—" He broke off and stared at her, as though seeing her for the first time.

"What is it?" she asked.

He gave her a sad smile. "You'll think I'm mad if I tell you."

She made a little gesture.

"I was thinking how beautiful your hair looks in the firelight." He looked sheepish and she couldn't control a giggle, in spite of the desperation of their circumstances.

"You mean, we sit here . . . in the middle of the night, in what must be the most dangerous place in all of the League, a powerful thurge is after us, and all you can think of, is my hair?"

He shrugged. "It was just a thought." Their eyes met across the fire and she smiled at him in spite of the situation.

"Do you have any others? Any that might get us out of this predicament?"

He shook his head. "Not at the moment, lady. Lie down and sleep. The dawn is still a fair ways off, and you need the rest. I'll keep the watch the rest of the night and try to think of some way to throw Diago off our track. Though to tell you the truth, discarding everything and going the rest of the way stark naked is the only thing that occurs to me at the moment."

"It's a little cold for that," she said as she settled herself in her cloak.

"Well," he said, with the same boyish look, "it was just another thought."

Chapter Thirteen

✦

The day dawned grey and overcast. Juilene shivered as they packed and made their way across the winding track, which led higher and higher into the rocky hills. Huge boulders rose on either side, striated with black and silver granite, and a few spindly pines hung by bare roots to the rocks. Once again, Juilene found herself wondering what kind of place the wilderness was. It was a wild place, untamed and raw, and the terrain seemed to change quickly and abruptly. The wind whined around the rocks, an eerie sound like a low mourning howl, and she glanced all around. She fingered the dagger she wore in her belt. It didn't seem like much protection, and here, between the high walls of rock, seemed like a perfect place for an ambush.

As if he heard the echo of her thoughts, Cariad paused

where the trail widened momentarily and handed her another dagger. "Here," he said. "Take this. I don't like the looks of this path—

"Is there another?" Juilene glanced over her shoulder.

"Not that I know of," he said. "And I've no wish to go exploring here, either." He turned and urged his horse on once again.

Juilene followed as closely as she could. The rocks leaned at crazy angles, some were squared, others lay in crumbled heaps. Building blocks, she thought, and with a chill, she realized that that was exactly what these boulders were.

"Cariad," she said, just loud enough for him to turn and glance over his shoulder, "what is this place?"

"The wilderness," he said.

"But—these rocks—these aren't ordinary boulders—"

"Yes," he said, "I know. I think this is the seventh city of the League—the lost city."

A chill went down her back at the name. "Shinqua'Lir?" she whispered. "This is Shinqua'Lir?"

"No one knows for sure," he said. "But it would explain why the wilderness is such a blasted place."

She peered around with morbid fascination. The lost city of Shinqua'Lir was only another legend, told to her by the nursery maids, scoffed at by her parents and Neri. It seemed that so much that her parents told her had been, perhaps not wrong, but at least not right, and that the legends that the nursemaids scared her with as a child were more real than what her parents would have her believe reality was. What sort of a world was this? Why had her parents not told her the truth?

She followed Cariad, lost in her own thoughts. All around her the ruins of a city so old its history had faded into the mists of time lay beneath the shrouded sky. Some even doubted its existence. But the legends said that once,

Shinqua'Lir had been the most beautiful city in all of the Sylyrian League—more beautiful and grand than Sylyria itself. And if that was true, could it be true that the grimmen were the remnants of the people who had once lived in that city?

So lost was she in her thoughts, she was scarcely aware that Cariad had reined his horse and was holding up his hand, listening intently. His face was fixed and grim.

"Cariad?" she whispered.

Before he had a chance to answer, she heard it, too. It was borne by the wind, a curious, low, snuffling sound, as though something was breathing, very near and very hard. And a stench was borne on the wind, so that she gagged and reached for her dagger, even as Cariad dug his heels hard into his horse's sides and cried out, "Ride!"

She dug her heels into the animal's sides and urged the little mare on, and their hoofbeats rang eerily against the rocks and stones, and down the streets of the lost city. She saw movement in the rocks and on the stones, and out of her peripheral vision, she saw squat, roughly human shapes emerge from behind the rocks, clad in rags and armed with rude weapons.

There were hundreds of the things, and Juilene knew that if they were caught, there would be no chance of escape. The things surged over the rocks and onto the track like a living tide. She crouched low on the saddle and urged the horse on. The little animal needed no urging. She had the stench of blood in her nostrils, and her ears were flat against her head as the little mare galloped for her life and Juilene's. The track was full of the things, and more were scrambling up and over and leaping down into the track. Cariad had his sword out, and slashed viciously at the grimmen who reached for them.

She bit down hard on her lips and prayed that the horses wouldn't trip or fall or slip on the rough track. Finally they seemed to have outrun the things. Their legs were clumsy and badly bowed and Juilene realized that that made it hard for the grimmen to pursue their prey.

Finally Cariad reined in his stallion. The little mare was heaving hard, but her nostrils were no longer distended, and she whickered and flung her head as Juilene tugged her to a stop. He looked back the way they had come. "I think we've lost them."

"Are you sure?" Juilene asked. She had no wish to encounter those creatures again.

He held up a hand, and except for the heavy breathing of the horses, there was silence. Juilene heard nothing but the moaning of the wind through the rocks. "Yes," he said at last. "I am. Let's walk for a while—give the horses a chance to rest."

Juilene slid off the mare's back. As her feet touched the ground, she once more felt horribly vulnerable. How could she and Cariad hope to survive if those things attacked them while they were on the ground? But Cariad was already guiding his stallion down the track, and so Juilene hastened after.

The wind blew harder and the shadows up ahead seemed to move of their own accord. So many things seemed to threaten. At every noise, Juilene jumped and turned over her shoulder. A fat drop of rain stung her cheek, and she gasped and clapped a hand against her face. The mare shied and whinnied.

Cariad turned. "Are you all right?"

She managed a weak smile. "Yes. Forgive me. This place disturbs me so—it would seem there's something hiding under every rock."

"Just stay close." He turned away and Juilene glanced down at her ring. In the dull light, it glowed a bright and fiery blue. She cast a quick glance around. Could there be more of those things?

"Cariad?" she whispered

He glanced back at her over his shoulder. "Yes?" There was the barest edge of impatience in his voice.

"My—my ring." She held her hand up and the sapphire blazed in the gloom. "There's danger—"

He opened his mouth and might have said something when a low snuffle came clearly to their ears. Cariad froze, and the blood turned to ice in Juilene's veins. He beckoned noiselessly. They turned down a street at right angles, and he peered right and left. He made a vertical motion and a jerky nod and Juilene understood they were to remount the horses. She swung up into her saddle, and at that moment, ten or twelve grimmen attacked.

The grimmen rushed forward with their crazy, staggering gait, and the horses screamed and reared. Cariad, half in the saddle, was thrown to the ground, and Juilene clung to her seat with all her might. The stench of old blood and sweat and worse reached her nostrils and she gagged. She glimpsed their red, beady eyes, the blaze of the tusks, the yellow teeth dripping with greenish spittle.

"Run!" cried Cariad. "Save yourself and the harp." He drew his sword and backed against the wall as Juilene fought for control of her animal. The things paused long enough to consider rushing Cariad and then Juilene, peering at them expectantly, and in that instant, Cariad swung his sword in a broad arc, and Juilene picked her small dagger from her boot and flung it as hard as she could into the back of the closest grimmen. It fell, howling, and one head rolled onto the ground. The others backed away as Cariad once again swung his broadsword. Juilene slashed at one that reached for her. It fell back, blood spurting from its hairy club-fingered hand.

Cariad's stallion reared and screamed a challenge of its own, knocking two of them down with a blow from its deadly hooves, and Cariad with another double-handed blow lopped an arm off yet another one, and sent a fifth toppling to the ground, blood spurting from his head.

Cariad grabbed at the reins of the stallion, and swung into the saddle. "Now," he cried, "ride!"

A jagged fork of lightning split the dark sky, and the thunder cracked so loudly the mare leaped forward. Juilene gripped the reins so hard, she thought her hands must bleed. They galloped over the rough and winding track as the rain pelted harder and the wind howled through the rocks.

The horses tossed their heads and snorted, and Cariad turned to Juilene. "We've got to look for shelter."

She pulled her cloak over her head and nodded. The horses kept their heads down, and slowly, as the rain fell and slashed at their faces, they made their way up the winding mountain trail. The rocks ended and the trail once more opened up, into a wide track bordered on both sides by scrubby, stunted pines that offered no shelter. Once out of the rocks, the wind howled with renewed vigor.

"Up there—" Cariad cried over the wind. "Come on— we'll try to make the other side of the hill." He turned back, and Juilene saw the blood on his face. The wind slashed the water against their faces in driving sheets. Gasping, Juilene clung to the reins with one hand, while she held her cloak bunched around her face. The water streamed in rivulets down her face, soaking her to the skin, seeping into the collar of her tunic. She was wet to the bone, and she was cold, and the horse slipped and slid in the downpour. "Cariad," she screamed over the howl of the wind, "we can't go on much more."

He turned back and his face was white and stark against the dark cloak. "Up ahead—up here—it looks like a hollow in the rocks." His voice echoed eerily in the wind, and Juilene shivered. What if more of those things were hiding? A gust of wind and a wash of rain ended all thoughts about that.

Stumbling and sliding, the horse followed Cariad into the shelter. Juilene slid off the saddle, and stood for a moment as water trickled down her back and dripped from her clothes. Everything she wore was soaked, the mare streamed with water. Puddles formed quickly at their feet. She saw that this was no mere outcropping in the stone. It was a cave, and the back of it was lost in the blackness. She wondered if anything else was there.

Cariad was peering into the dark with a frown. She peered over his shoulder, trying to see into the darkness. Nothing moved or stirred, and finally Cariad turned back with a shrug. "I think it's all right. It looks like a fine place for a nest of dwarf dragons, but I don't see any signs of them at all." He heaved a deep sigh, and glanced once more over his shoulder. "I don't like how far back that cave seems to go—goddess only knows what might be hiding back there. But we'll build a fire—that ought to keep most creatures at bay, at least until we can escape." He nodded toward her hand. "What about that ring of yours?"

Juilene glanced at her hand. The sapphire was dark. "Nothing. At least not now."

"Good. Then let's build a fire and wait out this storm. We can't go any farther in weather like this."

"But with what?" asked Juilene. The floor of the cave was smooth sand. "What will we build a fire with?"

Cariad spread his hands and looked annoyed. He looked around. "With—with that." He pointed to a low pile of firewood, neatly cut into uniform logs nearly hidden in the shadows.

Juilene swallowed hard. "How did that get here?"

He shrugged once more. "Who knows? Some traveler passing through, perhaps, didn't stay as long as he thought he would. Come, let's not waste time."

The fire cast eerie shadows on the ceiling and the rocky walls of the cavern. Juilene slowly straightened. Her clothes stuck to her wet body, and she shivered.

"Here." Cariad held out a blanket. "Take your wet things off and lay them out on the rocks to dry. You'll be more comfortable."

Juilene blushed, then hesitated. She drew a deep breath, thinking that she ought to say something, protest in some way, but the thought of shedding her wet clothing was more tempting than she could bear. She took the blanket Cariad offered and retreated to the darkness deeper in the cave. Cariad was hunkered down before the fire, his back turned to her. She bit her lip. What would Neri say, if she knew? A gust of air blew through the cave, whipping the fire higher and slicing through Juilene's wet clothes like a knife. What difference would it make, now, Juilene decided. Her fingers shook as she unlaced the tunic and breeches and peeled her wet underclothes off her damp skin. Quickly she wrapped the blanket around her body. She tucked the end securely into the folds of the fabric, and carefully spread her clothing out on the rocks.

She sidled past Cariad, and slumped down on the soft sand beside the fire. It was very clean, she noticed, no twigs or leaves or other debris. It was as if the cavern had been kept clean for a purpose. She glanced down at her ring. The sapphire was still dark, the flames dull in its surface. She twisted the ring thoughtfully on her finger.

Cariad got to his feet and retreated to the back to the cave. Out of the corner of her eye, she peeked at him as he stripped off his tunic and shirt. He was slim, just as she had thought, but his skin was crisscrossed with scars, and muscle curved over his shoulders and upper arms. His back was to her, and she couldn't see his chest. He bent, slipping out of his breeches, and she blushed, unable to turn away, at the sight of his tight rump. His thighs were covered with a fine coat of dark hair. She turned to look at the fire as he gathered his things, hoping he would attribute the rosy flush on her cheeks to the heat of the fire.

She barely raised her eyes to his when he joined her at the fire, the blanket wrapped tightly around his waist. He held another blanket in his hands. "Here," he said, holding it out to her, "use this around your shoulders. It's still chilly in here."

As he leaned over her, she saw the flesh of his shoulders was prickled with gooseflesh. He was just as cold as she. "We can both use it."

He raised on eyebrow, but shook the blanket out. Bits of straw flew in all directions. He squatted down beside her, one end tucked around his shoulders, and held the other out to her.

She snuggled into the dusty folds. The blanket was a little damp, and it smelled strongly of horses. But it was drier than anything she had been wearing. She was acutely conscious of his presence. The fire leaped up and a log split in a shower of sparks. She pulled the corner tighter over her shoulders and dared a peek at him.

He was staring into the fire, his chin on his knees. Wrapped in the blankets, he looked far more vulnerable than she had ever seen him. The ugly ridges of scar tissue marred the smoothness of his skin, and suddenly she remembered what he had told her about people tortured by magic. Could he have been one of them?

"Cariad?" She spoke his name softly, barely louder than the flicker of the fire.

"My lady?" He did not take his eyes off the burning logs.

"What—what sort of country do you come from? Is—is it very far?"

A shadow crossed his face and instantly she regretted

her questions. "Well," he answered finally, which surprised her. "That depends on how you look at it."

She cocked her head, glad that the conversation gave her an excuse to look at him. The hair curled in little tendrils at the nape of his neck, and suddenly she wondered how soft those curls would be. "That's an odd answer."

"My country"—he shook his head a little and gave a little grimace that might have been a smile—"you would find it an—an odd place."

"No odder than any other, surely. Odder than Khardroon? Stranger than Eld?"

"How many places have you seen, my lady?" He smiled at her this time, and in the firelight, the golden flecks within his eyes reflected the fire's warmth.

"Not that many," she admitted. "Until—until Lindos, I had never been outside of Sylyria."

He nodded. "That's the way things are done, aren't they? I imagine you never thought—" He broke off, as though aware he might be treading on dangerous ground.

"No," she replied, with a smile of her own to show she took no offense, "I never thought to go so far or see so much."

They lapsed into silence. The fire flared and snapped, and outside the storm screamed louder. Gusts of wind blew into the cave, and involuntarily Juilene shivered and moved closer to Cariad's warmth. His arm closed around her, and her body melded itself to his. The rough wool suddenly seemed very thick.

She raised her eyes to his. Her head fell back against his shoulder as he lowered his mouth to hers. His kiss was gentle at first, just the barest pressure of his lips on hers. She turned to him, wrapping her arm around his neck, and the kiss deepened as his tongue flicked over her parted lips. Eagerly, they strained into each other. He lowered her gently to the sandy floor, his arm beneath her head, and she twined her hands in his hair, even as their tongues twined together.

When he finally raised his head, her breathing was ragged, and the blanket had almost completely slipped away. She took his hand and guided it to her breast. His palm closed over the smooth mound of rounded flesh, and she raised her face to his once more.

"Stop me now, lady, if you wish," he whispered, his voice hoarse.

For answer, she clasped him closer and pressed her lips to his once more. He shifted, so that she was lying flat beneath him.

"Juilene," he murmured against her ear, "do you want this?"

She pulled away, stared into his eyes. In the dim light, the blue was nearly black, but the gold flecks within the irises reflected the light of the fire. Pleasure coursed through her, and desire and need and want, and her hands trembled as she caressed his shoulders, feeling the hard muscles beneath the soft, scarred skin. Her breath caught in her throat when she tried to answer. "You've no idea how much."

He bent his head and brought her close, and then nothing mattered at all for a very long time.

Juilene opened her eyes. The fire had died down, but the wind no longer howled at the opening of the cave. The woolen blanket beneath her itched, but Cariad's face was buried in her hair, and his arm encircled her and held her close against his chest. She was loath to move.

She must have made some sound, some gesture, for he stirred behind her and nuzzled her neck. She drew a deep breath and gave a little sigh of contentment. She brought his hand up to cup her breast.

"Mm," he murmured.

She arched back against him, and lay, staring at the rough rock walls on the other side of the fire, unable to put into words what she felt. Unexpectedly, her thoughts turned to Arimond. This was deeper, truer, in some way than anything she had felt for Arimond. What would he have done, she wondered, in the last days? Intuitively, she knew he would not have had the patience or the skill to take them through the swamps and fens of the wilderness. Lying in the circle of Cariad's arms, she knew that the memory of Arimond would always be dear to her, but that she had changed. She was no longer the girl he had loved. Would Arimond have approved of the way she had thrown the dagger? She doubted it. Arimond would have been horrified to learn that she carried a dagger, let alone that she had practiced how to use it. She could just imagine what he would have said if she had whipped out a dagger in his presence. He probably would have insisted she hand it over to him, before she cut herself with it. A soft giggle escaped.

Cariad stirred once more. "What's so funny?"

"Nothing," she said.

"Tell me," he murmured, his lips soft against her ear.

She sighed a little. "Just thinking about—" She broke off. She didn't want to mention Arimond to Cariad, lest it in some way upset him. She had no reason to think that it would, but she hesitated. "About before," she finished lamely.

"Before? Ah—and now it seems funny?"

She shrugged a little. "In some ways it does. All the things I couldn't do—all the things I was supposed to do—all the things I shouldn't do—"

"Like what?" His fingers kneaded the flesh of her breast.

"Oh—like lying naked in a cave next to a fire beside my lover." The words were out of her mouth before she could stop them. She flushed. Would Cariad mind that she had called him her lover?

"Ah—but what would it matter? If no one knew—"

"Someone always knew," she said, her body responding to his touch.

He made a little sound, which might have been a laugh, but when he spoke, he didn't sound amused. "Yes, I know. There was always someone to find out."

She turned to face him. "Cariad, I don't mean to pry, but—why did you come here? Where is your country and why are you here?"

A shadow crossed his face, but he picked up her hand and kissed it. "Juilene, can you bear with me, a little while longer? I want to tell you my story—I need to tell you my story. You've made me feel things I thought I would never feel again—better things than I have ever felt before. I never knew I could care about a woman the way I have come to care about you. But—" He hesitated, and she caressed his rough cheek.

"It's all right," she whispered. Her fingers twined in the little curls at the nape of his neck. "It's all right. I'm not going anywhere."

"Not without me, anyway." He smiled down at her, and gathered her close. Her eyes closed as he lowered his mouth to hers once more.

But before their lips could touch, a gust of wind hurtled through the cave, not from the front, but from the back, and the fire leaped and swirled in a blaze. Cariad half rose, gathering the blanket around himself, reaching for the dagger he had placed on the rock above their heads. The wind blew again over and around them, and sand swirled, choking Juilene in a cloud that seemed to sparkle in the light of the fire.

They both coughed, and Cariad covered his mouth and nose with a corner of the blanket, holding his dagger clenched in his right hand. "By the goddess," he muttered as the errant wind came again, this time blowing their hair over their heads.

Juilene seized a corner of her own blanket and sat up, gathering the folds around herself. Only the wind seemed to blow capriciously. In the flickering light of the fire, nothing else moved.

Then a voice boomed from the back of the cave, and Cariad caught her and held her close. "All hail the non-born knight! All hail the 'sayer who holds the harp! Hail the knight and hail the 'sayer! Welcome to my humble home!"

Juilene clung to Cariad, who glared suspiciously into the depths of the cavern. A light shone, a thin bright beacon, which seemed to beckon, and the wind blew around them, a gentle, beguiling breeze.

"What is it?"

"Who is it, is the question," Cariad answered, his face set and grim. "I don't like being spied upon—here, lady, dress yourself."

He ripped her clothes off the rocks where she had spread them and handed them to her. They were nearly dry. She crouched down and dressed as quickly as possible, while beside her, Cariad did the same. He straightened to his full height and unsheathed his sword. "Come." He held out his hand.

Unsteadily she rose, reminding herself that together, they had faced grimmen and the dangers of the wilderness. The words the voice had spoken reverberated in her mind. The non-born knight. Was it possible that Cariad was the non-born knight? Could it be true? She clutched at his hand, and followed as he led them back into the depths of the cavern.

The rocks rose on either side, and the sand beneath their feet gleamed whitely, leading them on like a ribbon. At their feet, cool air swirled and flowed about their ankles, and Juilene had the unnerving impression that the air was somehow sensate, somehow aware of what and who they were, and urged them on.

The rock tunnel led back quite a distance. The passage was narrow, but the walls were high, and when Juilene looked up, she could not see the top. Cariad said nothing.

At last the tunnel ended, and they stepped into a room brightly lit, carved out of the rocks. A fire burned in a deep pit, over which was suspended a huge pot of some sort of stew, for it bubbled and steamed, and the odor that rose from it made Juilene's mouth water. Cariad wrapped one arm around her shoulders. "Who's here?"

A slight form, garbed in a long robe of greyish homespun, emerged from some nook carved into the rock walls. "All hail the non-born knight," he said with a bow, spreading his hands wide. "All hail the 'sayer who holds the harp."

"Who are you, old man?" Cariad's jaw was tight, and he did not relax his guard.

The old man seemed to smile through the thick beard that flowed down his chest nearly to his waist. "My name—" He seemed to search his memory. "Ah, my name! My name lost all meaning long ago, but you may call me Ludi, if you will, young knight. Please, have a seat at my hearth, and a bowl of my broth, you and your lady both."

Juilene flushed at being called Cariad's lady. She drew a little closer to him and pressed against his side. Cariad was looking warily at the old man. "Who are you?" he asked.

The old man sighed. "Hm. So you know the difference between what a thing is called and what a thing is. And that is not a question easily answered. But most call me the old man of the wilderness—you've heard those stories, too, I think?" He smiled nearly slyly at Cariad.

Cariad narrowed his eyes. "I've heard them. Are you he or not?"

Ludi spread his hands once more. "I'm afraid I am. But please, it's not nearly so important who I am as who *you* are, young knight. And your lady looks famished. Won't you both sit and have a bowl of broth?"

Cariad cast a look around. Juilene could see nothing that would indicate any danger or harm. He nodded and slowly sat on one side on the firepit, keeping the exit to his back. She sat down beside him, crossing her legs in front of her.

Ludi whistled something tuneless under his breath. The errant breeze whipped around his head, making the unruly locks lift and dance, and Juilene had to bite her lip in order not to giggle. Whatever there was about this strange old man, he didn't strike her as dangerous, just odd. She glanced at her ring. The stone was dark and dull, and she relaxed beside Cariad, nudging him and pointing to the ring. He raised his eyebrow and set the sword down by his side, the hilt still close at hand.

Ludi waved his arms. "Away with you, sprite!" He shook his head in exasperation. "Air sprites! Ever deal with a sprite? Be grateful you haven't had one fall in love with you—" The fire in the pit rose in a shower of multi-colored flames. "Ah, my Imisine—you know I love you, too." He busied himself with spoons and bowls, ladling generous servings of the contents of the pot into the bowls. He passed them over to Juilene who handed one to Cariad. "Now, eat, my friends. Eat and then you may ask me what you will."

Cariad dipped his spoon into the broth and stirred it, as though reluctant to eat it. Juilene felt her mouth water once more. She tasted the broth, though it was more like a stew, gingerly. Flavor exploded on her tongue. She glanced once more at the sapphire ring, and with a little sigh began to eat.

"What's a non-born knight?" Cariad demanded, setting the bowl aside untouched.

Ludi raised his eyebrows, bushy and grey. "Ask her." He nodded at Juilene.

Juilene nearly choked in midswallow as Cariad glanced at her. "No, old man. You tell me. What's a non-born knight?"

"I think you know." Ludi smiled through his beard. "It's you."

Cariad glanced at the sword by his side. "I'll ask you once more—"

"It's Lindos's doom," said Juilene. She put her spoon down. "He can only be killed by a non-born knight. Arimond thought it was he, since he wasn't born the usual way. But it wasn't."

Cariad stared at her. "Lindos?"

"Aye, young knight. Gives you pause, doesn't it?" Ludi cackled softly. "You have a choice to make."

Cariad looked at Ludi, his eyes narrowed. "A choice?"

"It's in your power to end it, to change what will be—"

"Who are you, old man? How do you know these things?"

Ludi met his eyes evenly, and there was no trace of madness in the steady gaze. "It's not important who I am. What's important is what will be."

"You're talking about the future."

A chill went down Juilene's spine. There was an undercurrent to the conversation she couldn't understand, but something told her that it concerned Cariad's identity. Who was he, that Ludi called him the non-born knight?

"I am," said Ludi with a nod. "Choices made and choices spurned. Things which should not be, and yet are. Places not known, and yet sought. All these things—and more."

Cariad drew a deep breath. "What do you know of us, of me?"

"I know who you are, and who you aren't."

"How?"

"I can read the magic on you."

"And me?" Juilene interrupted.

Ludi looked at her closely. "There's no spell on you, little sister. You aren't bound by magic."

"But—but the spell—" She stared from the old man to Cariad.

"Can be lifted by one who loves you for yourself alone," murmured Cariad, not taking his eyes off the old man.

Shock went through her, made her weak. Could it be true? Was it possible that since they'd traveled through the wilderness the spell was lifted? She thought of all the things Cariad had handed her, offered her, given her. Nothing had ever affected him, and yet, she had thought it because of the spell he said he had from his uncle. "Why didn't you say something?" she whispered.

"I was afraid you wouldn't believe me," he murmured back.

She sat back, still shaken.

Ludi regarded them both from the other side of the firepit. "So many things left unsaid, young knight." He got to his feet. "There's a room—" He pointed. "Sleep there if you like. If not, sleep in the cave. No harm will come to you." He clapped his hands. "Come, Imisine."

A gust of air so concentrated it was nearly visible swirled around his robes. The old man laughed. "Yes, yes, let's be off."

Cariad half rose. "Wait—old man—"

Ludi turned back. "Yes?"

"You haven't told us anything."

"I've told you everything. The rest is for you to tell."
Without another word, the old man seemed to fade into the

rocks, his grey robes fading into the walls as though he had never been there.

Cariad sank down beside Juilene.

She dared a peek at him. His face was pale, and his eyes were shadowed. "Cariad—"

He heaved a deep sigh. "The old man was right. There's so much I must tell you. I—I just don't know how."

"Was he right? About the spell?"

Cariad lowered his eyes and color rose in his cheeks. "I never expected to feel what I feel for you, Juilene."

"But—you love me?"

He raised his eyes to hers and nodded. "From the first time I heard you in the inn, I think."

"But, I thought Lona—"

"You thought I loved Lona?" He sat back with a soft chuckle. "No, she's like a sis—" He seemed to choke on the word sister and hastily went on. "Like an aunt." He dropped his eyes and somehow Juilene knew a nerve had been touched. "No," he said again. "I don't love her like that."

She reached for his hand, and his fingers curled eagerly around it. "So, all this time—"

"All this time, I've tried to think of some way to make you safe. I knew Diago and Rihana were a danger to you, and I was so unsure of my own feelings. There's so much about me you don't know, Juilene." He broke off. "There's so much about me you may not like if you do."

"Cariad, how can you say that? You have no idea how I've felt these last weeks—how much I looked forward to your coming every evening—how much I hoped you'd speak to me—and tonight—"

He looked over his shoulder. "I'm not sure we should stay with this old thurge, or whatever he might be."

"Then let's go back to the cave."

"I want you to be comfortable. It may be a long time before we can sleep sheltered again." He got to his feet and picked up his sword. "Come."

She followed him to the place Ludi had pointed to. A low opening in the rock wall led to a room carved out of the rock. A low bed, big enough for the two of them, covered in blankets and piled high with pillows stood in the center of the floor. A lone candle cast huge shadows on the round walls. "You sleep," he said. "I'll keep watch." She opened her mouth to protest, but he stopped her with one finger laid across her lips. "It will be a long while before we have this chance again."

With a little frown of resignation, she ducked beneath the low opening. Inside, the ceiling was as high as the other room's. She glanced at the door. She could hear Cariad settling down once more beside the fire, doubtless his sword still held in his hand. She wondered if she should protest. The bed looked so inviting—she thought of their lovemaking earlier and a pang of desire went through her that was nearly painful. There'll be time for that, she scolded herself. She sank down on the bed and weariness overtook her, and was asleep before her head touched the pillow.

The fire guttered and burned, fed by some unknown, unseen source. Cariad watched the flames dance in the confines of the pit, and wondered how to tell Juilene his story. Would she believe him at all? he wondered. And if she believed him, would she recoil in horror when she heard it? Would she think him some beast, less than a man? Curse the old man for revealing him to Juilene before he was ready to declare himself. But wasn't it right, somehow? Shouldn't he have told her how he felt, before he had taken her?

But need and desire and want had overwhelmed him. The journey so far had been a torment. The sight of her, the smell of her hair, the sound of her soft voice, so musical, made him mad. He heaved a sigh, and fingered his dagger, drawing designs in the soft sand of the cavern's floor. Who was this old man?

"The prince keeps the watch."

Cariad leaped to his feet, sword up.

Ludi held up both hands. "Calm yourself, young prince. I mean no harm to you or to your house."

"How do you know who I am?" Cariad spoke through gritted teeth.

The old man hunkered down beside the firepit. His movements were smooth and deliberate, his face was calm, and in his eyes was no hint of the madness of earlier. "I am the lost thurge," he said simply.

"The lost thurge. The lost thurge of Gravenhage, who rebelled at the end when the original thurges and thanes agreed to sleep." Cariad shook his head. "You'll have to do better than that, old man."

Ludi spread his hands. "I can tell you no more than the truth, young Prince of Gravenhage."

"You look remarkably well preserved for what—over ten thousand years old?" said Cariad dryly.

Ludi nodded and smiled disparagingly. "I deserve that. And more. For I betrayed my goddess at the end, and all my friends."

"You still haven't told me how you know who I am."

"I know who you are because I see the truth. It is the curse of living these years, to see what lies beneath the outer face which all present before the world." His voice lapsed into silence, and he stared into the fire. "An extension of the thurge's doom, you see, is to see the truth. The truth is not often what we imagine it to be."

"So if you know that I am the Prince of Gravenhage, you know the circumstances which led to my being here? In this time and place?"

Ludi shrugged. "I see your sin. That's enough."

Cariad shifted uncomfortably. "I lost the woman I believed I loved, for all time, and the child we both wanted. Isn't that enough?"

"Enough what? Enough payment? Enough suffering? How should I know, my thane? I have wandered over this world for the last ten thousand years—and I will only be released when another comes to take my place. I ask you, is ten thousand years of torment not enough?"

Cariad smiled slowly. There was something about the old man, something indefinable, that he trusted in spite of all the reasons he could think of why he should not. "Then you know who she" —he jerked his head toward the alcove where Juilene slept—"is?"

Ludi nodded slowly. "I see the truth of her, as well, yes." He took a deep breath and hesitated. "You stand at a crossroads. You have a choice to make."

Cariad leaned forward. "What do you mean?"

"The harp she bears is the Harp of Dramue—the harp which all the Guardians of Eld have searched for these many years. But the time is not right to bring it back to Eld—the thurge who searches for you both knows exactly where you flee. If you stay upon this road, you may well lose the harp and your lives." He drew a deep breath and heaved a great sigh, and the flames in the firepit leaped higher. "But if you choose not to go to Eld—" He shook his head once more. "I cannot see the future, young thane. Only the truth."

Cariad leaned forward. "What are you trying to tell me?"

"You are the non-born knight of Thurge Lindos's doom. You are destined to meet him—and to kill him. I cannot see the way of it. But there is less risk of the harp being lost once more if you take another road."

"Another road? Not go to Eld?"

"Yes." Ludi nodded slowly, staring into the flames with puckered brow. "Choose another road. Seize your fate and ride to meet it."

"You would offer me counsel, wizard, without explanation. If the harp Juilene carries is truly the Harp of Dramue, then surely it will be better to take it to Eld as soon as possible, where the Wardens will see that it is kept safe."

"Do you think it chance that you were attacked today? Do you think the thurge who pursues you is any less determined than you are?" Ludi lifted his head and stared beyond Cariad's back to the tunnel that led to the outer cave. "He—and his sister—won't give up easily. You think because you've banished a few mere thurge-sent grimmen that the battle is won, and you and your lady can go on your way without fear? The dangers of the wilderness—"

"Are legendary. My uncle often told me tales. I know what lurks within it."

"Ha! Let me finish. The dangers of the wilderness are easily manipulated. Where do you think all the wild elements were banished, long ago? Do you think perhaps the goddess took them with her? That's not the way it works, boy. Any thurge with the desire to invoke the wild magic can find what he needs within these borders. Heed me, boy, and take another road, if you want to keep your lady safe."

"She knows the dangers," answered Cariad slowly.

"Does she?" Ludi met his eyes squarely. "The curse is lifted from her—by your own hand—but do you think Rihana and her brother have lost any interest in you? Don't you think Rihana herself can see the strands of her own work on you?"

A chill went down Cariad. "Surely—that isn't—"

"You ever see your handwriting, boy, from when you were a child? Looks different, but something of what it will become is in it, isn't it? This is the same in reverse—harder to spot, perhaps, but still there."

"And you think if we turn off the road to Eld—and go to another place—we can buy the time we need to save the harp and ourselves?"

Ludi nodded. "The harp's in danger, so long as the thurge pursues you. You must turn him away from you. And there's only one place you can go, where Diago will be loath to extend his magic—Sylyria."

"Sylyria—where Lindos reigns as Over-Thurge? Where I am his doom?"

Ludi nodded. "Wild magic is awake in the land, boy. You don't know what it feels like, but I do. All the wilderness sings with it—stirs with it—nothing is quite the same as it was."

"And this Lindos—I am meant to kill?"

"A thurge's doom is always true."

"Why will Diago not pursue us into Sylyria?"

"In order to find you, he has to use his magic. And that magic leaves a trail—a scent, so to speak. He won't do that—he won't want to draw Lindos's attention to himself."

Cariad sat back. The fire leaped and burned, as though no time had passed at all, and the cavern about him was utterly still. It was as if they had wandered into a bubble, where everything stayed the same.

"The storm is over," said Ludi. "It will be a fine day. But the paths are muddy; you must take care."

"You can tell me no more?"

"I can tell you only this—if you persist in going to Eld, the harp will most likely be lost before you get there. If you go to Sylyria . . ." His voice trailed off. "All that is, won't be." He spoke in a breathy whisper, staring transfixed into the flames. "Everything shall change—time itself is altered." He stared at Cariad, his eyes clouded and no longer clear. "I can see no more, young prince."

"Wait—can you tell me if there is anywhere else we can go? Parmathia? Albanall?"

"We can only hide from destiny so long, my prince. And yours pursues you on eagle's wings. The hound at the hunt is no more eager on the trail than your fate. And none of us escapes in the end. Leave the things you brought from Diago's house in my cave. The scent will grow cold—his purpose will be frustrated, and it will buy you a little more time." He rose, his joints creaking audibly like any ordinary old man's. "Your love lies waking."

Cariad glanced over his shoulder at the niche where Juilene slept, and when he looked back, the old man was gone. A chill went down his spine. He got to his feet, and a mantle of weariness seemed to descend upon him. He drew a deep breath and deliberately straightened his shoulders. He ducked down through the low opening.

Juilene lay in the center of the bed, her hair streaming on the pillows. She smiled when she saw him, and held out her hand. Swiftly, he moved to take it, and pressed a kiss upon the palm. "We have to leave," he said.

She nodded, her eyes still glazed with sleep.

He paused, wondering how to tell her of his conversation with the old man. "I've been speaking to our host," he began. "And he doesn't think we should go to Eld."

"Why not?" She sat up and stretched, and covered a yawn with the back of one hand. "Where are we to go then?"

"He thinks we should go to Sylyria." He waited to see her reaction.

Her eyes widened, and a smile broke out on her face. "Sylyria? Truly? You would take me home?" She flung her arms around his neck, hugging him closely. "Truly?"

He hugged her back, unable to resist the feeling of her body pressed against his. "It isn't that simple, Juilene. You heard what that old man called me last night—the non-born knight. That means I am Lindos's doom. We are fated to meet—at some point."

"And if we go to Sylyria, then you will, and all the people Lindos has hurt or killed will be avenged, and you and I can live happily . . ." Her voice trailed off when she saw the look on his face. "Forgive me," she said at once. "I have no right to expect—"

He caught her hands in both of his, and brought them to his mouth. "Juilene, there is no future I can imagine that does not have you in it. But things are far more complicated than you know."

"Then tell me," she said, sinking back on her heels. "Tell me all of it."

He picked up one curl as it lay over her shoulder. "I would that I could, my dearest love. And I will, I promise. I owe you that." He shook his head and turned away. "But right now, we must ride. Every moment we stay here is a moment we lose. The longer we stay in the wilderness, the longer we are vulnerable to attack from Diago. So come. The storm is over and Ludi says it is a fine day for travel. If my memory serves me correctly, we can reach the road to Sylyria by nightfall. What do you say to a night in a proper inn?"

Juilene smiled in spite of herself. A bath, a real meal, a wide bed—one shared with Cariad. "It sounds fine to me."

"Then up with you, lazy woman. The hour grows late."

He gave her a quick kiss on the cheek, and a light spank on the rump, and left her. He ducked out the opening and stood in the cavern. The firepit was empty. Nothing burned within it, and no ash marred the interior. But light streamed from an opening in the roof of the cavern, showering dust motes, and beside the empty pit, two loaves of bread and a flask lay on a piece of linen. Beside the linen, two traveler's packs were propped against each other, and resting beneath them both were piles of fresh clothing, carefully folded. Two pairs of boots, one much smaller than the other, leaned against each other. He knelt and touched the food. The flask was silver, blackened and dented in spots. It appeared very old, and the linen—he looked at the linen and a chill went through him. It was a crest he knew nearly as well as he knew his own. The crest of the Over-Thurge of Gravenhage was worked in faded thread.

Chapter Fourteen

୶ஂ৵

They reached the road to Sylyria long before nightfall. As if the storm had cleansed the land, they found the path muddy but clear. Cariad was wary and alert, his hand never far from the hilt of his sword, but the horses moved with relative ease across the sandy track.

At midday, they paused and ate the rest of the bread Ludi had left for them. There was more to the food than bread, Juilene thought, for it filled her with an energy that made her feel as though she could travel on for miles more. She looked all around herself with interest. Could it be possible that they were truly going home?

She gazed into the distance where she imagined Sylyria lay, imagining what her father and her brother would say when they arrived at the gates of Sarrasin. Oh, to be home, once more. To lie in the bed where she had grown up, to feel the clean white linen sheets, the blankets worn by use to a rich softness nothing else could match, to once more see and touch and know all the familiar things she had thought were lost to her forever. And old Neri, dear Nenny. She hoped the old woman had healed over the months of her absence. She would make the pain and suffering up to the old woman, somehow. Somehow she would find a way to make the old woman realize how much she loved and had missed her. And poor Reyerne, what would he say, when she returned bearing a harp thought to be—no, recognized by the crazy old thurge as the harp borne by the goddess herself.

"Juilene." Cariad's voice, gentle as it was, burst through the bubble of her reverie like a needle through silk.

She started. "Y-yes?"

"Come. We'd best be on the move again. I don't trust this land. We may have bought ourselves a few hours by turning off the track to Eld, but I don't trust Diago and Rihana either." He extended his hand and helped her to her feet.

She brushed the crumbs of food off her tunic. "Very well." She swung into the saddle with an ease that was new to her. Cariad mounted his own horse, and together they set off down the shady path.

"Daydreaming, were you?" His words intruded just as the pleasant bubble was beginning to enfold her once again.

She flushed. "Yes. I—I can't wait to see home again. I never realized how much I loved it, how much I would miss it, until I had to leave it."

Cariad's smile was grim. "Juilene—" He hesitated, as though searching for the words. "Everything may not be as you remember."

She turned to look at him. "Why? What do you mean?"

He drew a deep breath and hesitated once again. "The reports coming from Sylyria have not been good."

"Yes—I know that. I know of the war between the thanes and the thurges—but my father is a great thane— one of the most powerful and the richest. Wait until you see Sarrasin—it could withstand anything the thurges might send against it."

Cariad shook his head. "I hope for your sake you are right, my dear." He lapsed into silence.

Juilene gazed at Cariad with a troubled frown. It seemed that since last night—since yesterday—a distance had come between them, that their physical intimacy had not increased the familiarity between them, it had only served to distance them, somehow. A lump rose in her throat and she swallowed hard. But Cariad loved her; the curse was lifted, wasn't it? Or had the crazy old thurge been wrong? She blinked back tears and stole a peek at Cariad's back. He rode with a ramrod-straight back and a troubled frown. Something was obviously troubling him. She pressed her lips together and tightened her hands on the reins. She would speak to him that evening.

The shadows had fallen and the stars were shining in the black sky when they reached an inn on the road to Sylyria. Cariad had refused to stay at the first inn they had come to earlier in the evening. There was still a bit of light left in the sky, and he had insisted they press on, while the evening still had a bit of light left to it. Juilene had only nodded and said nothing. She wasn't sure of his moods, and she had no wish to say or do anything to further upset him. As the miles had increased, he looked more and more troubled. She only resolved to confront him as soon as they were settled for the evening.

In the courtyard, they slid off their weary horses and a couple of grimy stablehands came forward to take their reins. Cariad picked up their packs and together they entered the common room of the inn. Only a few travelers sat at the tables scattered throughout the room.

"May I help you, friend?" A small man behind the bar paused in pouring wine into high goblets.

Cariad nodded. "Lodging, if you have it. And a bath if you have it, and dinner."

The landlord nodded as he beckoned to a serving maid. "Right away, sir. The bath will take a few minutes, but I can show you a fine room, and dinner is hot and ready anytime. Will you come with me?"

Cariad gestured to Juilene. The landlord slid out from behind the bar and disappeared up a set of stairs to the right. They followed him. One lone candle burned in a sconce high at the top of the steps. "Be careful," Cariad murmured.

"Forgive me, sir," the landlord said as they reached the top. "Trade's been off these last months. We've had to make some small economies. But you'll see that my rooms are clean—my food is good, and my ale the best in the district."

"We understand," said Cariad.

The landlord withdrew a ring of jangling keys from the depths of his robe, and led them down the shadowy hall. He paused at a door in the middle of the corridor, inserted a key, and pushed it open. "Here you are, sir." He stood aside, allowing Cariad and Juilene to peek past him into the room.

The room was dark, and there was a chill in the air. Juilene could see little but the posts of a wide bed, and a table and chairs at the foot of the bed. Cariad grunted his assent. "That will do. You'll get the fire going, won't you?"

"At once, sir. And a bath—I'll have that brought up to the room and made ready. Will you want something to eat while you wait?" The landlord rubbed his hands together.

In glee, thought Juilene, or in the fear they might get away?

She looked down at her feet. The thin piece of carpeting looked threadbare. Small economies indeed.

"We'll eat now," Cariad was saying. "Bring us your best—we've traveled a long way."

"At once, at once." The little landlord eased past them and started off down the hall. "Been on the road awhile— I know how that is. Did a fair amount of traveling in my youth, I did, before my father passed on and left the inn to me. We have quite a reputation, you know—best ale in the district."

They had reached the bottom of the steps by this time, and Cariad paused and stripped off his gloves. "Bring us some of that ale, then, and a cup of wine for my lady, and a dish of whatever your cook is proudest of tonight." He smiled down at Juilene and guided her to a table tucked in an alcove by the fire, leaving the landlord babbling in their wake.

Juilene smiled in spite of herself. The timbers in the ceiling were black with age, and the hearth was big enough for both of them to stand upright. A log thicker than a man burned in the enormous grate. The place looked clean enough, she thought as Cariad pulled out a chair for her.

"Will you sit, my lady?" He whispered it in her ear, and his breath tickled the soft skin of the nape of her neck. His fingers caressed her briefly, and he bent and swiftly kissed her cheek.

She gasped.

"Is anything wrong?" he asked as he took his place beside her.

"N-no. It's just—" She looked down and twined her fingers together.

"Just what?" he prompted gently.

"Just that I thought you were angry with me all day. You

seemed so distant—so closed off. I wasn't sure whether"—
she bit her lip and finished in a rush—"if you regretted last
night, or not."

"Oh, Juilene." He covered her hand with his, and his
palm was warm. She looked at him, and saw the deep circles beneath his eyes. Suddenly he looked very weary and
older than she had ever seen him. "Forgive me. I've been
troubled these last days, that's true, but not because of you.
And believe me, I don't regret last night and I only hope
you don't either, because I was hoping—" He stopped and
grinned at her.

She raised one brow.

"I was hoping the same would happen tonight." His grin
made him look like a mischievous boy rather than a man
worn by care.

She flushed. "Well." She looked away, into the fire, and
tossed her hair over her shoulder. "I suppose it could—as
long as you aren't angry with me."

"How could I be angry with you?" He picked up her
hand and kissed it. "It's only—" He paused. "It's only that
when you have heard my story, you may be the one who
regrets last night."

She cocked her head as the serving maid set a brimming
tankard before Cariad and a clay goblet of wine in front of
her. "There you are, folks," the girl announced with a
cheery voice. "Supper'll be right out—do you want cheese
and butter with your bread?"

"Both," they answered together, then looked at each
other and laughed.

"Very well," the maid replied with a knowing smile, and
went off.

Cariad leaned forward and spoke softly, even though
there was no one within earshot. "I can't tell you here—but
tonight—later—I promise."

"Cariad, whatever it is, how could it be so bad that I

would regret last night? I love you," Juilene said, and as soon as the words left her mouth, she knew they were the truest words she had ever spoken. "It doesn't matter to me—what's past is done."

"Oh, my dear," he sighed as the serving maid approached once more, with two dishes piled high with steaming food, "would that that were true. Would that that were true." He turned away, then, even as the maid placed the food in front of them, and although Juilene's mouth watered, she hesitated. But there was a closed, pinched look about his lips, and she knew that she could ask all she pleased, and he would say nothing until he was ready.

She picked up her knife with a sigh. The meat was covered in thick brown gravy. Tiny pieces of herbs floated on the surface. She cut off a tiny piece and placed it in her mouth.

As the rich taste filled her mouth, she happened to glance up as another traveler entered the inn. He wore a worn cloak, and his face was obscured by a ragged beard. Everything about him suggested he had been on the road a long time. Then his cloak fell back, and the uniform he wore beneath it was revealed. Juilene's face paled as she recognized her father's colors. Cariad saw her expression and turned, still chewing.

"What's wrong?"

"That man—" Juilene whispered. "My father—those are his colors." She couldn't help but stare as the man shrugged off the cloak. There could be no doubt, for the badge he wore upon his chest was the crest of her father's house. She lowered her eyes by force of habit, and in that moment, the man happened to glance her way.

Their eyes met, and shock and recognition dawned in his tired face. "Lady Juilene!" he cried, ignoring the landlord's greeting. "By the goddess—Lady Juilene, at last!"

Cariad got to his feet. "Greetings, friend. Will you join

us?" He spoke quietly, his tone and his look full of meaning, and the soldier bit his lip, responding at once to the implicit warning.

In midstride, the soldier checked his step. "Thank you, sir. I will, with your permission."

Juilene stared, her food nearly forgotten as Cariad ordered another flagon of ale and another plate of food. She knew this man. His name was Skar, and he had been in her father' service more years than she had been alive. In the last few years, he had become the captain of her father's house guards—the most respected and trusted of all his men. "Skar," she whispered as the man approached, his travel-worn face alight with what could only be relief.

"My lady Juilene," he whispered, his voice hoarse. "I have searched for you since Festival—your father is sick with grief. I cannot believe I've found you at last." He turned to Cariad. "You will have the gratitude of Thane Jiroud, sir, if you have kept his daughter safe. May I know the honor of your name?"

"My name is Cariad," Cariad answered. "Sit with us. You look as though you've traveled more miles than we have."

Skar sank into the chair opposite Juilene. "With your permission, lady." He paused for a moment, looking across the room. "I never thought to sit at table with my lord's daughter. Whoever would have thought it?"

"I am so happy to see you, Skar," Juilene said. The reality of seeing someone from home, from her father, shocked her to the very core. So her father had never given up looking for her. "How is my father?"

Skar drew a deep breath and glanced at Cariad. The two men exchanged a long look and Cariad resumed his seat just as the serving maid placed another platter before Skar.

"Let the man have a bite to eat, love." Cariad picked up his own knife. "We have only just arrived ourselves, sir."

Juilene cut and chewed and swallowed her food automatically as the men dug into their portions. Skar's eyes were fastened on his plate, and as the moment dragged on in silence, she wondered what he wasn't telling her. "Please," she said at last. "Tell me what's happened at home."

Skar put his knife down and glanced at Cariad. Cariad nodded imperceptibly. "Give us the news of Sylyria."

The man sighed. His beard was more white than silver, and he looked very old. "I wish I could tell you, lady. But the border of Sylyria is sealed against the world. No one can get in or out. I have tried—chance brought me to this inn tonight. The pass is closed."

"Sealed?" Cariad leaned forward, his voice low. "What do you mean?"

Skar shook his head. "After Lindos—" His face twisted, as though the name itself left a foul taste on his tongue. "After he became the Over-Thurge, he ordered the borders sealed until all the troubles, as he called them, were over. I left right before his election. And I have not been able to get home."

Juilene glanced at Cariad. "Then—how will we get home?"

"You can't, my lady." Skar shook his head.

"What do you mean, sealed?" asked Cariad.

"He's used his magic, sir. The situation among the thanes was bad enough when I left. I have the feeling it's even worse now." He looked down, and Juilene knew the man felt he had abandoned his post.

"How was my father when you left?" Juilene asked softly.

"Worried sick about you, lady." Skar met her eyes with a sudden ferocity. "What happened to you? Where have you been all these months?"

"I—I had to run away, Skar. Lindos put a curse on me."

It was the grizzled soldier's turn to stare. "In the name of the goddess, my lady. Why didn't you go to your father? He would have done anything to help you."

"That's the trouble," she replied. "He couldn't have helped me—it would only have brought the curse down upon him. And I couldn't let that happen to my father—to anyone in Sarrasin. So I had no choice but to leave."

Skar's eyes narrowed, as though he couldn't quite believe that there was nothing that the all-powerful lord of Sarrasin couldn't accomplish, but he didn't challenge her. "Your father was sick with grief, my lady."

"I know." She looked down at her plate and toyed with scraps of food. She drew a deep breath and raised her eyes to his. "But the curse is broken, Skar. And now I can go home, without fear of harming anyone there." She smiled.

Skar shook his head. "I wish that were true, my lady. But I have tried more times than I can count to get over the border to Sylyria. And it's just not possible." He leaned forward and when he spoke, his voice was low. "But now—just this week I have heard rumors—rumors that the King is very close at hand—that one of the master-thurges is willing to help—" He broke off and glanced around, as though the room itself had ears. "There is a resistance forming. That's where I was headed. To the keep of a master-thurge named Deatrice."

Juilene raised her eyebrows in surprise. "Why," she said, "I know that lady—I was at her keep before the Year's End—" She glanced at Cariad, who stared into the fire with a grim expression. "Cariad, Skar is on his way—"

"I heard him." Cariad looked from one to the other. "The King is there?"

Skar shrugged. "I'm not sure. Close by if not yet there. I have heard that Deatrice allows certain people through at certain times of day."

"How do you know it's not a trap?" Juilene asked.

"It isn't," Cariad said softly, an unreadable expression on his face.

Juilene turned to him. "And how do you know that?" she demanded.

He met her eyes with a long look but said nothing. Instead, he addressed Skar. "And what else have you heard?"

Skar shook his head. "Little else. They say the King and what thanes he can gather are planning an attack upon Lindos—that this Deatrice and several of the other masterthurges have joined with the King, and will help in the assault. But other than that, I won't know until I get there." He looked at Juilene. "Come with me, lady. Even if your father isn't there—surely there will be someone who knows something of your father's fate. And you, sir—you, too, would be welcome. Every hand is needed in this fight."

Cariad drew a deep breath. "You're right about that, Skar. More right than you know." And for the rest of the meal he was silent, even as Juilene and Skar discussed a plan for the morrow.

The linen towels were frayed at the edges, but the water was hot, and the soap was fat and sweetly scented with herbs. Juilene slid down farther into the high-backed wooden tub and sighed. She felt as though she might turn to liquid. How long had it been since she had had a proper bath like this? Weeks, she knew, as she dipped down beneath the surface and let the hot water massage her scalp. The long strands of her hair floated and swirled around her. She picked up the soap and scrubbed herself from the top of her head to the tips of her toes.

Cariad and Skar lingered by the fire in the common room, though whether or not they talked, she couldn't imagine. Cariad's silence had worried her, had puzzled and perplexed her and made her realize how little she knew of this man whose actions proved he loved her for herself alone. He had become so very distant, saying little, so clearly absorbed in his own thoughts. Was it merely the thought of confronting Lindos? Or was it something more? He had confronted Diago without hesitation, and Diago had been nearly as dangerous.

She shivered at the very thought of meeting Lindos once more. And this time his power was even greater than it had been the last time. But wasn't that what they wanted?

What if the old man was wrong? she wondered. What if Cariad wasn't the non-born knight, any more than Arimond had been? After all, what in the world was a non-born knight?

She slipped lower into the water, and let it close over the top of her head. It seemed that she had been running for so long. She was tired. Dramue, bring me home, she prayed. If it's your will that everything ends by Lindos's hand, let us all be together, at least.

She had just surfaced when the door opened and she heard Cariad's step on the floor on the other side of the screen the landlord had had set up around the tub.

"Juilene?" He spoke with the same familiar gentleness she had come to expect.

"I'm here." She flung a few drops of water over the screen.

"Oh, I see." He peeked around the screen, and Juilene blushed and ducked down modestly beneath the water. "What are you hiding under there, my lady?"

She giggled. "Come and see." Her answer shocked her own ears. What on earth did Skar think of her appearance in the unchaperoned company of this obviously very virile knight? But then, there was so much more to think about— who cared, after all, what company she kept?

She heard the sounds of Cariad stripping off his clothes,

and before she could think much more, he was in the tub, leaning against the opposite end, the water lapping at the gold chain he wore around his neck and the curious medallion attached to it.

"Ah," he signed, lying back against the rim. He closed his eyes. His arms rested on the sides, and his knees broke the surface of the water.

Juilene rose and eased herself between his legs, wondering once more at her own boldness. He opened his eyes, and smiled. He gathered her close to him and bent his mouth to hers. The water steamed and swirled around them as the kiss went on and on. "Oh, my sweet." He caressed her damp hair.

"What is it?" she whispered. "What troubled you so all through dinner?"

He sighed. "Let me wash some of the stink of the road off me, and then I'll tell you. Everything. I promise."

The firelight flickered off the rim of the medallion, and Juilene picked it up. A crest was stamped into the gold, a noble crest, much like her father's. But where her father's was topped with a pair of crossed swords, this one was topped with a crown. His fingers closed over hers as she raised questioning eyes to his.

"Everything," he repeated. "I promise."

She backed away, her mind spinning, trying to remember everything she knew about the heredity markings of the noble houses. There was a strict precedence about the markings, and only the kings of the city-states and their heirs could wear a crown. Could it be, she wondered as she dried herself with the towel and wound her hair in a braid around her head, that Cariad could have stolen the medallion? Could that be why he seemed to behave as though he could never return to his own country?

She climbed into bed and waited.

He bathed with the same economy that marked all his

other actions. She heard the splash as he stepped out of the tub, the rustle of the linen as he dried himself. He stepped around the screen, a towel around his waist, the medallion gleaming on his skin.

"May I join you, lady?" he asked with his customary grave courtesy.

She moved over a little, eyeing the medallion suspiciously. He had taken it off last night, she was sure of it, and she wondered why he had taken such pains to hide it from her yesterday, when today he seemed determined that she should notice it. *Perhaps I can make this easier for him,* she thought. The mattress dipped as he dropped the towel and slid into bed naked beside her.

She brushed the back of his shoulders with the tip of her fingers. "What's this?" she asked, letting her fingers dance on the edges of the chain.

"It is the medallion of the heir of the royal house of Gravenhage," he said.

"How did you get it?"

"It was given to me at my birth," he said with that same simplicity. "I am the Prince of Gravenhage."

Her fingers fell away, and Juilene stared at him. "What did you say?"

"I am—or I will be, in my own time—the Prince of Gravenhage."

"Will be?"

"I know this story is going to seem quite unbelievable to you, Juilene. I only ask that you let me tell it, as best I can, in my own way as you told yours, and if you want to ask me anything, wait until I am finished."

She nodded. "All right."

"In my own country—which is Gravenhage—there is in this time a King named Mark. He is young and not very wise, and he leaves much of the ruling of the country to his young Queen, Mirta, and the various captains of his army, one of whom is a man named Keriaan. In less than a year, Mark will fall ill, and his young Queen will seek the company of this captain, who is mourning the death of his own young wife in childbed.

"Their love will bear fruit—and in less than two years, I will be born—and everyone will think—including Keriaan—that I am Mark's child—begotten by magic, and the help of a certain thurge named Galanthir, who is Keriaan's brother. Time will pass, and Keriaan, who will be gravely wounded in a battle on the borders of Gravenhage with a band of robbers, will retire to the country, taking his only daughter with him. And Galanthir will go to Eld, to study with the Guardians of the Sleepers. And no one, except my mother, will know the truth of my birth." He wet his lips, and looked down, and Juilene, who was trying hard to understand the sense of what he was saying, bit back a question from her lips.

"My mother will be hard set upon by the factions who would bring down the throne of Gravenhage. King Mark is increasingly unable to cope with the demands of his rank. Shortly after my birth, my mother is appointed regent of Gravenhage. But as I approach the year of my majority, the attacks intensify. For my own safety, I am sent to the mountains, and there, I meet Keriaan's daughter." His mouth twisted and a shadow crossed his face. "She is very beautiful—there is no one to tell me the truth of my parentage—and so we fall in love. And of that love, she bears my child.

"But then Galanthir arrives—Galanthir, who with my mother knew the truth and finds the abomination we have committed. Alysse and I—we stand at the brink. Our love is forbidden; she will have nothing to do with me; she finds a way to rid herself of the child, and in the process dies herself. And the scandal begins to grow—the whispers—and then Galanthir offers me a chance to escape."

"Escape?" Juilene asked. "How?"

Cariad twined his hands in hers. "Into the past. The Over-Thurge of Khardroon, Rihana, offered to help him—to help us. And before last night, I didn't understand why. But now I do and I see that whatever mistakes I made before—" He looked away, and his face was grim.

"Cariad—you're saying—you are from the future? How far in the future?"

"I was sent back in the year 9997."

"9997? This is only 9968 . . ." she whispered.

He nodded wordlessly.

She shook her head as if to clear it. "You mean to tell me, you come from the *future*? From a time that hasn't happened yet, because of—"

"Because I got my half sister with child. And if it were known that the child was mine—" He shook his head. "I was half-mad in those days—half-mad with grief. Rihana offered us a way out, and we took it, seized upon it, without care or realization of what it would mean."

"What does it mean?" she asked, confused.

"In my time, Lindos is the High Thurge of the Conclave. And wild magic is not a whispered tale—wild magic is real. But only Lindos knows how to use it." He held her hands so tightly she was afraid the bones would break. "Except for Rihana. Somehow, that witch also discovered the secret—and that's how she sent me back. And it was Ludi who made me see last night just why. She didn't send me back to save my house, or Gravenhage from disgrace. She sent me back to be the non-born knight. For in this time, I am not born."

His words faded into the silence. Juilene listened to the gentle snap of the fire, the soft creaks all around them as the ancient inn settled for the night. "So if we go to Sylyria—"

"When we go to Sylyria," he corrected.

"Does that mean you must meet Lindos?"

He looked away. "In my time, Lindos rules all of the League with a grip like iron. He has inflicted more pain, more suffering—Juilene, you have seen only the barest taste of a man held in check by nothing and no one. Every one lives in fear—even the highest of the thanes. No one—not the lowest beggar, the mightiest thane—dares incur his wrath. Remember what I said to you, about torture with magic? His dungeons are full of people—victims—he uses people to experiment with the wild magic—he makes the tales of the thurges of old seem tame by comparison. I would shudder to tell you some of the things I have heard—some of the things I have seen."

Her eyes fell on the ridges of scars that marred his shoulders. "Was that—"

He shrugged. "In the mountains, some of the things he's created escaped. I got these from a dwarf dragon—only it wasn't a dwarf anymore."

Juilene raised her eyebrows. The dragons were formidable enough. The thought of even one of them much larger made her shiver. "So—you don't exist yet?"

"Not in this time, not technically, no. But according to Galanthir, I will be thrown back into the future, when I am conceived. In about six months."

Juilene picked up his hand. "And—and what of me? Of us?"

"I have thought and thought, and I think there must be a way to bring you with me, Juilene. Somehow. I can't lose you—whatever happens in the future—and believe me, it isn't a pretty place—there's no one I would rather face it with than you. We'll find some way, I promise. If it worked once, it should work again. While the spell is on me, perhaps some other can read it—"

"So that's why you had to get away from Diago."

"Yes. And especially from Rihana—it's her spell, after

all. And she might not be much more than a child now, but—" He shook his head and gathered her close. For a moment, they clung together, and then he raised his head and looked long into her eyes. "Now. Can you accept what I have told you? And can you understand why I hesitated all this time to tell you?"

Juilene nodded slowly. "I can scarcely believe what you say. But—" she hesitated.

"But?" He bent his head.

"But I know I love you, Cariad, and no matter what happens, or where or when, I only want to stay with you—for as long as the goddess wills."

He wrapped his arms around her and pulled her into him, and their bodies molded beneath the snowy linen sheets. She closed her eyes, and his arms tightened around her, and his fingers stroked her wet, tangled hair. "I was thinking—have been thinking—that perhaps together, we should seek out a thurge, a powerful thurge, and explain my story—but now—" He broke off speaking and his fingers twisted the knotted strands of her hair so hard, she winced.

"But now," she prompted, pulling her hair out of his reach. "What more is there?" She rose up on one elbow and looked down at him.

He gazed back at her. "Tonight, listening to Skar—I realized that there's more to it than just me and Lindos." He glanced at the ceiling and then met her eyes once more. "Don't you see, Juilene? I know the end of the story. I know what happens—to Jarron and Deatrice and all the thanes and thurges who oppose Lindos."

She twined her hands in the sheets, suddenly very cold. "And what is that?"

"It's called the Rout of Arvon in the history books." He looked at her steadily. "Does that name mean anything to you?"

"Arvon," she echoed. "That's the name of the river that flows through Sylyria to the sea—you mean—"

"Jarron and all his men—all the thanes and thurges who fight with him—will be destroyed. There're even implications for my own family—my own country. My father was involved, too, for the King of Gravenhage sent troops to assist Sylyria, and the Over-Thurge of Gravenhage was part of it, too. I even know the date. And it's soon—very soon. So you see, Juilene, what my dilemma is? I think I understand why Rihana sent me here. She planned for me to clear the way for her. And the terrible thing is, I know what happens under Lindos, and I can't help but think that anything Rihana schemes will be even worse. But here I am now, and brave men and women will die, unless I help to prevent it. But what if it changes everything, in ways we can't begin to imagine? What if everything is altered so greatly, the future doesn't unfold the way it once did? Do you understand what I am talking about? What would you do, if you were me?"

"We can't let the King and all his allies die," Juilene declared. "What if my brother is among them? So many have died already—Sylyria will never recover if all the thanes and thurges who oppose Lindos are slain. How could you go back to your own time, knowing that you allowed all those deaths to occur, which you might have prevented. We must—you must do what you were sent here to do." She caught his hand and held it to her cheek.

He said nothing for a long time. Finally he sighed. "Yes," he said at last. "Though I am not so certain anymore exactly what it is that I am meant to do."

He reached for her then, and pulled her close, and covered her mouth with his. She gave herself up to his lovemaking, and all the while, she wondered just what he could possibly mean by that.

Chapter Fifteen

❦

The snow crunched beneath their feet and their breath steamed away in long white plumes. It seemed to Juilene that each step closer to Sylyria was at least one degree in temperature colder. The forest rose all around them, still and silent and starkly beautiful. The fir trees were covered in thick layers of snow. The horses' hoofs echoed flatly. Soon, she thought, soon. Goddess, see us over the border, she prayed.

The roads were all deserted. Juilene understood the shabbiness of the inn, the reason why the innkeeper had been so glad for their patronage. Truly, she thought, it must indeed be exactly as Skar had said—no one went in or out of Sylyria. The winter-bare trees that grew along the road-side provided excellent cover for robbers. But the men had decided such an attack was unlikely. Bandits would have been the first to take up residence in a more profitable location, and indeed, in the day and the night it took to reach Deatrice's keep, they had met no one at all.

She drew a deep breath, and realized that the air had changed in the last few paces. It was different, thicker somehow, and the trees up ahead seemed to shimmer and ripple. Skar stopped. "I'm not sure how much closer we can come on our own. Up there" —he pointed—"up there is the border."

As if at a signal, a dark-robed figure emerged from a stand of trees a few paces off the road. The figure looked substantial enough, but he, too, wavered against the trees. "You must turn back," he called. "Sylyria welcomes no one."

"Perhaps not Sylyria," replied Cariad. "But we had heard that Thurge Deatrice has welcomed others at her keep."

The young man stepped closer, and through the wavering air, Juilene could make out the glyphs that distinguished him as a demi-thurge. He glanced around, from right to left, and back again, and this time when he spoke, his voice was low. "State your names, travelers, and your business with the lady."

"I'm Skar, lately of Thane Jiroud's house of Sarrasin. I'll state my business to the lady, but I mean her no harm."

"My name is Cariad," Cariad said when Skar paused, "lately of the house of Thane Diago of Khardroon. And this—"

"I am Lady Juilene of Sarrasin." Juilene stepped forward, her shoulders squared and her chin high.

The name had an instant effect upon the demi-thurge. "Lady Juilene!" he cried. "Stand aside, please, off the road. T'will be an easy thing to raise this border for you, lady."

"And why is that?" asked Cariad, frowning.

"Because the mighty Lindos himself has put out her

name, with orders that she is to be admitted into Sylyria. Lindos wants you, lady. And I know my mistress will be pleased to talk to all of you."

Now Juilene gripped Cariad's arm as tightly as she dared. The antechamber was cold, as though the chill that pervaded the air outside seeped into every corner of the great keep. The small fire that snapped and burned in the polished grate did almost nothing to relieve the temperature. She had noticed that everyone they had seen since they had arrived at Deatrice's keep was wrapped in as many layers as they could stand to wear, and that even the house servants wore gloves.

But once there, the inner wards of the keep had been crowded, with men and women and children, all huddled around roaring fires. They had the look of refugees, thought Juilene, of people who had been forced to flee their homes and leave most of what mattered to them behind. And that was exactly what they were, she realized, people driven out of their villages and domains, forced to seek shelter at whatever thurge's keep would have them. And in this cold, this bitter, unnatural cold that gripped Sylyria in an iron fist, how many had died before they found an open door?

She had eyed the people speculatively. Huddled and shrouded as they were, in whatever layers of clothing they possessed, it was impossible to tell their rank. But they all wore the rough-spun garb of peasants—no thanes hid among the lot. What had happened to her father and the rest of her family? she wondered. It was impossible to think that living so close to Lindos's keep, the occupants of Sarrasin had been spared. What had become of the people she loved? Cariad and Skar had led her into the great keep, her harp cradled protectively in her arms.

Now the three of them stood shivering in the little antechamber, waiting for Deatrice to favor them with her company. They had been unsure as to their reception, but the servants who greeted them, the men who guided them to the keep, had been nothing less than courteous. Skar and Cariad had said nothing, though they had exchanged long looks, when they had not been asked to surrender their weapons.

But this cold, Juilene felt, was more than just a physical discomfort. It insinuated itself into one's very depths, and seemed to close around her heart, gripping her in a tightening vise of sadness and despair. More than once she had found herself thinking that all their efforts were hopeless, that nothing would come of it, that Lindos was surely unstoppable. So far she had managed to dismiss such thoughts for the nonsense they were, but she found it harder and harder to shake off the sadness that seemed to clutch at her like a sucker vine.

The door opened abruptly, and a tall, thin manservant, dressed in a dark blue robe bordered with the glyphs that marked him as a demi-thurge in Deatrice's service, bowed. "This way, good folk. The lady of the keep desires your presence." He stood aside.

"Shall we?" asked Cariad lightly. He gripped Juilene gently under the arm and led her out of the room. Skar followed, her harp in his arms.

The corridors were even colder than the antechamber. Their breath steamed lightly, and their footsteps echoed in the silence. At the doors of the great hall, which Juilene recognized from her visit, the demi-thurge bowed and stepped aside. "Lady Deatrice, the newcomers."

The smell of roasting meat made their mouths water. Along the length of the hall, fires roared in hearths so huge men could stand upright. Great haunches of meat turned on spits, and the fat sizzled and steamed. Juilene blinked. She had never seen the hearths inside a hall used for cooking.

And then her attention was diverted once more as a tall woman turned from a group clustered around a hearth at the very end of the hall, and she recognized Deatrice herself. The woman beckoned.

Deatrice was still as tall and pale and beautiful as Juilene remembered, but her companions looked like men who had spent a great deal of time on the road, for their garments were shabby and travel-stained. Juilene noticed that they all seemed to be clustered around one man, who sat in a chair beside the hearth. He turned as the sound of their footsteps echoed in the still cold air of the hall, and regarded the newcomers with interest.

Juilene's heart stood still. "Greetings," said the man in the chair, in a voice Juilene had heard many times before. "Countrymen."

Skar halted in midstride, and Juilene almost stumbled. She stared in disbelief as she recognized the man in the chair. "By the goddess," she breathed. She sank into the best curtsy her masculine attire would allow. "Your Highness," she breathed. This was the King, the King of Sylyria, whom all reports had said had gone into exile, fleeing from Lindos and his power.

Jarron smiled, a wry smile that did little to alleviate the deep channels care had carved in his face. But his voice when he spoke was kind, and his pale blue eyes burned steadily in his tired face. He did not look like a king in defeat. "Juilene of Sarrasin. You've led your father a merry chase, my girl."

Juilene shook her head, scarcely sure of what to say or how to begin. "Highness, I—I can explain everything—"

"I'm sure you can, child." The King smiled gently. "We are happy to see you safe. Your father will be greatly relieved."

"How is my father?" Juilene blurted. She had lived for

all these weeks with no idea at all, and the words slipped out heedlessly.

The King shook his head and smiled sadly. "Your father is a brave man who has borne the brunt of this war, my lady. Your disappearance was just the beginning. But he has stood firm, an example to all—both thane and thurge"—here he paused and smiled meaningfully at Deatrice—"who would honor the vows of their rank."

"But—but you do not know if my father lives?"

"He lives, lady, or so we believe. Lindos has claimed all your father's lands and possessions—your father and your brother have been stripped of all they owned. We think they are imprisoned in their own keep." The King paused once more, as if assessing the affect his words had upon her. "I wish I could tell you your father was in good health, and all was well."

Juilene drew herself up. This man had borne and lost as much as she, as much as her father, more, perhaps. She would not dissolve into tears. She would show the King and Cariad, and even this pale, proud lady thurge, that the daughters of the thanes of Sylyria were made of sterner stuff. She drew a deep breath and nodded. "At least there is hope he is still alive."

Jarron nodded approvingly. "Indeed, lady. And while there is life, there is hope. Your own arrival brings us more. Lindos is not indestructible. There must exist a way to contain his power, and restore the order of the League once more."

A chill ran up her spine as Deatrice stepped forward. "You keep strange company, my lady." She rubbed her slim hands together, considering. Her eyes lingered on Cariad, and Juilene tightened her hand in his.

"Will you tell us the names of your companions, my dear?" asked the King.

"Skar, of my father's house," Juilene said, turning and

gesturing to the lanky man on her left. "And this is Cariad, but lately of Thane Diago's house in Khardroon."

"Your Highness," said Cariad, with a bow.

"Of Gravenhage, you are, no?"

Cariad flushed. "Yes, Your Highness. I am."

"Hm. I would know that accent anywhere. Mark is my closest ally in all the League. In fact, one of your countrymen arrived here but late last night. He's still resting from the perils of his journey." Jarron stroked his short black beard. It was heavily shot through with pure white threads. The weeks of exile had taken a toll upon him, but he still was clearly a vigorous man of no more than forty. "In fact, you remind me—is it possible you are connected to the Queen's house?"

"Well . . ." Cariad flushed an even deeper red and let his voice trail off. He looked down.

"Ah," said Jarron, "forgive me, son. I didn't mean to embarrass you. These days my brains and my wits are addled enough. There are many fine men born of noblemen, whose mothers may not have been so noble. A man's connections matter little in times like these. Forgive me."

"But you, too, like the lady when she first arrived here, before the winter," said Deatrice, her eyes narrowed, "you, too—there's power magic on you, sir. Great magic . . ." Her voice trailed off and she cocked her head, a little puckered frown on her face.

"Yes," said Cariad. He glanced at Juilene, as if warning her to say nothing. "Magic I believe which will enable me to defeat Lindos—if I can get close enough."

Deatrice raised her brow, and the King leaned forward. A few of the men gathered around him guffawed softly and he quelled them with a glance. "And why do you think that, my young knight?"

Cariad squared his shoulders and drew himself up. "Because I am the non-born knight."

There were more mutters of derision from the men, but the King only stared and Deatrice sucked her breath in hard. Finally Jarron spoke. "I think it would be better if we continued the rest of this conversation in private." He glanced impatiently at the men who clustered close about his chair. "Away with you, all of you," he said.

The men drew back with guarded expressions. Skar bowed and touched Cariad's arm gently. "I go, too, lord." It was the first time Skar had ever addressed Cariad as anything more than an equal and Juilene was surprised.

Deatrice beckoned. "Come with me." She led the three of them, Cariad and Juilene and the King, down a short corridor and into a small room, which Juilene recognized with immediate distaste. Although a fire leaped in the polished grate, it was only marginally warmer than in the hall. Juilene pushed the unpleasant memories aside. What did any of that matter now? Eral was dead, and here she was, in the company of the King of Sylyria. Who could have foreseen the twists her fate had taken, or the role the goddess had in store for her to play?

She sank to the soft rug beside the hearth as the King and Deatrice and Cariad took chairs.

"I'm warmer here," she said when Cariad offered her a seat.

"So you think you are Lindos's doom?" Jarron demanded without ceremony.

"No, Your Highness," said Cariad. "I know I am."

"How do you know this?" Jarron pressed.

"Because," Cariad spoke slowly, as if measuring every word, "I am not from this time. I come from what will be the future of this present."

Deatrice gasped, and the King glanced at her. "What do you know of this," he asked.

She shook her head. "No-nothing. Such a thing as

breaching time would require knowledge which I don't have—which no one has, I thought."

Cariad nodded. "No one does, lady, not yet. But in the future—"

"Can you prove that?" Jarron asked. "Can you tell me something which has not yet come to pass?"

Cariad wet his lips. "I can tell you that right now you are planning for an assault upon Lindos."

The King blanched. "Yes?"

"Your efforts are doomed to failure, Highness. It will go down in history as the Rout of Arvon. You and all your supporters will be killed. And Lindos will make himself High Thurge of the Conclave."

Jarron breathed a long sigh, his eyes narrowed, his mouth grim. "Killed," he mused. He ran his eyes over Cariad, measuring and assessing. "So if I believe that you are the non-born knight, how can we turn this to our advantage?"

"I am impervious to magic in this time," he said. "I am not sure if that isn't part of it, or not."

"Impervious," asked Deatrice. "What do you mean?"

"I mean magic has no effect upon me, lady. Would you care to try it?"

She narrowed her eyes and glanced around the room, and Juilene knew that Deatrice would like to try it, itched to try it, and dared not. "The confines of this room are too close, my knight," she said, her voice nearly a purr. "There would be danger to the King and to your lady. But," she went on, addressing the King, "when I tried to—to assess the sort of spell he carries—it was almost as if he weren't there, in some way. I can understand how that would affect the magic's effect upon him."

The King drummed his fingers on the arms of the chair, thinking. Finally he said, "What thurge laid this spell upon you?"

"Her name is Rihana. And in my time, she is the Over-Thurge of Khardroon."

Deatrice wrinkled her brow. "Rihana? I never heard of her."

"You would not have, my lady," Cariad said, with that same gentleness Juilene loved. "She is yet not much more than a child. But she is the sister of Thane Diago, who is also a thurge."

Deatrice raised her brows. "Diago! I've heard of him!"

Jarron nodded and stroked his beard. "Indeed. And if his sister is anything like him—"

She's worse, Juilene wanted to say. But she kept silent, watching the three.

"Well," said Jarron, "let us not worry about a thurge who's yet a child. We have enough to deal with now. The situation here is—" He broke off and stared unseeing into the flames.

"If you are impervious to magic," said Deatrice, "Lindos is helpless against you. It would be an easy enough thing for you to kill him."

A chill went down Juilene's back that had nothing to do with the temperature of the room. Easy enough, Deatrice said. The words echoed in her mind, in Arimond's voice. Easy enough to kill him, Arimond had said. Easy. And now Arimond was dead. She raised her head. "We must not underestimate Lindos."

For the first time, the King looked at her and there was kindness and pity in his eyes. "No, Lady Juilene, we will not make that mistake. But we do have one advantage, I think, especially with your presence here."

"And what's that, Your Highness?" asked Cariad. "The layout of Lindos's keep?"

Jarron exchanged glances with Deatrice. "He's not at his keep," Deatrice said softly. She glanced at Juilene.

"No?" asked Cariad. "Where is he then? At the Over-Thurge's palace in the city?"

"No," answered Jarron, his voice equally gentle. He looked at Juilene and his eyes were kind. "He's taken up residence at Castle Sarrasin."

Juilene felt the words like a blow. The thought that the monster could have taken up residence in her father's own house—walked the halls her family had walked, sat and ate and slept within the very chambers she had known and cherished in her memory all these terrible months—twisted in her belly. Nausea washed over her like a wave, and Cariad was half out of his chair before she looked up once more. "I'm all right," she managed weakly.

There was a knock at the door, and the King called, "Enter!" his eyes still on Juilene's face.

A servant stood shivering in the doorway. "Your pardon, My Transcendence, Your Highness, but the young thurge from Gravenhage has awakened at last, and begs leave to join your company. And, Highness, one of your scouts has returned from the western districts."

Jarron got to his feet. "Then I will go and talk to him immediately. There may be something he can tell us that will aid in our discussions." He bowed to Deatrice and Juilene. "Transcendence, Lady Juilene. Will you excuse me?"

"Of course," Deatrice said, "though I must go as well and speak to my demi-thurges who guard the borders. Bring this lady and her knight hot wine and some seed-cakes, if there are any, and I will return directly."

The servant bowed and turned away, and with a rustle of robes, both Deatrice and the King were gone.

Cariad moved to the hearth. "So," he began.

A slight man, younger than Cariad, only a few years older than Juilene, peered into the room. There was something familiar about his face, some set of his chin, some lift of his eyes, and Juilene realized with a start that he had the same dark curling hair as Cariad. But he wore the robes of a thurge, and the thin border around the hem told her he was only a demi-thurge. "I beg your pardon, good sir, my lady, but I was told I would find the lady of the keep here? And the King?"

"So they were, sir, and will return shortly. Will you wait with us?"

The thurge stepped into the room his thick robes swirling around his ankles, and Juilene glanced at Cariad. He gripped the edge of the hearth with a white-knuckled hand and his face had drained of all color. Juilene started to get up, but Cariad motioned to her to stay where she was. She looked at him, a question in her eyes.

"My name is Galanthir of Gravenhage," said the newcomer, extending one hand courteously to Cariad. With a start Juilene recognized the name from Cariad's story.

"I am—" The words seemed to stick in his throat. "I am also of Gravenhage," managed Cariad. "My name is Cariad."

"Of Gravenhage?" repeated Galanthir. His voice was higher than most men's, but he gave the syllables the same lilting lift as Cariad did. "I am very pleased and most surprised to meet you here, my friend." He paused, cocked his head, and regarded Cariad. "Have we ever met before? I—I must confess, I don't recall your name—but your face—"

"My name is Lady Juilene of Sarrasin," said Juilene quickly.

Galanthir raised one coal dark brow. "Lady Juilene. Now I know your name if not your face. The lost lady— the songsayers have made you a legend in Gravenhage already, lady. Though I am very glad to see you've been found." A smile curved the serious mouth, and Juilene, gazing into the pale eyes, saw gentleness and humor, and something that reminded her of Cariad, and she glanced at her lover once more.

The two were turned in profile to each other, and with a start, Juilene saw exactly what it was. The two of them resembled each other, not so much that they looked like brothers, but the family resemblance was strong. No wonder Galanthir looked so puzzled.

"Thank you, sir," she said. She nodded and smiled and thanked Neri for all the hours of etiquette lessons that not even months of deprivation could erase.

"Will you sit, sir?" asked Cariad.

Galanthir nodded, and took the chair Deatrice had just vacated. "What brings you to this part of Sylyria, my friend?"

"I—I was in the serve of a thane of Khardroon," answered Cariad.

Galanthir cocked his head at Cariad. "Forgive me—I do not mean to stare at you, but surely, we have met—"

"Yes," said Cariad. He faced Galanthir. "We have." The eyes of the two men met but Galanthir said nothing, only waited. "Though strictly speaking, we have not met yet—but we will."

Galanthir raised one eyebrow. "Tell me who you are."

"My name is Cariad. I am the son of Queen Mirta and General Keriaan."

"Keriaan is only a captain," Galanthir said softly.

"He will be promoted very shortly, partly in reward for his part in the coming battle."

Galanthir stared at Cariad, then glanced at Juilene. Finally his eyes settled on Cariad, scanning his face over and over, as if searching. "Are you implying you've been sent here from the future?" Galanthir asked.

Cariad nodded and Juilene shifted her weight. There was something different about this young man. He spoke as calmly as if meeting someone who claimed to be from the future were an everyday occurrence. His next question surprised her even more.

"Did I send you?"

"No. You helped. I am, after all, your nephew."

The same wry smile flitted across the features of both men. Juilene slowly let out the breath she hadn't realized she was holding.

"Lindos's doom is the non-born knight," said Cariad.

Galanthir nodded. "And so here you are." He rose and paced before the fire, his robes swirling. "But—" His whole frame quivered with suppressed energy, and Juilene realized that despite his demeanor, Galanthir was anything but calm. "There're so many questions I have for you—" He stopped and turned and glanced from Cariad to Juilene. "But you—you are of this time, no?"

She nodded.

He ran a hand over his forehead and down his cheek. "So many questions—this raises so many possibilities—" He stepped in one direction, seemed to think better of it, and resumed his pacing in the opposite direction. Finally he threw himself into a chair. "Keriaan and the Queen—hmm—then—" He shook his head. "Ah, never mind that now. The fact is that you are here—no matter the circumstances of your birth. But let me ask you this, for I must know, in your time—where you come from—Lindos is alive?"

Cariad nodded. "Yes. Very much so."

"So by sending you back in time—to be the non-born knight—to bring about his doom—the future—your present—will change." Galanthir looked from one to the other.

Cariad nodded again. "Yes. I suppose you are right."

Galanthir frowned. "And whether that's a good thing or a bad thing—" He broke off. "I'm not sure there's time to consider all the implications." He sighed.

"No," said Cariad, "nor are we."

"What will happen here—according to the history that you know?"

"The forces of the King will be defeated. There will be a plan to force Lindos out of Sarrasin. But it will fail, and the King's army will be routed on the banks of the River Arvon."

Galanthir listened. "Jarron hopes that Gravenhage will come to his aid. But in truth—although Keriaan, Captain Keriaan, is poised upon the border, there will be no aid from Gravenhage. That is why I have come, by routes as dark and circuitous as any you have walked, my lady. Lindos has Keriaan's wife, Amanda, as hostage, and there are rumors that she is with child."

"The rumors are true," said Cariad softly.

Galanthir started. "How can you be—" He broke off, and his expression was grim. "Keriaan and Amanda have waited a long time for this child." Cariad said nothing, and Galanthir regarded him closely. "What else can you tell me?"

Cariad spread his hands. "Perhaps you would rather not know."

Galanthir laughed, briefly, without humor. "Surely you know nephew"—he spoke the word with bitter irony—"that what we would rather not has nothing to do with our present situation."

Cariad drew a deep breath. "You're right. Of course. Keriaan's wife, the lady Amanda, is indeed pregnant. She dies in childbirth, although her daughter is spared. Keriaan, when he hears of this, is so angered and distraught that against every order he rides over the border of Sylyria and rescues the infant, returning with her to Gravenhage. In the process, he manages to inflict a fair amount of damage to Lindos's reserves. His heroism is" —Cariad seemed to search for the proper word—"rewarded."

"By the attentions of the Queen?"

Cariad nodded briefly.

"And what of the Sylyrian King? What of Lindos?"

"Jarron is defeated." Cariad looked Galanthir squarely in the eyes. "A truce is reached—but the battle they are planning is remembered as the Rout of Arvon."

"I see." Galanthir turned away. "And why did the assault at Arvon fail?"

Cariad shook his head. "From everything I have understood, the mistake was to try and force Lindos out of his castle."

"It's not his castle," Juilene interrupted.

"Forgive me," Cariad said. "I should know better. But it seems to me that goading Lindos into moving was not the answer. Lindos must be taken by surprise—before he has time to work his magic—before he has an opportunity to strategize with his own thurges."

Galanthir nodded. "Yes. Now, if we can only think of a distraction—something to bring us in close enough—"

"I can think of something," Juilene said.

The two men looked at her. "And what's that," asked Galanthir kindly. He looked at her with the same expression one gave to an adorable child, and Juilene gritted her teeth.

"You heard what the demi-thurge said, who raised the border for us." Juilene looked at Cariad. "He said Lindos was looking for me. What if I go to Sarrasin, and pretend that—that I am coming back to him?"

Cariad frowned. "I don't like the idea of you as bait, Juilene. I don't like that at all."

"But what if we go with her?" asked Galanthir, who was looking at Juilene with new respect. "As emissaries from the King of Gravenhage?"

Cariad exchanged glances with Juilene. "I'm not sure I

like that. It smacks of what you tried once, lady, and failed. Surely you know that I would never—"

"Is my name mentioned in the history books?" asked Juilene. "Is my father's name, or any of my family?'"

"No." He shook his head slowly.

"Then maybe this is the way it should have been all along, Cariad. Maybe Arimond wasn't totally wrong in what he tried to do—only it was the wrong time and the wrong place and the wrong—"

"Knight?" supplied Galanthir.

She stopped in midspeech. "Yes. He wasn't the nonborn knight, but you are. And we know Lindos wants me. He'll let me in. And how can he not let you in? Would he dare to defy the King of another city in the League?"

"In my time, he would," said Cariad.

"But he's not that strong yet, is he? And you know we can stop him. Between the two of us—the three of us—" she paused to include Galanthir—"between us we can distract him so that he won't have time to make plans, and the Rout of Arvon will go down as the Siege of Sarrasin. And if Lindos can be stopped, then Sarrasin need not be destroyed."

Galanthir and Cariad exchanged a long look. Finally Cariad nodded. "We can discuss it with the King, lady. Though to bait a trap with you is not to my liking."

The bedroom they were given to share was cold. Juilene huddled beneath the covers, wishing Cariad would hurry. But he had still been hunkered down before the fire, discussing strategy and tactics with Galanthir and the King's advisers, and Juilene had felt useless and out of place. All evening he had said little to her, ever since that afternoon when she had suggested that she go back to Lindos. She knew he was upset with her, but surely even he could see that there were no guarantees of safety to anyone?

Deatrice and Jarron were nowhere to be found, and Juilene suspected that the thurge had chosen to entertain her highest-ranking guest in private. Well, why not, she thought. The thurges answered to no laws but their own—she knew that now—and who was to say that a woman who was a thurge should willingly bind herself to any rules of propriety.

She turned on her side, curling her feet up and under herself. The linen sheets were crisp and white and very clean, and the blankets were thick and smelled of summer herbs. But the cold pervaded every corner of the room, and the fire burning brightly in the grate did little to warm the air. The candles flickered as the door opened and closed. "Blessed goddess," Cariad muttered as he stepped into the room, shivering. "I've never felt such cold." She watched him strip and dive under the covers. Immediately he reached for her warmth. "There," he said, between teeth clenched to keep from chattering. "That's better."

She said nothing, only curled closer to him.

"What's wrong?" he asked, against the mass of her hair on the pillow.

"Cariad," she whispered. "What will become of us? Of you and me, once Lindos is dead?"

There was a long silence. "I don't know, Juilene. I will talk to my uncle—though it's hard to think of him that way—now, while he's so young. He's younger than I am. If there is any way we can be together—"

She snuggled deeper into the pillow. Waves of longing and sadness washed over her. The candles did little to brighten the darkness, and the thick blankets barely made a difference in the chill. A tear slipped down her face.

"Juilene?" His voice was tender. "Please—you must know I will do everything I can. I don't want to lose you, either—that's why—"

"Maybe it would be better if I did die in Sarrasin," Juilene said, her voice muffled by the pillow.

"What?" He forced her over, flat on her back. "Ah, Juilene, don't even talk that way. Don't even think like that. I can't bear the thought of losing you, of anything happening to you. Don't you understand that's why I am less than enthusiastic about this scheme which brings you right into Lindos's grasp? But—" He clasped her to him and held her close against his chest. "This is part of it, don't you see?"

She raised her head. "What is?"

"This despair—this sadness—this belief that everything is hopeless. Everyone is affected by it, though Deatrice and her thurges do what they can to mitigate the effect. Galanthir suggested to me privately that the border of Sylyria is sealed because the people believe it to be sealed."

"What? But you and I saw the border—"

"Yes, yes, I know we did, but the point is, Juilene, don't give up."

"I don't want to lose you and I don't want you to be angry with me."

"And I don't want to put you in danger."

There was a long silence, and finally she raised her face to his once more. "I cannot believe the goddess brought us together only to tear us apart."

"No." He smiled into her eyes. "Nor can I."

"Cariad," she said hesitantly, "I—I have been thinking—what if there should be a child—"

He drew a quick breath. "No, you needn't worry."

"Worry? I don't worry—I would welcome a child of yours—"

"No, you don't understand. In this time I cannot father children. Just as magic doesn't affect me—well, there are certain other things that are affected as well. But rest now, my sweet. Tomorrow is another long, cold day."

She settled down against him, turning the information

over and over in her mind. No child. And Cariad would go back to the future as soon as he was conceived. What then would she have of him? What, except her memories? She forced the sad thoughts away and closed her eyes. Goddess, send me sleep, she prayed, and for once, Dramue's answer came swiftly.

Chapter Sixteen

The snow was deep and the roads were rutted pits of ice. Juilene shivered and pressed closer to Cariad's warmth as the cart bounced over the deepest ruts and the horses staggered and fought for their footing on the pitted surface. The sun glared down, all light and no heat. Her eyes hurt. Could she have forgotten the depths of a Sylyrian winter? No, she realized. This was no normal winter. According to the calendar, spring should have made its approaching presence felt. This unnatural cold was Lindos's doing. Deatrice had explained something of the spell to them before they left. The spell lay over the land like a web, and in truth, as the hours passed, she felt as though they did push deeper into unseen barriers.

She squinted ahead, trying to see through the sunblindness. They couldn't be more than a few hours ride from her father's keep now. Along the way, the roads had been eerily empty. Not one soul moved across the barren landscape, and although the roads were packed down, there was no evidence, no signs that anyone had traveled upon them in a long time. What was happening here? she wondered once more as she huddled in the circle of Cariad's arm.

Why hadn't the League risen up against Lindos? she wondered as she watched Deatrice's heavily garbed servants urge the horses on once more. The whole League seemed to have drawn back, to allow whatever was happening in Sylyria to happen. Are they blind? she wondered as the cart lurched forward. Are they blind not to realize that what can happen in Sylyria can happen anywhere? Or are they all afraid of Lindos?

She glanced over at Cariad. His mouth was grim and drawn. Without the blankets and the thick cloaks Deatrice had provided for them, they surely would have frozen to death. Even the bandits who roamed the roads had been absent, and when she had questioned Cariad, he had replied with a furrowed brow: "Robbers require people to rob, lady."

And she had known for certain then that something had happened in her native city, something more terrible than she could imagine, and she had wished she had paid more attention to the lessons of the demi-thurge her father had engaged to teach her history and the uses of the power the long-ago thurges commanded.

"Does anything look familiar, yet?" Cariad interrupted her thoughts.

She glanced over at him with a start. "No—no, not yet. Everything looks so different now—this snow, this ice—"

Cariad nodded. "I understand, lady." He glanced around once more. "Not even a village—were there not villages on this road? There's been no sign at all . . ." His voice trailed away as a bitter gust of wind blew icy snow in their faces.

He tightened his grip on her. She watched as Cariad and Skar exchanged another glance. At least they were together. The thought of going to Lindos terrified her. She had no reason to doubt that what Cariad said was true—she believed wholly that he was the non-born knight. But so many things could go wrong . . . Her thoughts trailed off into a troubled jumble. Beside her, the harp gave a soft strum. She glanced down at her gloved hands. She had no doubt that the sapphire on her finger was glowing a vivid blue.

The road forked, and Cariad slowed the cart to a near halt and looked around. "Now which way?"

Juilene followed his gaze in all directions. On the distant horizon, a dark smudge rose against the bright white sky. "That way—I think."

"All right," Cariad said with a sigh.

Juilene bit her lip. "There should have been villages all along this road."

"Yes," he said as he flapped the reins. "I know."

"Deatrice was right." There was a little catch in her throat she couldn't conceal. "He's destroyed everything."

"He can't have destroyed everything, Juilene. What use is a land laid waste? The villages may have been destroyed, but the villagers are still alive—most of them, anyway. And the keeps of the thanes—he's left most of them intact—only has his own people in them. When this snow clears away, you'll see."

Juilene took a deep breath, willing herself to believe what Cariad told her. "If the snow ever clears."

"As soon as Lindos is dead, it will clear." Galanthir spoke from the back of the cart. Whatever spell Lindos had laid upon the hearts and minds of the people never affected him. He was quietly and unfailingly optimistic, even as depression settled upon Juilene, pulling her deeper and deeper into herself.

The cart bounced over the rough ice. Cariad kept one arm tightly around her. She smiled bitterly, remembering a time when she would have protested that such a display was not proper, no matter what the weather. So very much had changed. Everything had changed. She glanced back at the harp, strapped securely to the seat, wrapped in thick oiled skins. She had debated taking the harp with her when they went to Lindos, but the idea of facing the wizard without the strength the harp seemed to endow was more than she could bear. Who knew what awaited them? The harp thrummed a low note with each jolt of the cart.

As the road wound down into a low valley, she could see the high towers of the keep rising black against the white winter sky. She shivered uncontrollably. "Be brave, sweet," Cariad whispered. "Be brave."

They rounded a rise, and spindly, twisted trees rose on either side of the road, their bare branches reminded her of outstretched skeletal hands. Could that have been the little clearing where Arimond's friends had waited for her return; where she had watched and waited, and where Lindos had found her? She drew a deep breath and the cart lurched on.

The road threaded through the trees now, and the long blue shadows softened the blinding brilliance of the light, but the intertwining branches arching overhead reminded her of bars. But this was the road for home, she knew, and joy, great and unchecked, bubbled up within her, conflicting with her feelings of deep and utter dread.

Suddenly, the walls of Sarrasin rose before them, high and dark and somehow forbidding. Nothing moved upon the walls, no banners floated in the crisp air, the gates were locked and barred. Grey smoke leaked from the chimneys, wreathing the towers in grey clouds that shifted but never quite dissipated. She swallowed hard. Fear and despair descended on her like a shroud, and she tried to fight. I mustn't think this way, she told herself, over and over again. I mustn't let it affect me. If I let it, then Lindos has won.

Cariad pulled on the reins and the horses slowed to a stop. "We're here."

Galanthir scrambled up behind them, erupting out of the mountain of robes under which he had buried himself. "Look there," he said. "What's that?"

As the three of them watched from their perch in the cart, the great gates slowly swung open. Black-robed figures marched out in precise formation, and Juilene saw they bore no arms.

"Demi-thurges," Galanthir whispered. "And they're crawling with sprites."

Juilene squinted and saw nothing, but she remembered all too well the misshapen creatures that had lurked in the halls and corners of Lindos's keep. Bile rose in her throat as the memory of that night made her nauseous. I won't think of that night, she insisted to herself. I won't.

The thurges lined up on either side of the road leading up to the gate. "I don't see any sprites," murmured Cariad.

"Oh, they're there," answered Galanthir. "That's the trouble with thurge-sight. Sometimes you see things you'd really rather not."

A lone figure marched out from the keep, down the middle of the row of demi-thurges. He wore a long black cloak, bordered in red glyphs, but despite the richness of his apparel, it was clear from the markings that he, too, was only a demi-thurge.

"That's interesting," Galanthir muttered. "Are we to think that Lindos keeps no master-thurges by his side?"

The man paused halfway down the row. "State your business." He spoke without feeling or inflection.

"I say the songs the goddess sends," Juilene said, surprised how strong she sounded.

"There is no welcome for songsayers beneath this roof. Be off."

"I think your master will welcome me," Juilene said, thrusting her chin forward. "Go and tell him that Lady Juilene of Sarrasin has come home."

If the three expected a ripple of recognition to reverberate through the thurges, they were disappointed. Not one moved a muscle. "Interesting," mused Galanthir.

The demi-thurge turned on his heel and for a moment they thought they were dismissed. Then he raised his arm and beckoned for them to follow. Cariad sucked in a deep breath audibly and flapped the reins. The horses moved forward.

"Well," said Galanthir, "let's hope your name remains the charm it would seem it is."

And with a shudder and a sigh, Juilene nestled closer to Cariad as they passed beneath the gates of the home she had longed to see. A lump rose in her throat as the shadow of the gates fell across her lap. She felt as if her throat closed, as if she couldn't get her breath. Cariad made a little sound of encouragement. Shadows swirled within the courtyard, dark and sinuous, like grasping tendrils. Waves of darkness washed over her. Her limbs felt heavy, as though weights were pressing her down from all directions. She struggled to stay upright, but all her efforts against the spell were useless. She had just enough time to whisper, "Cariad" as her vision clouded and she crumpled in her seat.

The sound of singing brought her back. It was Neri's song, an old, old lullaby, one of her oldest memories of childhood, and the voice was Neri's voice. Her eyes fluttered open, and for a moment, everything was blurred, and then Neri's face came into focus. She gasped and tried to sit up, but the old woman pressed her shoulder down.

"Neri," she cried, "Nenny, it's you."

"Yes, yes," the old woman said, laughing and crying all at once. "Yes, child, it's me—and more's the blessing—it's you!"

Juilene struggled to sit up. She wrapped the old woman in a joyous hug. Neri felt thin, fragile, far more frail than she remembered. She pulled back and in the glow of one stump of a candle, which was the only source of light the room offered, searched the old woman's face. "Nenny, how're your hands? Were they very bad?"

The old woman smiled and pushed a lock of Juilene's hair behind one ear. "No, child, they healed. I'm fine. And so very happy to see that you are all right. You had us all worried sick about you, you know?"

"So I've heard. But what about Father? And Lazare and Eliane? Are they here? Are they all right? And Cariad and Galanthir—"

"Hush," said Neri, smoothing Juilene's cheek as though she couldn't bear to stop touching her. "All in good time, child. Your father will be much better once he sees that you're safe."

"Better? What's that monster done to him?"

Neri took both of Juilene's hands in hers. Juilene looked down and saw the red shiny scars, and bit her lip. "Child, you—you have to understand. Things have been very difficult with your father since you left. All the troubles, you see . . ." Her voice trailed off.

"What's wrong, Nenny? Is Father sick?"

Neri met her eyes with compassion. "Sick, yes. And heartsore, with worry for you. But ever since—ever since that—that man came here, your father's—"

"What's Lindos done?"

"He's not himself anymore." Neri shook her head and turned away. "He's not himself."

"What do you mean? He's sick?"

"He's out of his head, I guess you could say. He doesn't know where he is, most of the time, and much of the time he doesn't know who he is or who any of us are. But don't you worry—he'll know you, I'm sure of it, and that will make it ever so much better."

"Don't count on it." A younger woman's voice cut through the chill air, and Juilene looked up. In the doorway, Eliane, Lazare's wife, stood, a shawl clutched to her throat, her dress, threadbare and much patched. She hardly resembled the proper lady of her rank Juilene remembered.

"Eliane!" Juilene was so happy to see her again, she forgot the differences they had sometimes had.

The woman let her thin mouth bend just a little. "I'm glad to see you haven't suffered much, Juilene. You look wonderfully well for all your experiences."

Juilene sat back, shocked and more than a little hurt. "How—how are things here, Eliane?"

"Hasn't Neri told you? Awful, that's how they are. Terrible. Your father's a drooling idiot, Lazare's ill of some fever that won't break, I've nothing to wear from one day to the next, and you come dancing in, after giving us all months of worry, looking as fresh as tomorrow's rose." Eliane turned on her heel and stalked away, her thin slippers slapping against the floor.

Juilene turned back to Neri. "Is it really as bad as all that?"

Neri smiled sadly. "Things are very different from when you left, child. But you mustn't blame yourself. That's Eliane talking, not the rest of us. I know you and Arimond meant well. And even Lazare says matters were bound to come to a head, sooner or later. It was only foolishness that got you stuck in the middle of it all."

Juilene sat back with a sigh. "I didn't realize how you all would suffer, too."

"No, child." Neri shook her head. "Don't listen to Eliane. Of anyone, Lindos treats her better than the rest of us."

"Do you—do you see him?"

"No." Neri shook her head. "Not since—not since the first few days he came. He sends his minions."

Juilene smiled at the word. That didn't sound like Neri. "Minions?"

"What your brother calls his friends."

Juilene smiled in spite of her fears. Lazare was so much like her father. He would refuse to be cowed, and would fight with every method at his disposal. And if disdain were all he had left— She took a deep breath and tried not to think such despairing thoughts. "Will you take me to Father?"

Neri patted her hand. "I will, child, in a little while. But first, can't you tell me what's happened to you?"

Juilene glanced around the room. They were in one of the round towers. Although night had fallen, and the turrets outside were swathed in darkness, she could dimly make out the lights upon the walls. The lone candle spat greasy wax and gave off little light. "All right." She glanced down at her hands. The sapphire glowed gently, a pale, soft blue. Who would ever have thought that there could be danger for her beneath these roofs?

She took a deep breath, and told the story to Neri, leaving out a few of the more unsavory parts, such as Eral and Diago. There was no sense in upsetting the old woman. And when she came to the part about the harp and the songsayer, she didn't tell Neri how close to death she herself had come. She didn't say who Cariad was, or how he came to be there, or even that the harp she carried was most likely the Harp of Dramue. But from the woman's white face, and the little noises she made, Juilene knew the tale was quite lurid enough. At last she paused.

Heavy footfalls were coming down the corridor. Neri rose and stood in the doorway. A black-robed figure thrust a pitcher and a tray into her hands. The figure said nothing, just continued on its way.

Neri brought the tray back into the room and set it down on a low rickety table that rocked alarmingly at the weight. "Dinner." She smiled wryly.

Juilene got up. On a rough wooden tray lay a loaf of course bread. The pitcher was full of acrid wine, scarcely the stuff her father had allowed the servants to drink. She turned to see Neri pulling a ragged cloth from a chest near the bed. "This is all he gives you to eat?"

Neri nodded. "There's a loaf for all of us, and then gruel in the morning—that's all."

Juilene twisted her mouth. Had she expected anything more?

"Don't fret, child. We've enough. Though I doubt it's enough for the poor lady with child—the lady from Gravenhage. Truly, he's left us alone for the last weeks and things are better."

"Better?" Juilene rounded on Neri. "You call this better because he ignores you all? Leaves you to starve, I would say. Take me to Father, now, Neri. I want to see what's been done to him. And then you must tell me what you can of the lady from Gravenhage—where is she?"

The old woman pursed her lips. "She's in the tower opposite. On sunny days I see her walking on the battlements. I fear the bread and gruel is not enough for her." Neri's voice trailed off.

"I want to see Father."

"Very well," Neri said at last.

She beckoned Juilene down the short corridor, and in the doorway of another room, she paused. Eliane was sitting by a narrow bed. She looked up when she heard their foot-steps, and a frown wrinkled her brow. "He's sleeping."

Juilene tiptoed closer. "I'll not wake him." She leaned over her father, and could scarcely conceal her gasp of dis-belief. Could this wasted shell of a man truly be her father? This man's body looked caved in, somehow, as though the muscles and the sinews had collapsed upon themselves. His hair had been hacked off close about his head, and his mouth was slack, his nose thin and pinched. A thin line of spittle stained his cheek. She swallowed her tears and backed away.

She heard Eliane's snort of derision, and Neri's soft ad-monishment. Then she was back in Neri's room, her head buried in her hands. She had thought that if she left, no harm would come to the people she loved. Indeed, it seemed that they had suffered more than she. She pressed her fists against her eyes, forbidding herself to cry. Where was Cariad? she wondered. What had happened to him and to Galanthir? Had the ruse worked? Did Lindos believe that they were emissaries from King Mark?

It was a dangerous, deceitful game they were playing, and Juilene rose and paced to the window. Below her, lights flickered fitfully. Nothing else moved upon the walls, and no living person could be seen. She saw move-ment out of the corner of her eye, and she turned, her skirts swirling. Nothing. She remembered what Galanthir had said about the thurge sprites, and she shuddered.

Neri came in, softly closing the door behind her. "Eat, child. You'll feel better if you do."

Juilene sank down onto a low stool, the only chair the room offered. "I thought you'd all be safe if I left, Nenny. I thought you wouldn't suffer."

"Child, this isn't your fault. How many times do you need to hear it? Your father opposed Lindos—he would have done that whether you were here to see it or not. Do you think he would have listened to you?"

"No." She reached for the hunk of bread that Neri offered. It was stale and dry and tasted like ashes in her mouth. She looked around the room. Her harp, she realized with a start. What had happened to her harp? It had been in the cart. But where was it now?

She opened her mouth to ask Neri about the harp when a knock sounded on the door. Neri looked frightened. Juilene got to her feet. "I'll open it." She jerked open the door. A thurge stood silently. "What do you want?"

"The Lord Lindos commands your presence." The man eyed her with speculative interest, and Juilene tossed her hair over her shoulder. She was no untried girl. She stared back at the man, bold as she could, and he smiled, his uneven yellow teeth gleaming in the dim light. "Oh, you won't look so brazen when Lord Lindos sees to you, lady. Not so brazen at all."

Juilene said nothing, but refused to let her eyes drop. "Take me to him"—she hesitated the fraction of an instant—"minion."

Behind her she could hear Neri's soft chuckle all the way down the winding stairs.

Her father's audience room just off the hall was exactly as she remembered it. A lump rose in her throat, and she had to suppress a sigh as she followed the thurge through the great keep. It all looked the same as she remembered it, the very same, but the atmosphere was nothing like she remembered at all.

Now shadows seemed to gather and pool on the perimeters of the rooms and on the stairs, and she constantly detected movement on the periphery of her vision. She only prayed that the rest of the plan would work. She had heard them discussing it, Cariad and Galanthir. The King had begun to move his troops across the frozen landscape, even while the thurges and the demi-thurges under Deatrice set up the spells that hopefully would launch an attack long before Lindos was aware that any army stood within striking distance. Her skirts made a heavy whisper across the dusty floor.

The thurge stood aside and allowed her to pass in front of him, and then closed the door behind her. She heard the turn of a key in the lock. She blinked. The light of a hundred candles or more illuminated the room.

"So, my dear Lady Juilene, welcome home." His voice was the same sibilant whisper that made her flesh crawl.

She raised her face but said nothing.

"Well, well. I see you've changed. What brings you here?"

"Did you think you would keep me away from my house and my family forever?"

He smiled, bitter and cruel. "Do you take me for a fool, Lady Juilene?" He gave her title a subtle emphasis.

She shifted on her feet, uncertain of his meaning. "I think you're the cruelest man alive."

"But you came back." He raked her with his cold eyes. "Did you think you and your newest knight would stop me?"

A knife twisted in her heart, but she gripped the fabric of her gown and vowed he wouldn't see her fear. "We come as emissaries of King Mark. To find out the welfare of the Lady Amanda, whom he has heard is with child."

He laughed. "Emissaries of King Mark. You are amusing, my dear. Well, since the welfare of the Lady Amanda concerns you so, allow me to reassure you."

He opened the door and spoke in low words. Juilene heard a murmured assent. Lindos turned back to her with a sardonic smile. "Please, my lady. Sit."

She sank down, holding her back as straight as possible,

keeping her shoulders squared. A long moment passed and then she heard the patter of slippered feet and the tramp of boots. The door was flung wide, and a woman stood just outside the threshold. Lindos smiled. "Come in, my dear. You have a guest."

Juilene looked up. The woman's face was thin and pale, and beneath her dark eyes, her bloodless cheeks were smudged with deep circles. Her chilblained hands rested on the round swell of her huge belly, a belly grotesquely out of all proportion to the rest of her stick-thin body. She glanced past Lindos to Juilene, and an unspoken question was clear on her face.

"Allow me to present the Lady Amanda of Gravenhage, my dear." Lindos reached out and touched the lady's face caressingly, and she dodged his hand with a little cry of disgust. "Lady Amanda, the Lady Juilene. You've heard of her, I'm sure."

Amanda's eyes grew wide, and Juilene rose to her feet. "The King of Gravenhage, my lady, is most concerned for your welfare. Neither he nor your husband has forgotten you—they bid you keep a high heart."

Amanda drew a deep breath, closed her eyes, and opened them. "Thank you, my lady. You are most kind." She avoided looking at Lindos.

"Are you well?" Juilene thought the lady looked anything but well. No wonder what Cariad said would happen would come to pass. The lady looked as though she would hardly survive the walk back to the tower.

"I am well, enough. You may assure my husband, and my king, that I have not lost my faith in either." Her eyes blazed in her thin face, and there might have only been the two of them in the room.

"Oh," said Lindos, "I doubt the Lady Juilene will be in much of a position to do that—though I might allow the demi-thurge she brought with her to go back—"

"Demi-thurge?" Amanda looked at Lindos for the first time since entering.

"Your brother-in-law, Galanthir," answered Juilene before Lindos could speak. She wondered desperately if there were some way to get Galanthir to see Amanda. "He came himself."

"He's here?" Amanda whispered.

Lindos smiled. "For all the good it will do you, my lady, yes. He's here." He snapped his fingers. "Take her back."

Amanda pressed her lips together. "Tell him—tell him I am well, my lady. Tell him I have not forgotten my promises—please, lady?"

"Of course," answered Juilene as the door slammed shut.

"So," said Lindos. "You've seen her. And now what do you propose to do?" He sat down, leaned back in his chair, and raised one eyebrow. "Well?"

"Anything I can to stop you."

His expression did not change. "And how do you intend to do that?"

She only smiled.

At once he was on his feet, looming over her. "Don't try and play games with me, little songsayer. Whatever you think you might have planned—think again. You can only fail." He touched her cheek in the same caressing manner he had Amanda's and Juilene shrank back immediately. He smiled at her reaction. "Oh, not to worry, my dear. When I'm ready to take you, you'll thank the goddess the worst is over." He twined his fingers in her thick curls, and yanked her face closer to his. A knock on the door made him release her. "Well?" he barked without turning around.

The door swung open and a soldier stumbled inside, his eyebrows and beard covered in icy condensation. His boots were caked in snow. "Lord—" he began, his voice hoarse.

"Well?"

"There've been reports of movement along the River Arvon. It seems an army is moving into the area, through the southern foothills."

At once Lindos released Juilene and rounded on the soldier. "How many?"

"That's difficult to say, lord," answered the soldier with a hint of sullenness in his voice. "The snow—the ice—the cold—all make it hard for our scouts."

"Where are they?"

"Being revived," the man answered. "There are only two who made it back, and they're half-frozen. The physicians are with them now."

"Bring them to me as soon as they are able to stand."

"Yes, my lord." The soldier bowed curtly and was gone.

Lindos looked back at Juilene with narrowed eyes. "You know something about this, don't you? It's no accident you came now, is it? Emissaries of King Mark, indeed. Have you ever in your life laid eyes on the man?" His mouth twisted. "Little fool. Come with me. Allow me to show you your precious knight." He snapped his fingers and the door opened. He yanked her out of the room.

Down the darkened corridor, he strode, Juilene hurrying at his heels. His hand was like an iron clamp on her wrist, and he tugged her arm so viciously she thought it would break from her socket. They came to the stairs that led to the cellars below the castle and he started down, Juilene tripping behind him. Torches flared on the dank walls, and the chill that pervaded the air cut her to the bone.

They passed the kitchen levels and continued on, down to levels Juilene had never explored in all the years she had lived in Sarrasin. Her ankle twisted as they reached the bottom and he jerked her upright. She stifled her cry by biting down on her lip so hard she tasted blood.

He looked down at her with a sneer. "That's nothing

compared to what you'll feel when I have my way with you," he whispered.

She straightened up and pulled her shoulders square. She would never give this wretch the satisfaction of her pain, never. She stared at him with all the hatred she could muster.

He only laughed and jerked her forward. Water dripped from the ceiling and leaked down the walls. The stones beneath their feet were uneven and covered here and there with mold and lichenous growth. Rot pervaded the air, and offal, and something worse, something sickly sweet that made her gag every time a whiff of whatever it was reached her nostrils.

Finally they paused before a heavy iron door. A black-robed thurge stood before it. He nodded to his master.

Lindos ignored him and walked in. Juilene gasped. Cariad and Galanthir hung in chains, naked but for breech-clouts. Deep welts and bruises marred the whiteness of their skins, and blood oozed from deep wounds. Juilene bit her lip to keep from crying out. Cariad raised his head at the sound of Lindos's voice, and when he saw Juilene, he closed his eyes.

Lindos picked up a whip. "You thought to fool me, boy? I want to know the plot you're a part of—the name of the thurge who put you up to this—do you hear me? The name!" He cracked the whip. The long tail licked out, curled around Cariad's legs, and left a bloody trail in its trace.

"No!" Juilene cried. "No—please. Leave him alone—let him go. It was all my idea. Please."

Lindos turned to her, caressing the whip in his hand. "Do you think I believe that? There's the stink of a thurge all over him—and I want to know who it is that dares to challenge me." He turned once more and this time the leather lash snaked out and around and fell on both men. They twisted in their bonds, and Galanthir moaned.

"This is nothing," Lindos whispered, gripping her and forcing her to look at them. "Have you ever seen magic ripped off of someone? It's a painful process, trust me, and there are ways to make it even more so. But I might keep them around a few days more—because to tell you the truth, I'm enjoying it. And the sight of you, my dear, watching, is even more pleasure than I could imagine."

"Let me speak to him," she begged. "Let me talk to them."

Lindos raised his eyebrow. "What for? Talk sense into them? And spoil my fun?" He drew the handle of the whip down her cheek. "Well. I suppose there're all kinds of pleasure."

He walked out and shut the door. Juilene turned and looked at Cariad. "By the goddess," she whispered. "Can this be true?"

"Lady," whispered Galanthir. "There might be yet a way."

She drew closer, wishing she had water, salve, anything, to lessen their pain. "Listen to him, Juilene," croaked Cariad.

"He doesn't know—he cannot see—who Cariad is. He can sense the magic—he sees the spell but vaguely and it drives him mad. I think there's a way—for me to use my magic—to cut his bonds—but Lindos must be in the room. And you must not be—do you understand? I can't guarantee a great deal of control—" Galanthir swallowed hard.

"When will you do this?"

"We must do it soon," Cariad said, raising his eyes. "I am not sure how much more of this I can stand."

"But how will you kill him?" Juilene asked.

"Don't worry, Juilene. Just get him in here alone—and get yourself out."

The door opened and slammed shut. A dark-robed thurge stood just inside. "Time's up."

"They—these gentlemen want your master."

"Master's gone to his bed." The thurge leered at her.

"Then get him back," Juilene spat. Behind her, she heard Galanthir and Cariad stir in their chains. It had to be soon, she knew, before infection set in and made their wounds suppurate, and fever or worse struck them. What if they became like her father. Juilene stared the thurge in the eye, and something must have made the man back down, for he turned and left the cell.

"Good luck," she whispered to them both. She stood on tiptoe and pressed a gentle kiss to Cariad's mouth. "I love you."

"I love you too, Juilene."

Measured steps sounded in the doorway. "Touching little love scene." Lindos laughing low in his throat. "Well?"

"They say they'll talk." Juilene made as if to brush past him, but he caught her by the arm.

Galanthir met her eyes, and Juilene gave a quick nod. Whatever he would do, he should do, without care or worry for her.

"I am the son of the Queen of Gravenhage," said Cariad, his voice rough and harsh in his throat.

Lindos laughed. "The Queen? She's no older than you are—tell me something that's true."

"Use your thurge-sight," goaded Juilene. "You'll see it's true."

Lindos shot her a look but she met his eyes fearlessly. She was tired of being afraid. If they were all to die in this miserable dungeon beneath her father's keep, so be it. Better to die trying to stop Lindos than to live knowing they had failed.

He pushed her away and she fell, stumbling back to the door. Lindos shut his eyes, and in that moment, she saw

Galanthir's lips move. A powerful ball of fire erupted right over Cariad's head, and the chains melted. He dropped to the floor, the metal flowing off his skin like heavy syrup, with no more thought than if it had been drops of water. He rose in a half crouch.

Lindos raised his head and gazed at Cariad, and his face blanched whiter than the snow that lay so thick outside. "You!"

Cariad advanced. "Yes. I'm the one you were so certain would never come. I am the non-born knight."

Lindos wet his lips and backed away, his mouth working in the silent words of a spell. The air shimmered and sprites materialized out of every corner, crowding and crawling all over the walls, the ceiling, and the floor. Juilene shrieked as the misshapen monsters moved near her, but she saw they were converging on Cariad. Or they were trying to, for it seemed that though they tried to reach him, to touch him, their grabbing claws slid off him as easily as the molten metal had. He straightened to his full height, and grabbed for Lindos.

The thurge shrieked and waved his arms. Fire exploded all over the room, and Galanthir cried out as one of the fireballs hit him. The walls shivered and shook and tentacles reached up from the floor, whipping around Cariad's legs as uselessly as weeds on the bottom of a pond.

Cariad wrapped both hands around Lindos's throat, his teeth clenched, his face contorted. His arms bulged and the wizard struggled in his grasp. Juilene shrank back from the walls, screaming as a clawed hand reached from the walls themselves, questing blindly. Galanthir moaned in pain.

And then the tentacles faded, the fires flared out, and the thurge sprites disappeared in a blur of high-pitched screams. Cariad rose from the floor, and Lindos's lifeless body lay at his feet.

He looked at Juilene, his chest heaving. "It's done."

Epilogue

❧

The music floated on the warm summer air, soft as a far-away sigh, and the sounds of laughter rose and fell in predictable counterpoint. Juilene leaned against the stone railing of the balcony and drew a deep breath. The air was balmy and sweet, thick with the scent of thousands of candles and the fragrance of the white and yellow flowers of the darvion boughs that decorated the hall.

So much had changed in the last weeks. Her father's recovery was slow, but steady; every day he made progress. Now he sat in his chair overlooking the hall, his eyes missing nothing, his big hands flexing impatiently on his lap, as though he ached to be active once more. The King had come back to his country, the winter was over. Spring had come to Sylyria at last.

She heard quick footsteps behind her, and turned. Cariad

hesitated in the doorway, the expression on his face unreadable in the falling dusk. She held out her hand and
smiled. He walked swiftly to stand at her side. He picked
up her hand and kissed it. It was rare they were alone these
days. With Lindos's death and Juilene's reinstatement as
the daughter of a noble house, all their moments of privacy
were severely curtailed.

"There's been a message," he said.

"From whom?"

"My father."

She raised her brow.

"Oh," he said, "Keriaan doesn't know he's my father, of
course. But he's had the news of his daughter's birth—he's
coming to take the child and Lady Amanda home."

"That surprised you, didn't it?" Juilene asked.

"That he would come?"

"No. That she survived."

Cariad shrugged, and gazed into the deepening twilight.
"Yes. It did. It makes me wonder exactly what else has
changed. But I'm still here, and so—well, I guess I have to
assume I was meant to be here."

"Of course." She twined her fingers in his and held his
hand tightly.

"But there is something I need to talk to you about.
Galanthir and I are in agreement. I mustn't be here when
Keriaan comes."

"Where will you go?"

"Not back to Khardroon, and Diago, that's certain.
Though your father and the King believe, and rightly so,
that Diago and his sister must be watched, carefully, from
afar. I had another place in mind."

"Oh?" She turned to face him and waited.

"There's still the matter of the harp. The harp should be
taken to Eld. And perhaps the Guardians there can discern
something of the changes in the future which must have

come about with Lindos's death. Perhaps they can even tell me what's to become of me."

"Maybe you'll stay here—in this time—with me."

He smiled then, and pulled her close. "Nothing would make me happier. But in the meantime, the harp should go back to Eld, and I should leave Sarrasin."

"Oh," she said. "I don't want you to leave. I—I'll miss you."

"I don't intend for you to miss me, sweet. I want you to come with me. There's no better companion I can think of for the journey. And who else to bring the harp back to Eld, but one of the goddess's own?"

She wrapped her arms around his neck and raised her face to his. "And what of my father?" she murmured as his lips came down on hers. "How will he ever agree to let me go?"

Cariad laughed softly in her ear. "My sweetest love, you've survived some of the worst roads in all of the League. If anyone can handle your father, it's you. And besides, he'll not object to a wedding trip."

"A wedding trip?" She pulled back to stare at him.

He laughed again, and this time his laughter rang out across the courtyard. "Don't you want to marry me?"

"Of—of course," she said, nearly speechless with surprise. "But—but—what of the future—the present—the—"

He hushed her with a finger across her mouth. "Oh, Juilene, haven't you learned that the past is over, and the future is no more than a dream? We can't know for certain what will happen—I was sure Amanda would die and she lives. Lindos will never reign, and Diago and Rihana will find themselves closely scrutinized. Who can say what will be? There's only the here and the now that matters."

He gazed down at her, waiting for her to speak. But she only pulled his face down to hers and pressed her mouth on his, for there were no more words to say.

Also the author of The Power and the Pattern trilogy, *Daughter of Prophecy, Children of Enchantment,* and *The Misbegotten King,* ANNE KELLEHER BUSH holds a degree in medieval studies from Johns Hopkins University. She lives with her children in Farmington, Connecticut.